WITCH HAMMER

WITCH HAMMER

VÁCLAV KAPLICKÝ

Translated by John A. Newton

Harbinger House

TUCSON ✦ NEW YORK

HARBINGER HOUSE, INC.
Tucson, Arizona

©1963 Václav Kaplický; the heirs of Václav Kaplický
English-Language Translation ©1990 John A. Newton
All rights reserved
Manufactured in the United States of America
∞ This book was printed on acid-free, archival-quality paper
Typeset in 10½/13 Linotron 202 Sabon by Andresen Typographics
Designed by Harrison Shaffer

First English-Language Edition

Diacritics over Czech names have been omitted.

Library of Congress Cataloging-in-Publication Data
Kaplický, Václav.
  [Kladivo na čarodějnice. English]
  Witch hammer/Václav Kaplický; translated by John Newton.
    p. cm.
  Translation of: Kladivo na čarodějnice.
  ISBN 0-943173-59-0 (hardcover): $17.95
    1. Trials (Witchcraft)—Czechoslovakia—Severomoravský kraj—
Fiction. 2. Severomoravský kraj (Czechoslovakia)—History—
Fiction. I. Title.
PG5038.K39K613 1990
891.8 ' 635—dc20
                                        90-4311

✦ Translator's Note

This novel is based on real people, real places, and real events that occurred in North Moravia around the year 1680.

Now a thoroughly Czech part of Czechoslovakia, this region was then ethnically mixed, and indeed remained so until well into the twentieth century.

Historically it was a province of the Czech kingdom, but at the time described in this book, mere decades after an abortive rebellion of the Protestant Czech nobility and the ensuing turmoil of the Thirty Years War, it had become a firm part of the fiercely Catholic Austrian Hapsburg Empire.

Although some catholicized Czech noble families retained their estates, the language of power was German, especially in North Moravia, which had long been home to a population that was largely not Czech. Certainly, the urban manufacturing and merchant classes were dominated by German families, and many towns and settlements had purely German names.

Many of these names remained in use until relatively recently, as a glance at any contemporary map or gazetteer will confirm. However, following the mass transfer of Germans from Czechoslovakia shortly after World War II, Czech names were adopted for all geographical locations, and these, naturally, were used by the author in the original version of *Witch Hammer*.

I make no apologies for deviating from the author's usage in the translation of this book. It was his undoubted intention to make this a documentary work, and its authenticity was all the more powerful for his use of proper names which were recognizable for a modern Czech readership. But different rules apply for other readers.

Wherever possible, I have rendered the names of places as they were generally known at the time of the events described. Where the contemporary records indicate a largely Czech community (Olomouc, for example) I have retained the Czech name, but in the case of wholly or predominantly German communities I have elected to use the German names.

Similarly, with the characters of the book I have chosen to use the standard German spelling of many names, especially those of people who were clearly not Czech. Again, this is supported by the contemporary records. The author's usage has been retained, however, for obviously Czech characters and for the names and titles of some historically Czech noble families.

The book has also been very slightly abridged. This is due largely to the elision of a very small number of proper names and references which were incidental to the plot and could, in my opinion, have detracted from the flow of the work for the English-speaking reader.

A glossary of changed place names is presented at the end of this book for readers wishing to locate them on a modern map.

JOHN A. NEWTON

✦ *Acknowledgments*

Sincere thanks are due to a number of people without whose devoted collaboration and assistance this book would never have been written. Above all I am indebted to my friends Dr. František Spurný of Šumperk, František Hekele of Mohelnice, Břetislav Hůla of Dobřichovice, Dr. Václav Medek of Prague, Vítězslav Zeman of Jeseník, and particularly František Kotrle of Mohelnice, who introduced me to the idea of drawing upon the witch trials of North Moravia.

V. K. 1963

WITCH HAMMER

1 ✦ *The Wedding Feast*

Shortly after noon, the lead-gray skies began at last to shed their burden of snow, dispelling the bleak frost of the morning but casting a new pall of gloom over the little town of Schönberg. Inside the deanery, it became so dim that Susanne had to move her chair closer to the kitchen window to see her work. The young housekeeper was knitting stockings for the dean from thick, raw wool. For the church was cold, and he often complained of aches and pains: in his back, his joints, and sometimes also his heart.

Susanne did not need much light, for she worked from memory. All the same, she soon laid her work aside, rising to peer at the distant mountains, but seeing little for the snow. The wafting flakes reminded her of the sadness of the fall, of trees shedding their leaves.

A tiny mirror hung on the wall opposite, just big enough to fit her face. She turned to the precious glass and smiled. She was beautiful, it told her, far more beautiful than Marie, or even Liesel. Susanne sighed as she thought of Marie Sattler's wedding, taking place that very day. Liesel, Marie's younger sister, was sure to be married also before long, and so were all the other girls of Schönberg. But no one would marry Susanne Voglick.

No matter that the old dean was like a father to her, she was still a priest's cook. And people were evil-minded; they always imagined the worst about women who tended the clergy. So what good was her beauty?

The one thing every man sought in a bride, after property, was a good reputation. Though he himself might be the vilest of sinners, with not a single vein of goodness in him.

Suddenly she heard footsteps in the hall, followed by the click of the door handle. The dean appeared. Christoph Lautner was small and round with a scant head of hair, but eyes full of kindness and merriment.

"Aren't you ready yet? Did you forget we're going to the Sattlers'? Be sure to wear your Sunday best and perhaps you'll find yourself a husband!"

His voice was resonant, even youthful. After all, he was quite a singer, and when he sang the *Gloria* or *Pater Noster* at High Mass, no one in church could hold a candle to him.

"I'd really rather stay at home, Father."

The suggestion of a suitor had hit a sore spot. The dean noticed, lifted her head in his hands and smiled.

"You're not jealous of Marie, are you?"

"No!"

"So why don't you want to go? We always enjoy ourselves at revels, don't we?"

Susanne did not reply, and the dean, looking more carefully into her eyes, saw they were welling with tears.

"I want you to know I do understand," he said, clasping her shoulder. "We all have our troubles. *Nemo ante mortem beatus.* We shall find blessedness after death. But do you know what Solomon says, the wisest man there ever was? *Quis abstinens est, adjiciet vitam.* He who is abstemious shall gain in life. There's no need for a long face!"

"All the same, Father, it might be better if you went alone . . ."

"And then who would be there to keep an eye on me? Just you get yourself dressed and ready to go!"

Since her arrival at the deanery as a girl of thirteen, two days after the dreadful fire that had reduced all the rest of Schönberg to ashes, and when the dean's mother was still alive, Susanne had learned constant obedience. And so it was that she soon entered the dean's room, dressed as directed in her best clothes, to find him resplendent in a new cassock.

"Excellent! Now go and fetch Florian."

Moments later, the dean's manservant-cum-coachman poked his red face into the room.

"You desire my services, Gracious Father?"

"I want you to go with a lantern to fetch us from the Sattlers' house tonight. Don't forget to be there at a quarter to midnight!"

Florian scratched his bristled head and grinned from ear to ear.

"What's the matter?" the dean asked. "Something wrong?"

"Wouldn't that be a little early, Father?"

"You're quite right. Come at five minutes before twelve."

"But I think it will be quite a banquet . . ."

"That's enough of your thinking, Florian. Now off you go!"

✦ ✦ ✦

Kaspar Sattler, a master dyer and one of the wealthiest citizens of Schönberg, owned a splendid dye works, which had been rebuilt since the fire, and two fine houses besides. Like Lautner the dean, he was already in his sixties, but he was a handsome man and still had his admirers among the ladies. Tall and wiry, he had a small head and bright, penetrating eyes that lent themselves easily to a reproving frown, especially if the dyemen in his workshops had spoiled something. But today they were shining with joy, for he was marrying off his eldest daughter to the rich silversmith Johann Weber from Riessa. The event had to be the talk of the town; the ceremony in the morning had seen a church procession fit for a countess, and the wedding feast in the Sattlers' largest house that afternoon was another grand affair. There were several barrels of Moravian, Hungarian, and Austrian wines, not to mention malmsey from Cyprus for the ladies; all kinds of game delicacies, flesh and fowl; and plates laden with pies, pastries, and sweetmeats.

When, dressed in his long greatcoat and lambskin cap, the dean entered the Sattlers' banquet room, he was greeted with joyful cries of "*Vivat! Vivat* Reverend Father!" from all sides, for he was always good company, and everyone knew the party would be the merrier for his arrival.

The welcome was hardly less warm when the kind face of his housekeeper appeared behind him; especially from Liesel, who rushed to invite Susanne to sit next to her.

Helped out of his coat by Esther Rohmer the maid, Lautner stood beaming at the familiar faces awhile before patting down his hair and scurrying to the bride and groom to offer his blessing. Then he turned to the bride's mother. She was clearly beside herself with pride. Her lofty acceptance of his congratulations, almost as if she were the Countess of Galle herself, constrained him to smile. Once, many years before, this lady had been a frisky filly of a girl, and the dean, then but a mere Latin scholar in Olomouc, had been madly in love with her, almost worshipping the ground she walked on!

Johann Sattler, her eldest son, brought in a fine glass goblet, filled to the brim with fiery Hungarian wine. The dean accepted the honor and bowed to the newlyweds.

"Good health, happiness, and God's blessings!"

The whole company raised their glasses, all roared the toast, and the wine flowed.

The cream of Schönberg society had gathered at the Sattlers': the Lord Mayor, half of the town council, and three guildmasters, the grandest being Heinrich Peschek, a rich linen maker whose fortune was founded on tripp—a mock velvet, part linen, part wool, which had become the source of long contention between the flax and wool weavers. Too big to sit at a loom himself, Peschek was a powerful, bullheaded man with cold, calculating eyes. Next to him sat his wife Marie, Kaspar Sattler's sister. She also was large, with a big nose and a wispy mustache, but her eyes gleamed with kindness. Alongside her was the merry widow Weillemann, now married to Maisner, her third husband, a paper manufacturer like his matrimonial predecessor. Farther on, with his adoring wife Dorothea, sat Kaspar Hutter, the former district judge, lately relieved of office for presuming to release two village women charged with witchcraft. Then came the other town councillors and guildmasters with their wives, most of whom, fat as wardrobes, sat quite still, not daring to open their mouths. Finally there was the wealthy bachelor and soapboiler, Jan Prerovsky. Prerovsky longed for a wife, but so far his quest for a bride had been in vain, thanks to his bald head, protruding ears, and bulbous, red, snuff-encrusted nose. Liesel Sattler's father, it appeared to him, was not against bringing more money into the family. Prerovsky's eyes, therefore, were fixed upon her now.

Lautner, meanwhile, had fixed his upon the bride, intent on a little fun. Remaining on his feet despite offers of a neighboring seat from everyone in the room, he began a playful cross examination.

"Did the bride make sure to tread on the groom's toes at the altar?"

Marie blushed as her new husband answered for her.

"Yes, but only lightly!"

"She'll make up for it later!" the Lord Mayor roared.

"And how many fingers did she sit on in church?"

"Five," the groom replied.

"Five fingers? So the blushing bride wants five children! Don't forget, Marie, the first one must have me for a godfather!"

"And now, my friends," he continued, turning to the guests, "what about the altar candles? How did they burn?"

"Quietly," several voices responded.

"That's a good sign. So we can expect a tranquil marriage."

Everyone smiled, especially the bride's mother.

"And one more thing. Did the bridegroom put any coins into his boots?"

"A ducat in each shoe, Father," came the bashful reply.

"In that case you will always have enough money, and we can drink to your good fortune!"

Once again the guests toasted the bride and groom and recharged their glasses as the merrymaking began in earnest. Lautner settled down next to Kaspar Hutter but did not remain silent for long.

"Marriage, my friends," he declared, "is a sacrament. That's why the Devil tries so frequently to defile it. But women are often cleverer than a dozen demons. That's why Satan didn't allow the famous Doctor Faust to take a wife."

"That's the truth, Father. Cleverer than a dozen demons," affirmed the bass voice of the master of the potters' guild.

"Perhaps it would be fitting," he went on, spluttering as his wife prodded him in the ribs, "if His Reverence gave the bride and groom a few tips on matrimonial conduct."

"I wouldn't mind hearing some myself!" the widow Weillemann smiled.

"First, then, something for the bride," the dean began. "Let's hope she will learn from the old tale of a great Persian king, Cyrus by name, who won a famous victory in a war against the Armenian King Tigran. Not only did he win rich spoils, he also captured the king himself and the fair Armenian queen. But Cyrus was a gracious monarch and didn't ill-treat his royal captives. On the contrary, he often visited them and sometimes even invited them to dinner. One day at a banquet he asked King Tigran how he would thank him if he were to set his wife free. Tigran replied that such a favor would have been worth his entire kingdom if he had still possessed it, but as the kingdom was no longer his, he would give the most precious thing he had left—his honor. Cyrus marveled at this and granted liberty to both of them. When he was home again, the grateful King Tigran said to his wife: Tell me, what did you think of Cyrus? And the queen replied: Oh, dear husband, how am I to know? I never looked at him once, for I had eyes only for you!"

The men enjoyed this tale, though it took time for some of them to fathom the sense of it. The women smiled, keeping their thoughts to themselves.

"Now some advice for the groom, Father!" shouted Prerovsky. "Perhaps he'll need it soon!"

"The best example for him is surely Saint Joseph," the dean declared with a roguish smile. "What a quiet life of purity he lived in that little house at Nazareth, working hard at his carpenter's trade, making sure that in everything he did, his wife should come to no harm. Then, when she grew great with expectation of a blessed event, he compared her in spirit with Aaron's rod, which by itself had brought forth delightful buds and blossoms. That is a lesson for the bridegroom. Never hasten to doubt your wife."

"That's all very well," said the potter, "but how are five children to be born from a life of purity?"

"There will always be somebody willing to do the work of the Holy Spirit," remarked the thrice-married and much experienced widow Weillemann.

"Oh no, I wouldn't suggest anything of that sort," the dean made clear. "Things could end as they did with the adulterer described by another of our church's great teachers: There once lived a man who lay down with another man's wife. And at once his countenance became that of a beast and his semblance that of a devil. On his way home from the adulteress he met a herd of cattle, and the cattle were so afraid of him that they fled on all sides. And even his own wife, when she saw his face, took to her heels. Only when the sinner swore the holiest of vows never to violate the Sixth Commandment again, and when he began to make atonement, was his natural form returned to him."

"It's a pity things like that don't happen nowadays," the potter's wife sighed.

"Be thankful they don't," interjected councillor Peschek. "The world would be like a menagerie!"

The laughter was just subsiding as Fritz Winter entered the room to yet another joyful welcome. Fritz looked like a butcher: strong, brawny-necked, and red-cheeked. But he was a gingerbread man, and never a feast, fair, wedding, or baptism went by but he did not appear with a wicker basket slung over his shoulder, filled with gingerbread, marzipan candies, and all sorts of good things.

The table was already piled high with the finest of pastries, but almost everyone bought something more from the gingerbread man, whom they knew as the loving father of six children.

Mistress Sattler had her eldest son fill a large glass of wine for him. Thus honored, he wished happiness to the newlyweds, their parents, and all the assembled uncles and aunts. Then he swallowed the wine with gusto in one draft.

"Gentlefolk," he observed, wiping his mouth with the back of his hand, "here you are making merry, but you should have heard the preacher at Zöptau last Sunday! Father Schmidt's sermon was enough to make your hair stand on end! The time of Lent, he said, is Satan's harvest. We poor Christians should beware, for if we fall to temptation we'll suffer the torments of hell—boiling oil, fire and brimstone, molten pitch!"

Most of the guests smiled, but the dean listened with an inward frown. He knew of this joyless, prying priest who took every opportunity to fill his parishioners with the fear of hell. But Lautner knew also that all eyes were upon him.

"Of course," he began gravely after indulging in a generous pinch of snuff, "there is truth in what the parish priest at Zöptau says. Lent is indeed when Satan has the greatest opportunity to lead even the most God-fearing Christian into sin. Yes, we have to beware of his blandishments, for his insidious ways don't lead straight to iniquity. The Devil is a cunning hunter, scattering berries to the birds without showing them the net.

"My advice to you, therefore, is to follow Saint Antony of Thebes, who taught us how best to fight the Devil. When this saint was in the desert, the Devil often appeared to him in many forms—once as a bear, then as a wolf, at other times as a tiger. But Antony took his staff to these beasts and drove them away. One day a beautiful maiden appeared at his house. The Devil had assumed a disguise which could tempt even a saint. Antony couldn't use his staff on a woman, but he did know what to do. He ran straight to his house, shut the door behind him, and closed his ears and his eyes to the Devil's temptations outside. We too, my friends, should fight like Saint Antony . . ."

"In a word, Father," said the soapboiler, "we're not to set foot outside without a stick!"

"And as you're a bachelor, Prerovsky," councillor Peschek chimed in, "you'd better get yourself a strong front door!"

✦ ✦ ✦

Time flew, wine barrels emptied, voices rose, and cheeks reddened. One guest broke into song, then another. This was something for the dean, whose crisp voice was soon ringing louder than all the rest, for the wine had gone to his head, too. All Susanne's anxious glances were now in vain. Lautner threw his arms around the shoulders of his neighbors; others followed, even Liesel Sattler and Susanne Voglick, and before long they were all hugging one another as they sang and swayed to the music.

The bride's mother also sang, keeping half an eye on the dean. No, she was not at all sorry she had forsaken him in her girlhood. Her Kaspar was a real man!

At exactly five minutes to midnight, the door opened, revealing a lighted lantern, followed by the grinning face of old Florian.

"If you please, Gracious Father, your time's up!" his croaking voice announced.

Lautner immediately got up, meek as a lamb, and Susanne with him. The Hutters also rose to their feet. All protestations from the others were to no avail; the dean was not going to start the new day in a state of intemperance. Also in vain were the bold attempts to influence Florian by plying him with drink. Though he swallowed everything that was thrust upon him, he would not lose hold of his master.

And so it was that as the night watchman sounded the midnight hour on his horn, Lautner and the Hutters were already out on the street.

It had stopped snowing and there was a mild frost. The night was as black as pitch. Florian strode ahead, lighting the way; behind him walked Dorothea Hutter and Susanne, while Lautner and his closest friend Kaspar Hutter brought up the rear. They walked arm in arm for safety, but even so they rested awhile from time to time.

The Hutters went their own way from the corner of the street near the church, leaving Lautner, Susanne, and Florian to walk in silence up the hill and around the graveyard to the deanery.

Florian opened the door with his great key, ushering in first the dean and then the housekeeper. But Susanne danced ahead and ran up the stairs. At the top she turned, somewhat mockingly.

"What about your back and your heart, Father? Does anything hurt?"

"No!" he muttered, continuing laboriously up the stairs.

2 ✦ The Beggarwoman of Wermsdorf

It was still early for church, but the poor widow Schuch could wait no longer. Bent over her cherrywood stick, she left her little cottage below the hill. This was how she set out into the world, day after day, bag in hand, to beg a crust of bread or morsel of food from charitable folk she met on the way. But today was different: it was not done to go begging on Easter Monday, and she could not stay at home. Anyway, she had a more serious, and secret, task to perform.

Wizened as a dried pear and thin as a rake, Maryna Schuch was not really as old as she looked. Nimble on her feet, she had no real need for her stick. But how could she go begging without it? She had lost her husband in the fateful year of '63, when the Turks invaded Moravia. They took him away and he never returned. And the children? One after another they died, more of hunger than disease. But what was the point of bitter remembrance? Maryna no longer grumbled at life; she was long reconciled to such things.

As she came within sight of Dorothea Groer's house, she noticed that Dorothea herself, the village midwife, was standing outside waving.

The beggarwoman frowned. Had she changed her mind at the last moment? A pretty pickle that would be! She pressed on toward the house, wondering at the sturdily built woman whose coarse looks belied her soft and gentle hands. Hands that had given life to all the children of Wermsdorf.

"I've been waiting for you, Maryna. Hoping you hadn't forgotten," Dorothea said at last, her voice lowered.

This was a weight off the beggarwoman's mind, but she was careful not to show her relief.

"Have I ever forgotten anything?"

"When you leave the church, just mind you come straight here, Maryna!"

"As if I didn't know what to do!"

Zöptau was not far away, so Maryna Schuch had plenty of time to think as she went her unhurried way to church. She thought about Mistress Groer.

Dorothea was not a bad woman, but she too had had the misfortune to lose her husband, and without a man to look after it, a farmstead was doomed. True, she was strong, quite the equal of many a man, but midwifery took up so much of her time. Whenever they came for her, whatever she was doing, she had to go, and she was more often in other people's houses than her own. She did not give her services for nothing, and she was paid quite enough, but the farm was going from bad to worse. Now she was complaining about her cow. But how could the cow give milk when the manger was empty? The hay was all eaten, for there had been only a handful in the first place. Dorothea had had no time to mow the year before.

Of course she was not the only person who had no fodder for the livestock. There were other farmers, even young and strong men, in Wermsdorf, Zöptau, and elsewhere, who had nothing to give their cattle. But that was another story. The Lords of Ullersdorf had put down the peasants' revolt of '62 by beheading its leaders, and since then the serfs had been forced to slave for their masters from dawn to dusk, with not a moment left for themselves.

Now at least there would be new spring grass. But Dorothea was impatient and could not wait. Mistress David had told her the cow would give milk in plenty if only she fed her a consecrated wafer on a piece of bread. Giving the cow a proper feed would have been better than this hocus-pocus, but Dorothea was sure the wafer would be quicker and cheaper. She had tried it last year at this time, but spring had come earlier and the cow had eaten her fill of lush, fresh grass. Still, Dorothea was convinced the trick had worked. And who was Maryna Schuch to deny it, when Dorothea had promised her a quart of peas and some barley flour just for bringing her another wafer from the church? Why shouldn't she fetch it, for such a reward? The Good Lord would surely forgive an old beggarwoman if she saved her holy bread for Dorothea's spotted cow! Man may have been made in God's image, but cows were God's creatures, too, and sometimes far more useful. What was a needy soul to do when offered the chance of a whole quart of peas, and some barley flour for griddlecakes, and all for nothing?

Thus conversing with herself, Maryna Schuch finally arrived at Zöptau and made straight for the church to confess her sins, for only then could she attend communion.

It was still early and few people were there, but fortunately the priest was already in the confessional, listening to a young woman unburdening her soul.

Maryna stood in line behind her, thinking she would not have long to wait. But she did, and when the young woman finally rose after the priest's torments, she was as red as a turkeycock.

The old beggarwoman knelt in her place, lifting her eyes to the priest beyond the grilled window. He saw her and merely nodded. She launched into a catalog of sins, but he, perhaps not even listening, seemed to be uninterested. Her sins were always the same: she had taken the Lord's name in vain, told lies, broken a fast, occasionally taken something that was not hers.

The priest asked no questions, but administered absolution directly, even prescribing a very moderate penance—three Our Fathers and three Hail Marys.

Satisfied, Maryna went straight to one of the side altars and religiously recited the set prayers, adding one more Our Father for good measure. But she felt no relief as she whispered the words, for their significance was almost beyond her comprehension. She did not vow to reform, still less never to take anything from the gentry's estates. A rich man might sin a hundred times a day, so why shouldn't a poor person? But more than this, she wondered whether she would be given at least a handful of barley flour. When she got home she would cook herself griddlecakes and eat them while they were still hot. O God, hot griddlecakes! Lord, have mercy on us!

Meanwhile the church had filled with people from Zöptau and other villages of the parish. The beggarwoman looked for a suitable place to sit, in the back pew beneath the choir gallery.

Soon a small bell rang and from the sacristy a red-surpliced acolyte emerged, bearing an enormous missal, followed by the gold-robed priest, monstrance in hand. Festive music resounded from the choir, the organ droned, the lower registers blared, a flute and violin trilled, something else tinkled. The congregation struck up an ancient hymn.

Maryna Schuch stared at the priest as he went from one side of the altar to the other, now kneeling, now genuflecting, although why he should do this, she did not know. Far more interesting was the church itself. Eventually her gaze fell upon the large picture of Saint Laurence, to whom it was dedicated. The saint looked like such a nice man, but he was almost naked, poor thing. The wicked heathens had put him on a gridiron and set a fire underneath to roast him like a goose. Poor devil, Maryna thought to herself. Roasted alive because he didn't want to hand over the church's treasure to its enemies. That's what the priest had preached at Martinmas. She felt so sorry for this poor young man. How vicious people were, roasting a man on a gridiron as if he were a goose or a lamb!

The Mass, like the hill path to Marschendorf, went on and on, but the beggarwoman of Wermsdorf was content. She was no longer studying the picture of Saint Laurence but watching the priest as the sun glinted on his golden robes. Their beautiful color reminded her of the griddlecakes again, and she was seized with a ravenous hunger.

At last the time came to take communion, and those who had attended confession now knelt on the stone step at the wooden screen separating the presbytery from the nave of the church. Maryna knew her place; she did not push in among the first of the communicants but settled for a position on the far left, next to the door to the sacristy. Putting her stick to one side, she took a white scarf from her bag, set it beneath her chin, and patiently waited her turn.

Monstrance in hand, the priest stepped down from the altar and began administering the sacrament to those kneeling at the far end of the row.

She looked around. Still plenty of time. Directly opposite her on the altar step stood the acolyte, a red-cheeked, jut-eared boy. Not an ounce of goodness in him, she thought to herself. Then, in the doorway of the sacristy, appeared the sacristan himself— Bittner the weaver, a white-haired old man with a pink face and eyes like sloes. The beggarwoman did not like the look of either the weaver or the boy in the red surplice. Both of them were too close; they would easily notice her spitting out the wafer. But she knew how to do it. Like last year, she would place the scarf on the screen, and on receiving the sacrament she would bow her head and drop the wafer into it. Oh, to get it over and done with!

Opening their mouths like fish out of water, the communicants crossed themselves as the priest approached, before sticking out their tongues. Then they beat their breasts in humility.

Now it was the turn of the beggarwoman's neighbor.

Maryna crossed herself and opened her mouth. She heard the priest intoning something above her, then felt him place the host on her tongue. She closed her eyes, bowed deeply, and expelled it into her scarf.

The priest had not seen her, because he immediately turned back to the altar. Bittner also had observed nothing, because the priest had obscured his view. The only person who could have seen was the altar boy, but Maryna took solace in the fact that he surely had other things to think about.

Beating her breast and mumbling her unworthiness like the others, she cocked one eye on him. He had run to the sacristan and was whispering something. The weaver frowned, then glared at her. Something urged her to get up and run, but fear rooted her to the spot.

The sacristan was already upon her, gripping her shoulder, quietly ordering her:

"Come with me into the sacristy."

Maryna did not move.

"Come with me!"

At last she rose and hobbled round the screen, through the doorway, and into the sacristy. The whole church saw her, and everyone wondered why the sacristan had done the beggarwoman such an honor. Perhaps she had fallen faint from hunger.

Maryna Schuch was indeed feeling faint but not from hunger. Her face was a bloodless paper-white, her legs like hundredweights. But she kept a firm grip on the scarf containing the wafer.

Inside the sacristy, Bittner bade her sit down. Then:

"Give it here!"

She pretended not to understand. Bittner took the scarf and opened it. There lay the host, as white as snow.

"Miserable wretch!"

He hurriedly folded the scarf again and kept it clasped in his hand.

For a while the beggarwoman sat rooted to the spot, staring starkly, silently pleading him to do her no harm. Then, overcome by fear, she sank to her knees, her hands joined in supplication.

"I beg you, for God's sake, give me back my scarf and let me go. Have pity on a poor beggarwoman!"

The weaver merely shrugged his shoulders.

"Wait until the priest gets here!"

The priest! Woe on woe! Her spine chilled. She could hardly expect him to show mercy.

Maryna got up, then sank onto the bench and began weeping bitterly. She knew that whatever was to become of her, it would be to no good. But then she was seized with a desperate hope; as faint as gossamer, but a hope for all that. What she had done could surely not have been so wicked. She had not desecrated the holy bread, only put it into a clean cloth. She would give it back to the priest and gladly forego the promised peas and the prospect of griddlecakes. It would not be such a tragedy after all.

At last the priest returned from the altar and, noticing her, asked the weaver what on earth the old woman was doing in the sacristy.

Bittner sidled up to him, whispered something and finally handed him the scarf. The priest opened it and gazed at the host with a look of genuine horror. Then he turned to the beggar-woman.

"What's the meaning of this?"

She threw herself at his feet.

"Reverend Father! It's not my fault. Mistress Groer from Wermsdorf, her cow's not milking and old Mistress David told her to give it some holy bread . . ."

"Hold your tongue!"

Full of revulsion, the priest kicked himself free of her grasp and went to place the consecrated wafer back in the monstrance. Then, his thin lips tightly pursed, he paced the sacristy, deep in thought.

The weaver stood ramrod-straight as the beggarwoman remained on the floor, her frightened eyes following the priest. The altar boy tore off his surplice and raced to tell the people outside what had happened.

At last the priest stopped in front of the sacristan.

"Go and fetch the magistrate!"

The old man hurried to obey while the priest took pencil and paper and began writing furiously.

One note was addressed to the Very Reverend Christoph Alois Lautner, Dean of Schönberg:

"A dreadful thing has happened at Zöptau. Please come at once."

A second was addressed to His Excellency Adam Vinarsky of Kreuz, Sheriff of the Manor of Ullersdorf:

"I have detained a woman on grave suspicion of witchcraft. Awaiting your instruction. Schmidt, parish priest at Zöptau."

The beggarwoman had merely spoken of a cow not milking. The priest's zeal had seen to the rest. He knew the Devil lurked at every corner, and he regarded it as his sacred duty to fight him at every opportunity.

Johann Axmann, the village magistrate at Zöptau, entered the sacristy to be hailed with an abrupt command:

"Get two runners immediately! This woman is evidently a witch, in league with the Devil. And there are more besides her!"

The magistrate was a levelheaded man. Women were all diabolical as far as he was concerned, though Father Schmidt, whose own housekeeper was as ugly as Ash Wednesday, could hardly know about that sort of thing. And as for Maryna Schuch, he had known her for years. She would hardly go begging if she really knew how to weave spells!

"Why are you still standing there?" the priest thundered. "Go, there's not a moment to lose!"

This was the first time the sacristy of the parish church at Zöptau had heard the terrible word "witch." But within minutes it was resounding in the yard outside, echoing among the graves.

Soon it was to fill the village of Zöptau and spread far beyond, sweeping all the estates of Zerotin.

And no word was to be of greater dread.

3 ✦ A Dreadful Thing

Premek of Zerotin, Lord of the Manors of Gross Ullersdorf, Wiesenberg, and Johrnsdorf, had left on his death two young sons, Frantisek and Jan, who were made wards of their aunt Angelia, a Zerotin by birth. Having no children of her own, she took scrupulous care that the property of Premek's heirs remained intact and saw that the young Zerotins were given a good upbringing. A devout Catholic herself, she brought them up in the spirit of the Roman Catholic Church. She went so far that neither boy was allowed to know that their father had undergone conversion to the redeeming faith of Rome only in 1652, and then on pain of forfeiture of all his possessions, or that during the Czech rebellion and the ensuing Thirty Years War, many Zerotins had held prominent positions in the anti-Catholic and anti-imperial camp.

A lady of some vigor, the Countess of Galle prospered, thanks to her reliable manager, Sheriff Adam Vinarsky of Kreuz, as well as to her treasurer, Frantisek Vrany, and her burgrave, Kristian Mayer. She was also given considerable assistance in educating her wards by the learned yet still quite young parish priest of Ullersdorf, Thomas König.

The countess deplored the moral decay, coarse nature, and backwardness of her serfs without realizing who was mostly to blame. She did admit the sad consequences of the Thirty Years War and the legacy of the Swedish occupation, but it never occurred to her that the greatest guilt was borne by her own utter failure to improve their condition. On the contrary, she only deepened their misery by relentlessly increasing taxation and feudal labor to make good the losses of previous years.

Along with other authorities, the Countess of Galle was convinced of the paramount need to promote Roman Catholicism. With great admiration, therefore, she followed the efforts of Count Liechtenstein, bishop of Olomouc, who, mindless of the cost, had restored neglected churches, established new priests' houses, and striven to attract more young men to the priesthood.

But the serfs of Zerotin knew very little of the countess or the young heirs to the estates. For them, authority was represented by Sheriff Vinarsky. Whatever their station, all trembled before him. Resolute and uncompromising, he served his mistress faithfully— though naturally enough he made quite sure his own pockets were well lined.

When, on Easter Monday, he received the urgent message from the priest at Zöptau, he smiled. Here was a pretty Easter gift for her ladyship! This would give her something to worry about, and why not? She would look after the witches, and at last he would be left to look after the estates!

First, he glanced at himself in the mirror, for he always took very good care of his appearance. He was a man in his prime, squarely built, swarthy skinned, dark haired, with a fine eagle's beak of a nose. Nothing, he knew, would escape the countess's eye. He adjusted his cravat.

She received him directly. The sheriff wore an expression of extreme concern as he bowed deeply and kissed her hand.

"I know I am disturbing you, Your Ladyship, but I cannot withhold from you a most unpleasant matter. I would be most grateful if you read for yourself this most urgent letter from Father Schmidt, parish priest at Zöptau," he said, handing her the note.

The countess took the slip of paper and read it in silence. The word "witch" disquieted her considerably. She had often heard tell of women who had abandoned the Almighty and allied themselves with the Devil, but she had never yet seen a real witch. And now one had appeared on her estates! This was a matter that clearly had to be investigated, and a report would have to be sent immediately to His Grace the Bishop.

"Where is this woman?" she urged. "Have her brought to the castle straightaway. And Father Schmidt. And send for Father König."

The sheriff had not been mistaken. Nothing could occupy the countess more fully than this report of a captured witch. He could have handled the matter himself, of course, but this would have deprived the countess of the impression that she was in command. Women were a cross that had to be borne, and the older they were, the heavier the burden. But he knew how to handle her!

Back down in the castle courtyard, he ordered a carriage to be got ready and directed one of the castle clerks to drive to Zöptau to fetch the woman and the priest.

From her upstairs window the countess watched the preparations, wondering about the witch who would be brought back. This was a person who, body and soul, had sold herself to the Devil. What did she look like? Did she stink of brimstone and pitch? Try as she might, the countess could not begin to imagine.

✦ ✦ ✦

As this was going on, the second runner was delivering the other note from the priest at Zöptau to Christoph Alois Lautner, Dean of Schönberg.

The dean read the note once, twice, and still shook his head. Something dreadful had happened at Zöptau. But what, Schmidt had failed to say. Just like him, the crack-brained fool!

Lautner had never held the priest at Zöptau in any high esteem. In fact, he had little time for any of the younger clergy with whom the Consistory had filled the parishes. They were learned and fervent, to be sure, but they had not an ounce of understanding of the people. Instead of leading their flocks, they ordered them around; instead of winning them over for the cause of goodness, all they knew was to hound them with fear; too often they threatened them with hell, instead of approaching them with kindness.

Something dreadful had happened at Zöptau. But what? And to whom? To Brother Schmidt?

Lautner was of a good mind to add a few pungent words to the note and have the waiting runner take it back to Zöptau, but he decided otherwise. He was aware that Schmidt enjoyed some standing at the Consistory; perhaps he had even been secretly commissioned to spy on him, for such things were not unknown. There was nothing for it but to go.

The runner was already making to leave, but the dean, pressing a *Trinkgeld* into his hand, bade him stay.

"Wait a moment and rest your legs. You'll be riding back to Zöptau with us."

All that remained was to order Florian to prepare the carriage.

The horses raced hell-for-leather and in half an hour they were at Zöptau. The dean had Florian draw up in front of the priest's house, where Schmidt's old and ugly housekeeper was waiting for him. She had some disturbing news. A few minutes before, a carriage had come from the castle; it had taken Father Schmidt to Ullersdorf, and the dean was to follow as soon as he arrived.

This was evidently no small matter. Lautner asked no questions but got back into the carriage and instructed Florian to drive on to Gross Ullersdorf.

On the way, the old dean racked his brains in vain. What could this be that could not wait until after the Easter feast?

Had Thököly's Hungarian rebels spilled into Moravia again?* Had the Turks begun a new campaign against the Emperor? Or had the Plague, an increasingly frequent topic of conversation, appeared nearby? It was raging in Southeast Europe and Transylvania, and many cases had been reported in Hungary. But why should such reports have reached the parish priest at Zöptau before the Dean of Schönberg?

---

*Count Imre Thököly led an abortive Hungarian revolt against Austrian domination in 1677–78.

Florian thundered into the castle courtyard. Nothing unusual was to be seen. Only a gold-braided flunky who hurried straight to the carriage and asked the dean to follow him into the castle. The other gentlemen, he said, were already waiting for him.

Gentlemen, waiting for the Dean of Schönberg? What sort of gentlemen could they be? Confounded Schmidt! Why hadn't the man written anything more specific?

Though gently inclined, the wooden staircase they ascended was still quite a climb for an old man, so the flunky who bounded ahead had to pause for the dean several times.

Finally, Lautner was led into one of the many rooms on the second floor.

Inside, seated at an oval table, were Vinarsky the sheriff, Vrany the treasurer, Mayer the burgrave, König the parish priest at Ullersdorf, and Schmidt. All seemed to be waiting for something.

"You've led me a merry dance, gentlemen," said the dean, forcing a smile. "What in heaven's name is going on?"

The sheriff nodded to Schmidt, motioning him to speak. The priest from Zöptau raised his head stiffly, careful not to look Lautner in the eye.

"A dreadful thing has happened," he intoned.

"That is indeed what you wrote me," observed the irritated dean, "but I still don't know what this thing is, or whom it happened to!"

At this the door opened again and the Countess of Galle herself entered, accompanied by a rustle of silks and trailing fragrance, like a spray of jasmine in the breeze.

All the men sprang from their seats and bowed low. With head erect and a faint smile on her lips, the countess bade them in a firm alto voice to sit down.

They settled noisily in the high-backed leather chairs, the countess taking her place at the head of the table. Her heavily powdered hair hung in plaited tresses on her bare shoulders, and a string of pearls graced her neck. She gazed around the table, like a monarch presiding over a council of state, as the men strove to

assume an air of unworthiness before her, especially the small and
jittery figure of Vrany the treasurer, who hunched himself so
small that he was hardly visible above the table.

Curious to know what would happen next, the bemused
Lautner winked at his good friend Father König, but even he bore
the expression of someone in audience with a bishop.

At last the countess turned to the priest from Zöptau and
asked him to describe what had occurred.

Schmidt stood up, wiped his perspiring forehead with his
hand, and swallowed nervously, his huge Adam's apple describing
a ludicrous dance on his scrawny neck. But as soon as he opened
his mouth, the Dean of Schönberg knew that this had nothing to
do with the Turks, nor with Thököly, nor even the Plague or other
pestilence, but with some kind of domestic matter. Perhaps, he
began to suspect, Schmidt had even concocted something to in-
gratiate himself with the countess.

Occasionally faltering, Schmidt began to recount what had
happened that morning in church at Zöptau, describing the beggarwoman of Wermsdorf as a foul fiend and her deed as the depth
of degeneracy. The more he spoke, the more convinced Lautner
became that Brother Schmidt from Zöptau was making a mountain out of a molehill. But it was a most dangerous mountain:
Schmidt was saying that this was not just one beggarwoman but a
whole gang of sinful women who had sold themselves to the Devil
and against whom the sharpest action was needed.

Schmidt's announcement over, the room was plunged into a
stunned silence. The countess eyed the gathering with an eerie
smile. Everyone seemed to be thunderstruck, except for Sheriff
Vinarsky, who stared at the wall as if counting the roses on the
yellow wallpaper. The most pathetic figure was the treasurer,
whose air of consternation suggested he had somehow consorted
with all the witches of Wermsdorf.

It was up to the dean, as the eldest and spiritually most au-
thoritative person present, to have the first word.

"The charges pressed here by my brother from Zöptau

are surprising," he observed. "Has this woman been cross-examined?"

"Only by me," Schmidt admitted rather reluctantly.

"So it is essential that she be properly questioned as soon as possible!"

"That's no problem," announced the burgrave. "The witch is here at the castle."

"Have her brought in!" decided the countess.

The treasurer, who sat nearest the door, sprang up and ran into the corridor to alert the footmen as Father Schmidt resumed his story.

"Even now it gives me the shivers when I think of it," he told Father König. "Nothing like it ever happened to me before!"

"That shows you are yet young, Brother," Lautner commented, retaining his smile even as he saw the flicker of a frown cross the countess's brow.

The countess was not overly respectful of this paunchy priest who was so lacking in courtesy. He seemed far too worldly, more like a village magistrate or a tradesman. And to cap it all, he had a young cook who everyone agreed was extremely beautiful. The young priest from Zöptau was different; his housekeeper was ugly. She cast him an encouraging glance.

"I would venture to suggest, Your Reverence," Schmidt stammered, "that youth is the determining factor. What we have is a crime that outweighs all others. Regard not them that have familiar spirits, neither seek after wizards, to be defiled by them, says Leviticus. And in the book of Exodus we read: Thou shalt not suffer a witch to live!"

The dean smiled at this shallow theological scholarship.

"That is indeed what the Scripture says, Brother," he observed. "But don't you also know the proverb: He who readily believes is easily misled?"

Before Schmidt could think of anything to quote in reply, the door opened and Maryna Schuch, the beggarwoman of Wermsdorf, was pushed roughly into the room by a bailiff.

The old woman now appeared even smaller than she was. Her beady eyes, like those of a caged mouse, flitted from one face to another but saw only hostile stares. Her stick and her bag had been taken away, and now she did not know what to do with her hands. She hung her head and wiped her tear-stained eyes with her sleeve.

"Is that her?" inquired the dismayed countess. Heaven knew what kind of demonic being she had expected, and here was an ordinary old countrywoman.

The others also were clearly disappointed. Lautner alone was not surprised, having formed a clear image of the witch of Wermsdorf from Schmidt's account. He felt sorry for this poor woman who could hardly stand, and he appealed to the countess to permit her to sit down.

The countess had always made a show of Christian love, but this time a new frown of suspicion crossed her brow. So the fat dean felt compassion for a witch! Seeing for herself, however, that at any moment the old woman might escape interrogation by collapsing of her own frailty, she nodded to the priest of Ullersdorf, who willing proffered a chair.

Maryna sat down. She did not have enough courage to look again at the grand company she had seen on entering the room. Instead, she gazed down at her tattered shoes. She was very ashamed, even afraid to breathe.

Once again it was up to the dean, as the senior member of the clergy present, to have the first word.

"Tell us your name."

The old woman feebly told them who she was, also where she was from, where she lived, what her husband had been, and how he had gone astray. There was nothing disquieting in what she said.

"And now tell us, as if you were at confession, how it was with the consecrated host."

Lautner's voice was gentle and kind, and gave her courage. Quite coherently and straightforwardly she told them what had happened.

Everyone could see she was telling the truth, with nothing concealed or clouded. To Lautner particularly, everything was clear. What kind of witch was this? Only a poor woman who wanted to earn herself a little living. Far greater guilt was borne by the midwife, but even in her case there could be no question of witchcraft, only of the widespread popular superstition that the host, transmuted into the body of Christ, had miraculous powers. The people had to be taught; absurd superstitions had to be explained, not branded immediately as black magic. If the priest at Zöptau had had more forethought, he would have resolved the whole matter quietly, without troubling the countess or the sheriff, without sending for the dean, and mainly without stirring up the entire neighborhood. As things stood, it was even possible that in his precipitancy Schmidt had also sent a message to the Consistory! Lautner wanted to help the old woman, but before he could speak Sheriff Vinarsky was questioning her.

"What do you know about the woman Groer?"

Maryna Schuch looked up at the sheriff and immediately hung her head again. His voice had shown no trace of compassion, and now she saw the severity of his eyes. Undaunted, however, she answered truthfully, telling all she knew. She spoke well of Mistress Groer, who had only wanted the holy bread because her cow wasn't milking. If Mistress David hadn't given her such advice, she'd never have got into trouble.

"And who," asked the sheriff, raising his voice further, "is this woman David?"

The beggarwoman could picture her now, haggard, yellow-faced, and bent-backed, at home with her bearded billy goat and two tomcats. It was all Mistress David's fault that she was sitting here now.

"She's an old witch!" she spat.

Schmidt was exultant: "A witch!"

"A witch!" echoed Vrany the treasurer in astonishment.

The sheriff tossed a smug glance at the countess, as she strained to get a better view of this heinous fiend.

"On what grounds do you consider Mistress David to be a

witch?" asked Lautner, brow knitted, determined to help the old woman.

Realizing that perhaps she had said something wrong, Maryna hesitated. The priest of Zöptau closed in.

"Not to answer is to commit a mortal sin!"

"She can charm away diseases," Maryna faltered. "She mends broken bones. She sees to sick animals . . ."

Like so many other old village women, thought Lautner to himself. But Schmidt was already on his high horse.

"And do you know where she gets these powers?"

Maryna shrugged her frail shoulders.

"That I don't!"

"And does this woman David stay at home nights, or is she often away?" urged the priest of Zöptau. "Does she have night visitors?"

The beggarwoman gazed at him in amazement before smiling weakly: "And who would go visiting her, Father? She'll soon be threescore and ten!"

The sheriff could hardly contain his mirth as the countess averted her eyes to the ceiling in embarrassment. The more she listened to this cross-examination, the more disconcerted she was. This witch, the first she had ever seen, exuded no horror; and if she had met her in front of a church she would surely have thrown her some coins. She tried questioning her herself.

"Are you aware of the despicable deed you have done?"

"I'm sorry I did it, Your Ladyship," Maryna replied tearfully. "If I'd known what would happen, I'd never have promised Mistress Groer a thing . . ."

Even the countess knew this had to be the truth.

Things seemed to be turning to the beggarwoman's favor, until the zealot of Zöptau intervened again.

"Your Ladyship must not believe a single word from this artful slattern. It's only a sham. Before committing her terrible deed she attended confession, and in the confessional she looked as contrite as she does now. She acts like a poor wretch, but clearly she is prompted by the Devil himself. She lays blame on the woman

David, but who knows how things really are! I say we shall hear no truth until the thumbscrew squeezes it from her!"

Lautner shuddered at the fanatical hatred of his brother priest from Zöptau.

"Revealing the truth should not be our task," he declared, "but that of a court. I don't believe we need detain this woman here any longer."

Against his expectations, the countess nodded. Lautner observed with some satisfaction that Schmidt was choking with rage.

Summoned by Vrany the treasurer, the bailiff arrived to take the beggarwoman away; but she lingered in the doorway, and the dean noticed that her plaintive gaze was directed at him.

"Do you have anything else to say?" he asked.

The old woman raised her tear-stained eyes to the elderly priest who was the only person to have spoken kindly to her.

"I haven't eaten since yesterday, Father. I did have some crusts of bread in my bag, but they took it away . . ."

"The impudence of her!" erupted Schmidt.

Lautner took no notice, but looked appealingly to the sheriff.

"No, we won't let her starve," Vinarsky pronounced. "She will have what's due to her."

The beggarwoman gone, the room was now filled with an uneasy silence, broken at last by the sheriff.

"We'll have to send immediately to Wermsdorf for the midwife and for the old crone! And we'll also have to start looking for an experienced judge."

"Does anyone know of one suitable?" the countess asked.

It occurred to Lautner that his old friend Kaspar Hutter, former presiding judge in Schönberg, would be just the man of good sense and experience that was needed; but before he could utter his name, the priest of Zöptau rose to his feet. Lautner knew this would be bad. If Schmidt proposed anyone, it would be someone after his own heart.

"There is an advocate in Olomouc who was once an inquisitor," he began.

Lautner caught his breath again. Boblig! He should have known!

"Who is he?" asked the countess.

"Master Boblig of Edelstadt. He is also well spoken of in the Consistory."

"Go and see him," ordered the countess, turning to Sheriff Vinarsky.

Lautner felt a grim foreboding, an anxious tightening of his heart. But he said nothing, not even when two footmen brought in refreshments. The others were surprised, for they knew the Dean of Schönberg as a most convivial table companion.

The dean maintained his silence as he traveled home, accompanied part way by the priest from Zöptau. He could not help feeling that with the impending arrival of Boblig, a man he knew to be proud of his forty years as an inquisitorial judge, some wicked work was afoot.

Lautner bade Schmidt a frosty good-bye, resolutely declining the invitation to stop by at his home, and he breathed a sigh of relief when he was at last alone in the carriage.

He ordered Florian to drive slowly. The countryside was bathed in evening sunlight. Everywhere he looked, new life was forcing its way out of the earth. White and yellow flowers were appearing in the meadows, and by the wayside water gurgled in the ditches, tiny streamlets trickled down the hillsides. How beautiful, how logical, how ordered it all was! Nothing was superfluous, everything had purpose and reason. It was as if only mortal men could exempt themselves from the natural laws that gave order to all things. Man often destroyed man for no serious reason at all.

Poor beggarwoman of Wermsdorf, if she were to find herself in the clutches of Master Boblig of Edelstadt! Yes, in the words of the prophet Isaiah: Woe unto them that decree unrighteous decrees!

4 ✦ The Devil Comes in Many Forms

Sheriff Vinarsky did not know Master Boblig personally but became acquainted with him only when he went to Olomouc to see him. The shabbily dressed old lawyer did not create a good impression, and his hunchbacked assistant Ignatius was positively repulsive. All the same, Vinarsky confided to him the reason for his call.

Boblig followed his account without interruption, merely nodding his head and tugging at his chin. Only when the sheriff had finished did he declare that this was an exceedingly serious matter that demanded an experienced arbiter. He would be pleased, therefore, to take up the case. But it could only be on his own terms, the most important being that no one was to obstruct him in the exercise of such a grave responsibility. In any case, he had to have time to prepare some necessaries, and he and his assistant would not be able to leave until the following day. Vinarsky had no choice but to accede.

Early next morning, all three set off in the castle carriage, bound for Gross Ullersdorf.

The strange thing was, at no time did the old advocate mention the reason for the journey—the three imprisoned women of Wermsdorf. Instead, both on the road and in the many wayside inns they stopped at, he constantly questioned Vinarsky about all manner of other things: how big were the estates of the house of Zerotin; how many serfs; what income derived from the farmland, the forests, the iron-forges of Zöptau; how old was the Countess of Galle; what relatives did she have; what was her relationship to the Bishop of Olomouc; who was the priest at

Ullersdorf? The sheriff was most taken aback by an inquiry about the countess's largess. It seemed to him that he was beginning to understand this grand lawyer, and he was angry with himself for not checking his credentials before agreeing with Schmidt's proposal to appoint him. But he was angrier when he looked at Boblig's assistant. The countess was terrified of cripples, and the sight of this hunchback would make her leap out of her skin!

Boblig finally fell silent only as the castle loomed ahead, guarded by its lofty eight-sided watchtower, topped by neat battlements, and bedecked with a metal banner bearing the heraldic lion of the house of Zerotin. Now he only stared, evidently satisfied. But his contentment was even greater when the carriage drew into the courtyard, bounded on three sides by four-storied arcades, their ponderous arches borne by a succession of elegantly spindling Tuscan pillars.

He would have stared longer, but the sheriff, afraid the countess might see Boblig's assistant from the window, led them quickly into the castle and ushered them into a guest room, asking the advocate not to let Ignatius out for the time being.

After a while, the sheriff, now changed out of his traveling clothes, returned and asked Boblig to go with him to see the waiting countess.

Angelia of Galle was ready to receive her guest in the small drawing room in the left wing of the castle. She had paid considerable care to her appearance, for she wished to look her best for the great personage she was expecting. So it was with some consternation that she eventually greeted Master Boblig of Edelstadt. He was a disappointment in all respects. She had imagined him to be a noble and learned doctor, a cannibal-converting missionary from distant lands, someone who resembled the priest at Zöptau more than the Dean of Schönberg. Boblig was in such contrast to her expectations that her self-control momentarily faltered. But then it occurred to her that this inquisitorial judge perhaps deliberately paid no attention to his outward appearance or to what people might say in order to dedicate himself more devotedly to his pious task. Still, she could not quite rid herself of a disagreeable feeling as she looked at his unshaven cheeks, his unkempt gray beard, the shabby clothes, and the bloated belly that bore witness to anything but the renunciation of worldly pleasures.

Her guest bowed politely, kissed her outstretched hand, and barked a few courteous words. But he eyed her so piercingly as he did so that she felt quite unwell. Inviting him and Vinarsky to sit in deep armchairs, she seated herself on a chair that was somewhat higher. Now it was her turn to study Boblig. Illuminated in a full beam of sunlight, he looked even worse than before. Indeed, the longer she looked at him the further he seemed removed from her original image of a zealous defender of the faith. Instead, although she strove not to believe it, she could not escape the impression that this was a debauched and decrepit old man, nothing more.

"I have come to do your bidding, milady. I have left all my affairs at home and I await your instructions," Boblig said, his voice old and tired.

"Master Vinarsky has surely informed you . . ."

"Yes, milady. He tells me you have three persons under suspicion of witchcraft and that you need to establish their guilt. I am entirely at your service, milady. *Nil mortalibus ardui est,* as Horace sang. No height is too arduous for mortal men. For forty years I held the office of inquisitorial judge. I have a wealth of experience."

"What puzzles me," said the countess, "is that these three witches don't look like witches at all."

Boblig chuckled condescendingly.

"Appearances, milady, are often deceptive. Many's the time in my long life I've been convinced of that!"

The countess averted her eyes, suddenly alarmed by this man who seemed to be reading her mind, leaving her weak and helpless. She wanted Vinarsky to say something, but it was Boblig who continued.

"For many years, milady, I have fought the Devil, and I have to admit, *nolens volens,* like it or not, that the Devil is exceedingly cunning, far more cunning than anyone of little experience could believe. One of his remarkable powers is that he can assume the very form that most accords with his evil ends. The more intent he is on evading recognition, the more inconspicuous he becomes. Only common fools believe he always goes about as a huntsman's boy or a merry miller's lad, or that he only takes the shape of black cats, bearded goats, owls, bats, toads, and other vermin. Were that to be so, our task would be easy. But it is not so. The Devil often assumes even the form of a beautiful woman!

"Perhaps, milady," he went on, moistening his lips, "I can give you an example. Once, in Germany, the Devil found his way into a monastery in the form of a lovely maiden. So irresistible was the devil-woman that she led four abbots in succession to commit carnal sin. Saint Serenus and Saint Equitius saved themselves from the same fate only by having a certain operation to extinguish their impure desires . . ."

Sheriff Vinarsky gritted his teeth at this, while the countess gazed chastely at the toes of her shoes. Boblig licked his lips again and resumed his discourse.

"Cases are recorded where the Devil took the form of a pious man of God, renowned for a life of purity. According to reliable witnesses, he once assumed the appearance of Saint Silvanus, the holy Bishop of Nazareth, and in his shape attempted to seduce the fairest girl of the diocese. Luckily he was surprised before the deed was done and quickly hid under the bed. When the people of the house dragged him out, he claimed he was the real bishop, so they let him go. Then the real Saint Silvanus had the Devil's own job proving his innocence. It was only by his performing a number of miracles that his followers were convinced it had not been him at the girl's bedside but the Devil in his form."

The sheriff was enjoying this enormously, but the countess was becoming more and more embarrassed. She did not know whether Boblig was talking in earnest or in jest. She had certainly not thought an eminent inquisitorial judge would behave like this! There he was, talking about the Devil, the archenemy of mankind, while the sheriff—she couldn't help noticing—could hardly keep a straight face. Vinarsky obviously did not believe it had been the Devil and not Saint Silvanus at the girl's bedside. And perhaps Master Boblig didn't believe it either! She had had quite enough of these doubtful stories.

"But we are forgetting our own case, sir," she interrupted. "Would you be willing to carry out a proper investigation?"

"Why else, milady," replied Boblig, gripping his chin, "would I have undertaken such a journey? I am honored to be of service and to be permitted to reside for some time in your magnificent castle. Nothing will give me greater pleasure than to join you in confounding the enemies of our Holy Faith. Perhaps, milady, you recall the story of the prophet Habakkuk, whom the Devil dragged by his hair from Judaea to Babylon . . ."

"Thankfully," interjected Vinarsky, regarding Boblig's bald head, "the same fate could not befall you, sir."

For the first time, the flicker of a smile crossed the countess's face. But Boblig's expression remained grave.

"I am fond of jokes, sir," he said, "but it is inadvisable to sport with the Devil. To this day, they will show you a stone in the Church of Saint Sabina in Rome, weighing several hundred-weights, which was hurled by the Devil at Saint Dominic. It was only thanks to the Guardian Angel, who rushed to spread his wings, that Saint Dominic's life was saved!"

This was the kind of story the countess liked. She now looked at the advocate more warmly. Boblig took immediate advantage, changing his tone.

"Forgive me, milady, but the journey was long and my throat is a little parched. If you were to provide a little something to slake my thirst . . ."

The countess was taken aback. This man, whom she had known for hardly half an hour, was behaving under her own roof as if he were one of the family. But at the same time she did feel guilty for not offering anything to her guest. She blushed, rang for the chambermaid, and ordered her to bring wine. Then, to cover her embarrassment, she began talking about something else.

"I would like to know, Master Boblig, your conditions for undertaking the investigation."

The advocate raised the thick brush of his eyebrows.

"My requirements are negligible, milady. Of course, you have to bear in mind that witch trials are not ordinary criminal trials. An inquisitorial court is a place of battle against the Devil himself.

And the Devil, milady, is exceedingly cunning. He is a past master at concealing his evil deeds, carrying them out in the remotest of places, without witnesses, and at the dead of night. The judge, milady, has to be even more cunning and employ methods which are not used at other trials. He must be very experienced; he must not allow himself to be swayed by the words, looks, gestures, or outward appearance of the suspect; he must be a man of honor, closed to inducements of any kind. The inquisitorial judge must also be heartless, showing no pity, even to his own mother or daughter. What is more, of course, he must also know all of the law, both of the crown and the Church."

The countess listened attentively. It seemed to her that Boblig was a man who knew his job and did it well.

The chambermaid brought in a pitcher of wine and two goblets. Without waiting for an invitation, Boblig grasped the pitcher and poured drinks for himself and the sheriff. He raised his glass.

"Prosit!"

The countess was astonished at this behavior. But she was utterly appalled when she saw how the wine vanished down Boblig's throat.

"Hungarian wines are usually better than Moravian," he remarked, wiping his mouth with the heel of his hand.

Once again the countess blushed. She had never had a guest like this before.

"There is one thing, milady, I should point out," Boblig said, pouring himself more wine. "A tribunal will have to be set up. Apart from me as director, the law states that there must also be a *procurator fiscalis*, a secretary, and two or three associate judges. Further, the court regulations of Emperor Ferdinand III decree that persons condemned by an inquisitorial tribunal may not be *concremiret*, that is to say, burned, without the approval of the Court of Appeals in Prague. That means every such trial is protracted for several months, thus considerably increasing court costs. There are, of course, means by which an experienced inquisitor, with acquaintances at the higher court, may accelerate such decisions."

The countess, who had had some experience of the courts, was starting to be worried by the prospect of the fees. She glanced at the sheriff.

"About how much would such a trial cost?" he asked.

Boblig frowned.

"One does not think of money in trials such as these, sir. Higher interests prevail: the Holy Faith, our Holy Church, our bounden duty to the Lord, the uncovering of satanic intrigues. Besides, my own terms are exceedingly modest. A daily retainer of one thaler and full board and lodging, that is to say food, drink, and warm accommodation. I used to receive two thalers a day . . ."

"That's quite in order," said the countess quickly. "I trust we will give you no cause for dissatisfaction."

"I have already heard tell of your generosity, milady," Boblig bowed.

The countess bit her lip, sensing the mockery in his words.

"Perhaps we should set up an inquisitorial tribunal right now," she offered, immediately proposing Sheriff Vinarsky and her treasurer, Vrany.

The sheriff added the names of Mayer, the burgrave; Richter, the manager of the iron-forges; and Zeidler, the forest warden. Boblig did not object.

"Isn't that rather a lot?" the countess asked.

"Members of the tribunal are also paid a daily fee, but at half rate, milady, and then only when the tribunal is actually in session. I shall not be taking too much of their time," he replied soothingly.

But the countess was not altogether at ease, for she was quite capable of reckoning. If the trial were to last three months she would have to dig deeply into her purse, and her dismay at this prospect could not be concealed. But determined to be bold to the end, she changed the subject and asked Boblig whether he had seen the three women who were under suspicion.

"Not at all, milady," he smiled, revealing the ruins of his teeth. "Above all, I hastened here to pay my deepest respects to your good self. Besides, the experienced inquisitor never sets eye upon the accused before the interrogation, to avoid any predisposition to sympathy or mercy. But that is not to say the sheriff cannot tell us how the women are conducting themselves in custody."

Vinarsky was brief: "One weeps all the time, one flies into rages, the third just glares in silence."

"One weeps, another rages, the third glares," Boblig repeated, nodding his head. "That alone is proof of their guilt!"

Both the countess and the sheriff stared in disbelief at this astonishing pronouncement.

"Witch trials, milady," explained Boblig, "differ from other proceedings. To the inquisitor, everything has to be suspicious, and mere suspicion itself is often proof of guilt. Might I inquire who is observing these three suspicious persons?"

"Our executioner, Master Jokl," the sheriff informed him.

"I very much doubt," muttered Boblig, "whether he has sufficient experience. It was clearly foresighted of me to bring my assistant, whom the sheriff has already seen. Ignatius is not an altogether handsome fellow, indeed he's a wretched hunchback, but as a custodian and observer of these despicable persons he'll have no equal. He'll note every word, gesture, and expression! All those who have sold themselves to the Devil bear his mark, and Ignatius sees even the slightest sign. I remember one witch in particular who'd long concealed the Devil's mark, but my assistant found it sure enough!"

"And where was it?" asked the inquisitive sheriff.

"In the most secret place of all, sir," Boblig leered. "Ignatius will furnish the details!"

By now the countess was as uncomfortable as she was impatient. The wine pitcher was now quite empty, and she hesitated before deciding resolutely not to order the chambermaid to bring more. She had seen enough of this strange advocate and was finding him increasingly repulsive.

Boblig easily read all of these things in her face. He stood up.

"So the arrangements are concluded," he declared. "I shall begin the interrogations tomorrow without further ado. I have nothing more to say for the moment, except perhaps that before departing from Olomouc I left word with the bishop's secretary, Schmidt, where I was going and what task awaited me."

This was pleasing news for the countess. If His Grace the bishop was informed, then surely everything was in order. She smiled sincerely and Boblig respectfully kissed her hand.

The advocate and the sheriff left the room together and strode in silence down the open corridor to the stairs. Suddenly Boblig halted and clutched the sheriff's sleeve.

"You didn't tell me, my friend," he hissed, "that generosity wasn't one of your mistress's virtues!"

"I'm sure you'll see you're not shortchanged," the sheriff retorted, his own opinion of the inquisitor now quite clearly formed. "And now will you be needing anything else from me?"

Boblig fumed.

"I'd like to meet this master executioner of yours!"

"You'll meet him soon enough!" said the sheriff, and hurried off.

Boblig remained for a while surveying the courtyard from a window before clattering his own thunderous way down the loose-paved, red-brick corridor. Finally he stopped at a large oil painting of a nobleman from the reign of Emperor Rudolf. The inquisitor smiled at the portrait, then slowly returned to the room that had been placed at his disposal.

His assistant was asleep. Boblig shook him out of bed.

"It seems we have quite a nice little place here, Iggy. It'll take some time for the big shots to get used to us, but we're patient. You'll see, we'll be singing the words of Saint Peter in the end: *Bonum est hic nos esse.* It's grand to be here! And now pull yourself together and get me the local executioner. We have to find out who he is!"

Ignatius went out, leaving his master to take his place on the bed.

A moment later came a dreadful commotion. Boblig, who knew what it was, chuckled.

Servants, cooks, chambermaids, all were fleeing in terror from the hunchback. Susanne Stubenvoll, wife of the castle cellarman, was so frightened when she saw him that she began to shriek: "Satan! Satan!"

The inquisitor listened from his room, his belly quivering in fits of laughter.

5 ✦ The Inquisitor Sets to Work

Heinrich Boblig had learned many things during his long inquisitorial career, one of them being that witch trials should never be hurried. Such procrastination, he claimed, derived from Christian love and permitted offenders to live that much longer. In truth, however, it was to suit his own pocket. But wishing to present himself well at Ullersdorf, he began his interrogations there the day after he arrived.

Shortly after first light, Master Jokl, the Ullersdorf executioner, was ordered to take all three Wermsdorf women to the courtroom, where the inquisitor and his assistant were already installed. A short while before, Boblig had inspected the room and its adjoining torture chamber with considerable satisfaction. The Zerotins of Ullersdorf had indeed furnished their castle admirably in this respect. Entered by way of an almost equally large anteroom, the courtroom itself was a spacious chamber on the uppermost floor with a number of windows on its northern side, an oil-steeped beamed ceiling, a huge tiled stove, two chandeliers with many candles, a long oak table, and a dozen oak chairs. The walls were covered with blue wallpaper and decorated with a series of oil paintings, mostly portraits. The torture chamber, separated from the body of the courtroom on the eastern side by a thin wooden partition, was richly equipped with all that was necessary for the executioner's trade. Beyond this chamber, for offenders awaiting interrogation, was a small cell reached by a secret stairway so that prisoners might be brought in without offending the eyes of the assembled gentry.

Before the executioner brought the women in, the inquisitor and his assistant positioned themselves in a corner where they would not immediately be seen by the accused.

Soon they heard footsteps in the torture chamber as Jokl, accompanied by Umlauf, the ruffian of a jailer, led the women through. Once inside the courtroom, they were lined up facing the windows to catch the full light of day; then Jokl and Umlauf stepped back.

Boblig strode out from his corner, crossed the entire room to the north wall, then turned and leered, shaking his head and licking his lower lip. Finally he asked them, one at a time, their names and ages.

Then he stomped across the room again. Suddenly he halted and ordered Jokl to take all three women into the torture chamber.

When the door had closed behind them, Boblig took a pinch of snuff, blew his nose loudly into a red handkerchief, and wagged a finger at his assistant.

"Well, Iggy, what do you say?"

"Ragtag and bobtail. No trouble at all!"

Boblig agreed. He also was not particularly satisfied with these women. All they had to do was squeeze them ever so slightly and they would sing. Perhaps the big one would put up a fight, but not the other two. Within a week they could be on their way back to Olomouc, the interrogation over, and their journey to Gross Ullersdorf wasted! It was not, therefore, necessary to exert any undue pressure on the accused. There was plenty of time for that. Meanwhile the countess should be given more opportunity to demonstrate her generosity and so gain merit in the eyes of the Lord!

"Have the executioner bring the big one in!" he told the hunchback.

Dorothea Groer was not calm as she stood before the inquisitor, but she was not altogether terrified either, for the few days she had spent in her cold, filthy dungeon had not worn her down. Besides, she was the youngest of the three women, healthy and strong, and far more resilient. Moreover, she trusted firmly that the punishment would not be so bad as to be unbearable. Certainly she did not expect the worst. After all, there would always be babies being born, and they would need her special skills.

Surely the authorities wanted as many new serfs as possible for their estates, and there was no other midwife for miles around!

But when she looked more carefully at this potbellied, bald-headed, toothless gentleman, his viridescent eyes showing no trace of sympathy, her self-assurance melted. Her legs weakened.

As if knowing how she felt, he bade her sit down. He said it with a smile, gently, almost as a friend. Dorothea stared wide-eyed, sank onto a rough chair, and began desperately to hope against hope.

The inquisitor smiled faintly and spoke again, this time almost like a priest at confession.

"The deed that you have done, Dorothea Groer, is a great sin. This you surely know. But we don't want to punish you too harshly. We want to show mercy. We'd like to set you free, but we have to know you're sorry for what you've done. And the best way you can show you're sorry is by telling us the truth about yourself and everything you know about the others."

Boblig took another pinch of snuff, stood by the window and looked out for a while, his back turned, giving Dorothea a chance to make up her mind. Then he turned suddenly and his voice was even kinder than before.

"So tell us."

"I don't know what else I should say, sir," she replied with tears in her eyes. "I've already told the whole truth. I wanted to give the cow holy bread so she'd give more milk. I know it was a sin now, and I'm very sorry. If I'd known what trouble it would cause I'd never have done it."

The inquisitor nodded his head, as if believing every word. Then he asked:

"We know you committed the same sin last year. And what happened then? Did the cow really give more milk?"

"She did, sir!"

"Are you sure it was the consecrated host that caused this to happen?"

"What else, sir? It's the body of Our Lord, and Jesus can do anything. How could He not have done it?"

Boblig pursed his lips with another of his faint smiles. This woman was no fool. She appeared to be speaking the truth, but more likely she had considered her answer very carefully. She had had plenty of time to think in her dungeon.

"Are you a Catholic?"

"Yes, sir. I go to church every Sunday and to confession three times a year, and I always say my prayers."

"So tell me then, did you confess your sin when you fed the cow the consecrated host last year?"

Dorothea Groer lowered her eyes and shrank back in frightened silence.

Ever so slightly, Boblig raised his voice.

"Without lying, tell me: to whom did you give last year's host?"

"I've already told you, sir. I gave it to the cow, on a crust of bread."

Boblig's voice now rose to a roar.

"Liar!"

"The Lord's my witness, I'm not lying, sir."

"You are lying! And you're taking in vain the name of the Lord whom you have deceived! You took the host to your gallant on the Petersstein. What's the name of this swain of yours? Come on!"

Dorothea stared in wide-eyed, uncomprehending amazement.

"Answer me when I ask a question!"

"I don't know what you mean, sir."

Boblig turned his back on her again and looked out of the window. Then suddenly he turned.

"Did you often go to the Petersstein?"

"Do you mean the big mountain, sir? I've never been there ever, sir."

The inquisitor glanced at the dark corner where his assistant was hidden. Knowing his moment had come, Ignatius emerged from the shadows, grimacing grotesquely. Dorothea Groer buried her face in her hands, terrified out of her wits.

"Have you forgotten me?" he chuckled.

Dorothea felt her flesh creep. She shook her head. Never in her life had she seen a hobgoblin such as this.

"Don't you remember," Ignatius bleated, "how we were together on the Petersstein? How we received the host as black as night? And how we drank wine from cows' hooves? And how we used to dance afterward? Hehehe! And what happened then? Don't you remember that either?

"No, no!"

Boblig nodded to Ignatius, who immediately withdrew. Then, placing his hand on her shoulder, he said gently:

"Dorothea Groer, we know everything. Nothing can remain secret from us. But we're in no hurry for you to admit everything. You have plenty of time to remember. In a week we'll call you again. Then you'll surely tell us what you were doing on the Petersstein and who was there with you. But now you can go."

He winked at the hunchback, who sprang back toward the prisoner. She was so devastated she could no longer stand. Ignatius clutched her arm. Suddenly he screeched:

"The mark! The mark!"

Stretching out a finger, he touched a small wart on her neck with his long, twisted nail.

"The mark of the Devil! And so soon revealed!" The inquisitor smiled.

The midwife of Wermsdorf left the courtroom reeling like a drunkard as the world swam before her eyes. Now she knew her interrogation was not because she had given her cow the consecrated host the year before, but because they regarded her as a witch.

Hardly had the door closed behind her when the inquisitor raised his voice to his assistant.

"We had plenty of time to find that mark, Iggy! There's no cause for haste. Now, have them bring in the second one!"

Ignatius scowled and went to fetch Maryna Schuch.

The few days she had spent in jail had had a terrible effect on the beggarwoman of Wermsdorf. Now a mere heap of shriveled skin and bones, she was hardly able to stand, and her hands shook as they wiped away her tears.

"Sit down," the inquisitor began, his voice kind again.

She gladly obeyed and, once seated, lifted her head to look at this gentleman who had spoken so nicely. It seemed to her that this was someone who could help. Without more ado she sank to her knees and clutched Boblig's feet.

"Have pity on me, kind sir," she implored. "Have pity on a poor old woman who never did anyone any harm but was herself pushed aside and persecuted by ill fortune all her life. For years I've lived from charity, sir, as a beggar. I know I did a terrible sin when I wanted to take the holy bread to Mistress Groer, but don't judge me too badly. Poor people like me have to take the best of what's going. They've no choice if they don't want to go hungry. Even a dog eats the meat first, before chewing on the bones. Have pity on me, for your own sake, sir!"

Boblig was a callous man, but for one brief moment as he stood above this wretched old woman he felt something like compassion. But an instant later he wrenched himself free.

"Stand up and stop crying. No one will hurt you if you tell the truth!"

Now a little calmer, she got up from the floor and looked the gentleman trustingly in the eye as he posed his first question.

"Tell me, do you believe in witches?"

"How couldn't I, sir? The reverend father at Zöptau preaches such fine sermons about them."

"And have you ever seen one?"

"No, I haven't, sir."

"And what about Mistress David? You did call her a witch, didn't you?"

Maryna remembered with alarm what she had said in front of the countess. That had been because she was angry at Dorothea David for getting her into trouble. But now things were different. She had seen Dorothea in the little cell by the torture chamber, so utterly broken and deathlike that all her anger had dissolved. What was she to say now?

"We know all about Dorothea David," the inquisitor continued. "We know about her long involvement with the occult. We know she could do a lot of things other people can't do. She healed the sick, made love charms, caused cows to stop milking, summoned the wind . . ."

"She could do most of those things, sir, but I never heard of her summoning the wind."

"And how do you think she did all of these unnatural things? Only with the help of the Devil!"

The beggarwoman crossed herself and stared at the inquisitor.

"I didn't know that, sir."

Boblig frowned and raised his voice again.

"Let's have less of this pretense! You knew all right, and you're no better yourself!"

"Sir!"

"Why didn't you go to the reverend father and tell him what Dorothea Groer wanted you to do? Why didn't you tell the magistrate? Whosoever knows of the Devil's work and does not denounce it is himself a servant of Satan and shall be cast into the fires of hell!"

"But there were others who knew what she was doing," she countered desperately, "and they didn't tell anyone either!"

"Their time will come, too! But do you know why you're here now? To confess to your own dealings with the Devil!"

"Me?" Maryna quaked. "Me, with the Devil?"

"There's no use denying it. How many times did you go to the Petersstein? And what did you get up to when you were there?"

As if Maryna Schuch had not heard of the Petersstein! Famous in folk tales, this mountain was the legendary meeting place of swarms of witches every Walpurgis Night. Most flew there on broomsticks, it was said, but some went astride goats, and yet others rode in carriages of gold. But how in the Lord's name could this gentleman think she was a witch? She knew no spells!

And she could never scale such a mountain! She had enough trouble as it was, just tramping to Marschendorf! She shook her head.

"I was never there, sir."

"Did you see there a creature who was half goat, half man, by the name of Urian?"

"Urian?" repeated the beggarwoman, thinking aloud. "That's a name they give to the Devil!"

"There you are, you know him well!" Boblig smiled. "You'll remember everything, just you see! And if you speak the truth, we won't punish you severely."

"But I don't know this Urian!"

"Oh yes you do! And you'll have plenty of time to remember him, back in your dungeon! Now I want you out of my sight. But remember: When I summon you again, you'd better know who you were with on the Petersstein!"

Boblig motioned the hunchback to take her away to the torture chamber.

Once she had left, he went back to the window and looked out. The sun was beating down and the waters of the river Tess shone like a mirror. The countryside was a blaze of color, full of life and joy. But inside the courtroom all was gloom, ancient dust, and stale air. The inquisitor scowled. He had interrogated two of the accused and the third was to come. They would resist for a time, but in the end they would admit everything. Meanwhile, they were of no interest. Just sour-faced, foul-smelling hags. Even to look at them was a pain. If only the third one were better looking, but she was the ugliest of all!

Ignatius led her in.

Dorothea David shuffled, hanging from his arm, sorely missing her stick. She was indeed ugly, more ugly than both the others put together. Her face was yellow, as if suffused with bile; her body was bent, and the veins of her hands stood out like cords. Only her eyes were bright, but they saw neither the inquisitor nor his assistant, for they were burning with fever and merely gazed absently into the distance.

With the help of the hunchback she sat down on a chair and placed her hands on her knees before staring ahead at a picture on the wall, a portrait of a lady toying with a lapdog.

Boblig leaned over the old woman, his eyebrows raised in concern. Taking great care not to touch her, not even with his clothing, he shouted in her ear.

"Do you know who I am?"

She sat stock-still.

"You are known to have signed yourself in blood to the Devil. Do you hear me?"

She remained still as a statue. Boblig lost his patience.

"We know your powers are from Satan!"

Again she made no response.

"You have renounced the Holy Faith, you have intercourse with the Devil, and you keep him at home in your cottage in the form of a bearded billy goat and a black tomcat. Confess!"

For the first time, Dorothea David turned to the inquisitor, her eyes ablaze.

"And who," she asked in a hollow voice, "are you?"

Boblig frowned. He knew from experience that these things happened, but he had not expected to meet such a miscreant on his first day at Ullersdorf. Devil's whore! Who was she to ask him questions?

"Who am I?" he returned, seizing the opportunity. "Don't you know me? I am your master. My name is Lucifer!"

The effect was awful. The old woman sprang in terror from her chair, flailing her arms.

"Lucifer! Satan!"

Ignatius stifled her shrieks with his hand, but she continued to howl and wave her arms. Hearing the noise, Jokl hurried in.

"Take this rabid bitch away," the inquisitor spat.

Boblig of Edelstadt was furious, unsure whether Dorothea David was demented or whether the Devil was cleverly using her as a tool against him. Ordinarily he had no trouble dealing with village witches. A few interrogations, several months in solitary confinement, then the thumbscrew or Spanish boot, and the matter was resolved. That was the way it would be with Groer and the beggarwoman, but this third hag could be a problem.

"Let's go," he said, turning to his assistant. "We've done enough for today."

They left the courtroom and emerged into the fresh air of the open corridor outside. Suddenly Dorothea David was forgotten. Boblig was hungry, and he was also thirsting for a goblet of good wine. He strode ahead, the hunchback hurrying in his wake. Soon they had clattered down the stairs and were on the broad first-floor corridor that led to their room.

Walking toward them, on their way from daily Mass in the castle chapel of Saint Michael the Guardian Angel, was the Countess of Galle, accompanied by her two nephews.

As soon as she caught sight of the inquisitor she determined to force a pleasant smile. But before she could, she felt the tight grasp of her younger ward's hand, while the older one pointed at Ignatius.

Now the countess saw him, too. So this creature, only vaguely resembling a human being, was Boblig's assistant!

Boblig bowed low and hurried toward her, as if not detecting the expression of revulsion on her face.

"We have just begun the interrogation of your subjects, milady," he said.

"And what have you found, sir?"

"That they are witches, milady, beyond the slightest doubt!"

The countess gasped.

"And the person behind you?" she asked.

Boblig assumed an expression of humility.

"Why, that's my assistant, Ignatius. You will remember, milady, I told you he was not an altogether handsome fellow. But what a good and gentle Christian soul he is, and how he suffers his misfortune . . ."

"He gave me quite a surprise, sir," the countess said stiffly and continued down the corridor without another turn of her head.

But the young Zerotins could not resist another look at the

hideous assistant. As if anticipating their stares, Ignatius glowered, and bowed and scraped before them.

"Come along, Iggy, don't frighten the boys!" his master called. "You've a far more important task. Get me something to eat and drink!"

6 ✦ *The Visit*

After lunch that day, the dean sat down at the desk in his room to work on his Sunday sermon. He had selected as his text the familiar words from the 11th chapter of Saint Luke, verse 14: *Et erat Jesus ejiciens daemonium, et illud erat mutum.* And he was casting out a devil, and it was dumb.

The sun was shining brightly on the rough paper, and a titmouse sang by the window. Lautner wondered why he had chosen such a cheerless theme. Nature was awakening to new life. Soon, when the grass had burst forth, the trees blossomed, and the songbirds flown in from the south, all the land would be transformed into an earthly paradise.

The window overlooked the graveyard surrounding the parish church. There, too, the dean observed, spring was announcing its imminent arrival. He resolved to go there to see if the primroses had appeared on his mother's grave.

Just then came a fierce jangling at the door. A replacement for the old door-knocker, the bell was often to be heard at the oddest hours of the day and night; yet the sudden ringing this time seemed to herald something disagreeable. There on the threshold, surely, stood not a poor petitioner craving solace but someone accustomed to giving orders! The dean got up and looked out the window. All he saw was an empty carriage, to which was harnessed a pair of young, well-fed horses.

The gruff tones of Florian echoed from the hallway on the first floor, answered by an equally unpleasant voice from outside. Now he heard the sound of the kitchen door. Evidently Susanne also was going to see who had arrived.

The dean left his room and saw a man panting up the stairs, eyes to the floor, dressed in a long coat edged with fox fur.

He waited. At last the stranger raised his head—and Lautner's blood froze.

At the top of the stairs the man swept off his cap.

"My name is Boblig!"

"I thought I recognized you."

"Indeed?" Boblig unbuttoned his coat and stared Lautner mockingly in the eye. "I am now at Ullersdorf," he continued, "and I couldn't resist coming to pay Your Reverence my respects."

"I am honored, sir," said the dean, forcing a polite reply as he noticed yet another strange figure ascending the stairs. Underneath a ridiculous hat was a hunchback with a crooked nose, broad mouth, and eyes as sharp as thorns.

"My assistant, Ignatius," explained Boblig. "Unpleasant to behold, but faithful and very reliable."

If the Dean of Schönberg had not believed in the existence of the Devil, one look at this strange creature would have convinced him.

"Don't you like him?" Boblig smiled, revealing the blackened stumps of his four eyeteeth. It occurred to the dean that here was a wolf, or at least a mad dog.

"A sorry fellow, I'm sure."

"Sorry? That's where you'd be wrong, Father. If you could only see him at his food or drink! Or when he gets his hands on a wench!"

Boblig grinned and turned to the hunchback.

"You don't have to be with us now, Iggy. Go to the servants' quarters, and I'm sure the dean will have something sent to you."

Obedient as a trained hound, Ignatius turned and scampered down the stairs into Florian's room, as if the deanery were his own.

Boblig stood for a while in the doorway of Lautner's room and peered inquisitively inside. Fixed to the wall was a large crucifix that reached almost to the ceiling, with a red-glassed lamp burning before it. Several open books and sheets of paper lay on the oak desk. Another small table and three upholstered chairs completed the furniture, and shelves filled with more books ran along the walls.

"A nice place you have here," he remarked. "But rather a lot of books, I see."

"There can never be enough books, sir!"

"I have my experiences. Too many books burden the brain."

Lautner had no intention of arguing with Boblig about books. He invited the visitor to take a seat, then went to ask Susanne to bring food and wine and attend to the visitor's assistant.

When he returned, Boblig was standing at his desk, studying— the impudence!—his draft sermon.

"A very fine passage you've chosen, Father." He smiled. "Casting out devils is my old vocation. Perhaps you've heard."

"Yes, I did hear that the Countess of Galle had invited you to Ullersdorf. I also know you were an associate judge at the tribunal in Freiwaldau when the famous, or rather infamous, Ferdinand Zacher was inquisitor. More than two hundred people were burned at the stake, including little children. All of them disciples of the Devil! You certainly have much to your credit, sir!"

Boblig sensed the sarcasm.

"You do me an honor, Father, by appreciating my merits," he replied in the same ironic tone, displaying the remains of his teeth again. "But there are many people, of course, who regard witch trials quite differently."

At this he finally took off his coat and laid it on an empty chair. Only now was he revealed in his full ugliness: a decrepit old man with the bloated belly of a pregnant woman. But his figure was still not as repulsive as his head, which reminded Lautner of an ostrich. The scalp was bare, with just a few tufts of hair above his ears; the tired eyes were sunk deep beneath thick black brows; the nose was bulbous and red; the cruel lips puckered. As for his clothes, his jacket was threadbare; his trousers tattered; his shoes, long unbrushed, were scuffed.

Could this tired old derelict really be a notorious inquisitor, with hundreds of human lives on his conscience?

The visitor was continuing his listless inspection of the dean's room when Susanne entered, radiating freshness and youth, and carrying a small pitcher of wine, two glasses, and some cake on a silver tray.

"Oh!" Boblig exclaimed, taken utterly by surprise. His eyes lit up, his body straightened, his lips pursed.

Susanne blushed. She would have liked to stick her tongue out at this ugly old man, but as he was the dean's guest she pretended not to notice his lecherous looks and left the room as quickly as she could.

"Pretty!" observed Boblig as soon as the door had closed behind her.

The dean frowned. One look at the old man's eyes told him—the shame of it!—what was running through Boblig's mind. Nevertheless he attempted to respond.

"She's an orphan," he said, pouring out the wine. "We took her in after the terrible fire of '69. She wasn't yet thirteen years old . . ."

"A charitable deed, I'm sure, Your Reverence. A point in your favor on Judgment Day, I would hope!"

No, it was no use explaining anything to this cynic. He would not understand. His soul was too black. Lautner chose not to reply, therefore, but invited his guest to take a glass.

Boblig did so eagerly.

"I wonder, Father," he asked, taking a sip, "whether you have any idea why I've come to see you?"

His voice was quite different from before. Sure and firm, it was now the voice of an inquisitor.

"How should I know?"

"I won't keep you in suspense. But I must say you do have good wine. That's something I found long ago—it's always priests who have the best wine. Of course, that applies also to bishops, *per consequens*—they usually have even better wine. Excepting the Bishop of Olomouc, where I come from. Count Liechtenstein doesn't drink more than one glass of ordinary Spanish *vino tinto* a day. It only goes to show: the younger the bishop, the better the wine."

Boblig laughed heartily at his own joke, eyeing the dean as he sat uncomfortably on the edge of his chair.

"But to let you know, at last, why I'm here," Boblig continued, his tone changing yet again. "Does the name Giuseppe Francesco Borri mean anything to you? That man is serving a twenty-five year sentence in the dungeons of the Castel Sant'Angelo in Rome. He will never see the light of day again. I understand you knew him . . ."

"May I ask why you are so interested, sir?"

"Personally I'm not interested at all. But the bishop's palace received some sort of inquiry from Rome and, as I was leaving for Ullersdorf, His Grace's notary took me into his confidence . . ."

Lautner winced at the nonsense of such a suggestion. Why should the bishop's notary need such an intermediary? What on earth was this fellow up to? He reached mechanically for his snuff bottle and took a large pinch.

"Aren't you going to offer me a little snuff, Father? What's your favorite? Buntschi?"

"No, Brasil."

"Also excellent, though a little harsh. But to get back to this Italian . . ."

"Of course I remember him," said the dean firmly. "It was in 1671, I think, or perhaps the year before. I know the town still lay in ruins after the fire. The only building left standing was this one, the deanery, and a small cottage nearby. Late one evening, in foul weather, a carriage pulled up outside. Two gentlemen got out and asked to stay the night. There were no inns in the town then, and no other suitable lodgings for such gentry, so I had no choice but to take them in. One of them was a captain of horse in the imperial army by the name of Scotti, the other was Giuseppe Borri, a nobleman from Milan. I gave them both something to eat, and only then did I find out that the Italian was actually the captain's prisoner . . ."

"I trust you got on well!"

"Very! Borri was an enthralling talker, especially on the subject of medical science and alchemy."

"And didn't he tell you that the Inquisition in Milan had found him possessed by the Devil and had sentenced him to death? And that with the help of the Devil he'd escaped and fled the country, leaving them to burn his effigy instead?"

"No, he said nothing about that. Later, though, I heard he'd once saved the life of His Majesty in Vienna. Borri was taken to the Emperor when Leopold was almost at the point of death. They say he had hardly stepped into the bedchamber when he knew the cause of his illness. All the candles were burning with a green flame, and he sensed they were giving off a poisonous odor. So he ordered the wax lights to be changed and the windows to be thrown open. Afterward, they found that all the candlewicks in the Emperor's bedchamber had been steeped in arsenic. The Emperor is supposed to have rewarded him with a life pension of two hundred ducats and a letter of recommendation to Pope Innocent."

"And is that all you know about him?" Boblig asked, toying with his glass.

"He was a man of learning. Beyond that I know nothing."

"A man of learning!" Boblig laughed. "Learning always stinks of heresy. That learned gentleman of yours was an arch-heretic. He presented himself as a Catholic reformer. He said he wielded the sword of the Archangel Michael himself. But under that veil of holiness and learning hid the very Devil. The truth came out, sure enough: he stayed in Hamburg, Copenhagen, even the court of Kristina, Queen of Sweden!"

"I know nothing of that. As a guest of mine I must say he behaved impeccably. Captain Scotti himself paid him every respect."

Boblig suddenly fixed Lautner with a piercing glaze.

"Did he by any chance leave anything in your safekeeping?"

"Absolutely not! Nor did he ask whether he could. Anyway, the captain never left us alone for a moment. There were six people sleeping in this room at the time," said the dean.

"I don't understand why," he continued excitedly, "if this matter is so important, I was not summoned to the Consistory myself,

and why you, sir, of all people, should have been sent to question
me! The bishop's own advocate, so far as I know, is Doctor
Mayer!"

"I've told you, it was a coincidence. My journey to Ullersdorf . . ."

"How anyone could be interested in who stayed the night at
this parish eight years ago, I can't comprehend. Do you have some
sort of suspicion, sir?"

The advocate waved his hand, as if brushing away an insect.

"Let's forget it, Father. If you say the heretic left nothing here,
all is well. You know what surprises me? How your town has
risen up again in these few years! It's even more splendid than it
was before the fire!"

"The people of Schönberg work hard."

"And now I see their coffers are full again!"

"*Humilibus Deus dat gratiam.* God giveth grace to the humble,
as the Apostle Peter says."

Boblig reached for his glass and sipped some more wine before
replying.

"But I have other experiences," he said. "I never concerned
myself too much with theology, but my understanding is that
riches are largely the work of the Devil. You know better than I,
Father, how many times the Bible extols poverty above wealth.
It's easier for a camel to pass through the eye of a needle than it is
for a rich man to enter the Kingdom of Heaven . . . Isn't that
so?"

"Your quotation is correct," Lautner explained. "But if you
were better acquainted with the Scripture you would know that
nowhere is wealth directly proscribed. Riches simply present
more opportunities for sin."

"Let's not get involved in theological disputes. I've had a look
at Sattler's new dye works. The town's flourishing. The people
must be prospering. What's Master Hutter doing, now he's no
longer a judge?"

The dean gave a start.

"He farms."

"Hutter is dangerous: a rationalist, too free-thinking. Self-evidently witches were brought before his court, yet he had the audacity to acquit them! He wouldn't have got away with it so easily anywhere else!"

"Hutter is an honest and just man!"

"So why, may I ask, was he discharged from office?"

"Because of his verdict on those muddled women. The charges were absurd. They admitted they flew to the Petersstein on broomsticks. It was laughable. Not even my coachman believes such nonsense!"

"You think so?" asked the advocate, a peculiar stress in his voice.

"I know many things from the works of learned men," insisted the dean. "Men who have witnessed witch trials first hand!"

"Hmm! And I say to you, Your Reverence, that if you haven't served as an inquisitorial judge for forty years as I have, you know precious little! I've seen countless people burned at the stake who I'd never have thought were in league with the Devil. Yet they proved to be witches, every one!"

"Because," said Lautner with unconcealed irony, "they all confessed!"

"And how else could they have been condemned? There were respected ladies among them, sometimes even people from the Church. Even they confessed, Your Reverence!"

"Of course, after being tortured! The point of the Inquisition is not to mete out the law or to see that justice is done but to exact confessions. Isn't that so?"

"What else can it do?" The advocate smiled. "I understand you also studied law in Vienna, so you're no layman. I'm sure you're aware that a witch trial isn't concerned with an ordinary crime, and the judge, therefore, can't be guided by ordinary rules and regulations. The people he has to deal with are almost always obstinate and cunning. What's more, they can rely on help from their diabolical ally."

"I'm well aware of *Malleus maleficarum*, *The Witch Hammer*, and also the works of Martin Delrius. Dreadful books!"

"Oh! You've read *Malleus maleficarum?* And yet you have doubts?"

"My dear sir, I have no doubt that God, whom I serve, is more powerful than the Devil. Do you know the Gospel according to Saint John? If a man is not of God, he can do nothing."

"I'm not an expert in theology," replied Boblig, fixing the dean with his shining green eyes. "But in my forty years of witch trials I learned that even the staunchest disciples of the Devil often claim to speak in God's name. However, let's leave such matters aside . . ."

But once again Lautner interrupted, this time returning the inquisitor's fierce gaze.

"I'd like to ask you something. Do you believe all the people you burned at the stake were truly disciples of the Devil?"

"Believe?" echoed Boblig, his face twisted. "There's a word that belongs to theology, and I'm no expert in that field, as I said. I'm a lawyer. But I can assure you, Father: not only did the people whom you are defending confess, their guilt was also confirmed by the testimonies of others . . ."

At that moment there was a shriek from outside, as if from the servants' quarters.

The dean rushed out onto the landing, just as his housekeeper Susanne ran from the kitchen. The screaming was from Boblig's hunchbacked assistant. Old Florian, red in the face, was holding him by the scruff of his neck, cuffing him again and again. Ignatius, his face contorted into a ludicrous grimace, yelped and stamped his feet, flailing his arms.

"Let him go, Florian!" cried the dean sternly. "Whatever's happened?"

"He's like a beast out of hell!" the coachman replied. "I feed him, polite and proper, give him two glasses of wine, and just the one for myself, and what does he do? Instead of behaving like a guest, he's full of indecent talk. The shame of it, Father. And in a priest's house! Then he asks me if I've seen on you or on Miss Susanne any marks. Secret marks that don't bleed if pricked! As if I don't know what he's aiming at, the scoundrel!"

The dean frowned, went downstairs without a word and squeamishly touched the hunchback's shoulder.

"Was that supposed to be a joke?"

Ignatius lifted his head and emitted a piercing laugh.

"A joke! Hehehe!"

Suddenly there was a smacking sound from above. The dean looked up to see Susanne standing on the landing, as red as a peony, with Boblig beside her, wincing and rubbing his hand. The stumps of his teeth protruded like wolf's fangs.

"What's going on?" the dean called upstairs.

Susanne spun round and in one leap was back in the kitchen.

"Nothing," said Boblig, beaming again. "Just whisking a fly from your little maid's cheek."

Lautner understood. He knew Susanne's temper, and now he also knew Master Boblig of Edelstadt. But not a word passed his lips as he made his way deliberately back up the stairs.

He entered his room, and Boblig, without waiting for an invitation, followed him.

For a moment neither spoke. The advocate donned his cap and slowly drew on his shabby coat. But he was in no hurry to leave. Once again he gazed around the room, studying the books lining the walls, slim volumes and weighty tomes, all bound in leather. He could not resist taking some at random from the shelves.

"Aristotle, Euripides. This one's all theology, this one's all law," he muttered. "Look, here's *Corpus iuris civilis, Summa iurus canonici, Oeconomia iurus!*" He crossed to another shelf and reached for a large, evidently well-thumbed book.

"Adam Tanner, *Theologia Scholastica*. Never heard of it."

Then he took a smaller volume.

"*The Aurora*, by Jakob Boehme," he droned, shaking his head. "Another one I don't know!"

He laid the book down, took another, and read its title.

"*Cautio criminalis, seu de processibus contra sagas liber.* Langenfeld. Hmm. Don't know that one either!"

Lautner was worried. If Boblig were to reach farther to the floor, he would find plenty of books he would surely know, for they could be considered *libri haeretici,* works of heresy. The dean hoped his bloated belly would prevent him bending down.

Suddenly Boblig looked up.

"As I told you, Father, too many books burden the brain. Just one is enough for me!"

"And what would that be? The Bible, perhaps?"

"Not at all, Father. The book you mentioned yourself: *Malleus maleficarum!*"

The advocate laughed. But it was no mirthful laugh. It struck terror. That is how the Devil must laugh, the dean thought to himself.

"Good-bye, Your Reverence," Boblig said. "I hope this won't be the last I'll see of you!"

Lautner accompanied his guest outside, his knees buckling, his pulse racing. He felt a roaring in his head. Florian and Susanne were nowhere to be seen. The hunchback was already sitting in the carriage.

The coachman cracked his whip and the carriage jolted off along the bumpy pavement. Lautner returned to his room. Forgetting Susanne and Florian, he thought of the books Boblig had taken from the shelves. Surely he knew Boehme, the Lutheran philosopher, and Langenfeld and Tanner, whose books were fierce attacks on the methods used by those who conducted inquisitorial trials. It was impossible for Boblig not to know these books. He had lied. But why? He had also lied, certainly, in the matter of the gentlemen from Milan. Why? What was he up to?

Then Lautner went into the kitchen. Susanne sat sobbing, her head buried in the arm of her chair.

"You lost your temper a little, my dear," he said softly.

She sprang out of the chair.

"I should have knocked his head off, the filthy goat!"

The dean slipped away. Susanne was right. He would have gladly granted her absolution if she had done just that. That slap alone had been worth at least ten Our Fathers.

7 ✦ Ripples on the Surface

The arrest of the three old women from Wermsdorf caused an unprecedented commotion. Witchcraft was the topic of the day at Zöptau on Easter Monday, and it remained so when the burgrave, a clerk, and two bailiffs from Ullersdorf arrived a few days later to ransack the suspects' homes, looking for disappearing ointments, magic dust, and all the other tools of their trade. But however hard they looked, they found little, only some dried herbs and roots in Mistress David's parlor, a bearded billy goat in the pen, and an old black tomcat in the hall. They took the goat back to the castle, but the cat escaped and was never seen again.

Life at Wermsdorf gradually began to return to its old course after the burgrave's departure. For many years Mistress Groer had practiced her midwifery to everyone's satisfaction, Mistress David had treated their ills, and even the beggarwoman Schuch had never seriously offended anyone. The people of the village had never seen them do anything suspicious. If the Devil had rewarded them as he had done Doctor Faust of Wittemberg, of whom they had heard so much, Maryna Schuch would hardly have had to go begging or the others to lead such a hand-to-mouth existence. Dorothea David had set broken bones and treated diseases, had healed sick animals and men by incantations. But even she had not been able to cure all ills, just as Dorothea Groer had been unable to save every newborn child.

But spring was in a hurry this year. The fields were drying before their eyes; there were other things to worry about. Besides, manorial overseers and bailiffs were going into the countryside, reminding the people of their most baneful responsibility—feudal labor.

Eusebius Leander Schmidt, the zealous priest at Zöptau, did not have to work on the manorial estates. He spent his time now poring over Floriand de Remond's thick treatise on the origin, rise, and fall of heterodoxy, amazed at how many vexations the Church had suffered. Whenever he looked out the window to rest his eyes, he saw his own parish church. Even *that* house of the Lord, he recalled, had been built by heretics. The horns of the Devil were everywhere! The three witches of Wermsdorf were surely not alone in his parish. The others would have to be rooted out!

When, the following Sunday, he mounted the pulpit, he knew his duty.

He began his sermon with a quotation from the prophet Jeremiah, who, long before the birth of Christ, had warned the Jews to beware of diviners, dreamers, enchanters, and sorcerers. Then, moving to the time of Christendom, he spoke of the changes in the Devil's ways that more than four hundred years before had compelled the Holy Father Gregory IX to declare a crusade against Satan and his disciples.

"Even then," he ranted, his sunken eyes burning as if from a fever, "there were many who had renounced Christianity and denied the Son of God. They turned their backs on the Lord, the sacred cross, and the holy relics, and instead bowed down to the Devil. He would show himself to them in the shape of a hideous toad, sometimes of common size, sometimes as large as a duck or a goose, but most often as large as a loaf of bread. And they would kneel, mark you my words, to kiss its anus or its mouth, taking its very tongue and spittle into their own mouths! And at the same time as this toad there would appear also a man, an apostate, fallen from God, so thin that it seemed all the flesh had fallen from him, leaving only a skeleton drawn over with skin. Even him they kissed, so losing every remembrance of our Catholic faith from their hearts. Thus changed, they would sit down to feasts at which a tomcat, as big as a dog, would appear. One after another, the beasts that were once men would kneel to kiss the cat's behind. And when they had finished their long litany to the cat, they would douse all the lights and, regardless of age or kinship, join themselves in the most loathsome fornication. When the lamps were lighted again, a creature would step out from a dark corner; below the waist as hairy as a cat, but above the waist as radiant as the sun—Lucifer himself . . ."

The congregation gazed in awe as they heard these blood-curdling things. No one doubted their truth, not when they came from the reverend father himself, and from a church pulpit, too.

For a very long time Father Schmidt vividly described the bestialities of Devil worship. Only when he was quite exhausted did he moderate his tone.

"Parishioners, brethren and sisters! Everything in the world that is bad, evil or sinful, or harmful to body and soul, is the work of the Devil; and everything that is useful, good, fine, and noble, is the work of the Lord. I know what troubles you. You grumble about your poverty; the illnesses that torment you; the barrenness of your land; the gales that blow away your roofs or uproot your fruit trees; the hailstorms that sometimes leave you with not an ear of corn to reap from your fields; the floods or the drought; the plagues that kill your livestock; the famine that can follow the failure of your crops. Just consider: who can cause you all of these evils? Perhaps you think it is Almighty God, punishing you for your sins. But are your sins really great enough to deserve such punishments? After all, the Lord God is a merciful, kind, and loving Father to his children! No, all of the evils that befall you must needs be the works of the Devil, for the Devil's greatest joy comes from his confounding the good works of the Lord . . ."

The priest's words were an awesome revelation to the packed congregation. Poor to a man, tribulation was all they knew. Their rock-strewn fields yielded little, the meager crops often destroyed by rain or hail. Their cattle perished, disease was rife, there was hardly ever enough grain to last the year. Some toiled at the manorial iron-forges and smelting furnaces, or risked their lives as woodmen in the forest, or log-haulers on the steep mountain-side. All were sorely punished by a lifetime of drudgery, poverty, and often hunger. And this was the work of the Devil!

The priest paused to give each of his parishioners sufficient time to recognize the cause of their poverty. Then he continued.

"Three women from Wermsdorf have been found to be in league with the Devil, the archenemy of mankind. They have already been handed over to a righteous judge, and none of them can do you further harm. But I ask you, my friends, could those three women, now in custody awaiting punishment, have been alone? Aren't there more of them among you? Perhaps not all the witches of our parish are under lock and key; perhaps there are other vile souls who have sold themselves to the Devil and are still helping to spread his evil in our parish! So be on your guard! If you suspect anyone, seize them, or waste not a minute but come and tell me their names! This you must do, each of you, for your own sake, for your salvation and for all the community, in the name of God the Father, the Son, and the Holy Spirit. Amen."

His flock was so appalled they forgot to beat their breasts during the Mass that followed. They were thinking of the preacher's words, and of their neighbors and friends, any one of whom might be in league with the Devil.

Later, when the service was over and little knots of people remained standing outside the church and by the graves of their loved ones, no one spoke of anything but the sermon. Everyone had some kind of enemy. What if they, too, were disciples of the Devil, along with Maryna Schuch, Dorothea Groer, and Dorothea David?

The only person present to keep a clear head was Johann Axmann, the village magistrate at Zöptau. He said nothing in front of his neighbors, maintaining his silence until he got home.

"As I recall," he winked to his wife Dorothea over lunch, "most of the evil that ever befell us came from the castle at Ullersdorf. And I can't believe that's a house of the Devil—though I'm bound to say plenty of folk there look the part!"

"Rather you say nothing, husband," she hushed, "or the reverend father will get to hear of it!"

The church at Zöptau had indeed been packed that Sunday, and having heard the priest's message, no one kept it to himself but passed it on. So people throughout the parish were soon observing one another with suspicion, and neighbor was regarding neighbor through quite different eyes than before. What, after all, if she were another Mistress David of Wermsdorf?

But still the priest waited in vain for someone to come forward with a name. Only later did some scoundrel push a slip of paper into the church charity box. On it was the name of his housekeeper . . .

Reports of Father Schmidt's sermon reached the Dean of Schönberg directly after he heard from Father König that the inquisitor Boblig had begun his interrogations at Ullersdorf Castle. This was disturbing news. Schmidt's fervor, unbridled by prudence or discretion, was grist to the mill for Master Boblig, who made a lucrative living out of other people's misfortunes. At this rate, the tranquil countryside around Schönberg could soon become a living hell. No one would be sure how he stood in the eyes of his neighbors; denunciations would follow denunciations; just as in Silesia before, even husbands would condemn wives simply to get rid of them. But what was the dean to do?

As Schmidt's superior, Lautner could go to Zöptau to give him some fatherly advice, or summon him to Schönberg. But would it help? Schmidt was a fanatic.

The dean came to no conclusion. Instead he worked his next Sunday sermon into a polemic against the priest at Zöptau. It was not the Devil, he declared, but God who directed the run of the world and the destinies of men. And God was love. However great the sin or the sinner, He in His omnipotence, goodness, and mercy could forgive. The more one suffered in this vale of tears, the greater was one's hope of eternal bliss in the hereafter. Not through hatred or suspicion could people be bound to one another, but through love, self-devotion, and fellowship.

But such words were all too commonplace. Even in Schönberg there were many who also lived in dire straits. They saw how the rich burghers disregarded the Lord's Commandments, and how most of them worshipped Mammon in place of the Lord. And was not Mammon also the name of a devil? Words were but as light as feathers; deeds were of far greater substance. There was indeed more evil than goodness in the world!

Realizing his sermon could not possibly equal the force of Schmidt's preaching, Lautner turned for advice to his closest friend, the former judge, Kaspar Hutter. He proved to be far less faint-hearted.

"If you throw a rock into a pond," Hutter told him, "there is a splash, and there are ripples on the surface. But in a while everything is once more as it was. The best thing would be to have Schmidt transferred to another parish."

The advice was sound, but if it were to be followed, the dean would have to have powerful friends in Olomouc. Or perhaps, thought Lautner, he might use the influence of an old friend from his student days. Now the Dean of Müglitz, Vojtech Winkler enjoyed the bishop's highest confidence.

But it wasn't just a matter of Father Schmidt. A far greater problem was posed by the inquisitor. Not even the experienced Kaspar Hutter could advise the dean how to get rid of him.

"The only possibility, as I see it," he suggested, "is for Father König to persuade the countess to send him back. But would an advocate as cunning as Boblig allow himself to be dismissed?"

✦ ✦ ✦

That same day, Lautner was invited to the home of Franz Ferdinand Gaup, Schönberg's new district judge, whose newborn first son was also the dean's godchild. Lautner could not refuse, but he was loath to go, for the judge was not a good friend of his, having come by his position only through Hutter's suspension.

Gaup's elbows were as sharp as his shoulders were broad. Hardly forty years of age, he had thrust his way to a judgeship, though many citizens had enjoyed greater seniority and rank. A large, fat-bellied man, he had an affectation for grandness, covering his sparse hair with a wig, and on great feast days—when he discovered they were de rigueur at the imperial court in Vienna—dressing in red stockings.

This man of ambition was unable to look anyone directly in

the eye, but flinched from nothing that could advance his career. Lautner did not like him. His past held many dark secrets, the only certainty being that he must have had powerful friends in high places. Otherwise he could hardly have been made a district judge.

The Gaup family house on the town square was of stone, with an upper floor built of timber. Everything inside was, as people were beginning to say, à la mode: costly furniture, polished and inlaid with mother-of-pearl, walls full of sacred pictures, everywhere charming bric-a-brac, but nowhere, Lautner noticed, a trace of a book. But that was usual in almost all the burghers' families. Only here and there would one find a prayer book or simple almanac.

The other guests at the Gaups' house included the old Sattlers and Heinrich Peschek. But it was the dean to whom Gaup paid the most attention, and he unashamedly and publicly explained why. Above all else, he proclaimed, he wanted his son to grow up to be a churchman, for only a member of the clergy could attain high status without the benefit of an aristocratic title.

Good food and wine was to be had in plenty, but the company was neither merry nor jovial. Even Lautner, renowned for his humor at such gatherings, was not his usual self.

And no wonder, for conversation turned to the case of the witches of Wermsdorf. Kaspar Sattler and Heinrich Peschek declared clearly that they found the charges hardly credible. What had the women done that was supernatural? Whom had they harmed? One of them had wanted to feed a consecrated wafer to her cow so it would give more milk, nothing more. It was just a foolish superstition. She deserved strict punishment for abusing the sacrament—but it was nonsense to accuse her of witchcraft! Peschek added that he, an old man, had seen much of the world and many kinds of people in his time, but he had never ever met a devil in any shape or form.

One of the other guests was the diminutive figure of Sebastian Flade, clerk of the Schönberg district court. Clever and very pious, he was also a little the worse for drink.

"If anyone's ever seen a devil," he laughed, "I'd say it must be the dean!"

"And indeed I have seen one," the dean retorted gravely, as all eyes turned on him. "Tiny, thin, bristly-haired—I'd say it was the spitting image of our dear court clerk."

The guests smiled. Fortunately, Flade also took the remark to be a joke.

"And where did you see him, Father?" he asked.

"It was when I was parish priest at Nieder Mohrau," Lautner began. "There was a very pious but quite intrepid farmer. Every winter he smoked meat and bacon in his kitchen chimney. One morning he got up to hear a strange noise coming from the next room. He ran into the kitchen and stopped in his tracks. There by the hearth he saw a creature, quite black, with flashing teeth. But he wasn't afraid. 'Who are you?' he asked, and the beast whined: 'I am Belial.' The farmer was a little unnerved, but he stood his ground. 'And what are you doing here?' he asked. 'I've brought you some bacon,' said the creature, handing him a whole side of bacon. 'No, keep it,' said the farmer, 'or give it to someone who has more need of it. I've plenty of my own in the chimney.' The devil said not a word, but dashed out of the house as if the dogs were after him. Only days later did the farmer admit the devil had offered him his own bacon and run away with it when he refused. Next Eastertide, one of my parishioners told me at confession how he'd stolen a side of bacon, and that was how I got to know the farmer's devil."

"And what penance did you give him, Father?" asked Gaup.

"Three Our Fathers and three Hail Marys. He was only a poor man, with half a dozen children and no land of his own. And the farmer really did have plenty more meat up the chimney!"

The story went down well, not so much for its humor, but for its undertone. Everyone recognized that not even the dean gave much credence to demons. Gaup alone was dissatisfied, both with the mildness of the penance prescribed for a common thief and with the way the dean had made light of the Devil.

"Master Boblig of Edelstadt, who is investigating the witches at Ullersdorf," he said, "would, I think, take another view of such things!"

The remark was as much in jest as it was meant seriously, but it came as an icy blast to the whole company. So the district judge, who would always side with anyone who could advance his career, knew the inquisitor! The two of them could well work hand in hand. The dean's humor was now gone for good. He took a deep draft of red wine, but it was bitter to the taste.

A new guest arrived—Christoph Zeidler, forest warden from Ullersdorf, burly and garrulous, with a gingery beard that came down to his waist. Bellowing greetings to everyone present, he pumped Gaup's hand before draining a large glass of brandy to the health of his newborn son. Then he turned to the others.

"I've brought some news from Ullersdorf. The three hags have confessed! They're witches! Once a year they flew to the Petersstein on broomsticks and got up to some fine tricks! I'm thankful it's not on my patch, I can tell you!"

Silence. The dean squeezed his knuckles until they cracked. He could feel the stares of the Sattlers and of Peschek. He observed the suspicious smile on Gaup's face and the astonishment of Flade, the court clerk. At the same time he imagined the dreadful fate of the three women from Wermsdorf and reflected with utter certainty that Boblig would not rest now. A renowned inquisitor such as he would hardly have gone to Ullersdorf on their account alone. He would not be content until more victims were found.

"Well, Father," asked Gaup, "what do you say to that?"

"What do I say? I saw Schuch the beggarwoman, and many of you know Dorothea Groer and the muddled Dorothea David. I don't believe any of them was possessed by the Devil!"

The judge's face twisted into an incredulous frown.

"And if they confessed?"

"My friend, you may hold the office of presiding judge in our town, but I'm afraid you know very little about inquisitorial courts!"

Gaup's face reddened as Sattler and Peschek smiled.

Lautner saw no reason for staying any longer.

Out on the street, the air was as clean and heavy as old wine. Rivulets trickled along the pavement, remnants of a sharp spring shower. Several small boys were building earthen dams, trapping the muddy water into tiny pools.

The dean paused to watch. If only the flow of filth from Zöptau to Gross Ullersdorf could be stemmed as easily as this!

As he made his way home, he thought back to the learned nobleman from Milan whom he had once sheltered, but who was now serving a cruel term of twenty-five years at the Castel Sant'Angelo. Borri had quoted the great physician Paracelsus: the highest principle of medicine is love. No physician was ever born without it.

Physician! But should not the same be said of a judge? And what of a priest?

He would have to go to Müglitz to see Brother Winkler.

8 ✦ A Scream in the Night

What Zeidler said at the christening party was not true, of course, but merely a report of what the inquisitor had proclaimed all over the castle: that the women from Wermsdorf were witches, beyond the slightest doubt. But if the truth were to be known, Boblig was in no hurry to conclude his investigation. He enjoyed being at Ullersdorf Castle. The food was excellent and the drink, though it could have been better, was plentiful. He did summon the prisoners again and frighten them with another cross-examination, but they were not pressed too hard for a confession. He did not even consider torture. Everything in due course, he told his assistant.

But he could not be accused of idleness. Above all he wrote a long letter to His Grace the Bishop of Olomouc, Count Liechtenstein, grandiloquently informing him of the gravity of the case with which he had been entrusted. He knew the bishop and knew his secretary even better. Schmidt could be counted on to take the liveliest interest in any mention of heresy or magic. Not so much because he was personally concerned about witches at Wermsdorf, but because it would give him the chance to attract the bishop's attention to himself. As always, Boblig of Edelstadt was thinking far ahead.

He also wrote another letter, to which he attached equal importance. This was to the Court of Appeals. He urgently needed the approval of the Law Lords in Prague before he could officially begin the witch trial at all. But he did not doubt for a moment that such approval would be given, for heresy and witchcraft were still supremely punishable crimes.

All was going well for Boblig except one thing. The senior officials at the castle had noticed the reserve with which the countess treated her guest, and so none of them ventured to approach him themselves. Neither Sheriff Vinarsky, nor the burgrave, nor even the treasurer had visited him in his quarters, still less invited him to visit them. And the sheriff had such a delightful daughter Elisabeth, and the burgrave had such a jolly wife! There was nothing for it, Master Boblig of Edelstadt had to spend the evenings and long nights in the company of his assistant.

This evening, as usual, no one had invited the inquisitor for dinner. So, like the day before and the days before that, he and his assistant dined alone in their quarters, stuffing their bellies with prodigious quantities of excellent sausages, washed down mightily with rather less excellent beer. As he ate, the inquisitor cheered himself with memories, plucking tidbits of stories from the distant past, like currants from a cake. After the beer he poured himself wine, and the more he drank, the more maudlin he became, until in his own stories he was all but the greatest benefactor the world had ever known. Ignatius knew him and did not interrupt. He was drinking far less than his master, for he knew his duty. When the inquisitor stopped talking, he would lay his head on the table; then he would have to be dragged off to bed.

Boblig was telling the tale of one of his victims in the town of Neisse. Or was it Görlitz? He had officiated at so many places, he tended to confuse the names. But he remembered this witch very well and always recalled her in his drunken melancholy. Though he knew the story like the Lord's Prayer and could tell it himself in his master's own words, Ignatius sat and listened as if he were hearing it for the first time.

"That was no woman, Iggy, that was a goddess! Ah, what's the use of describing her! She was no ordinary, grubby country girl, but the wife of a respected town councillor who was master of a guild of artists. She'd been the model for his Madonnas, with and without child. And yet we still had to send her to the stake! When I first saw her, I remembered the wise advice of the Dominican friar Henrich Institoris, that an inquisitor should never set his eyes on the accused until he has extracted a confession. *Qui vivra, verra.* He who waits shall see. We had to strip her naked to find the witch mark. Can you imagine it, Iggy? She looked like a statue of the finest Carraran marble. If you'd seen her, Iggy, you'd be drooling. I almost was. She struggled, though. Fought like a tigress. Tried all sorts of things. Once she sank to her knees before me and begged me to save her life. You know, Iggy, the Devil comes in many different forms, but this was too much. I had to fight to overcome myself. To the last moment that witch hoped she'd escape death. Even when she was tied to the stake, surrounded by dry logs. The executioner stood with a flaming torch, waiting for my order to light the oil-soaked wood shavings. And she was still hoping. She cried out to the monk who'd prepared her for the execution, and I couldn't help going to her one more time. 'Would you like to confess your sins again?' he asked. I noticed how he couldn't bring himself to look her in the face. Even he was afraid of her eyes. 'No, I've already made my confession,' she said. 'So would you like me to celebrate Holy Mass for your soul?' he said. 'Even if you say no, I'll still say three Masses for you.' And he bowed his head further. 'Oh no,' she sobbed, 'I only want extreme unction. If I'm given the last rites, I'll live on, I know it!' The monk bowed so low, you could see the little shaved circle on the crown of his head. There was nothing I could do but order the executioner to delay no longer. But I admit to you, Iggy, at that moment, even as the shavings were lighted, there was nothing I wished more than for the heavens to open and a cloudburst of water extinguish the flames . . ."

Boblig groped for his glass.

"But master, you were still very young in those days."

"Young! I suppose you're right, Iggy. Now I'm old—but still not too old to see her when my eyes are closed, as if she were alive before me now. What a beauty! Beauty has immense power! Did you see the cook when we were at the deanery in Schönberg? You know, she reminded me very much of that witch in Neisse. Beauty, Iggy, is dangerous. Beauty, *quod bene notandum,* note this well, is the work of the Devil."

Ignatius was not fond of anyone talking of beauty, not even his master. He regarded it as mocking his own fate.

"If beauty is the work of the Devil," he observed with irony, "then you and I must be children of God!"

Boblig stared at his hunchbacked companion with bloodshot eyes. Then he burst into gales of belly-shaking laughter, seized his glass, and drained it to the dregs.

At this there was a timid knock at the door.

"Come on in, don't be shy, the pitcher's empty!" shouted the inquisitor, assuming this was Stubenvoll the cellarman, coming to see whether he should replenish the wine.

But it was not the cellarman. The man who appeared was not particularly big, but he was strong, especially his arms. His head was round and completely shorn, his neck was squat, his forehead low, his eyes broad slits on either side of a red, turned-up nose.

The inquisitor recognized him immediately as Jakob Hay the master executioner, otherwise known as Jokl. This was a pleasure. Any visitor was welcome, even an executioner, for three made company.

"You've come at just the right time," he said. "Sit down, Jokl. Iggy, pour the man a drink if there's still a drop left!"

The bewildered visitor remained standing, ill at ease. No judge had ever invited him to his table before. This one was treating him as an equal.

"Come on!" Boblig repeated his invitation. "We're in the same trade, aren't we?"

Jokl saw that his host was considerably the worse for liquor. He sat down on the edge of a chair and accepted a glass from Ignatius.

"*Prosit,* Your Honor!" he said, and took a modest sip.

"What's on your mind?" the inquisitor asked.

Jokl stroked his thick neck for some time.

"I wanted to tell you, Your Honor, that the—uh, trade is bad."

"What's so bad about it?"

"The money, Your Honor."

"Just you wait!" laughed Boblig. "We didn't come here for nothing, you know! You'll soon have so much work, you won't know where to turn!"

Jokl merely sighed.

"What's the matter?" Boblig asked.

"It's getting to be a long wait, Your Honor."

"Does this mean you're not satisfied with me?" Boblig smiled.

"Not at all, Your Honor. But you can afford to wait, you have money flowing in . . ."

"And you don't?"

"Yes, but only a trickle. I get paid one kreuzer a day for each prisoner for food and another two each to keep them in irons. I have to give them a little bread to keep them from starving, and then what's left for me? Forgive me, Your Honor, but it really does seem to me you're too gentle with them. Not once have you ordered torture. Now, if I were to use the thumbscrew or the Spanish boot, I'd get eighteen kreuzers, and for the rack I'd get thirty-five . . ."

"I get the idea, you scoundrel," Boblig chuckled, "I get the idea!"

"If you were to take pity on a poor master executioner, Your Honor . . ."

Boblig puffed out his chest, stood up and pounded the table with his fist.

"Master Jokl, your request will be granted!"

Then, turning to Ignatius, he shouted: "Where in hell is that cursed cellarman? Get him to fetch another pitcher of wine!"

The hunchback scurried out. Boblig leaned over to Jokl.

"You have to be patient, my friend," he whispered, "like me. *Post nubila Phoebus*, as the Latin scholars say. The sun shines after the rain. But I put it another way: The stake burns after the trial. You are going to get not kreuzers, Master Jokl, but thalers! How much do you get for one burning?

"Ten thalers and something for my lad."

"There, you see? Thirty thalers are on the way!"

The hunchback returned, with Stubenvoll in tow. Boblig saw at a glance that Ignatius was carrying an empty pitcher.

"Where's the wine?"

"Begging your pardon, sir," blurted the cellarman, his face a twisted grin, "but one way and another you're already over the burgrave's limit . . ."

Boblig flushed crimson, seized Stubenvoll by his lapels and shook him violently.

"You damned rogue, guzzling on my account and then blaming it on the burgrave! You taste our wine at least three times before we ever get it, you shameless thief! So no more sour looks from you, and fetch some more wine! The best!"

"I'll ask the burgrave, sir."

"There's time enough for that tomorrow. Now I want wine!"

Stubenvoll left the room, gritting his teeth. Never had he served such a guest!

"That man," heaved the inquisitor, "is a suspicious character."

"Too fond of scowling," chortled his assistant. "That's an evil sign."

After a while the cellarman returned with a pitcher filled to the brim. He set it down without a word and left.

"See? There's no point being polite to such villains," commented Boblig, recharging his glass and passing another to Jokl. "Here, drink, build up your strength! *Bibamus!*"

The glasses clinked, the wine gurgled down.

Boblig wiped his mouth on his sleeve and leaned over to Jokl again.

"You know what? When we've drunk this, we'll have some sport with the old scarecrow, Mistress David. See if you can straighten her out a little!"

"What, now?"

"Didn't you just ask me if you could?"

"But I've always carried out torture only in the presence of the court, Your Honor!"

"I am the court, you dolt! And I judge *igni et ferro*, with fire and iron, understand? *Alii sementem faciunt, allii metent.* I sow and you reap! Now, pull yourself together and take the witch to the torture chamber. You know which one, don't you? The one with the bent back!"

"David."

"That's her! The one who calls me the Devil! We'll see what she says when you put her on the hoist!"

The executioner shrugged his shoulders, but did not leave the room.

"It's nighttime, Your Honor. Everyone's asleep. We might wake the countess . . . !"

"Go! I'm the judge, and I'm ordering you!"

Master Jokl hesitated no longer, but left to do as he was told.

A moment later, Boblig himself got up and lurched off with Ignatius for the courtroom, hiccuping violently. So violently that he had to rest several times on the stairs.

"That wasn't wine, that was stale slops," he muttered. "Mark my words, Iggy, that scoundrel of a cellarman will pay dearly for this one day. Dearly! Just you remind me if I forget. But I won't forget . . ."

"Quiet, we'll wake the countess," hushed the hunchback.

Boblig cursed and spat on the floor.

At last they reached the courtroom and went straight through into the torture chamber. Boblig sank onto a chair while Ignatius lighted a number of candles. The inquisitor's blood-tinged eyes spotted a chair opposite, its seat and backrest pierced through with a hundred and fifty sharp nails. He was still thinking of Stubenvoll, and now he saw the cellarman sitting in that chair. Its nails were ripping into his buttocks, thighs, back, and arms.

There was a noise from next door and suddenly Jokl emerged, half carrying the old woman David.

She was now just skin and bones, but her eyes still glared brightly. When she saw the inquisitor she screeched:

"The Devil, tormentor of Christ the Lord!"

"Foul creature!" Boblig hurled back. "You'll soon be singing another song! Master Jokl, do your duty!"

Jakob Hay was truly a master of his craft. First he gagged the prisoner by pushing a pear-shaped block of wood into her mouth, then he tore off the rags that clothed her ancient, emaciated body. Only Ignatius appeared to be animated by the dreadful sight.

Next he bound her legs, then twisted her arms behind her

back, tying them tightly with the same cord. Finally he secured a stout rope to her arms and ran it over a roller-pulley fixed to one of the ceiling beams.

Boblig went to the prisoner and ordered Jokl to take the pear from her mouth.

"We know you went to the Petersstein. How many times did you have intercourse with the Devil?"

Dorothea David's face was contorted with pain, for the tight cord bit deeply into her skin. She appeared not to understand what the inquisitor was saying. As far as she was concerned, he was the Devil. The blubbery lips, the barking voice, the bloodshot eyes! Her whole body shook, but she kept her silence.

"So the bitch won't talk! Jokl, begin!"

The executioner pulled on the rope hanging from the pulley. At first he pulled gently, but then as the rope became taut he began to tug. The old woman gave an agonized yelp as her body, crooked for so many years, began to straighten.

Boblig motioned Jokl to slacken the rope.

"Are you going to talk?"

She fixed her eyes on the inquisitor. For a moment she was silent, then she shrieked: "Lucifer!"

"Haul away, Jokl!"

The executioner had arms of steel. Again he pulled on the rope until it was as taut as a bowstring. Then he slackened it suddenly. There was a sharp scream as Dorothea fell with a back-wrenching jerk, then all was quiet. She had lost consciousness. Her body slumped, her head sank, and if she had not been tied up she would have crumpled on the floor.

Boblig stared in annoyance. He had not expected the torture to end like this. He looked reluctantly at the executioner.

"That will have to be all for today," Jokl said.

"Throw her in the dungeons!" Boblig growled. "Get her out of my sight!"

After that he paid no more heed to Dorothea David or to Jokl. He clutched his assistant's hand.

"You, take me home!"

They both lurched from the chamber and passed through the courtroom and the anteroom beyond. Outside on the open corridor there was already some light, but the stairway that descended from it was as black as pitch.

Halfway down the stairs, Boblig stopped.

"Did you see the Devil, Iggy? Just as she was about to confess, he took away her senses. That often happens. The Devil has great power, Iggy. Always with God's indulgence, of course. When we get back to our room you'll have to fetch another pitcher. This calls for a drink!"

"Come on, master."

Treading very carefully, they finally arrived at the first floor. Boblig leaned, panting for breath, on one of the stone pillars that supported the upstairs corridor. Outside in the gloom he saw a dim figure crossing the courtyard bearing a heavy burden. Master Jokl was carrying the prisoner back to her cell.

Suddenly the whole yard resounded with an awful, inhuman scream. Dorothea David had regained consciousness.

Ignatius dragged his master back into the stairway as windows and doors were flung open on the upper floors.

Only when silence returned did Ignatius bundle the inquisitor into his room and put him to bed.

9 ✦ Mere Chaff

The sun was already high in the sky; the dew was long dry, and in its place the sweat of laboring serfs now moistened the manorial fields of Ullersdorf. But the inquisitor was still sprawled fast asleep on his bed, his bare torso exposed to the daylight. His chest wheezed, and his snores were punctuated by occasional whistling noises, like a saw cutting through wood that is full of knots. Someone tapped on the door.

Ignatius, long awake and dressed, hurried to answer on tiptoe, in order not to disturb his master.

It was Jokl, and he was plainly worried.

"I must see His Honor straightaway!"

"You'd better wake him yourself, then!"

Jokl strode to the bed and shook him soundly. The snoring ceased. Boblig awakened, forced open his rheumy eyes, fixed them on his visitor and—Ignatius marveled—did not shout at all.

"Ah, Jokl! What do you want?" he said, stretching himself.

"Your Honor, it's the witch we had in the chamber last night . . ."

"What's the matter with her?"

"She's dead, Your Honor. I found her cold on the straw this morning . . ."

Boblig shook himself, sat up and stared, scratching his hairy chest.

"We must have overdone it," Jokl sighed.

"What do you mean, we?" exclaimed Boblig. "If she's dead, it couldn't have been anyone but the Devil. He was the one who broke her back!"

Jokl did not share his confidence.

"The Devil?"

"Are you doubting what I say, you dolt?" the inquisitor thundered. "A fine executioner you are! This is a common occurrence! In Zuckmantel we once arrested a young overseer's wife, and the Devil broke her back before a week was out! You surely don't think hoisting the woman was enough to kill her, do you?"

"I don't know what to think, Your Honor."

"There you are! The Devil is afraid lest his disciples betray his secrets. The more a witch knows about him, the more likely he is to break her back during the interrogation or to see her off some other way. That old witch must have known plenty. Get rid of her somewhere, Jokl, but don't let too many people see you!"

The executioner nodded and left.

Boblig sprang to his feet.

Ignatius knew his duty. Taking up a pitcher of water, he poured some over his master's hands. Boblig washed his face, head, neck and chest, and an instant later he was dressed.

"Breakfast?" asked the hunchback.

"No, there's no time now."

Ignatius shook his head. It was not very often that his master went without breakfast.

Boblig strode out of the room, marched solemnly down the corridor to the countess's wing of the castle, and there asked the chambermaid to take him to her mistress.

The maid disappeared for a few seconds before returning to the door and inviting him in. Boblig was flattered. What respect he had acquired! But when he entered the countess's room he was less agreeably surprised, for she already had a visitor—Father König of Ullersdorf. Neither was smiling.

Boblig bowed.

"Forgive me, milady, for the interruption, but I was in a hurry to bring you some rather unpleasant news," he said, his deep voice even coarser than usual.

"I am ready," said the countess coldly.

"One of the three persons accused of witchcraft has died . . ."

"Without receiving any spiritual solace," interjected the countess, even more frostily than before.

Boblig frowned. He saw that his haste had been in vain. Some-one had given her the news already. He should have known there could be no secrets in this castle!

"Her back was broken by the Devil, milady . . ."

Father König looked him sharply in the eye.

"Did this happen during torture?"

The inquisitor glared back. He hated this little priest.

"With the benefit of my experiences," he replied calmly, "I can state that such cases are not exceptional. The Devil has often been known to take the lives of people who might bear witness against him. It happens with God's indulgence, of course, but why it happens is a theological question, and one I am not competent to answer."

The countess peered silently and unnervingly at the inquisitor. Then she spoke.

"During the night I heard a frightful scream from the court-yard. Do you think, sir, that it could have been the Devil? That the Devil himself was in our castle?"

"It could have been none other, milady. Of course, this too was surely only with God's indulgence. The reason, I would sug-gest, was to test our mettle; God requires more from us than mere humility. And I would say that for me also it was a call—for the swiftest action against those who have entered the service of the Evil One."

"But you acted yesterday, didn't you?" remarked Father König. "And your efforts appear to have been insufficient."

Before Boblig could reply, the countess spoke again.

"You should have sent to Olomouc for the Capuchins long ago. They would have protected us from the Devil's powers. And perhaps the prisoners would have confessed sooner!"

"Perhaps also yesterday's torture would not have been neces-sary," the priest added.

Boblig could hardly contain himself. He felt like a mouse caught in a trap. The countess and the priest knew everything, to the finest detail. But from whom? Jokl, or one of the jailers? He was incensed by this little priest who would have looked far more at home in a shoemaker's apron than a surplice. This priest, he had heard, was a good friend of the Dean of Schönberg. Well, he would see about that! Meanwhile, however, he had to keep calm. He bowed.

"I will summon the Capuchins immediately."

"I'd like to point out just one more thing, Master Boblig," said Father König. "According to the law, torture is permitted only with the assistance of a tribunal."

Boblig puckered his lips.

"I don't believe I require any lessons in the law, Your Reverence. As an inquisitorial judge I am well aware of my rights and responsibilities."

The inquisitor was outwardly composed as he left the countess's quarters, but his blood seethed. Not for a long time had he been so shamed and humiliated.

He slammed his own door behind him. Ignatius cowered in a corner as his master paced the room in silence. He knew trouble when he saw it.

Suddenly Boblig stopped, seized his assistant by the lapels, and screamed, his voice breaking.

"What do you think, Iggy? That we've grown stupid in our old age? That a jumped-up little priest like König can play high and mighty with us? That we can hand over to someone else and quickly retire? Are we of no more use, mere chaff? Are we, Iggy?"

"No, master."

"Of course we're not! We'll show them who we are! We'll show the entire manor of Ullersdorf! Let no one dare suggest we don't know our business! Our memory still serves us well. We know what not to forget, and we know who not to forget!"

Ignatius said nothing. Even Boblig fell quiet. But after a while he spoke again, and this time it was his usual voice.

"The Devil took one ugly old hag from us, Iggy. But we're going to find a hundred others to take her place."

Ignatius saw the worst was over.

"Younger ones?" he smiled.

"Younger ones!"

Then Boblig told his assistant to get breakfast.

"See if they have any beer soup!" he called after him.

10 ✦ *Gathering Clouds*

Few people were privy to the strange and mysterious happenings at Ullersdorf Castle, and wild speculation abounded, especially when two Capuchin monks arrived from Olomouc and settled in at the castle. Bearded and somber, they dressed in hooded brown habits and wore rough sandals on their feet. One of them was called Carolus, the other Crescentianus. Every day they said Mass at the parish church or the castle chapel; every day they bathed in the nearby sulfurous pool, of whose curative powers the great physician Thomas Jordan of Cluj had written a laudatory discourse.

At first, the strange monks aroused only curiosity among the people and here and there some ridicule and scurrilous suggestions regarding the nature of the diseases they were treating. But the humor soon subsided when more women were arrested by the bailiffs and accused of witchcraft. First they took Maryna Züllich, the well-known miller's wife from Weikersdorf; then old Anna Föbel from Kleppel and Barbora Kühnel from Reitenhau, and finally Marie Petrova, wife of the senior estates manager at Johnsdorf. Now everyone knew for certain why the Capuchins had come—to help the inquisitor.

These arrests were in the surrounding countryside, so no one could tell whether there was any truth in the charges. But then the bailiffs began dragging away women from Gross Ullersdorf itself. The first to go was Agneta Kopp, a farmer's wife who for years had lived in peace and friendship with all her neighbors and whose herbal knowledge had been called upon and appreciated by everyone. The next was Susanne Stubenvoll, wife of the castle cellarman. The village was overwhelmed with panic. Mistress Kopp and Susanne Stubenvoll were respectable and decent women;

they went to Mass and to confession, they took communion. Now, all of a sudden, they were arrested as witches who served the Devil. Surely they could not have been arrested without just cause. But how was it that no one had noticed anything about them before? Whom was it still possible to believe? Who was in the service of God, and who the Devil?

The awful tidings spread from Gross Ullersdorf on all sides, and it was as if dense clouds, impervious to the sun, were gathering over the far-flung estates of the house of Zerotin. In all other respects this was a favorable season, with plenty of work to be done in the fields, the forests, the iron-forges and lumberyards. But the people were losing their appetite for such things. They lived in the shadow of a cloud and talked about nothing but the mysteries that were beyond their understanding: about the witches and devils, sometimes helpful, mostly harmful, that appeared in the most varied forms; about all sorts of apparitions and secret marks; about inexplicable or unnatural things they had seen or experienced. At work and at home in the evenings, people cast their minds back to past events which had remained unexplained, especially stories of blood-sucking vampires. They recalled the story of Barbora Polnar, the Schönberg weaver whose veins, even after her death, were found to be coursing with fresh red blood, a sure sign she had been the victim of a vampire. They remembered also Marie Sponnar and Regina Gärtner, who had taken to hunting for hidden treasure with the help of dark forces and who escaped burning at the stake only because they were acquitted by Kaspar Hutter, when he was district judge. But who was to know the real truth? They remembered cows that suddenly stopped milking or fell victim to disease; people who had been given the evil eye by a stranger; others who had been afflicted by evil spirits or who had died of a fright. Suddenly the world appeared to be a playground of unknown and insuperable forces, and mankind was at their mercy. Where could any certainty be found, where could one seek protection, when so often the Devil's disciples wore masks or were able to transform themselves, like old Agneta Kopp or Susanne Stubenvoll? The manor was overhung with the oppression that precedes a terrible storm. Human fantasy assumed enormous wings, and even the most levelheaded people of Gross Ullersdorf began losing their powers of reason. One began to suspect another; people were afraid to leave their homes at night; they were frightened of their own shadows; every noise was suspicious, and every black cat, goat, toad, snake, or other beast could be Satan in disguise.

Master Boblig of Edelstadt had pledged himself to pursue this case with utmost vigor, and he had not spoken in vain. But it was not out of zeal that he fulfilled his pledge, but more out of a desire to prove to himself and to others that in revealing evildoers of all kinds he had no rival. The two Capuchins, he discovered, were of considerable assistance, especially Brother Crescentianus. The elder of the two, he had a gray goatee, a soft velvety voice, and eyes as blue as chicory flowers.

This monk took charge of Maryna Schuch, the beggarwoman of Wermsdorf. There was no need for him to use even the thumbscrew, the lowest degree of torture. In the course of hour after hour of kind and gentle conversation, he convinced her that the more she admitted, the more mercy she could expect and the greater would be her chances of forgiveness—and that eternal heavenly bliss would be her reward. Weakened in body and soul by her imprisonment, no longer knowing the difference between truth and lies, she confessed to everything, even to sins she could not possibly have committed. She might have stood up to torture, but the soft voice of the Capuchin was something she could not resist. No one before had spoken so nicely to her, no one had behaved so kindly. But when Brother Crescentianus asked her whom she had seen at the witch-swarms on the Petersstein, she could not remember a single name.

"Didn't you see Mistress Petrova from Johrnsdorf?"

No, Maryna had not seen her, but that was not to say she could not have been there! Marie Petrova, she had heard, was a wild sort of woman and enjoyed a drink, and Maryna had also heard on more than one occasion that she was a bit of a devil. And so she named her, even though she did not even know her personally, for Johrnsdorf was a long way from Wermsdorf.

Her denunciation of Susanne Stubenvoll followed a similar pattern.

"Was the cellarman's wife also at the witch-swarms?"

"I don't know her."

"But you must have seen her there! You mustn't deny it if you wish to be forgiven!"

"Yes, I saw her!"

But it was a different story with Dorothea Groer. So far she had been uncowed by hunger or by solitary confinement, unconvinced by the younger Capuchin and obstinately unimpressed by Boblig of Edelstadt. Not until Master Jokl pulped her thumbs and crushed her legs in Spanish boots, with wedges inserted to increase the pain, did she submit, naming a number of people who, like her, had served the Devil. As a midwife, she knew all the women from far around. Now, more from self-pity than from a desire to do anyone harm, she named names. She had to, or the torture would have gone on. The names she gave were of women who, when they required her services, had not treated her with the respect she deserved.

And so, hurriedly, new cells had to be prepared at Ullersdorf Castle, and new assistants had to be provided for Master Jokl. Boblig's promises began to find a terrible fulfillment.

The journey from Ullersdorf to Schönberg took two hours. Twice a week, on Wednesday and Saturday, the farmers and cottagers of Ullersdorf went to market to offer their wares. Now, besides butter, eggs, curds, and cheese, they also brought alarming tidings. The tradesmen of the town, and even more their virtuous wives, listened eagerly to these thrilling stories, but no one was afraid. The power of the authorities at Ullersdorf did not extend to Schönberg, which was under the protection of Prince Liechtenstein. So neither Boblig the inquisitor, nor the two Capuchins could strike any fear in their hearts, and many of them, especially Winter the gingerbread man, poured scorn on what they regarded as old wives' tales. In any case, the townspeople were not in the habit of sympathizing with country folk. They preferred to ape the gentry, who opined that the harder one beat the peasantry, the hardier they became.

Kaspar Hutter, the former district judge, was alone in having a far more sensitive ear for their stories. He followed them with grave concern and a daily deepening fear for the future, for his own experiences told him this smoldering fire could flare into a blaze from which even Schönberg might not escape. If his evil doings were allowed to go unchecked, the inquisitor Boblig would hardly stop at the town walls. It would be a tragedy far worse than that of '69!

Few people knew what was going on at Ullersdorf, but Hutter came to be among them. He heard the details from the dean, who had himself heard them from Father König when he was in Schönberg. König had borne witness to the methods used by Boblig in his ruthless endeavor to incriminate his victims. He had described the tortures. He had told of the death of old Dorothea David. Such cruelties had been practiced by the inquisitors in German Silesia fifty and more years before. Quite evidently, Boblig was practicing them again.

For two whole hours, the old friends sat across a table, sipping sour wine, seeking means to counter the unfolding tragedy. But in the middle of their quest they were interrupted. Liesel, the younger daughter of Sattler, the master dyer, rushed into the deanery as if pursued by a swarm of hornets.

"What's the matter, my dear?" asked the dean.

"The soapboiler's come to visit my father!"

The two men burst into laughter.

"You're not running away from him, are you?"

Liesel was verging on tears.

"Prerovsky wants me to marry him."

Again they laughed, but then the dean became serious.

"And you don't want to?"

"I'd rather drown myself!"

"Now hold on awhile, Liesel," the dean smiled. "The water's still far too cold!"

"Anyway, why don't you want to marry him?" asked Hutter, half jesting, half serious. "He's a fine catch, isn't he? I'm sure he has plenty of money. And you know what they say: an old shoe soon wears out. Then you'll be able to afford a new one of your own choice."

But Liesel had no heart for humor. Her face clouded, and her eyes welled with tears.

"Don't cry," the dean hushed. "You'll see, there'll be no rain from this cloud."

"Father, if you could come to our house . . ."

Lautner glanced at Hutter. Why shouldn't they pay a visit to the Sattlers? It was Saturday afternoon, the master dyer was away from his cauldrons, and a friendly chat with him would not appear amiss. Hutter was thinking the same.

"Run along to Susanne, then," said the dean, "and stay with her until I come back. We'll go and see your father."

Liesel answered the dean with the thankful look of a happy but helpless lamb again. The two old men returned her smile, and they, too, were happy. They understood. Prerovsky was much the same age as themselves. What would a lovely young thing like her do with such an old man? Anyway, he was bound to be more interested in money than a bride.

The unexpected guests at the Sattlers were given something of an embarrassed welcome. No one likes to have outsiders present when delicate matters such as one's daughter's nuptials are under discussion. The master dyer knew quite well why Prerovsky had come and was not altogether against his becoming his second son-in-law.

Fortunately, Prerovsky had begun his conversation at a point far removed from the real purpose of his visit and was still talking about his clergymen brothers, specifically the priest at Bisenz in South Moravia.

Lautner eyed him with admiration. The bald soapboiler wore a new dark blue coat of Dutch cloth, a lace neckerchief, and silver-buckled shoes; but he had lacked the courage to don a wig.

"Dressed for a wedding, I see!" the dean smiled. "And about time, too, my friend!"

Prerovsky cringed, as if caught in the act. He blushed and opened his maw of a mouth.

"Indeed, Father, it *is* about time!"

"And I declare we've just seen your bride," interjected Hutter. "Being chased by a demon, by the looks of her!"

"Please," cried Prerovsky, wiping the perspiration from the nape of his neck, "don't say that word!"

It had meant nothing before, but now the mere mention of it turned everyone's thoughts to Ullersdorf. There was a moment's silence. It was as if the oppressive atmosphere that hung like a black cloud over the district had suddenly penetrated the Sattlers' parlor. Both master dyer and soapboiler were abruptly oblivious to all thoughts of a wedding. Prerovsky was the first to speak.

"Have you heard about Rozina Blahaskova of Weikersdorf?" No one had.

"I heard it from my journeyman this morning," he continued timidly. "They say Blahaskova accused herself of witchcraft. She told the magistrate that last year she had intercourse with three devils on the Petersstein. They say one was called Balthazar, another Ambrosius, and the third Aureos . . ."

"Blahaskova?" said the dean. "Isn't that the woman who's not right in the head?"

"That's what my journeyman says. She's been deranged for years," Prerovsky agreed. "The magistrate took her in, but she escaped and ran to the Capuchins at the castle. And something else I know: she's the sister, or cousin, of a woman already under arrest—Mistress Züllich, the miller's wife."

"No wonder people are going insane," said Sattler.

"As far as country people are concerned," the dean thought aloud, "there are devils everywhere nowadays. Everyone suspects everyone else. It's like a plague."

"You know," broke in Prerovsky again, "I've asked my brother prior about these things, and he says it's not true a person can have power from the Devil, because the Devil himself is in God's hands. That means everything in the world is governed solely by the will of God."

The dean smiled, and the soapboiler felt a little ashamed for his sermonizing. But there was no need to be.

"Your brother is unquestionably right," said Lautner. "But what your wise brother says, and what other Christian teachers also tell us, doesn't stand for anything at Ullersdorf. The only thing that counts there is what Boblig and the Capuchins say!"

"And what does that mean?" asked Prerovsky.

"It means that you, I, Master Sattler, Liesel—anyone—can be deemed by them to be an evildoer, a witch, and be burned at the stake!"

"No!"

"Perhaps you've heard what happened years ago in Zuckmantel. If not, you can ask your brothers. Many people were burned there, even a soapboiler."

Prerovsky was so aghast that he quite forgot the purpose of his visit. He left soon after, without mentioning Liesel at all.

Sattler felt offended. Having weighed all the pros and cons, he had already decided to give his consent to the marriage, and many people knew it. Prerovsky had come dressed to the nines, he'd talked and talked, but he'd said not a word about Liesel! Perhaps he'd been ashamed to speak in front of the dean and the judge, but why should he have been? Stupid fool! Even older and balder men than he got married! Was the master dyer to give his daughter to a fool?

Lautner and Hutter also left soon afterward, when some drapers arrived to discuss business with Sattler.

The two friends made their way back to the deanery. Liesel was rid of her unwanted suitor for the time being, but otherwise they had learned some unpleasant things. They were both thinking of Rozina Blahaskova.

As they arrived, laughter rang out from the kitchen. How they envied the girls' cheerfulness!

"I'm becoming more and more unhappy about this," said

Hutter as they sat down in the dean's room. "It's like a fishpond when the sluicegates are opened. The water drains away, the fish gather at the deepest point, and the net closes in!"

The dean took a pinch of snuff and stared long at his friend's hand on the table.

"But we're not carp or pike, to be caught by a dragnet," he said at last. "I'll go to the bishop!"

Hutter heaved a skeptical sigh.

"Bishop Liechtenstein," he said. "I've tried that myself. He's not a bad man, but if there's a whisper of heresy, his ears prick up, and he runs with the hounds!"

"Yet it's my responsibility to tell him what this advocate from Olomouc is doing."

"And you would dare to go to him alone, Christoph? Don't forget that in any court, church or secular, whoever stands up for a heretic is himself guilty of heresy! And the bishop isn't well disposed to you, anyway!"

"Thank you for the warning," said the dean, smiling, "but I still haven't forgotten everything from my law studies. And, anyway, I wasn't thinking of going to see the bishop alone. I know he doesn't like me. I was thinking of doing it through my friend Winkler, Dean of Müglitz. We sat on the same form at Latin school in Olomouc."

"That's not a bad idea, except for one thing. Your old friend is a weakling."

"You don't know him as I do, Kaspar!"

Hutter was visibly crestfallen as he made his way home after his conversation with the dean. He did know Winkler, and better than Christoph Lautner thought. And he had had his own experiences with the bishop.

The dean also was subdued, no longer so sure of his friend Winkler. Yes, even he had sometimes detected more bluster than boldness in his old classmate.

At times of uncertainty, Lautner usually turned to the Scripture for guidance. He opened the Bible at random and set his finger on the page. It was the 18th verse of the 10th chapter of Saint Luke:

" . . . I beheld Satan as lightning fall from heaven."

The dean felt a gentle creeping of his flesh. I beheld Satan . . . Yes, even he had seen Satan, in the shape of Heinrich Boblig of Edelstadt, witch-judge. Who was the Devil? Certainly he existed, when both the Old and New Testaments spoke of him in so many places. According to the Scripture he was strong, powerful, and clever. Almost like God. He had to be, to be able to tempt Christ, the Son of God. Taking him to a high mountain, he had shown him all the kingdoms of the world and said: "All this power will I give thee, and the glory, if thou wilt worship me." If the Devil could make such promises, he was indeed stronger and mightier than God!

The dean gasped, shocked at his own train of thought. Mightier than God? What nonsense! Then another thought struck him. How was it that in bygone days—and this was well documented—it was possible to drive out the Devil and resist his temptations with just a few drops of holy water or by the mere mention of the name of Jesus or Mary? According to the old stories, this would dispel the Devil's power like a puff of smoke. Yet today's disciples of the Devil, who were burned at the stake by inquisitors such as Boblig, went to church, crossed themselves with fingers dipped in holy water, attended confession, and took the sacrament! And the learned advocate Boblig condemned them like thieves, murderers, or arsonists. Worse, actually, because while arsonists could be given mercy, witches could expect nothing less than an ignominious death. God or the Devil? Who was the more powerful? Was God truly so almighty and the Devil truly so black as he was painted? Was not everything merely an invention, like so many other mysterious things which ceased to be mysterious when human reason unraveled their secrets? Was not the true God quite different from the one described in the Old Testament? Was He not rather as Jakob Boehme, the poor cobbler from Görlitz, knew Him? He wrote that no book could impart more divine wisdom than a walk through a meadow in bloom. And was he not right? Was not all else mere legend, passed down from distant forebears?

The dean trembled as he realized where his thoughts had taken him. To doubt the faith was a dreadful sin, especially for a priest. Was he not like the man who claimed there was no God and no Devil, for neither one nor the other had come to his aid when he called them?

He sank onto the hassock in front of the crucifix.

Lautner did not hear the door open as Susanne and Liesel peered inside. The girls had come to invite the dean to dinner, but when they found him immersed in prayer, they closed the door quietly again and went away.

At last he rose to his feet, calmer and happier for his meditation. Yes, the cobbler from Görlitz was a very wise man; he had found God where others saw only grass or flowers.

"I'm hungry!" the dean cried as he entered the kitchen, to find the table already laid for dinner. Then he leaned over to Liesel:

"Don't worry about a wedding for the time being, my girl. Your suitor didn't even have time to say what he wanted!"

If he had not been the dean, Liesel would surely have hugged him for joy.

11 ✦ Old Friends

As they prepared to set off for Müglitz, the Dean of Schönberg noticed Florian tie a large truss of hay to the back of the carriage and prepare a hefty sack of forage for the journey.

"Why so much hay and oats?" he smiled. "We'll be back by the evening."

"I know what I'm doing, Father. They won't give us a thing at Müglitz."

"What do you mean? The dean always tells Stephan not to scrimp and to feed the horses as if they were the bishop's!"

"That's true, Father. That's what the dean says, but Stephan never gives them more than two handfuls of oats. I reckon the two of them are in collusion."

Lautner burst out laughing. And well they might be, he mused. Vojtech was known to be a skinflint, though heaven knew why he should be. Look what age had done to the young prankster! Back in their schooldays in Olomouc he'd been the life and soul of any practical joke there was. And once, when they stuffed a dead mouse into a teacher's pocket, he'd almost been expelled.

The weather was dreary. It had rained throughout the day before, and there were puddles of dirty water everywhere. Yet Lautner's spirits were high as he took his seat in the carriage with its broken springs. But the fact was he was looking forward more to the journey than to seeing his old friend.

Florian drove at an amble through the town. Not only because it was difficult to trot along the narrow streets, but because he liked to see the friendly passers-by stop respectfully and shout their greetings to the reverend father—for a little of that respect fell on him and his horses.

As soon as they had passed through the muddy suburbs and the last few cottages were behind them, Florian smacked his lips and cracked the whip. This was the sign the horses, well brushed, fed, and rested, seemed to have been waiting for. Thrusting out their hindquarters, they snorted, reared their heads, and fell into a trot that was a joy to behold. Even Prince Liechtenstein, whose own stud stallions were brought from as far away as Friesland, could have envied such a team as the Dean of Schönberg's. High on the box seat, Florian was almost bursting with pride.

They soon found themselves amid fields and meadows where sheaves of mown grass lay in long rows, not yet scattered for fear of the rain. The dean gazed out, and the more he looked, the lighter became the burden that lay on his heart. Nowhere could man feel such relief as below the vast vault of heaven, amid the beauty of nature!

Farther on came the silver ribbon of the little river March, strengthened by the waters of its tributary, the Tess; and the sound of church bells in Bludov. Now all the dean's worries and fears began to dissolve as if it had all been just a bad dream. He knew every inch of this country from his childhood, and every spot within it held memories. Nowhere, he thought to himself, was there a finer place than this corner of Moravia, wreathed to the north by the Altvatergebirge range and washed by the waters of the March and a dozen smaller streams, all teeming with cray-fish and trout. Just one thing was wrong: if only the sun would come out!

"Hey, Florian, what do you think? Is it going to rain, or will it brighten up?"

"It'll brighten, Father! Look over to the west, it's breaking already!"

Yes, the clouds were breaking, and the sun was shining through. Perhaps, thought Lautner, there would also be a brightening of another kind! If only Master Boblig and the Capuchins from Olomouc were to leave Ullersdorf, everything would be different!

Now the terrible man with the ostrich head was firmly back in the dean's mind. He stopped looking at the countryside and thought of the inquisitor of Ullersdorf. Where did the man find such malice? Where? All of a sudden it seemed to Lautner that the answer was remarkably simple. Surely it was because people like Boblig never walked the field paths when the grain was ripening; they never took time to stand in the meadows when they were in flower; they never walked of an early morning through the woods when they resounded with the singing of the birds. Instead they lived their lives with others of their kind, in closed rooms, gorging themselves with rich food and fine drink. If only they went out more often into God's good world and left their creature comforts at home!

Lautner was reminded of the old tale of the once-mighty Assyrian king, Artaxerxes. Defeated in battle, ravenously hungry and racked with thirst, he found refuge in the squalid hovel of a poor peasant who could offer him only a crust of barley bread and a mug of water. The king was used to a life of pampered luxury, but he declared that no delicacy had ever tasted so good, and no courtier had ever been so kind as this peasant. Every proudling, every swellhead, every tyrant should at least once in his lifetime find himself in such a plight as Artaxerxes. Then they would be humbler, and more humane of heart; and the world would straightway be a happier place.

The journey passed quickly. The clouds withdrew to the east, and in the west a patch of blue sky appeared. And just as the sun shone through, the deep green spire and the two red-painted onion domes of Müglitz pierced the horizon. Then came the town itself, as if cowering before the great spire and church, almost immersed in the tall grainfields.

Lautner had often been to Müglitz but had never felt at ease there. This was the edge of the great plain that stretched as far as the very heart of Moravia, and only the wreath of mountains to the north reminded the dean of his hill-country home. Most of all, he missed the forests, but even the air here on the plain seemed to him thicker and heavier.

Florian cracked his whip as they approached the Hohenstadt Gate, and they flew like the wind into the town beyond. Inside, however, he eased the reins, for he wanted the people to see who was coming. Even in the bishop's own town everyone knew the Dean of Schönberg. Once again, people on the streets stopped to greet the old clergyman as he passed by—and far more sincerely than if it had been their very own Dean Winkler.

The carriage crossed the handsome town square, turned right toward the graveyard, and halted in front of the two-storied stone deanery. Even before Lautner alighted, a tiny upstairs window opened and Winkler's head appeared.

"What a visit this is! My brother dean from Schönberg!"

It seemed to Lautner that this rasping voice expressed less joy than it did surprise and curiosity. Just like Vojtech! He was probably thinking what this visit would cost him!

Lautner waved to his friend and without more ado went straight into the fine building. As he went up the broad stairs he clearly heard his brother dean calling:

"Stephan, where are you? We have guests! Give some forage to Dean Lautner's horses. And no scrimping! As if they were the bishop's!"

The Dean of Schönberg remembered what Florian had said and laughed to himself.

Winkler was already waiting on the upstairs landing, leaning on a stout stick. His face was pale, and his whole body seemed swollen.

"You're wondering what's the matter with me," he said, after the customary priestly embrace and kiss of welcome. "It's the gout! It started in my left big toe, then it was behind the instep, then in my knee, and still it moved higher. My dear brother, I thought I'd never stand the pain! Powders, all sorts of tinctures and ointments—nothing helped. I suffered for a whole two weeks, and only yesterday it began to ease. Just think, *amice*, for two weeks I've hardly eaten a thing!"

The Dean of Müglitz was indeed a sorry sight.

"I hope you'll soon be better now!"

"And so do I. But it's kind of you to come and see a sick friend. Visiting the sick is a good deed in the eyes of the Lord!"

"Unfortunately I didn't know you were ill, so I'm afraid I've won no favor from the Lord this time. In fact I came to ask a favor of you."

Lautner observed a chill tightening of his friend's face as he spoke, and though Winkler loudly ushered him on, his voice bore an unmistakable trace of concern.

They entered a very large room, crammed with furniture. An unmade bed—evidently the dean had just risen from it—stood by the window. The air was thick and stuffy, and heat streamed from a great tiled stove.

"Sit down for the moment, I'll call the housekeeper," Winkler said, tugging twice on a little bell-rope.

She bustled into the room, as round as a barrel, with a small black mustache.

"Kathy, bring us some refreshments."

For a while they sat and looked at each other in silence. It was impossible for either of them not to think back to when they had shared a form at the old Latin school in Olomouc. In those days they had been full of life, restless as a pair of snakes; now they were old men. How many years was it? What changes they had seen! And how they themselves had changed! Were they still old friends, or was their friendship merely a fading memory?

The tubby housekeeper brought in a dish of roast meat slices, a pitcher of wine, and some poppy-seed cakes, wished them an enjoyable meal, and then withdrew, as quiet as a ghost.

Lautner was hungry after his journey and tucked into the food with gusto; but his host was even more ravenous, as if wanting to make up for all those fourteen hungry days at one sitting. Nothing, it seemed, was of greater importance to the Dean of Müglitz than food.

They raised their large glasses in a silent toast, and Lautner was astonished. Winkler, he observed with alarm, drank all of his in one draft! Had he become a tippler and a glutton? People who loved food and drink above all else were lost souls when it came to the nobler things of life! For a brief moment, Lautner had the notion that he had come in vain, but it was an idea he instantly dismissed. He could not condemn his friend simply because he was enjoying his food after an illness!

"You said you wanted a favor," said Winkler, unable to suppress his curiosity.

"I'm sure you know what's happening in my parishes," Lautner began with some distaste. "The Countess of Galle summoned to Ullersdorf an advocate from Olomouc, by the name of Master Boblig of Edelstadt."

"The famous witch-judge? I know him!"

"The very one. The man has been in Ullersdorf but a few weeks, and the whole district is now gripped with fear. The castle dungeons are overflowing, the people are terrified. No one knows who will be incriminated next. And how far is it from Ullersdorf to Schönberg!"

"I understand that for you, as dean, it's not a pleasant business," Winkler frowned.

"It's not me I'm worried about, Vojtech. It's the women who are charged with witchcraft, when they aren't witches and can't possibly be so! I simply can't remain silent!"

The Dean of Müglitz drew himself up and stared aghast.

"I hardly think that without due cause such an experienced inquisitor . . ."

"It's simply because he *is* so experienced! Most of his victims are just poor countrywomen. Of course they're riddled with superstition, certainly they're no ladies of virtue, but to say they fly to the Petersstein on broomsticks and have intercourse with the Devil—that's pure nonsense! Neither children nor fools could believe that!"

Now Winkler was even more appalled.

"Do you realize, *amice,* what you're saying?"

"All I'm doing is telling the truth!"

"You no longer believe in the existence of the Devil?"

"I'm not saying that at all. The thing is, Vojtech, if the Devil does have the power to use people—and I very much doubt he does—he chooses others to spread his evil, not the kind of poor old women Master Boblig would have as witches!"

Winkler shook his head in disbelief.

"The Devil, *amice,* doesn't choose. You know the Scripture, you've read many papal edicts. You've read Saint John Damascene, the Golden Speaker, you've read Saint Augustine, Hilary, Thomas Aquinas, Gratian, and dozens of others. You know as well as I that the history of the Holy Church and the lives of the saints are chronicles of struggle against the intrigues of the Devil. Every heresy is the work of the Devil!"

Winkler was incensed.

"But the history of the Church, Vojtech," remarked Lautner dryly, "ought to be something else!"

For the Dean of Müglitz, this was outrageous. Lautner's words stank of heresy. Now he guessed what his friend wanted of him. No, a thousand times no!

"Just what do you want from me?" he said coldly.

Lautner knew it was a forlorn hope. Winkler would not raise a finger to help him. But he had to be sure.

"I know, Vojtech, that you are held in high esteem by His Grace the bishop . . ."

"I've never shown the slightest disobedience. That is all."

"Because I know how the bishop respects you, I thought you might have a word with him and ask him to exert his influence over the Countess of Galle to see Boblig withdrawn from Ullersdorf. There would be peace; the people would look only to their work again; there would be no more mutual suspicion."

Perhaps quite involuntarily, a smile of contempt appeared on Winkler's face as he gazed at his brother dean. As if he were being addressed not by an old friend, but by some kind of seducer. The silence became unbearable. Finally he spoke.

"Don't ask me to do that!"

"Is it so difficult for you to point out to the bishop what unseemly things are happening in his diocese?"

"Above all," shouted Winkler, "that's the business of the countess, not His Grace the bishop! And even if it weren't, do you honestly think I should contradict such a competent witch-judge?"

"And what if everything Master Boblig says is a lie?" replied Lautner, also raising his voice. "Is it not our priestly duty to fight it?"

"I am willing to fight against lies and superstitions, yes. But the Devil, witches, and heretics—these are no inventions or superstitions. They're real! Or have you come to believe the Devil is just a figment of man's imagination? What about the prophets, Moses, Hosea, Isaiah, Jeremiah? What about the entire holy Scripture? Do you think that for centuries they burned witches out of mere superstition? No, witches are instruments of the Devil, to be purged by fire, and that's the way it's been since the world began! Do you think I am to set myself above the apostles, the Sovereign Pontiffs, the teachers of the church? You may have taken leave of your senses, but don't expect the same of me!"

The Dean of Müglitz was a frightened man. Aware that all hope of his support was lost, Lautner simply stared at him in amazement, striving to comprehend what prevented such an educated man from using his common sense. Perhaps he was afraid of losing his comfortable position. The Dean of Müglitz held the richest prebend of the whole diocese of Olomouc, and Vojtech Winkler had become too accustomed to the good life. Now he was frightened, lest the very shadow of disobedience touch his person and deprive him of his comfort. But did he really believe everything he had been told, or was he just pretending? He had been a yes-man since the day he was ordained. He had had an easy ride, his standing with the bishop had risen year by year. But had it entirely clouded his mind?

"You are invoking the Holy Spirit, Vojtech," he said, with a gentle irony. "I have not taken leave of my senses; I have used them. And that is not a sin."

Winkler stood up and began banging his stick angrily on the floor.

"What's the matter with you all? Not long ago I heard the same talk from Brother Pabst at Römerstadt. And they say Brother König at Ullersdorf is another one. Things have been said about both of them at the bishop's palace! And now you, too, Christoph!"

This was startling news. Things had been said about Pabst and König at the bishop's palace . . . And perhaps not only about them, but also about him, the Dean of Schönberg—only Winkler did not want to say. Or perhaps Winkler himself was now going to talk to the bishop? He would have to stop him.

"My dear friend," he said, his voice friendly again, "we grew up together. Never was there any enmity between us, and neither should there be now. I would say only this: Please understand that our duty in this world is not just blind obedience. We do serve— we have to serve—but above all we have to serve as shepherds to our flocks. And one more thing I would ask you to consider: The world does not stand still. You said witches have been burned for centuries. Unfortunately you are right. But is that cause for witches to be burned for more centuries to come, until the very end of the world? Do we know, beyond doubt, that all these women were in league with the Devil? Just read Adam Tanner's book, or the work of another learned Jesuit—Langenfeld, who for years held the office of confessor at an inquisitorial court. They, and many other learned men besides, rejected belief in witches. I say again, Vojtech, the world does not stand still! There was a time when it was said the Earth was flat, like a pancake floating in a celestial sea, but today we know beyond doubt that it's round. It was always said that the sun moved around the Earth, but now there are grave doubts about that also! And what about a hundred, two hundred years from now?"

Winkler stared as if he were being addressed by a lunatic.

"That's why," continued the Dean of Schönberg, "we cannot stand passively by when we see such absurd and preposterous things. We know that people were often burned at the stake, hundreds of thousands of them, not so long ago, in Italy, France, England, and especially in the German lands. We ourselves re- member the inquisitorial courts in Zuckmantel and nearby Freiwaldau. Afterward it seemed the witch-fires had died out, and common sense had at last prevailed. But now, all of a sudden, Master Boblig is preparing new ones at Ullersdorf. Are we to let him do it? Are we to look on in silence as this foreigner disgraces our homeland?"

Winkler responded with a resolute gesture of rejection. But then he spoke, and his voice also was gentler than before.

"Brother, you are talking nonsense. It is none of my business, and it is none of yours either. You know that nothing happens unless it is God's will. Can you or I presume to know the dispensation of Providence? All who perished at the stake in the past were burned only with the indulgence of the Lord. And if new ones are to perish, they, too, will burn only with His indulgence. Our task is to strengthen our faith by humility and obedience, not to dilute it by idle reflection. *Omnia opera mala a cogitatione procedunt.* All evil deeds are preconceived!"

"That's not what Saint Augustine said." Lautner smiled. "He said: *Omnia opera, vel mala, vel bona,* that is to say, all deeds, be they evil or good, *a cogitatione procedunt.* And I would add to that the words of Saint Matthew: *Vae vobis, scribae et pharisaei!* Woe unto you, scribes and Pharisees!"

The Dean of Schönberg knew he was wasting his time. He rose to go but stopped as he reached the door.

"I'll have to ask the bishop for an audience myself," he said.

"You mustn't do that!"

"Why not?"

"I'm warning you, Christoph!"

"I don't understand. Why shouldn't I go and see the bishop?"

Winkler tugged nervously at his beard before whispering his reply, as if betraying an awful secret.

"Perhaps I shouldn't be telling you, but you aren't highly thought of at the bishop's palace."

Lautner knew this already, but coming from Winkler it was cause for alarm.

"And what do they say about me?"

"That you're too well liked among the people."

"And that's something bad?" Lautner laughed.

"Christoph!" Winkler shouted abruptly, and his voice seemed sincere as he gripped Lautner's hand. "I'm advising you as I would my own true brother. Hold back! Don't poke your nose into things that don't concern you! Perhaps your enemies are waiting only for you to make a false move so they can destroy you. You're already an old man. Leave the fighting to the young ones. *Tace pro pace!* Keep quiet and give yourself some peace!"

Had Winkler said everything? Was he speaking sincerely, or was it a sham? Lautner no longer believed his old friend. He pulled himself away.

"*Qui tacet, consentire videtur,*" he said coldly. "Keeping quiet means appearing to agree. And I can't agree! I can't!"

"Silence is golden!"

"It's not our duty to be silent but to set an example to those who are younger than we are. We're both old, and we hold responsible office. I think there's no more to be said. God be with you, Vojtech!"

Lautner left the room, found Florian, and ordered him to harness the horses.

Soon they were on their way out of Müglitz. The sun shone brightly on a landscape full of blithe and brilliant colors; but the Dean of Schönberg, huddled in a corner of his carriage, noticed nothing. It occurred to him that instead of going to Schönberg he should be going to Römerstadt to see Pabst, the parish priest. He was younger, more resilient, and it would be easier to talk to him than Winkler. Besides, he had to warn him. But the hour was already late, so he let Florian drive on.

On the way, however, Lautner's spirits revived, and as they approached Hohenstadt he tapped Florian on the shoulder.

"You didn't tell me what happened with the fodder, Florian!"

"As I said, Father! Two tiny handfuls, and no hay!"

"I suppose Stephan took ours!"

"That's right! Stephan and the dean had it all worked out!"

Lautner fumed as he thought of the coward, glutton, and miser they had visited, and was glad that Müglitz was now far behind them. After a while he tapped Florian's shoulder again.

"Florian, do you believe in God?"

"How could I not believe, Father, when I'm your servant at the deanery!"

"And the Devil?"

"No, Father. I'd have to serve Master Boblig or the Dean of Müglitz for that!"

"Florian, Florian! I think we'll have to take out that sharp tongue of yours!"

But the coachman's reply had delighted him. At that moment, Florian was far closer and dearer to him than Vojtech Winkler—and all the prelates of the diocese—had ever been.

12 ✦ *The Castle Coach*

Some days later, Florian found himself with a considerable thirst, which he decided to quench at Nollbeck's, an inn on the square up the hill from the church. On the square, his eyes lighted on a splendid coach in front of Judge Gaup's house, or rather on the handsome pair of chestnut horses harnessed to it. Always the horse-fancier, he forgot his thirst and headed straight for the coach. It bore the painted lion emblem of the house of Zerotin— but one coat of arms was like any other for Florian; it was the horses he was interested in. These chestnuts, he had to admit, were quite the equal of the dean's. Beautiful beasts, a perfect match, each with the legs of a roe deer and the neck of a swan. How old could they be? He was about to open one horse's mouth to look at its teeth, but as he touched the bridle a surly voice rang out from the box seat.

"Clear off! They're not for sale!"

Only now did Florian notice the coachman from Ullersdorf, a rude fellow with saffron-red hair but with the demeanor of a man of far higher station.

"Bastard!"

Florian stormed off, with not another look at either the horses or their driver.

But one thing puzzled him. Who had come to visit Judge Gaup in the castle coach? Surely not the countess herself?

Nollbeck's, a coaching inn, stood at the lower end of the square, directly opposite the Town Hall. Just inside was the tap-room, with a large window commanding a view of half the square; at the back, two steps higher, was an open area known as the best room, with paneled walls and ceiling, for visiting merchants and the local gentry.

It was still early. Only three burghers were sitting in the best room, playing cards, while down in the taproom, seated at the dining table, two evidently hungry teamsters and their boy were engrossed in their food, and their pitch-caulked wooden mugs, brim-filled with good Schönberg beer. At another small table near the door, however—and here Florian had to suppress a gasp—sat a hunchback, the creature who had recently visited the dean.

Fortunately, the hunchback had not noticed Florian's arrival, and Florian took a seat where Ignatius would not be able to see him. It occurred to him that this could be a chance to learn something.

He was very surprised to see that Ignatius was sitting with a little man whose bones almost rattled in his skinny frame. It was Hanus Vejhanka, a weaver from Hermesdorf, who seldom set foot in the inn—and could hardly afford to, he was so poor. He had half a dozen children to support, and everyone knew that no cottage weaver had ever become rich.

Florian noticed with distaste that Vejhanka was pouring more down his throat than he could ever hope to earn at his loom. And with Iggy, too! He wouldn't be taking any groschen home now—only a hangover!

What the dean's manservant did not know was that Vejhanka was the hunchback's guest. A short while before, the weaver had been wailing on the square, claiming to have been cheated—and all of a sudden this odd little fellow had appeared and taken him to the nearest tavern.

Now, filled with rage and self-pity, he was pouring out all his sorrows to the stranger: As usual, he had delivered good cloth, in fact excellent cloth, yet Kaspar Sattler had docked him six kreuzers because he said there were flaws in the work. Nothing of the kind had ever happened to him before. It wasn't so much the loss of the six kreuzers that bothered him—what hurt far more was that he'd been cheated.

Out on the square, the weaver's wailing had been ignored. But now, seated at the table in the inn, he had someone who was not only listening with both ears, but nodding at everything he said. Who he was, or what he looked like, was of no consequence.

Florian knew Vejhanka, and paid little heed to his talk. What interested him was the hunchback. What was he looking for? Why wasn't he at Ullersdorf? Evidently he was waiting for his master. Florian tapped his head in self-annoyance—now it was clear who had come in the castle coach and who was now visiting the district judge. This would surely be of interest to the dean!

In the meantime, his ears were pinned back and his eyes were peeled: not a word or a movement was to be missed, for Iggy was surely up to no good.

But the weaver was doing most of the talking. Now his rage had subsided for the moment, and he was whining about the hard life he led, about the sufferings from which a poor man, whatever he did, could never escape. Then his anger overcame him again; his voice rose and his knuckles beat into the oak table. The teamsters took no notice, and neither did the card-playing burghers. Only the hunchback smiled, and from time to time he pushed a full mug across the table.

"Here, have a good drink!"

The more the weaver drank, the more he was devoured by his own sorrows, and the greater was his grudge against the cause of his misfortune—Kaspar Sattler, the rich master dyer.

Sattler ran not only a dye works but also a thriving trade in cloth and yarn. Quite understandably, he bought as cheaply as possible and sold at the highest price. Many weavers and spinners worked for him in and around Schönberg—the best, in fact. For whatever else could be said of him, he always had ready money and never ran up debts to his suppliers. But he was also very strict and rejected shoddy goods.

Vejhanka was on the verge of tears again.

"A lovely piece of cloth it was! It could have gone straight onto the Emperor's table in Vienna! And that swine docked me six kreuzers! Does he have any idea what it's like, living with so many children, working your fingers to the bone? All that bloodsucker thinks about is his moneybags! The more impoverished we become, the richer he gets. That's how he can lay on a feast when he marries off his daughter! What's it to him if a weaver has nothing to feed his children? But one day he'll end up like us, food for the worms—and may they give him no rest in his grave!"

"Drink! Wash away the worms!"

Vejhanka finished his drink, and Ignatius motioned the inn-keeper to bring another.

"One of these days the Devil will take him, money and all!" the weaver continued, his boldness growing as he saw the full mug on the way. "He may look as honest as a saint, but he's a scoundrel all right! There's no fairness when one man spends his whole life dog-hungry, and another has sausages for breakfast!"

The innkeeper had heard enough of Vejhanka's slanderous outbursts against the town councillor and former Lord Mayor. He touched his shoulder.

"That's enough, Hanus. You don't know what you're saying. Time to go home!"

"And why should he go?" rasped the hunchback, raising his own mug to toast the weaver. "A fine potman you are, sending your customers home! Have another drink, my friend, if you feel like it!"

Vejhanka raised his mug in return, and for the first time took a proper look at his hideous companion.

"Who are you? I've never seen you before."

"And what concern is that of yours? Don't you like my company? Just drink! Potman, another mug."

Vejhanka heard and obeyed.

Ignatius also drank, but not so greedily. His face was even more twisted than before, and his eyes gleamed with malice.

"Tell me," he said, after wiping his mouth with his sleeve, "who do you think is the richest man in Schönberg?"

"The richest?" pondered the weaver. "Why, it has to be Satt-ler, the one who stole six kreuzers from me. He built himself a new dye works, he's got houses all over town. And bags of money."

"And who else is wealthy?"

Vejhanka stared blankly at his companion.

"So tell me!"

"Peschek's very rich," Vejhanka went on, rather less willingly. "He makes fabrics—tripp, serge, fustian. A lot of weavers work at home for him. He's another one who docks their pay for the slightest thing!"

"And who else?"

"They say Prerovsky the soapboiler's well off."

The teamsters at the next table were still eating, uninterested in the drunken talk. But the innkeeper was alert. He did not like the questions this hunchback was asking. Why should he want to know these things? Florian also was perplexed.

"And who would you say is the cleverest person in town?"

The weaver scratched behind his ear for some time, unable to think. Then he seized on a name.

"The cleverest is the dean. He's comfortably off and he doesn't have to do anything!"

Ignatius guffawed, the innkeeper laughed, and so did one of the teamsters. But Florian frowned. He could not allow the reverend father to be insulted! But the hunchback was already posing another question.

"Which woman in Schönberg has the sharpest tongue?"

Vejhanka needed no time to work this one out. "All of them!"

Everyone laughed at this. Even Florian.

"And who among them rides a broomstick to the Petersstein?"

This was insidious. Though Vejhanka's head was clouded with drink, he sensed the grave danger. He stared more carefully at his companion, and he was suddenly afraid. The town was full of witch-talk, and here was a creature who, if he had horns, would be the image of a devil. Perhaps he had hooves in place of feet. Lord be with us and deliver us from evil!

The innkeeper moved to intervene. Florian, the only man present who knew who the hunchback was, also stood up. But just as he was about to seize him and hurl him out of the door, he saw through the window that Master Boblig was standing outside Gaup's house. He was looking up and down the square, evidently searching for his assistant. For Florian, nothing could have been more welcome.

"Your master's looking for you!" he said, bearing down on the hunchback.

Ignatius lifted his head, recognized the dean's servant, remembered the blows he had received at the deanery, and took fright.

"Don't gape at me, look out of the window!"

The hunchback did as he was told, saw that his master was waiting impatiently outside, grabbed his hat, and in one agile leap was at the door.

Fortunately, Florian was prepared and seized him by the lapels before he could run out of the door.

"Hold on!"

"What do you want?"

"Who," asked Florian, "is paying for the drinks?"

Ignatius squirmed, fretted, and fumed, but there was no escape. He reached for his money pouch and counted out a few groschen. Florian counted with him.

"That's not enough. What about the drinks the weaver had?"

"He drank them himself, so he'll pay for himself!"

"You little wretch! You ordered them, so you'll pay for them!"

Ignatius was well aware that all resistance would be in vain. He was held in a viselike grip, and he knew what to expect if he did not pay. Reaching again for the pouch, he took out a gulden and tossed it at the innkeeper, who caught it adroitly in midair.

"Now be off! And don't come back!" bawled Florian, hurling him out of the door.

At this, even the teamsters stood up from the table to look out the window as the hunchback scampered ridiculously over the bumpy pavement and got into the coach with his master.

Florian quickly drank up and hurried straight back to the dean to tell him what had happened. Strangely, the reverend father did not laugh when he heard of the hunchback, the weaver from Hermesdorf, and the advocate Boblig but appeared to be listening with consternation. What interested him most was whether Boblig really had been visiting Judge Gaup.

Straight afterward, the dean dressed and left, telling Susanne he was paying a brief call on Master Hutter.

13 ✦ *The Bathkeeper of Ullersdorf*

Inside the coach, Boblig sat in long and silent meditation, without so much as a glance at his assistant. The hunchback observed his master from the corner of his eye. Boblig was rarely so pensive, and Ignatius was afraid to move lest he disturb him. The horses were going at a trot, and the coach shook as it trundled along the uneven road, but the inquisitor remained lost in thought. Only when they had passed the turning for Reigersdorf did Boblig turn to the hunchback with a question:

"Well, Iggy, what do you say to Judge Gaup?"

"What do I say? He's too good for a dump like Schönberg. He ought to be president of the Court of Appeals!"

"Hmm."

Again, nothing. Only the snorting of the horses and the rocking of the coach.

Just before Reitendorf, the hunchback could no longer contain himself and broke his silence.

"I wonder if you know, master, who are the richest men in Schönberg?"

"Tell me, I'm curious!"

"Sattler, Peschek, and Prerovsky."

"Iggy, Iggy! Tell me something new!"

"So who's the cleverest man in Schönberg, then?"

"If you lived there, that would be easy. But no, tell me."

"It's Lautner, the dean!"

"I wouldn't have said that. I would have said rather his manservant, the one who gave you a drubbing!"

Ignatius resolved to disturb his master no more after that and kept silent for the rest of the journey to the castle. Boblig, he thought, was not his usual self.

This observation was reinforced by his master's odd behavior back at the castle. After only a light meal, Boblig went straight to his desk and immersed himself in papers.

Ignatius had to prepare three candelabra, each with three new candles. This was astonishing. Was his master going to work all night? Or was he expecting a visit?

Dusk fell, Ignatius lighted the candles, and in their yellow glare Boblig assumed the features of a wild apparition. His eyes vanished into the deep hollows below his thick, protruding brows, and his bald skull reflected the flickering flames.

Ignatius retired into the anteroom, quiet as a ghost, only occasionally glancing out at his master in case he needed anything.

After his discussions with Gaup, Boblig had decided to put his court papers in order. He determined how many people he held in custody, wrote down their names on special cards, and noted for each of them their age, place of origin, and the progress made by his investigations. It was surprising that only four hearings had in fact been concluded, allowing for just four verdicts to be arrived at and sent to the Court of Appeals for approval. These hearings concerned the beggarwoman Schuch, the midwife Groer, the miller's wife Züllich, and Dorothea David—on whom the Devil himself had served sentence by breaking her back. The inquisitor crossed out the names of these four women, as a sign that they were beyond redemption.

But there was still many others who were not yet crossed out. The inquisitor studied them for a long time before his eyes lighted on the name of Marie Petrova, the wife of the estates manager at Johnsdorf. She was not so old, only a little over forty, and at one time must have been very attractive. Master Jokl said she was still hoping for a happy ending. She had been put to torture twice and confessed satisfactorily, but as soon as the pain was over, she always retracted. Evidently she needed a few more weeks of Jokl's rations and regime. The countess had asked about her twice. The best thing, definitely, would be to leave her to ripen, like a pear on a tree.

Then Boblig spotted the name of Dorothea Biedermann. Fifty years old, barber's wife and keeper of the bathhouse at Gross

Ullersdorf. He took a large pinch of aromatic Seville, a gift from Master Gaup.

"That could be the one!"

He looked at another name: Barbora Göttlicher of Gross Ullersdorf, forty-three years old, papermaker's wife.

"No, first we'll interrogate the bathkeeper," he said and called to his hunchback: "Get Master Jokl here at once!"

Jokl soon arrived and Boblig spent half an hour giving him orders. When the executioner left, the inquisitor rummaged through his papers for a while, then undressed, snuffed the candles, and lay on the bed. A quarter of an hour later, the room resounded to his deep snores.

✦ ✦ ✦

Down in the castle dungeons on a bed of musty straw lay the wife of the village barber, the bathkeeper Dorothea Biedermann. She had lost all sense of time in the total darkness; she did not know exactly how long she had been detained and had no idea whether it was day or night, weekday or Sunday; she suffered hunger and cold, vermin and filth.

Only once had she been subjected to interrogation, but it was curtailed because the inquisitor had been unexpectedly called away. She grieved for her husband and children. Once the executioner's assistant had smuggled in a piece of paper from her husband. "Trust in God," it read. But surely, if the Lord could see into the dungeons of Ullersdorf, He would have done something by now!

As the days passed, so did Dorothea's faith in God and in her fellow human beings. Many times she prayed, but it brought her no peace. She suffered pains in her chest and a severe cough. She often wept, sometimes softly; at other times she howled. Several times a day she asked herself whom she had ever harmed, that God was punishing her so. At the beginning she had thought it was all some kind of mistake that would soon be explained, but now her faith was gone. The glimmer of hope reminded her of the firefly that flew and glowed, then settled, and the light was doused.

Dorothea's melancholy was disturbed by the jangle of a key in the door. This, she thought, must be the executioner's boy with her food—the daily ration, a crust of greasy, black bread and a pitcher of water. The door opened, and in the glare of a lantern Dorothea did indeed see the boy with the food, but he was not alone. Behind him was Jokl. Her heart raced and her head swirled. It struck her that today something extraordinary was going to happen.

The boy went out, leaving her to the executioner.

"Get up," he said, gently.

The bathkeeper rose, her legs trembling from weakness and emotion.

"You're going for questioning."

It occurred to Dorothea that this could be the end of her suffering. Suddenly she was strong.

"Make yourself presentable!"

Dorothea ran her fingers through her hair and shook the straw from her dress. It was all she could do. If only she had a mirror! But perhaps it was best she had none, for the sight of herself would surely be a shock to her eyes.

Jokl was in no hurry to go. He had something else to say.

"If you listen to me, you can make it easier for yourself during the interrogation."

"But I never did anything!"

"The judge is going to ask you about the ladies from Schön- berg who used to go to the bathhouse," continued Jokl, as if not hearing what she said. "Give all their names, but whatever you do, don't forget Mistress Sattler and Mistress Peschek . . ."

Dorothea Biedermann had once been a strong and robust woman, and even now she could still walk unassisted, though she had to hold the handrail at times as they ascended the stairs. But the harsh morning sunlight of the cloistered corridor was almost more than she could bear. Her head swirled, and it all seemed to be a dream. The bright light blinded her eyes, the fresh air numbed her senses, and she would have fallen if Jokl had not caught her.

The executioner of Ullersdorf was a rough man, but he was moved by the sight of this woman he had known so well. Dorothea had been vigorous, talkative, and cheerful. But now she was a shadow of her former self; her cheeks were sunken, cadaverous. But there was no time for pity.

"Come on, come on," he said, but not so rudely as usual. "And don't forget what I told you!"

The judge was waiting for her in the courtroom, sitting at the table with his back to a window that faced the sun. Jokl stood her directly in front of him, in the full light. Boblig glared at her, wrinkled his nose, and turned to Jokl.

"Make sure she gets fresh straw! What a smell!"

Dorothea felt deeply ashamed. She had always prided herself on her cleanliness, and she knew how dirty and repulsive she must look now. She quite understood why the judge took a noseful of snuff.

"Sit down," he said, making sure he stood as far from her as possible.

The bathkeeper sat down, placed her hands in her lap, and lowered her head. Her heart convulsed with anxiety.

"How long have you been in custody?"

"I don't know. I've lost count of the days, sir."

"And why are you here? Don't you know that, either?

"No, sir!"

"It's all a mistake!"

Dorothea Biedermann lifted her head, not noticing the mockery in his voice. Mistake was the only word that registered. For the first time in ages, a gleam returned to her eyes. Perhaps this would be the end of her suffering! O God! Perhaps soon she would see her children and husband! She would be rid of this loathsome filth; the sun would shine again!

"You were the bathkeeper at Gross Ullersdorf," continued the gentle voice of the judge. "Did many women come to you to bathe?"

"Many, sir. Especially in the summer."

"And did they strip naked in front of you?"

Dorothea nodded, though she did not understand why he had asked such a question. It was shameful for her to speak about such things, however old the judge was.

"Were there any women from Schönberg among them?"

"Quite a lot."

"Were they generous?"

"Some yes, some no."

Dorothea had no idea where these questions were leading. All she was thinking of was Jokl's advice.

"Which one was the most generous?"

"The master dyer's wife, Mistress Sattler. Her sister-in-law, Mistress Peschek, was quite generous as well."

Boblig wrote their names on a piece of paper with a lead pencil.

"And who else came to bathe?"

"Mistress Weillemann, the papermaker, Mistress Hutter, the judge's wife . . ."

Again, Boblig recorded their names. But the bathkeeper was becoming increasingly confused. Why was he asking such things? Nevertheless, she gave the names of her other customers, quite unaware that she might be doing them harm.

"And now tell me the truth, as if you were kneeling in the confessional or even standing at the Last Judgment. You saw all these ladies naked. Did you at any time observe anything suspicious on their bodies?"

Dorothea shook her head uncomprehendingly.

"What I mean is some special mark, such as a wart, a pockmark, a large freckle, something like that."

Mistress Biedermann gazed open-mouthed. Why did the judge want to know? She sensed he was not asking out of curiosity but that something wicked was afoot.

"If you tell me everything truthfully, you will be doing yourself a favor. Perhaps I'll be able to grant you freedom!"

Freedom! He would release her from this loathsome prison, and she would be with her husband and children again! God, why not tell him everything she knew? After all, what was so bad about somebody having a pockmark or a wart?

"Well, can you remember?"

"I remember Mistress Sattler had a large wart under her left breast."

"There, you see," the judge purred. "Marie Sattler has a large wart below her left breast! And her sister-in-law?"

"She has a small wart on her left side, below the waist."

"Good! And the others?"

"Every one has some kind of birthmark, sir. I've seen lots of women, and they've all had some kind of mark. They're in all sorts of places, sometimes big, sometimes tiny as a poppy-seeds."

"Good, good," interrupted the judge, continuing to make notes. Then he went right up to her, fixed his gray-green eyes on hers and stared in silence. Dorothea lowered her eyes, feeling her hopes leaving once more. God, what could this awful man want from her?

"You surely know," he said slowly, "what those warts mean. You know full well that they are no ordinary warts but the *signum diabolicum,* signs by which the Devil marks those who have given their souls to him. Don't look at me as if you didn't know! You can't fool me! Tell me, why didn't you go to your confessor and tell him? I'll tell you why: you couldn't, because you also were in the coven. You are one of them!"

Dorothea half rose from her chair, wondering if she had heard right. It was too awful and unexpected. So the judge thought she was a disciple of the Devil! She had revealed that the generous ladies of Schönberg had warts on their bodies, and now the bailiffs would surely be on their way to arrest them! But she'd also said that all the women had such marks! Lord, why was this man staring at her? Why had he so suddenly changed?

Boblig was giving her time to remember. Then he spoke again, and this time his voice was friendly once more.

"I'd like to help you, Dorothea Biedermann, even though I know that you also are not without guilt. Your children need a mother, and I'd like to be merciful for their sake. For that, how-ever, you will have to testify truthfully, in front of witnesses and before the whole court, what marks you saw."

Dorothea nodded. What would she not do for the sake of the children? Anyway, she would only be testifying to the truth.

"Good! But that's not all. Furthermore, before the judge, wit-nesses, and the whole court, you must testify that both Mistress Sattler and Mistress Peschek smeared themselves with special ointments!"

"But I anointed them myself!"

"That's excellent!" exulted the judge. "Do you know why they smeared themselves with those ointments? To become invisible and to be able to fly to the witch-swarms on the Petersstein!"

Now at last the bathkeeper understood. The judge wanted her to testify that Mistresses Sattler and Peschek were witches. The blood rushed to her head.

"That's not true! All I anointed them with was oil of camphor!"

The judge raised his eyebrows and pursed his lips. The image of Lucifer, he took a pinch of snuff and then leisurely wiped his nose. He said firmly: "What I said is true, and you will testify before the court! Do you hear?"

"Have mercy, sir!"

She sank to her knees, but Boblig took no notice. He went to the door of the torture chamber and thrust it open to reveal Master Jokl, ready and waiting.

"Take her!"

The executioner lifted her up and led her inside. Dorothea caught sight of the chair that was run through with sharp nails; she heard the executioner's boy playing with the jangling chains; she knew what awaited her and shrieked in terror.

"Does she get the thumbscrew?" asked Jokl.

Boblig glared at Dorothea.

"You will be spared the torture if you tell the court the truth. You have a moment to decide."

"I'll tell everything!"

"Take her away, Jokl!"

Outside on the corridor, she wept uncontrollably, her whole body convulsing, her legs refusing to obey. It was some time before she became calm enough for Jokl to lead her back to her dungeon.

"Don't worry," he urged, "the inquisitor won't do anything to you if you do what he says!"

"But he wants me to . . ."

"He knows what he wants. And you have to submit!"

Moments later, Heinrich Boblig also left the courtroom. Back in his quarters room he swallowed a glass of wine and wagged a finger at the hunchback.

"Remember, Iggy, you told me yesterday that Sattler and Peschek were the richest men in Schönberg. And now the bathkeeper, Dorothea Biedermann, has just testified that their virtuous wives both bear the *signum diabolicum!*"

The hunchback looked at his master in wonderment. Now he knew why Boblig had been so quiet the day before. He had been preparing to pounce. Like a cat stalking a mouse.

"The weavers who Sattler buys cloth from think he's a bloodsucker. One of them said he was the Devil himself," said Ignatius, remembering the drunken Vejhanka.

"That's good news too, Iggy. The weavers will be on our side. Right now, though, it's not him we're after, it's his wife. And all we know so far is that she has a wart below her left breast!"

The hunchback grimaced:

"We often used to get by on far less evidence!"

The inquisitor laughed and tweaked his assistant's ear—a mark of especial pleasure.

"You scoundrel!" he said.

14 ✦ *Mockery or Menace*

What had Master Boblig of Edelstadt been discussing with the district judge? For both Kaspar Hutter and Lautner, this was the key question. Both felt that this had been no courtesy visit, and something was being hatched. But what? The easiest thing was to ask Gaup directly. Lautner had always maintained good relations with him and had even been godfather to his first-born son, so he could go and see him any time, or stop him on the street; but the dean did not want to do this. If the judge still had a little decency, he would come himself. But the days passed and Gaup did not come. Was this not the best evidence that his conscience was not clear?

Lautner decided he might be able to find out something from Father König. One day, therefore, he determined to travel to the parish of Gross Ullersdorf as if on a visitation and had his carriage prepared for the journey. But just as he was about to set off, Susanne appeared, ushering in a visitor. It was Judge Gaup.

The district judge looked even grander than usual. He wore a glorious lace cravat and a brown coat of costly Dutch cloth, tight enough to burst; and his buckled shoes shone like a dancing master's. The bloated ruddiness of his cheeks was offset by a splendid powdered wig. Though he conducted himself respectfully, his respect, it seemed, was directed more to the dean's holy cloth and seniority than to his person.

"I've been meaning to come for several days, Your Reverence, but I had many things on my mind. But, of course, you could have come to me, to see your little godson," he said somewhat reproachfully.

The dean's face brightened. He had done Gaup an injustice. The judge was nearing the completion of his new house, and there were always problems with craftsmen. Apart from a certain smugness, Gaup looked much the same as usual. Lautner smiled with anticipation: His guest was about to divulge what the villain Boblig had wanted.

Gaup sat down and looked around as if he were in the room for the first time. The dean guessed how he felt: He didn't know how to start. It was no pleasant task.

Finally the judge spoke, but he began with a topic far removed from what the dean had been expecting.

"I've come on account of that plot of land below the Old Gate. Since the fire it's been waste ground, overgrown with weeds . . ."

The dean raised his eyebrows, not only surprised, but offended.

"You mean where the house I was born in stood, and the piece of garden behind it?"

"The very place, Your Reverence. It would come in very useful for me, and you're hardly going to build on it, are you?"

"What makes you think that, my friend?"

A little cloud fluttered across Gaup's face, and Lautner noticed.

"At your age? And who for?"

Lautner gritted his teeth. Not for himself, certainly. But why couldn't he build, for example, for Susanne? Why should everything in town be gobbled up by Master Gaup? Especially his birthplace and the plot of land his father had farmed so many years before!

"That's something I'm sure we'll be able to discuss in a neighborly fashion," said the dean, "but another day, I'm afraid. You must have seen Florian with the carriage outside. I have a visitation at Ullersdorf."

"That's quite another matter. I mustn't keep you from your duties," said Gaup, suddenly making to leave. "I'll come another time."

He had not said a word about Boblig's visit. Had he forgotten out of his own covetousness, or had it been deliberate? And if so, for what reason? The dean decided not to let his visitor leave so easily. This was a chance he had to seize!

As they paused in the doorway, he drew his guest aside. "You are a modest man," he said. "You haven't told me about your own recent visitor, Master Boblig of Edelstadt. I understand he is the most powerful man in the land of Zerotin!"

Lautner saw he had scored a bull's-eye. The judge drew breath sharply, clutched at his beard in embarrassment, and blinked several times.

"Yes," he replied eventually, as if the inquiry had hardly been of any importance. "Master Boblig of Edelstadt did come to see us. Just a chance visit . . ."

"And didn't he tell you about the witches, and how his interrogations were going? Nobody seems to know the truth, and there's so much talk, isn't there?"

"There was no talk of that between us, Your Reverence."

The dean was now utterly convinced that Gaup was not speaking the truth and that he had discussed with Boblig things he either was not allowed, or did not want, to divulge.

Lautner detained his guest no longer, and the judge swaggered out, even more aloof than usual. The dean watched him go, knowing that this was a man to beware of.

He sighed, said good-bye to Susanne, went downstairs, and got into the carriage. Florian cracked his whip, and the horses set off at a trot along the narrow lane around the graveyard and directly to the square toward the Old Gate. And then past the scattered cottages and gardens of the suburbs and onto the Reitendorf road.

The roadway was dry, the horses almost danced with exuberance, and Florian had to work hard to keep them in check. The dean curled up in a corner of the carriage and stared out, first on one side, then on the other, deep in thought. The day was overcast, the air seemed thin. Cattle, sheep, and goats were grazing on the cleared fields. Shepherds were kindling small fires.

The Dean of Schönberg was usually fond of chatting with Florian as they traveled, but today he was silent, lost in his own thoughts.

Florian had something on the edge of his tongue. Finally he grew tired of waiting for the dean to speak.

"Are we going to the castle, Father?" he asked, turning to his passenger. "Or to the priest's house?"

"The priest's house!"

That was all he said. Florian was disappointed, for he enjoyed conversing with the dean. He decided that if the dean was not going to start a conversation, he must begin himself.

"Is it true, Father, that the advocate from Olomouc has had more than a dozen women locked up as witches?"

"That's what is said, Florian, but who knows if it is true."

"You remember Miss Kühnel, who used to cook at the old priest's house at Ullersdorf? They say she's one of them."

"That's what I've heard also."

"But it doesn't make sense to me, Father. Is it possible for a priest's cook to be a witch?"

The dean did not answer directly.

"Do you believe, Florian," he said, "that those women are in fact witches?"

The coachman scratched behind his ear.

"You know, Father, when they're old women, there might be something in it. It's always best to keep clear of old hags!"

"And stick to younger ones?" the dean smiled.

"If you like. I know it's different for you, Father, but we ordinary men don't live on clouds, we live by our natures, and we can't change that. Even the birds of the air, when they feed, have to come down to earth!"

The carriage was already nearing the first homestead of the village of Reitendorf.

"Are we going to stop at the priest's house at Reitendorf?"

"Some other time."

The horses trotted on, and the carriage made swift progress along the flat road. In the distance to the right loomed the wooded foothills of the Altvatergebirge and behind them the high mountains themselves—the Altvater, the highest, and the notorious Petersstein, slightly lower. The dean smiled wryly at the nonsense of it all. On the night before the feast day of Saint Philip and Saint James, it was said, witches gathered there in a great assembly. Old women flying on broomsticks or riding on goats or hares! Even old Miss Kühnel was supposed to have gone there, though she was as round as a cabbage and could hardly breathe for her bulk. Perhaps she, too, would confess to Master Boblig that she had ridden to the Petersstein on a hare or had flown on a bat!

To the left, amid the bright green of the landscape, was the conical hill they called the Sentinel, covered by a patchwork of tiny strip-fields and graced by the grand castle of the Lords of Zerotin.

It was Jan of Zerotin who, with great pomp, had begun to build Ullersdorf Castle a hundred years before; but he did not finish it, and neither did his successor. Everyone who visited it was amazed by the lightness and artistry of the arcades around both wings and the main castle keep; but no one understood why, on its southern side, the castle courtyard remained quite open, its appearance marred by a series of plain stables and outbuildings. Just as a century before, carriages entered the courtyard not via an imposing gateway, but through a common stake fence. But the octagonal watchtower, crowned by three squat, shingle-roofed, domed spires, was complete. Proudly dominating the countryside around, a galleried rampart ran around the base of the lowest spire, from which a sentry held constant vigil over the seat of the powerful Zerotins.

Now the sentry observed the approaching carriage and immediately signaled to the guards in the courtyard below with a small red flag.

But it did not occur to the Dean of Schönberg to go inside. He had no intention of meeting the inquisitor, and if it had been at all possible, he would have gone miles out of his way to avoid the castle.

But it was not possible, and the road obliged him to go almost to the riverbank that was the boundary of the castle park. Just a short trip across a little bridge and the dean would have found himself in a quite different and far grander and delightful setting. But for whom was it more delightful? Certainly not for the prisoners who had Jokl the executioner to contend with.

As if sensing what his master was thinking, Florian urged the horses on; and soon the castle, surrounded by the little river Tess and by Ullersdorf brook, was behind them.

In a while they came to the scattering of buildings that was the old Göttlicher paper mill.

"They say Mistress Göttlicher is another one who's been taken to the castle," said Florian.

Lautner merely nodded his head and stared out at the yard of the papermill. Everything looked the same as usual. The water roared, the rag-engine clattered, children were sailing model pine-bark boats down the mill stream, an old dog lay basking in the sun.

Some time later, the carriage arrived at the other end of the village, at the fine church with its massive pillars and low tower. The priest's house, a modest, two-storied, red-brick building, its front elevation turned toward the mountains, stood nearby. In the winter this was a blustery, snow-swept place, but now in the summer it was beautiful.

No sooner had the carriage stopped in front of the priest's house than two kind young girls appeared to greet the dean. Elisabeth and Anna-Marie were both related to the parish priest, and the eldest of them acted as his housekeeper.

"Father Thomas already has a visitor," she told him, "but he will be pleased you've come. Come inside!"

"Who's with him?"

"Master Göttlicher, the papermaker."

"Poor fellow," said the dean, entering the house.

Inside, priest and visitor were engaged in somber discussion. Göttlicher had the bearing of a man of gentility but was clearly desolated by the tragedy of his wife's arrest.

He recognized the Dean of Schönberg, and straightaway a glimmer of joy appeared in his eyes. Here is the dean, his face said, he is more than a priest; his word will be more powerful.

"Reverend Father," he began, his voice bleak, "they've taken away my wife and accused her of witchcraft. I've been to the castle twice to see the sheriff, but they didn't even let me near him! Please, if you would only put in a word for my wife with the countess . . ."

Father König looked on miserably, his head bowed low, like a man who could not help, even if he wanted to. He was overwhelmed. Things were beyond his power.

"Unfortunately," he said, "today the countess is leaving for Wiesenberg."

The dean placed his hand on the papermaker's shoulder.

"I did hear about your misfortune. If only God could grant you joy! But I'm afraid that whatever we say to the countess, it cannot be of help. She wasn't the one who put your wife in jail. It was Boblig, the inquisitor. And we are both weak against him!"

Tears appeared in Göttlicher's eyes.

"Do you know who accused your wife?" asked Lautner.

"If only I did! She was never a witch! She went to church every Sunday, she attended confession, she took the sacrament. She never left the house at night because she was afraid. She slept with me in one bedroom. I saw her every movement. How is it possible they have her as a witch? Such a good and righteous woman!"

Tears streamed into the eyes of the old man. The dean was sorry for him, but how was he to console him?

"Don't cry, friend," he said, "all may yet be explained and put to rights. God never abandons anyone who has faith!"

The papermaker's face hardened.

"But how can I have faith in a God who allows such terrible things?"

"God allows even worse things, Göttlicher! Was not his only born son crucified with two thieves? And think how many saints have died as martyrs!"

"Go home," König urged the papermaker. "I'll stop by tomorrow."

"We'll do all we can to help you," the dean added.

The old man left, but his disappointment was obvious. He had lost his faith in both of them; he no longer believed anything and he relied on no one.

The priest cried out in helpless rage as the door closed.

"Barbora Göttlicher is the sixth woman in my parish already! But how many more? And whose turn will it be tomorrow?"

"Have you spoken to Boblig?"

"I went to see him, but it did no good. He sent me away like some kind of servant. Told me to take better care of my flock!"

"And the countess?"

"She's a frightened woman. Boblig repelled her from the start, and ever since the death of old Mistress David she's been terrified of him. He wouldn't flinch from accusing her of witchcraft, too, and she knows it. That's why she's going away with the young lords to Wiesenberg."

The two clergymen stood for a while in silence, acutely aware of how powerless they were. Finally the dean spoke.

"We're left with the last resort—an appeal to Bishop Liechtenstein!"

König shrugged his shoulders.

"And what if the bishop believes Boblig rather than us?"

"But are we mere chickens to allow our throats to be slit without a murmur? What kind of shepherds would we be if we allowed a wolf to ravage our flocks the way Boblig is ravaging our parishes? We simply have to show this villain that he can't do whatever takes his fancy. Yesterday Mistress Biedermann, the bathkeeper, today the papermaker's wife, tomorrow perhaps your housekeeper Elisabeth, or her sister."

Suddenly they heard the crunching of wheels outside the priest's house. König peered out of the window and gasped in horror.

"Boblig!"

Even Lautner trembled. The inquisitor was the last person he had expected to meet at Gross Ullersdorf. How had Boblig found him? Evidently the sentry on the watchtower had recognized the carriage and told Boblig or his assistant. But why had he followed him? What did he want?

The shapeless figure of the inquisitor was standing in the doorway, a look of surprise on his face.

"Oh, I had no idea, Father, you had such a guest! But I'm so pleased to see you. I simply had to come, as you seem to be avoiding me. Such a nice place you have here! A beautiful view of the mountains, and I'll wager you can even see the Petersstein from here! And those two charming female creatures outside!

Believe me, gentlemen, if I weren't an inquisitorial judge I think I'd like to be a priest at Gross Ullersdorf!"

Boblig talked and talked, and every one of his words was a poisoned barb. Lautner's face drained of color, then reddened, then blanched again as the inquisitor smiled. König gritted his teeth.

"Well, aren't we going to sit down and have a drink?" said Boblig, reminding the priest of his duty as a host.

König took the hint, offered the judge a chair, and hurried out of the room.

Boblig's face grew grim.

"You, too, dean, must be wondering what's going on in this parish. I would say your flocks are not well tended, and your inferiors certainly require more supervision. But God forbid," his tone changed, "that I should rebuke you. That's not my business," said the inquisitor.

"For me," he continued with a smile, "it only means more work, and I'm not afraid of that. Can the Petersstein really be seen from here?"

Lautner found Boblig's talk hard to bear. He sensed the mockery and the menace in his words. But personal feelings had to be put aside. What mattered now was that at last he had an opportunity to speak to the inquisitor from the heart.

"I have just been speaking to Göttlicher the papermaker, whose wife you have imprisoned on suspicion of witchcraft. I know them both, and I cannot believe that Barbora Göttlicher could have been in league with the Devil. And my impression, Master Boblig, is that you do not believe it either."

Boblig's face lengthened.

"What a strange thing for a trained lawyer to say! I am an experienced judge, Your Reverence, and I know very well when I can believe with certainty in the prisoner's guilt. It's after the interrogations and the confrontations, and when the verdict has been approved by a higher court. Only then, with a clear conscience, may I declare the guilt or innocence of the accused!"

"May I ask you something, sir?"

"As always, I am at your service."

"In your wealth of experience, has it ever happened that you actually acquitted someone?"

Boblig laughed, revealing the rotten stumps of his teeth.

"No, it has not!"

The dean raised his eyebrows.

"And don't you think that's odd?"

A wicked gleam appeared in Boblig's eyes.

"No, I don't. If the trial is conducted correctly, if the judge doesn't allow himself to be blinded by the words of the accused, by her appearance, and by her relatives and friends; if he is unrelenting and incorruptible, and if he uses all means permitted by the law, he must always obtain a confession. And that, as you know, is sufficient at inquisitorial trials. In addition, there is usually the testimony of witnesses. *Nil mortalibus ardui est,* says Horace, if I'm not mistaken. No height is too arduous for mortal men. There are many evils on this earth, Your Reverence. The Devil is mightier than many would believe!"

"And don't you think, sir, that sometimes you must pull up the wheat along with the weeds? That with the guilty you must also destroy the innocent?"

Boblig curled his lower lip.

"You sound almost like an *advocatus diaboli.* You surely know, Your Reverence, that when witches' advocates rise too fervently in defense of their clients, they lay themselves open to grave suspicion! Nothing, after all, happens without divine indulgence—and if it did happen that innocent persons were burned at the stake, it would be God's will. Indeed, they could even be regarded as especially fortunate, for it would be an honor bestowed by God Himself."

The sophistry was horrifying.

"And what of the judge's conscience?" Lautner's voice, though he did not realize it, hissed more sharply than the wind on the Petersstein. But the advocate smiled. He knew his foe was utterly vanquished.

"Why trouble yourself with such notions, Your Reverence?

The judge, after all, is no more than an instrument in God's hands!"

The dean felt he would vomit. Never had he met such a cynical man. Nothing would have given him greater pleasure than to spit in Boblig's face. He would ask no more questions, for the inquisitor knew all the answers in advance.

At that moment, fortunately, Father König returned, bearing a large tray. On it was a pitcher of wine, glasses, and cakes.

Boblig cried in surprise.

"And where are your lovely housekeepers? Two women in the house, and the priest serves his guests himself? This is unheard of!"

"They have a lot of work," replied the priest, his eyes to the floor.

"That's a pity," sighed the inquisitor. "Even an old man such as I likes to see a good-looking girl or two!"

He raised his glass, sipped the wine, and rolled it on his tongue.

"Good! Far better than the stuff that scoundrel Stubenvoll serves at the castle!"

The dean held his glass in his hand, but did not drink. He was staring at the inquisitor as if wanting to engrave his image forever in his memory. As he stared, he forced himself to look for a tiny spark of goodness. If only he could find at least a glimmer of light! Even the tiniest spark could be blown, with care, into a fire. But there was no kindling here, only rottenness and slime.

Suddenly Boblig turned bodily and looked the dean straight in the eye.

"I'd like to tell you something, Your Reverence. Beware of your flock in Schönberg. Some of them wear horns beneath their caps!"

This was so unexpected that for a moment the dean quite lost his breath.

"I know no one whom I could suspect," he said, pulling himself together at last.

"Perhaps you're not looking closely enough," replied Boblig, reaching for his snuff bottle.

"Perhaps," said Lautner, determined to hit back, "you were told something by Master Gaup, the district judge?"

"Not at all, Your Reverence. All I know is what many of the accused have been revealing to me."

This was a crushing blow, like an ax thudding into the chopping block. König's hands fell to his sides as he looked to the dean with the desperation of a drowning man.

The dean was trembling, but he still found strength to quote the words of Saint Ambrose:

"Mihi cumulus iste suspectus est. The very enormity of what you say is suspicious."

Boblig crashed his glass onto the table.

"Would you doubt my words, Dean? And you, Reverend?"

"My trust," whispered Father König, "is in God alone."

The dean was silent, his teeth clenched tight.

Boblig got up and looked out through the flowers that filled the window ledge.

"You do well, Reverend!" Then he chuckled: "But do look after your housekeepers. The Petersstein isn't far away. And sometimes even young girls can be obsessed with a desire to go and have a look!"

He made to leave.

"But now I won't disturb you any longer in your pious work. We'll find an occasion yet for a pleasant talk!"

The two clergymen stood like carved saints, neither of them able to muster a reply. Did he mean what he said, or was it a threat?

The wheels of Boblig's coach crunched into motion below the window of the priest's house. Only then did Lautner and König come back to life. They sat down and talked, as if a great burden had been lifted from them. No longer were they in any doubt whether danger threatened. Boblig had convinced them of that.

✦ ✦ ✦

When the Dean of Schönberg was on his way home, he came across a crowd of people milling around a ditch on the other side of Göttlicher's paper mill. The Ullersdorf Castle coach lay overturned, its shaft broken and a rear wheel fallen apart.

One of the women of the crowd told him what had happened. The horses had reared, and the inquisitor, who was in the coach, had fallen out and hit his head. But it was surely nothing serious. Master Boblig hadn't waited for the coachman to calm the horses but had taken to his heels and run off to the castle.

Lautner gazed up at the heavens, observed by his coachman. The dean noticed that Florian's bristled cheeks were shaking with mirth.

"One would think, Florian, that you didn't believe in divine retribution!"

"I believe all right, Father," he said. "But they say the mills of God grind slowly, and this was devilish quick work!"

"I'd say this was proof . . ."

"And I could tell you something else, Father."

"What?"

"Oh, I don't know," said Florian and cracked his whip.

Florian had a secret that the dean was never to know. When Boblig's horses had been standing in front of the priest's house at Gross Ullersdorf, he had fed them the little green pill he got from a Gypsy the year before in exchange for tobacco. The Gypsy had told him these pills turned even the gentlest of horses into wild beasts. And he'd been right. But why tell the reverend father? Let him believe in divine retribution!

15 ✦ Crown Witness

When Ullersdorf Castle had been built on the site of an old water tower at the end of the sixteenth century, no one had thought to build a jail there. Or perhaps the builder had, but the marshy ground precluded deep foundations; and without a basement there could be no underground cellars to use as dungeons. He sought to remedy this by building a place of detention on the lowermost floor of the octagonal watchtower, the result being a quite large cell with a round-arched ceiling and stout walls. But even this prison was unsuitable because the door from it opened directly onto the castle courtyard, and the frequent weeping and wailing of the prisoners was not a pleasant thing for their lordships' sensitive ears. Besides, it soon became clear, especially after the revolt of the Zerotin serfs in the year of '59, that this prison was too small. So work began with utmost speed on a more spacious jail at one end of the extensive block of stables. Here, too, the foundations were hardly a yard deep on account of the waterlogged soil, but the walls were thick and the ceilings sturdily vaulted.

Altogether there were six cells: three had windows to the south, two fronted the castle courtyard, and the last was a windowless dungeon. The windows were of course mere slits, hardly half a cubit high, fitted with stout, sharp-pointed iron grilles. Moreover, they were boarded up from the outside, and light could penetrate them only through the tiny cracks between the planks. Outside the windows a guard kept watch. Inside the building, a narrow passage led between the two rows of cells to a larger guardroom with rough benches and a table. Now not even this jail was big enough, and so yet another building was under construction below the hill in the park.

Three women were awaiting their fate in the first cell on the left: Maryna Schuch, the beggarwoman of Wermsdorf; the midwife Dorothea Groer, and Maryna Züllich, the miller's wife from Weikersdorf. Their trials were already over, and the verdict and court records had been sent to the Court of Appeals in Prague for approval. Now no one accorded them any special attention, except when one of them was taken to the courtroom for a confrontation. Otherwise they received a regular hunk of coarse bread and a pitcher of water, and sometimes the young jailer, Friml, smuggled them a bowl of soup from the castle kitchen or gave them the remains of his lunch. Their long imprisonment, the interrogations, the torture, the hunger and cold, the constant persuasion of the Capuchins—all this had long since stripped them of all will or reason. None of them hoped for anything anymore. They no longer knew the difference between truth and lies, fact and fiction; and they even began to believe their own testimonies. Their behavior was passive, except when Master Jokl stopped by to look into their cell: then they trembled and pressed themselves against the cold walls, for fear of new torture. They were scarcely human beings anymore.

The next south-facing cell also housed three women: Barbora Kühnel, who had once served as a cook to the late Father Leopold of Gross Ullersdorf; old Agneta Kopp from Gross Ullersdorf; and Anna Föbel from Kleppel. All of them had undergone interrogation and torture but in their cases the inquisitor had not yet elaborated his verdict. They, too, had lost hope. But they had not been imprisoned for as long as their neighbors, and weeping and wailing could still often be heard from their cell. Sometimes they would even pummel on its oak door, and a jailer would have to come and restore order with his boot or with a horsewhip.

Three more women were in the third cell of the row: Susanne Stubenvoll, the wife of the castle cellarman; Marie Petrova, the wife of the estates manager at Johrnsdorf; and Barbora Rotter, the young daughter of the church baker at Gross Ullersdorf. This cell was the warmest, because it neighbored the stables; moreover, its inmates were generally more comfortable because, in return for bribes, the jailers occasionally brought them a little better food. Mainly, however, none of them had yet ceased to believe; everything, they were sure, was a terrible mistake that would ultimately be happily resolved.

Not so in the next cell, facing the courtyard, where just two women were detained. Barbora Kranichl, whom everyone knew as the Black Woman, was a swarthy, untamed, wild woman who confessed to everything under torture, but always recanted as soon as the thumbscrew or Spanish boot was removed. Back in her cell, she would hammer on the door and accuse the judges, especially the pot-bellied, bald inquisitor, of being in league with the Devil themselves—for which reason alone, she said, they tormented and tortured righteous Christians. Barbora's cellmate was Katerina Rabovska, ordinarily a mild-mannered woman, made meek by a lifetime of drudgery. And so she behaved in her cell, except sometimes when the torment became too much for her; then she raged as if bereft of her senses and continued until the jailer tied her up and stuffed her mouth with a gag.

Dorothea Biedermann, whose trial was still in progress, was kept in solitary confinement, and so was the recently arrested Barbora Göttlicher. In her case the dark dungeon was not only a means to break her firm resolve; her plight was to enable the executioner to exact a fat bribe from her rich husband.

But this comparatively feeble woman, Boblig found, could draw on almost unbelievable reserves of strength and resistance. Interrogations and courtroom confrontations were to no avail, and neither were Jokl's threats or the Capuchins' powers of persuasion. She was consistent in her claim that she did not know the beggarwoman Schuch, she did not know Mistress Groer, the midwife, and she had never been friendly with Mistress Züllich, the miller's wife. She had never been to the Petersstein, she had always led an orderly life, she had observed all the commandments of the Church, and she called on the parish priest at Gross Ullersdorf to testify on her behalf. Not even the thumbscrew could change her tune. And so she remained in the darkness of solitary confinement. The judge knew he could wait, for time was on his side. Dark dungeons, his experience told him, softened even the hardest of men, so why should the papermaker's wife be different!

After the Countess of Galle's departure for Wiesenberg, Master Boblig of Edelstadt effectively became the sovereign lord over Ullersdorf Castle. Sheriff Vinarsky, the burgrave, and the treasurer had already seen enough of him to recognize the danger of resisting his rule. Anyway, howling with the wolf was not only convenient, but sometimes even entertaining.

Today the inquisitor had convened the entire tribunal in order to conclude the trial of Dorothea Biedermann. But the event was in fact less because of her than for the benefit of the members of the tribunal. Boblig wanted them to see some exciting theater, and he was to be the star of the show.

The full complement of judges sat at the long, white-cloth-covered table and peered uneasily around the huge courtroom dimly illuminated by the small windows on the north wall. But the room brightened as soon as the grim-faced Stubenvoll set a large glass before each man and began to serve Austrian white wine.

Then the inquisitor's assistant, Ignatius, entered with an incense burner to ward off evil spirits—though the real purpose of the fumigation was to suppress the smell of the prisoners under interrogation.

The last to arrive was the director of the inquisitorial court, Master Boblig of Edelstadt, dressed to the nines, for a change, in a new blue cloth coat, wide breeches, new shoes, and a lace collar. And a wig. This, thought Sheriff Vinarsky to himself, surely covered the bump Boblig had received when his coach overturned by Göttlicher's paper mill.

Ignatius sat down at a small table, where paper, inkpot, and several well-sharpened quill pens were prepared. But no glass of wine. He barked sternly to the cellarman, who immediately rectified his grave error.

The doorway to the torture chamber opened and Jokl appeared. He, too, was in full glory, dressed in a red tunic, black breeches and a small fur cap.

Finally the inquisitor ordered:

"Bring in Dorothea Biedermann!"

The executioner stepped outside, and Master Boblig of Edelstadt went to the judges' table, grasped the largest glass and drank half of its contents in one draft.

"Stubenvoll's improving," he said.

Everyone laughed and nodded nervously. They were all feeling a little uncomfortable. This was the second time they had met as a body, the first being the pronouncement of the verdict in the case of Schuch, Groer, and Züllich. On that occasion they had all been startled by the three women's conveniently clear confessions of guilt. It was that convenience, rather than a fear of the inquisitor, that had led no one to venture an inquiry into what had gone before. Only the sheriff, Adam Vinarsky of Kreuz, formed his own opinion, but he kept that to himself.

The executioner suddenly flung open the door and pushed Dorothea Biedermann inside, escorted by a jailer.

A hush fell over the white-clothed table. Each of the judges knew the bathkeeper, and knew her well. But none of them could now be sure that this was really her. What they saw was a wretched, bent, old woman, holding aloft a pair of crippled and festering thumbs. But she did not see them. Her gaze was fixed on the window, and on Gross Ullersdorf beyond.

The gentlemen of the tribunal looked on in embarrassment; Zeidler, the forest warden, tugged on his long red beard.

Then the inquisitor opened the proceedings.

"In nomine Patris et Filii et Spiritus sancti . . ."

"Amen," replied the company of judges as if they were in church.

Boblig drew in his stomach and stood in front of the accused.

"Do you promise before the inquisitorial tribunal to reply truthfully to all the questions that will be put to you?"

Dorothea felt a choking in her throat and a bitterness in her mouth. She could not speak, and it was all she could do to nod her head.

"First of all, tell us what your name is and how old you are!"

It was some time before Dorothea could open her mouth. Then she replied, so softly that the gentlemen at the table could hardly catch what she was saying.

"My name is Dorothea Biedermann. I was the bathkeeper and I'm fifty-two years old."

Boblig glanced at the hunchback to see whether he was writing this down.

"Are you married, and for how long?"

"I've been married twice. The first time was over thirty years ago."

"Do you have children? How many? And where are they?"

"I had six children with my first husband. Three of them died as infants, and one son died just before you had me arrested. A daughter died a year ago, leaving just one son from my first marriage. I had two more daughters with my second husband, and both of them and my son are at home."

Boblig waited until the clerk of the court had written everything down, then he went on: "How often did you attend confession and communion?"

"At least twice a year, once at Eastertime and once at Christmas."

"When did you last go to confession?"

"On Good Friday, at Gross Ullersdorf. I confessed to Father König."

Nothing exciting had happened so far. Just dull, droning questions and soft, straightforward answers.

Suddenly Boblig's voice changed.

"You have already admitted that you used to go to the Petersstein. Is that so?"

Now the judges were more attentive. They knew that this answer would be conclusive.

Dorothea Biedermann answered in the same tone as before.

"Yes, I was there."

A deep hush fell on the courtroom, broken only by the scratching of the hunchback's quill.

"What did you do there?"

The bathkeeper, it seemed, could not find the right words. There was a long silence. Too long. Master Jokl gave a little cough from the door of the torture chamber. And, lo and behold, Dorothea Biedermann immediately opened her mouth.

"It was fun. We frolicked and danced. And we drank beer."

"And you yourself, what did you do?"

"Frolicked and danced—and drank beer."

The forest warden tugged at his beard again. Richter, the forgemaster, swallowed in anticipation.

"Did you have a gallant?"

"Yes."

"And what was his name?" asked the judge, more sharply now.

"His name was Balthazar."

"Tell us what he looked like."

"He's young and handsome, with a green gamekeeper's cap and shiny boots."

"Who took you to the Petersstein the first time, and how did you get there?"

"Balthazar took me. On a billy goat. We were there in a trice."

The inquisitor found these answers quite satisfactory, but Sheriff Vinarsky gave a faint smile. The treasurer and the burgrave looked at the floor. Zeidler, the forest warden, wore a puzzled frown. He knew how perilously steep the mountain was. To be there in a trice, and on a goat? Incredible!

But Boblig was pressing ahead with his interrogation.

"You have already testified that you took the sacred host with you. Where did you put it?"

"I took the wafer from the Easter communion. I put it in my shoe."

The sacred host, in her shoe! The judges were incensed.

"Why did you put the sacred host in your shoe?"

"I put the sacred host in my shoe to help me frolic and dance."

Now even Sheriff Vinarsky wore a frown.

"Did you pray to your gallant?"

"I used to call him: Black as night, white as light, beloved Balthazar, take me to the Petersstein."

The inquisitor paused, while the hunchback wrote all this down. Then, censoriously:

"Are you aware, Dorothea Biedermann, that in so doing you forfeited everything? The Almighty Lord, the Virgin Mary, Mother of God, the sacrament of the baptism, the other sacraments?"

"Yes, but I trust that in the Lord's mercy my sins will be forgiven on Judgment Day . . ."

The silence in the courtroom assumed a new and suffocating gravity. The treasurer stared aghast at the bathkeeper; whether he wanted to or not, he had to believe her, however incredible her testimony was. The burgrave reached in agitation for his snuff bottle; the forest warden tugged his beard even more furiously, while the forgemaster squirmed on his chair.

Boblig went on:

"And now, Dorothea Biedermann, if you so trust in the Lord's mercy, I want you to name all the people you saw on the Petersstein. And be careful not to leave anyone out!"

Dorothea's worst moment had come. She had learned by heart the names of about twenty people, some of whom she knew, others not at all, but now she found to her alarm that she could not remember a single one of them. Beads of perspiration stood out on her temples.

"Speak!"

"On the Petersstein I saw the beggarwoman Schuch from Wermsdorf; I saw old Mistress David and the midwife, Groer . . . And I saw the miller's wife, Mistress Züllich from Weikersdorf . . . And I saw old Agneta Kopp from Gross Ullersdorf, and Katerina Rabovska, and the Black Woman . . ."

Then she was quiet.

"Remember! Wasn't there also someone from Schönberg?"

This was a surprise for the other judges. Could there be witches in Schönberg also?

Dorothea swallowed in silence, and at this there came a jangling of chains from the torture chamber.

"Yes, I saw Marie Sattler, the wife of Kaspar Sattler, the dyemaster—he was there, too, with his daughter . . . And I saw Marie Peschek, with her husband Heinrich. And I saw Judge Hutter's wife, the widow Weillemann, and the soapboiler, Prerovsky . . ."

This was like a bolt from the blue. All the members of the tribunal knew Sattler the dyemaster, Peschek the clothmaker, and Prerovsky the soapboiler. They knew them as respectable citizens, without a blemish on their character. Now they were described as disciples of the Devil. The bathkeeper had obviously taken leave of her senses!

Boblig looked up in triumph. How about that for a surprise, his face said. But that's not all I've prepared for you! So pin back your ears and keep a firm hold on the table, or you'll find yourselves falling off your chairs!

"And didn't you ever see anyone else on the Petersstein?"

She hung her head.

The hush was unbearable.

But still Dorothea was silent. Until she heard a cough from the torture chamber.

Then she spoke. Hurriedly, as if afraid she would lose her memory at any moment.

"I saw Father Pabst, the priest from Römerstadt, with his cook. I saw Father Lautner, the Dean of Schönberg, and his housekeeper, Susanne Voglick. They all had the sacred host in their shoes, they all danced."

This was too much. Zeidler sprang up in a rage and went up to her.

"You've made it up! That simply can't be true!"

The inquisitor frowned, caught the forest warden by the shoulder, and led him back to the table.

"Your responsibility, Master Zeidler, is to listen. I am the person who is conducting the interrogation! You must remain calm. You are going to learn even worse things than this!"

Dorothea stood transfixed, her eyes directed at the ceiling, her thumbs upraised. For one brief moment it occurred to her to cry out, to say that everything was a lie, and that the inquisitor had forced her with torture to say those things, but in that split second there was a jangling of shackles from the torture chamber. Dorothea knew that this was the executioner's warning. She began to tremble.

Boblig's harsh voice was addressing her again.

"What else did the Dean of Schönberg do there?"

"The dean played a tune on a whistle, Master Peschek played another instrument, Father König played a flute . . ."

"So you saw Father König also?"

"Yes, he was there with both his cooks."

This exceeded everything! The treasurer, the burgrave, and especially the forest warden muttered and frowned. Boblig threw them a sharp look and laughed malevolently.

Then he went up to the accused and looked directly into her eyes.

"Dorothea Beidermann, are you well acquainted with Father Lautner, Dean of Schönberg?"

"I came to know him only too well," she whispered.

"What do those words mean—'I know him only too well?'"

"I'm an old woman. It's not decent for me to say it in front of so many gentlemen . . ."

Boblig pressed her no further, merely motioning to his clerk to make a careful note of everything. Only then did he pose his next question: "Would you be able to look the dean in the face and repeat to him what you have told us?"

"Yes," replied the bathkeeper softly. "I would like to tell him to his face that I saw him on the Petersstein, among the witches."

"Would you swear, cross your heart, and hope to die, that you have told us the truth?"

"Cross my heart and hope to die. I saw the dean on the Petersstein, and his cook Susanne."

"And Father Pabst?"

"I saw him, too, and his cook."

Dorothea Biedermann no longer had any more strength. At any moment she could collapse. The jailer, Friml, had to support her to prevent her falling, and Master Jokl, observing everything from the doorway of the torture chamber, brought her a mug of water. Dorothea gulped it down. The interrogation continued.

"Tell us, does every witch have some kind of mark?"

"Every witch must have a mark, to make her recognizable to evil spirits and to other witches."

"Tell us, how often did you join with this swain of yours, Balthazar? And how long was he your gallant?"

"I've known him for thirty-seven years. He came to me every week."

"By whom did you have your children?"

"My children are by my husbands. I could have only flies, bumblebees, wasps, or moths by Balthazar . . ."

This revelation aroused revulsion at the judges' table. Richter the forgemaster spat in disgust.

Once again, Dorothea was overcome with weakness. The time had come for the inquisitor to conclude the interrogation. Boblig raised his voice:

"Are you, Dorothea Biedermann, willing to confirm before anyone that what you have testified here, of your own volition and without the use of torture, is the truth?"

"Yes." Her voice was barely audible.

"Cross your heart and hope to die?"

"Yes."

"Would you be able to say it to all the people whom you have named, to their face?"

"Yes."

Not a muscle moved at the judges' table. The silence was so deep that one could hear the creak of the ceiling beams.

The inquisitor took his time. Everything had gone exactly as he had planned.

"Bring in Mistress Göttlicher for a confrontation!"

The executioner bowed and went out, and the jailer led Dorothea aside. The inquisitor withdrew to the table and drank a full glass of wine in one draft. Then, with a faint smile on his lips, he looked at the members of the inquisitorial tribunal.

16 ✦ *Confrontation*

It was not altogether clear to Jokl why the inquisitor was sending for Mistress Göttlicher. The papermaker's wife had not confessed, and interrogation so far had elicited only negative responses or silence. Did Boblig think she would volunteer a confession if the bathkeeper incriminated her before the full tribunal? Jokl had his doubts—but who could tell with this strange judge?

He unshackled her by torchlight in her dark prison cell and led her, bewildered, into the harsh light of day. It took some time before she accustomed herself to the brightness, but when she did, she directed him a look of utter scorn. For him this was the most persuasive evidence that her imprisonment had left her quite uncowed.

Appropriately to his vocation, the executioner was usually rough and rude to his prisoners, but with Barbora Göttlicher he made an exception. Like everyone else at Gross Ullersdorf, he knew her as a lady of utmost respectability and kindliness—and like everyone else, he had always treated her with civility, retaining some of this respect for her even after she was put in his charge. He gave her extra rations, he did not shout at her, he did not overtighten her shackles, he did not even use the familiar form of address when speaking to her.

In the passage outside her cell he said: "During the last torture, madam, I was very gentle with the thumbscrews."

The papermaker's wife looked instinctively at her contused thumbs, then at the executioner. Was this an attempt at extortion? She did not consider his remark worthy of a reply.

"I'd like to give you a friendly warning, madam," he continued in the same tone. "I advise you sincerely to reply the way the inquisitor wants. I wouldn't like to have to work on you again. Next time I'd have to tighten the screws far more."

"Do you want something from me?" she asked with unconcealed disdain.

"Not I, but master Boblig. He wants you to confess. It's hopeless to resist. You'll have to confess anyway, in the end. In our court there's no choice."

Mistress Göttlicher gritted her teeth and did not reply.

"Come!"

The papermaker's wife strode resolutely ahead, her head held guiltlessly high. She needed none of Jokl's support, not even when they climbed the stairs. Only when they were inside the torture chamber did her steps falter as she saw the inquisitorial tribunal at the long table through the courtroom door. She felt a rush of blood to her head and was suddenly very weak. She knew the sheriff, the treasurer, and the burgrave by sight; but also among the judges was the forest warden, Zeidler, and he was a good friend of her husband's. Many hours had he sat with him at the paper mill, and now he was going to judge her. How would he behave? Would he tell the truth, or would he be holding his tongue? He was looking at the floor, pretending not to see her. This was a bad sign!

Master Boblig of Edelstadt was sitting with his back to her, engaged in conversation with the sheriff. He did not even look up when they brought her in. Evidently he did not think her worthy of it.

After a while, he turned around, eyed her sharply from head to toe, stood up, and slowly bore down on her.

Barbora Göttlicher had never seen him so dressed up before. His gray-wigged head suddenly reminded her of a death's-head moth. She had found one once on the pillow of her firstborn son, shortly before he died.

Boblig was experienced enough to recognize that this victim had not lost her self-control. Perhaps, it occurred to him, he had been overly hasty. He had wanted to dazzle the tribunal with a judicial masterstroke, softening her like wax in the heat of his questioning, melting her self-assurance, relentlessly compelling her to confess. But now he saw that the papermaker's wife was decidedly not yet amenable to such a procedure, and there was no turning back. If necessary, however, Master Jokl was here with his instruments. The Spanish boot or the rope-hauling torture, *strappado,* would help where the thumbscrews had failed. This frail woman was used to a life of comfort; she could not hold out for long.

He nodded to Friml, the jailer, who pushed Dorothea Biedermann forward.

Only now did the papermaker's wife see the old bathkeeper, but it took some moments before she recognized her. Instinctively, she remembered the executioner's words on leaving the jail, and her skin crept.

Boblig went up to Mistress Biedermann, pointed to Barbora Göttlicher, and asked her:

"Dorothea Biedermann, do you know this woman?"

"I do," she replied softly. "It's the papermaker's wife, Barbora Göttlicher."

Now the judge turned to the accused.

"Do you, Barbora Göttlicher, know this woman?"

"Of course. It's Dorothea Biedermann."

Boblig turned again to the bathkeeper.

"Tell Barbora Göttlicher to her face whether you saw her at the gathering of witches on the Petersstein."

Barbora plainly heard what he said. She looked anxiously, not daring to breathe, at the mouth of the old bathkeeper. Dorothea was honest, she had never harmed anyone. Surely she would never say anything that was untrue. She had never been on the mountain.

Dorothea gave a sidelong glance, evading Barbora's eyes. "Yes," she said, as if from a dream. "I saw her on the Petersstein. It's true!"

Barbora Göttlicher's eyes opened wide with horror. Had she really heard this, or were her senses deceiving her? Surely it was not possible for the bathkeeper to claim what was not true!

"And what did Barbora Göttlicher do there?"

The courtroom resounded to the croaking voice of the inquisitor. "She frolicked and danced, and drank beer!"

The room dimmed before Barbora's eyes. It was as if some unseen hand were squeezing her temples in an iron grip. But still she maintained her composure. Dorothea, it occurred to her, had evidently gone mad. She looked at her. No, she had not gone mad. She was lying. She was lying because she had to. Why otherwise was she so conspicuously exhibiting her crushed thumbs? Barbora now realized why Jokl had urged her to testify just as the judge wished. O God!

"With whom," the inquisitor's voice was booming, "did Barbora Göttlicher dance on the Petersstein?"

"With her gallant."

"Tell her, Dorothea Biedermann, to her face, what her gallant's name is."

"Father Thomas."

"And who, Dorothea Biedermann, is Father Thomas?"

"Father Thomas is the parish priest, Father König!"

Barbora Göttlicher did not see the gentlemen sitting at the table, she did not see the awesome death's-head judge. Her eyes were fixed on the bathkeeper with her upraised, scab-encrusted thumbs. She felt the hot blood coursing to her head, she saw the dark spots dancing before her eyes, she felt her legs buckling. The terrible charge was like a great rock hurtling down a hillside straight toward her.

Master Jokl, who was standing at her side, caught her just in time. But the judge took no notice. Stepping right up to her, he stretched out one hand; the fingers were outspread, and on one of them was a gold ring.

"Did you, Barbora Göttlicher, hear what Dorothea Biedermann said to your face?"

She looked fearfully into the eyes of this dreadful man and made no reply.

"Do you admit you were there on the Petersstein?" The inquisitor spoke with growing insistence.

Still she kept silent, and as she stared into his eyes she suddenly felt that this was the Devil. The real Devil, the one in the Bible, the one who tempted Christ on the mountain. But how was it that only she, and no one else, could see him? Not even the hawkeyed Master Zeidler!

"Answer when you are questioned!"

Barbora Göttlicher felt the touch of the executioner's hand on her side. This had to be a warning, urging her to speak and not to inflame the judge against her. Even the mournful gaze of the bathkeeper seemed to be saying: Speak, all is in vain! And the forest warden? His hands were cupped in front of his eyes. Oh, the coward! The traitor!

The judge twisted his face and barked:

"Speak!"

Barbora Göttlicher opened her mouth.

"I was . . ."

And at that moment everything went dark again. She did not finish the sentence, but crumpled into unconsciousness. And this time not even the executioner could catch her.

Boblig sprang back as if he had trodden on a snake. He had not expected such a turn of events.

"Take the witches away!"

Friml the jailer bundled off the bathkeeper, Jokl gathered up the papermaker's wife, and shortly they had all disappeared through the door of the torture chamber.

Boblig stared at the floor, legs apart. Then he took a pinch of snuff and went to the judges' table. Without looking at anyone, he grasped his glass, but it was empty. And so was the pitcher.

"Wine!"

Ignatius jumped up and ran for wine.

Only now did the judge look at the mortified faces of the inquisitorial tribunal. Then he burst into laughter.

"Gentlemen!" he cried, his voice brash and overloud. "Your eyes are as wide as little lambs! But what's happened? The witch had a confession on the tip of her tongue, and the Devil struck her dumb. He simply made her swoon to stop her testifying. It's an old Satanic practice, and we judges are used to it. We know what to do. Things could be more unpleasant, of course. Sometimes the Devil even strikes a witch dead during torture, because he's afraid she'll confess—that's what happened with the old woman David!"

Boblig's theatrical smile could infect no one at the table, for the interrogation that they had seen had left a profound impression. Mistress Göttlicher, whom they all knew, was no common country woman, and they continued to hold the highest opinion of her.

This the inquisitor knew; and he was aware that his most important task now was to retain their respect.

"Gentlemen," he continued, "I'm sure you would be amazed at some of my experiences, and those of other inquisitors! We've had people who put up a saintly resistance to the harshest of tortures, steadfastly refusing to confess their crimes against God and mankind. But their outward saintliness proved to be only a mask. In the end we always found incontrovertible evidence that the Devil himself had sustained them. As a rule, they were the persons who were his most devoted disciples. The Devil doesn't wish them to defile themselves, to be taken from his power through a holy confession. Years ago, in Ravensburg, one stubborn witch commended others to boil newborn boys and eat them, to make themselves immune to the pain of torture so they would betray nothing."

The inquisitor's words defied belief. No one at the judges' table had the stomach to comment.

Ignatius entered, followed by Jakob Fleischner, the cellarman's assistant, carrying a large pitcher of fresh wine.

"Where's Stubenvoll?" asked Boblig.

"I don't know," replied the assistant.

"Probably weeping for that witch of his!" laughed Boblig and began to pour out the wine himself.

"Let's drink a toast to our pious work, my friends. *Bibamus!* Drink!"

The other judges raised their glasses politely and drank, but all they tasted was a sour bitterness; only Boblig took pleasure in the wine.

Zeidler, the forest warden, spoke out:

"Master Boblig, it may be that all this is simply beyond me, but I've known Dorothea Biedermann and Barbora Göttlicher for a good many years, and I've never known more respectable women in all of Gross Ullersdorf. Barbora was never anything but good to everyone. Yet now the bathkeeper tells her to her face that she's a witch. How is it possible? The Devil doesn't do good but evil!"

Boblig looked at him with a smile.

"The fact is, it's the most respectable who are usually the most suspicious! I could recount many cases from my own experience, but I'll settle for just one. On a certain estate in the diocese of Basel, near the town of Gewyll, lived a very respected and very pious lady, the wife of a farmer, the embodiment of virtue! But then she admitted to the Inquisition that for a full six years she had shared her bed with a gallant, an incubus. She even lay with him beside her sleeping husband and had intercourse with him three times a week, on Tuesdays, Fridays, and Sundays, and on feast days also. In the seventh year she was to fall to the Devil, body and soul. But God in his mercy permitted her to be imprisoned before the time was up, and she made a full confession in jail. She died in the flames, but God certainly accepted her with grace because she gladly went to her death. She told her confessor that if she were given the choice of death and liberty, she would choose death, merely to escape the power of the demon. It would be a bad judge, sir, who would allow himself to be swayed by the outward appearance of the accused! That's why they used to put masks on the faces of persons standing trial, to prevent the judge from being tainted with pity."

The men at the judges' table stared long at the inquisitor. His strange reasoning was indeed beyond them; it instilled neither respect nor admiration, but fear.

After a while, Sheriff Vinarsky of Kreuz said: "Forgive me, Master Boblig, but I know little of theology or of the law. Perhaps that's why I can't understand how even a priest, a holy man, can be held to serve the evil spirit. We heard Dorothea Biedermann pronounce a terrible accusation against three clergymen, and we all know them well . . ."

Boblig cast a sideways glance at his questioner.

"They would not be the first clergymen to fall victim to black magic. Bishop Philip Adolphus held office for eight years in Würzburg, and during that time some nine hundred witches, women and men, were burned in his diocese. And among them were eighteen clergymen! The Devil derives especial pleasure from the capture of a priest's soul!"

The sheriff was not giving in.

"But how could God allow it?"

"God allows every person, even clergymen, the freedom to choose. If a priest prevails over the Devil, the Lord makes a saint of him, and if he does not prevail, eternal damnation awaits. Do you want an example? In the Rhineland, in the town of Ober-weiller lived a parish priest by the name of Hässlin, who didn't believe in witches. He said they were just figments of the imagination. But otherwise he was a pious man, so the gracious Lord determined to cure him of this one heresy. One day He made sure that an old hag should confront him as he crossed a narrow bridge. When the priest didn't get out of her way in time, the woman began to shriek: 'Just you wait, preacher, you won't get away with this!' And indeed, that very night the priest felt cruel pains below his waist, which grew worse and worse. Finally he couldn't move and remained quite paralyzed for three whole years. Then the old hag was put before the Inquisition, where she voluntarily confessed that she had bewitched him. Hardly had she burned in the flames when the pains left him, and once again he could control his limbs. From then on he spoke of witches with respect and assisted the inquisitorial tribunal whenever he could."

The sheriff nodded, but it was evident he was not satisfied with the answer.

Now the treasurer asked a question:

"And doesn't the Devil sometimes try to win inquisitors to his cause, Master Boblig?"

Boblig pulled a serious face.

"We live in a world that seems bent on destruction, where evil thoughts prevail, and where the power of love is ebbing away. No wonder, then, that we see a growing impudence on the part of the demonic forces. Inquisitorial judges, therefore, have to be granted special divine protection. The question you have raised, sir, was also posed by the elders of Ravensburg. They asked witches at the stake why they hadn't bewitched their judges. And the witches truthfully replied that they had tried to do so many times but always in vain. And when the elders further asked why this was so, they replied that the powers of darkness, whether they be named Belial, Beelzebub, Behemont, Asmodeus, Mephistopheles, Leviathan, or Mammon, were not enough for us inquisitorial judges. Gentlemen, I have lost count how many times, day and night, during my forty years as an inquisitorial judge, the demons have raged below my windows, howled like dogs, bleated like goats, and screeched like apes. But they could never exert the slightest power over me as a servant of righteousness, praise be to Almighty God!"

After this solemn statement, no one dared make any more remarks. Only after some time did the forgemaster ask whether this divine protection also extended to the members of the inquisitorial tribunal.

"It does indeed," Boblig declared. "But of course, only if the members relinquish all pity they might have on the accused, and—which is most important—if they divulge nothing of what they have learned to anyone. Nothing would help anyone who defied this edict. They themselves would have become disciples of the Devil and would be dealt with accordingly!"

The inquisitor had finished. He peered at the awestruck faces around him, reserving his most piercing gaze for Zeidler, the forest warden. It appeared to him that he was the least trustworthy.

17 ✦ *The Net Closes*

When, during Master Boblig's visit to the deanery at Schönberg, Lautner had pointedly inquired whether he had ever acquitted anyone wrongfully accused of witchcraft, the question had appeared ludicrous. Could such an experienced inquisitor as Boblig have been deluded? Had it not been said of him that he was *leo, qui querit, quem devoret*, the lion who seeks whom to devour? And not only seeks, but finds!

Even the respectable and pious Barbora Göttlicher was to confess eventually. And not only did she confess: she also named others who had attended the witch-swarms on the Petersstein, among them the castle cellarman, Johann Stubenvoll, and the old and faithful castle housekeeper, Barbora Drachsler. The whispered story among the servants was that Stubenvoll had been accused of witchcraft only because he had served Master Boblig bad wine, and Drachsler because she had given him disagreeable meals; but in asking the Countess of Galle to consent to the arrests, the inquisitor referred to both of them as especially dangerous and cunning disciples of the Devil.

The inquisitor was selective, arresting only those he considered to be of especial consequence, because the new jail was still not yet finished. Even so, the number of detainees was rising fast. Inside the castle, people went on fearful tiptoe; some bowed deeply to Boblig and even to his hideous assistant; others, as soon as they saw them, avoided them. The inquisitor himself was blissful. The whole castle rang with his voice and laughter, both during the day and in the depths of night, when he caroused with his assistant.

At this time there occurred an incident which, though trifling, had a powerful effect on the inquisitorial judge. Late one afternoon he took it into his head to take a stroll to the sulfurous springs of Ullersdorf. He and his assistant were making their way to the pool along the bank of the little river Tess, thickly over-grown with aspens and willows, when suddenly a stone, as large as a fist, hurtled from the thicket, missing Boblig's head by a hair's breadth.

That was the end of the visit to the baths. The inquisitor took to his heels and fled back to the castle, stopping only when he reached the safety of its splendidly sgraffitoed walls.

"Wasn't that the Devil?" Ignatius inquired ironically, gasping for breath as he caught up with his master.

"That was no Devil! More likely some villain after revenge for the cellarman or that fat housekeeper!"

"We ought to find out who it was!"

"So go back and look!"

The judge crossed the courtyard despondently, made his way to his room, entered, and slammed the door so violently that it almost flew off its hinges. And straightaway he began to dictate a letter for Her Ladyship the Countess of Galle, who was still lin-gering at Wiesenberg. The letter declared that his life was under constant threat from enemies overt and covert, and if he was to continue his onerous task, his safety would have to guaranteed. Hence the request that at least one castle musketeer be reassigned as his bodyguard, with immediate effect.

Hardly two days passed, and at the countess's behest Sheriff Vinarsky ordered the strongest and ablest musketeer, a hulking fellow by the name of Barta, to act as Boblig's shadow; he was to stay with him at all times, and in the event of an attack was to shield him with his own body.

Nevertheless, the stone-throwing incident accelerated Boblig's resolve to expand his base of operations.

The dank days of fall came to Ullersdorf; the mountains faded into the mists, the land was drenched with the autumn rains, and the air was filled with the smell of rotting leaves. At Ullersdorf Castle there came an abrupt halt to the interrogations, confronta-tions, and examinations by torture. Instead, Boblig sat at a wide table, filling sheet after sheet of fine paper from the Göttlicher mill with his shaking, barely legible scrawl. But these were only drafts; the final copy was made by Ignatius, who sat at another table, transcribing the texts neatly in his own pointed hand. Boblig devoted special care to the writing of his first letter, addressed to His Grace the Bishop of Olomouc. In it he wrote that, to his greatest amazement and regret, his interrogations of divers persons accused of black magic at Gross Ullersdorf had revealed that three venerable clergymen of the diocese of Olomouc, viz., the Very Reverend Dean of Schönberg, Christoph Alois Lautner, further the parish priest at Gross Ullersdorf, the Reverend Thomas König, and the parish priest at Römerstadt, the Reverend Johann Franz Pabst, had attended gatherings of witches on the Petersstein. This grave charge was supported by the attached transcriptions of the testimonies of five convicted women. Finally, he entreated His Grace most humbly to order, without delay, a rigorous investigation into the aforementioned priests and called for their immediate arrest.

Ignatius took great pains over this assignment, embellishing all the capital letters with such flourishes that even he was not quite sure what they stood for.

"Master," he could not resist saying as he finished, "aren't we firing too high? The higher the climb, the harder the fall!"

Boblig stared round-eyed at his assistant.

"Fool! Nothing ventured, nothing gained! He who asks for little gets nothing!"

Remarkably, Ignatius did not hold his tongue.

"But master, we're dealing with three clergymen! This is a far cry from some old woman from Ullersdorf!"

"Fool, do you think I don't know that? But can't you see, those priests are the greatest danger we have to face! They're disbelievers, followers of condemnable writers who regard witch trials as lucrative enterprises for inquisitorial judges. Look, Gaup told me Lautner's mother's sister was supposed to be burned as a witch, and Schmidt, the bishop's secretary, told me about Pabst's aunt. Get this into your ass's head: both of those priests have more than enough reasons to stand against us and our pious work. And something else: When we were at the deanery in Schönberg, I saw piles of books. That's always suspicious. Just a cursory glance revealed quite a number of books that could well be *libri haeretici*. If we don't get those worthy priests, then they will certainly get us! Understand, Iggy?"

The second letter was addressed to Christoph Philip, Prince Liechtenstein, the Lord Protector of the town of Schönberg. Grandiloquently, and again supported by transcriptions of the interrogations, Boblig described the wretched state of affairs that had come to prevail in his city and he requested the prince to set up, as soon as possible, a special inquisitorial tribunal in Schönberg also.

✦ ✦ ✦

Soon afterward, the most splendid of coaches set off from the castle. In front sat a coachman clad in richly embroidered livery, at the rear was the musketeer, Barta, and inside was Boblig with his assistant. The coach went like the wind and did not halt until they reached Judge Gaup's house in Schönberg.

Such a luxuriously appointed coach immediately attracted quite a crowd of onlookers, but the inquisitor deemed none of them worthy of a single glance. Signaling only to the musketeer to remain on guard outside, he entered the house like a prince, accompanied by his assistant.

Gaup was taken quite by surprise. Such a grand visit, and he was dressed only in his house tunic and slippers! Flustered and ashamed, he immediately ushered them into the best parlor and shouted for all the candles to be lighted, although it was not dark at all, frantically scouring for ways to honor his unexpected visitors. But the friendly Boblig restrained him. First, he said, presenting him with two bulky packets, sealed in many places with red wax, he wanted the judge to see that these were delivered as soon as possible, because it was immensely important. Only then did he let Gaup go to attire himself more appropriately and to prepare refreshments.

After a while Gaup returned, this time dressed to the nines, and joined Boblig at the table, on which wine and cakes had appeared.

The district judge strained to amuse his guests, but somehow his efforts came to nothing. He was clever enough to know that Master Boblig of Edelstadt had not come just to deliver the mail. He was bringing tidings. Good or bad? He strove in vain to find clues in the inquisitor's face.

Only during the third glass of wine did Boblig level his gaze on the fretful judge.

"Since our last conversation," he said, "much has changed. I have something to tell you, *amice*, that may give you cause for disquiet."

Gaup pricked up his ears. He did not like this tone at all.

Boblig turned to his assistant.

"Have a look, Iggy, to see if anyone's listening at the door!"

This in itself was disquieting. The judge's fat cheeks reddened imperceptibly and tiny beads of sweat appeared on his high forehead. He was as taut as a bowstring.

"It's a serious matter," Boblig began, when Ignatius had assured him that no one was listening at the door. "I consider it my duty to warn you as a friend that your name has cropped up during the latest interrogations at Ullersdorf."

Gaup fidgeted in fear on his chair. He opened his mouth, but nothing came out.

"Yes. Two of the witches testified that among certain other citizens of Schönberg whom they had met on the Petersstein was your good self."

"I swear to God that's a lie!" Gaup's face was now deep crimson.

"A lie," Boblig echoed, softly.

For several long seconds he gloated, stroking his chin, raising his dense eyebrows, staring at the squirming judge, but saying nothing. Gaup was to be his lickspittle, and the little lie was doing the trick perfectly.

"I know," he said at last. "It's impossible to believe everything the witches say. They often give the first names that come into their head."

Gaup's face broadened into a grin.

"I'm grateful to you for refusing to accept such vile testimony. I swear to God, sir, that it is indeed a lie, and I'll be beholden to you for the rest of my days."

This was just what the inquisitor wanted. The time had come to tighten the screws even more firmly on this whimpering toady. People will do many things out of fear, but even more out of ambition.

"I've come to see you, *carissime amice,* to ask you whether you would accept the post of associate judge at an inquisitorial tribunal for the town of Schönberg, if you were nominated by Prince Liechtenstein. A tribunal is going to be set up soon, it would appear, and I took the liberty of proposing you."

Gaup sprang from his chair.

"Sir!"

"For the time being, my friend, you have nothing to thank me for. But please see that His Eminence receives the packet I entrusted to you as soon as possible. I hope you are acquainted with the duties of a member of an inquisitorial tribunal?"

Gaup recited like a schoolboy:

"I know the law. Primarily the statute of 1656. For witchcraft, practiced by a person in league with the Evil One, and whereby harm is done; for sorcery which denies the Christian faith and conduces to devotion to the Evil One; and further for carnal intercourse with him, there is but one punishment—death by burning alive. Only in quite exceptional extenuating circumstances, and when no great harm is done, and this by persons who are sincerely sorrowful for their foul deeds, may the punishment be mitigated by prior strangulation."

A smile appeared on Boblig's face.

"You do indeed know the law well, *amice,* and for that reason I would like you to become my right hand if an inquisitorial tribunal is set up in Schönberg . . ."

Gaup showed off a little of his Latin:

"I will be faithful as a dog, *canis fidelis!*"

"*Exquisite!*" cried Master Boblig of Edelstadt, raising his glass. "*Per amicitiam nostram!*"

"To eternal friendship!"

Boblig drank his wine and placed the empty glass on the table.

"Of all the people of Schönberg, you were the one I knew I had to select!"

"You made the right choice!"

The hunchback merely sipped his wine and smiled in silence.

18 ✦ *Audience*

Father Elias Isidor Schmidt, the assiduous and fervent secretary to the Bishop of Olomouc, was the first person in the bishop's palace to read Boblig's terrible charges against the three clergymen of the diocese. Schmidt had long held them in distrust for their libertarian ways, and for some time he had been compiling his own dossier against them. Indeed, it was he who had informed Boblig of Pabst's aunt. Now, as he read Boblig's letter, he felt vindicated. He had foreseen everything, while others had been deaf and blind! But how the bishop would react to the letter was quite another matter. His Grace had become irritable and obstinate in his old age, and had often made decisions which were quite contrary to all expectations. If only he, the secretary, could attend to this whole business by himself! But even that was possible—if he were to present the papers when the bishop was engrossed in other work and unwilling to occupy himself with unpleasant matters. Then he would mark them with the initials E.I.S. To be handled by the secretary.

Count Karl of Liechtenstein-Castelkorn, Bishop of Olomouc, had been so preoccupied with various building projects within the diocese that in recent years there had been some lapse of fervor in his spiritual stewardship. He had also been devoting more and more time to his favorite and dearest subject—paintings. He could sit for hours in front of his gallery's latest acquisition, carefully scrutinizing every brushstroke, every shade of color, every detail of the drawing.

Today the bishop was in raptures over his most recently acquired painting, depicting the return of the prodigal son. Now, thought Father Schmidt, was an appropriate moment. He glided noiselessly into the bishop's study, laid Boblig's papers on the table, and remarked that this was a most urgent matter. Nothing more. Then he went directly to the picture, studied it with interest for a moment, and finally announced that it was evidently a rare work.

The bishop smiled. His secretary understood the art of the painter about as well as he did the art of a blacksmith. He took Boblig's papers in his hand but immediately laid them down again and returned to the picture. The secretary saw that things were going just as he had foreseen. He no longer needed to admire this picture that did not interest him and was free to leave. He disappeared as quietly as he had come.

The bishop did not even notice him go. He looked again at the picture on the easel, squinting at every detail. The canvas was not very large, it lacked the kind of gold, ornamented frame that he liked, and the biblical theme was an old one, treated countless times by various artists; but this painting had something special about it, and the longer he looked at it, the more it enthralled him. Not so much for the whole picture as for two details within it. The artist had been quite unclear in his depiction of the Old Testament Hebrew father, who seemed to be stooping forward, while his son, a young man, knelt on both knees, craning toward him. Even the body of the son was quite roughly drawn. Evidently the artist had not been concerned with the figure of the father or of the son but had concentrated all his art into the old man's hands, which were pulling his son to him. They were old man's hands, with bulging veins, crippled fingers, and dry, wrinkled skin—but what vital and sensitive hands they were! In them and through them the painter had expressed all the love of a father for his lost son, all the joy of his unexpected return, all the gratitude to Him who had guided the steps of his lamented child. They were loving hands, hands that showed gratitude.

The light was falling directly onto the picture, exposing every detail, every shape, every shade of color. This picture could be viewed for hours, days, perhaps even months. For one moment the bishop dared to compare his own hands with those of the old man. And what a deplorable comparison! His hands were old

also, but how cold and dry they were, and how heavy! There was
nothing to lighten them, neither love nor gratitude!

The second detail, elaborated with masterly perfection, were
the feet of the returning son. Actually only the soles of his feet,
with their chapped and hard skin, dirty and poor. How many
paths had those feet trodden, how many rocks, how many swamps
and marshes? What sufferings had they borne before they found
the way home! They were imploring feet; they begged for mercy,
and, even more than eyes and mouths, they wept and wailed!

That was why the bishop gazed so long at this strange painting; and only when his eyes wearied did he recall with distaste
that his secretary had brought some urgent papers. He picked
them up again and began reading. And he was soon so riveted by
what he saw he even forgot the new picture. Initially Boblig's
pompous style bothered him, but then he saw only the facts, and
they were stunning. His brow furrowed.

Bishop Liechtenstein was a learned man. He had gained a
doctorate of laws in Ingolstadt, and he had served as canon in
Olomouc and Salzburg. When, more than twenty years before, he
succeeded Archduke Karl I Joseph as bishop of Olomouc, he had
but one aim: to culminate the work of one of his great pre-
decessors and counter-reformers, Cardinal Franz of Dietrichstein.
He strove with almost unbelievable fervor to sweep away the last
remnants of Lutheran heresy: he restored the priests' houses, he
sent missionaries to all corners of his diocese, he personally un-
dertook numerous visitations, he required the priests to lead the
most exemplary lives, he spared no expense. He elaborated and
printed a firm set of rules for the clergy and saw to it that every
priest abided by them. He diligently confiscated and burned all
harmful books, ecclesiastical and secular, which did not help rein-
force the Catholic faith. Among them, and especially widespread
in the mountainous country to the north of his diocese, had been
many books on witchcraft and sorcery.

Twenty years after taking office, he was satisfied. There were
no longer any non-Catholics in his bishopric, all the parishes had
incumbent priests, the power of the Church in public life and in

the life of every individual was decisive. The people flocked to the churches, and the churches themselves glittered with silver and gold, rang with sweet music, and were fragrant with incense.

Then, at last, the bishop could devote himself to matters close to his heart. Above all, he launched himself into a thorough restoration of his palace, and the Italian architect Fontana became his closest companion. He took it upon himself to reconstruct the old castle of the Thurzo family in Kromeriz by incorporating a picture gallery and an archive. He also took a keen interest in history and topography, and established contacts with other learned men—Thomas Pesina of Cechorod, Bohuslav Balbin, and Peter Lambeck, the Viennese imperial counselor and historiographer.

But now, reading Boblig's report, the bishop felt as if the sunshine of recent years had been obscured by a dense cloud. For so long he had been lulled by the belief that all in his diocese was in the best of order. And now he was reading of rampant heresy, even among the clergy! Why had no one warned him of the investigations at Ullersdorf? Why had it been left to some Heinrich Boblig of Edelstadt—a man evidently more zealous in his defense of the faith than the entire Consistory! And this man was accusing three priests! Terrible!

The bishop was already reaching for the bell to call his secretary and chide him; but then he pulled his hand back and began to read carefully the attached testimonies of the convicted witches. And now something of a sneer crossed his face; he began to have misgivings. The testimonies of these women were almost identical, as if one person had spoken through many mouths. The witches on the Petersstein had frolicked, danced, and drunk beer and joined with their gallants in carnal intercourse. Only one had further testified that Lautner had played a double bass, while others had played bagpipes, whistles, and a flute. That was all. The witches had needed the sacred host in their shoes to help them frolic and dance.

The bishop had followed many witch trials in days gone by, he had studied all the relevant papal edicts on witchcraft, and he had read many books about black magic. He knew that the Black Sabbath, the gathering of the witches on the night before Saint Philip's and Saint James' Day, was not such an innocent affair as that described by Barbora Göttlicher or Susanne Stubenvoll. But the Ullersdorf witches had said nothing of any gravity. At most they had mentioned their gallants. Otherwise they had frolicked, danced, and drunk beer! The bishop pondered. Either this inquisitor Boblig was a fool and could extract nothing else from these witches, or perhaps they were not witches at all, just rather confused, muddled women. But it wasn't just the women. The inquisitor was very specifically accusing three priests, among them even the distinguished Dean of Schönberg, Christoph Alois Lautner! Master Boblig would surely not have dared bring such a charge without grave reason!

The bishop shuddered. He did know of cases where even clergymen had concluded a pact with the Devil, but they were exceptions. Could something like this be happening right now, in his very own diocese? He recalled the papal bull of Innocent VIII, *Summi desiderantes affectibus,* which directed that witches were to be sought out, prosecuted, and tried most severely. He recalled Emperor Maxmilian's law, laying down the punishments for those found guilty of witchcraft: burning alive, boiling in oil, quartering, hanging, and interment alive. And he remembered also an old work by two Dominican monks, *Malleus maleficarum, The Witch Hammer,* still valid as the basis of struggle against disciples of the Devil. If, just one day ago, anyone had mentioned that work to the bishop, he would have laughed. But now it was different. These were no longer things of the past but of today. Urgent and very much alive.

This was dreadful!

The bishop knew Dean Lautner well, and the priests König and Pabst only superficially. He strained his memory, recalling that he had already heard some unpleasant things about all three from von Bräuner, the suffragan bishop, and also from his secretary, Schmidt. It took a while for him to recall exactly what those things were, but then he remembered. All three, it was said, had young cooks, and this was arousing indignation in the priesthood. Even the old Dean of Schönberg, they said, had a young cook. The bishop frowned. My fault, he told himself. I have neglected many things, and now here are the fruits! And Dean Lautner— one of the most learned priests of the whole diocese! Twice the bishop had visited the dean. The first time had been before the great fire. He had made the best impression on his superior, and together they had reminisced about Salzburg and Graz, where Lautner had studied divinity. The second time he had visited him was after the fire that had consumed the whole town, only the deanery having escaped the flames, as if by a miracle. The dean had behaved impeccably, doing everything he could to help the people. His good reputation in and around the town had been growing ever since. Later, of course, reports had reached the bishop that Lautner was perhaps too close to the people of the town and had cultivated too many friendships. There had also been criticism of his preaching, which was concerned almost exclusively with general morality rather than theology. But the criticism had come from Schmidt, parish priest at Zöptau, who clearly wanted to succeed to the Schönberg deanery himself. The bishop could remember nothing else of any consequence. Anyway, he asked himself, why should the dean have made a pact with the Devil? He had quite a lucrative prebend, almost as big as that of the Dean of Mülitz! Moreover, he was an old man, and elderly people tended to value a quiet life above all else. No, this letter of Boblig's could not be taken at face value.

Now, finally, he reached for the bell.

Father Schmidt entered and gave the bishop an inquiring look.

"Tell me," said the bishop sternly, "who is this Master Boblig of Edelstadt?"

Schmidt told him.

The bishop listened attentively, but his eyes instinctively wandered to the painting on the easel. He wanted to be hard, but the picture softened his heart. He smiled at the secretary, who was himself looking unusually stern, and said in a voice that was almost kind: "Write to Master Boblig that his accusation is so serious as to warrant grave misgivings. The whole case must be investigated thoroughly and everything most conscientiously considered. Only then might it be possible to proceed to the measures that he proposes."

The secretary bit his lip. He had expected something different from this.

"This Boblig fellow," added the bishop, "must not get the idea that he can deal with clergymen in the same way as he deals with common village women! And as far as you are concerned, I want you to maintain the strictest secrecy. Give the papers to Doctor Mayer for legal scrutiny and have those three priests summoned here!"

The secretary bowed deeply, took the papers, and left in dismay.

The bishop watched him until he was gone, then returned to the picture. Lo, the father had forgiven his prodigal son. Could we also forgive? We who prefer to burn, boil in oil, quarter, hang, bury alive! But how otherwise could we fight the Devil? Did not Moses decree that witches were to be destroyed by stoning, for to treat them otherwise was an abomination unto the Lord?

At that very moment, a visitor was arriving in his secretary's office. It was a priest, a thickset man with a large head of thinning gray hair. As he entered, he noticed the secretary quickly hiding a bundle of papers in his desk. Only then, and none too kindly, did Schmidt look up to see who had come.

"I am Dean Lautner of Schönberg and I would like to see His Grace the bishop!"

The dean would have had to be blind not to notice the look of sheer surprise in the secretary's eyes. Why was he startled? Lautner remembered the Dean of Müglitz and his horror when he proposed requesting an audience with the bishop. What was there to be so afraid of?

"His Grace is extremely busy. An audience has to be requested in advance," Schmidt whined, looking at the floor.

"I am aware of that," the dean insisted. "Nevertheless, I would like to be received. It concerns an extremely grave matter."

"May I know what it's about?"

Lautner had long distrusted the secretary and was not going to fall for this trick.

"His Grace is my immediate superior. And precisely because it is a grave matter, I do not require an intermediary!"

His voice was firm and self-assured. The secretary was at a loss. Was he, or was he not, to take Lautner, a man accused by Boblig of witchcraft, to the bishop? But then a thought struck him: Having read the inquisitor's report, the bishop might well change his decision. Dean Lautner might even be thrown into detention today, with no fuss!

"I'll try," he said, and left.

He had not even offered the old priest a seat. This small point confirmed for Lautner that the secretary was not inclined to him at all. But what about the bishop? Lautner felt like a small schoolboy waiting for his master before a viva voce examination. Had he done right to request an audience? He would soon know. But could he have delayed a meeting with the bishop any longer? Boblig had already paid two visits to Gaup. And König's reports from Gross Ullersdorf were yet more ominous. König had heard from Umlauf, the jailer, that Boblig's line of questioning was now being directed against the burghers of Schönberg. There was no time to lose. Only the bishop could put a stop to Boblig's rampage. Unfortunately, however, Bishop Liechtenstein was not the man he had once been. Before, he had made all his own decisions, but now he had surrounded himself with many people, and he himself was interested most of all in buildings and pictures. The main person at the bishop's palace appeared to be the suffragan bishop von Bräuner and, of course, also the secretary, Schmidt. It had always been possible to talk openly to the bishop, but what about his officials? Evidently they were all pulling together, but their aims did not always coincide with the wishes of the bishop.

The secretary returned, a forced smile on his face.

"Come with me. His Grace has made an exception and will see you immediately."

Lautner strode with some excitement down the corridor to a door guarded by a footman, who opened it to let him inside.

And so the Dean of Schönberg found himself in a spacious chamber, standing opposite a wall full of magnificent French tapestries, dominated by shades of olive green. The air in the room was warm and scented. The bishop sat at a great table, bathed in light, his purple cassock and biretta strongly offsetting the yellowness of his cheeks. The bishop's eyes were cold and carefully followed his visitor's every movement. Lautner almost froze.

Nevertheless, he maintained his dignity and strode ahead, stopping only directly in front of the bishop, where he bowed deeply to kiss his sapphire-studded gold ring. Then he remained standing, waiting for his superior to speak first. But Liechtenstein said nothing and merely gestured to an armchair covered in green brocade.

The silence lengthened. The bishop was still staring into the dean's round face, as if striving to read all of his secrets. He could read many things from pictures, so why not from faces? Moments before, he had learned that dreadful accusations had been made against this old servant of the Lord. Now the alleged disciple of the Devil was but two paces away from him. Was it true, or was it mere tittle-tattle? What did his face say? But however carefully he looked, the bishop saw nothing more than a round head and healthily ruddy cheeks, graying hair, and calm, level eyes. The dean looked more like a farmer or a craftsman than a clergyman! No, not a sign of evil in him.

"Tell me," said Liechtenstein at last, "why you have come." His voice was soft; neither stern nor especially kind.

Lautner had had plenty of time to prepare for this audience and had no cause for any pretense.

"I asked to see you, Your Grace, to report on some events in my district and to ask you for help." His voice was calm and bore no trace of humility.

"I shall be pleased to hear what you have to say," said the bishop.

This was encouraging. Lautner smiled inwardly as he thought of the fears expressed by his friend, the Dean of Müglitz. Then calmly, in a matter-of-fact way, he explained what had happened on Easter Monday at Zöptau and the woeful events that had followed.

The bishop listened patiently, without interrupting. Only when Lautner finished did he stroke his chin and say coldly:

"Do you wish to add anything?"

"I would like to say, Your Grace, that for months the whole district has been living in a state of great agitation. The people are full of fear, and no one is certain whether he, too, will be accused of such a dreadful crime as witchcraft. I am afraid that the advocate Boblig is concerned more with personal gain than with service of the Holy Faith. I know many of the accused, and Father König of Gross Ullersdorf knows all of them. They are hard-working, respectable women who have abided by the commandments of the Church. Many of them have been held in jail for long months, without hope that they will be granted freedom. Advocate Boblig takes no trouble to find reliable witnesses but satisfies himself only with the testimony of other accused people who have confessed under torture."

"Does this mean that neither yourself nor Father König believe that the women imprisoned at Ullersdorf made any pact with the Devil?"

Lautner saw the pitfall in the question. He replied cautiously.

"I believe, Your Grace, that my opinion is not of consequence. Something far more sinister is afoot. I wish to make it known to Your Grace that Master Boblig of Edelstadt uses brutal and inhuman practices to compel anyone whom he does not favor to admit to the most loathsome crimes. It is repugnant, Your Grace, not only to common reason, but also to the commandments of the Church. That is why I ventured here, to beg your assistance. I feel a great responsibility to God and to my own conscience for the lives of persons who are unjustly accused."

These were fearless words. Lautner moistened his lips, and this time it was he who sought to read from the bishop's face what he was thinking.

"You do know, of course," said Liechtenstein uncertainly, "that what goes on at the castle at Ullersdorf is not within my jurisdiction."

The bishop was evading the issue! He was fleeing his responsibility! This only made the dean even bolder.

"The gravity of your word, Your Grace, would be decisive for the Countess of Galle. It was she who sent for Master Boblig in the first place and she who is generously rewarding him!"

"That may be so," said the bishop begrudgingly. "And I can even allow that you were led here by the noblest intentions of Christian love; but at the same time I cannot deny that fraught things have been taking place in your district. How long ago did we eradicate the heresies that had sprung up in our diocese! And now, when the weeds are surfacing again, the Dean of Schönberg, instead of coming for help against heresy, speaks out on behalf of those under suspicion or even those who have been convicted! Should the principle here not be: *Qualis rex, talis grex?* Howsoever the king, so the herd! The Devil does not slumber!"

The dean reddened, but his reply was equally resolute.

"Above all else, Your Grace, the Devil is temptation. And the advocate Boblig arouses temptation by his every deed. Thus he perhaps serves the Devil more even than those whom he accuses!"

The bishop had not expected the Dean of Schönberg to speak so fearlessly and with such assurance.

"Is there anything else you wished of me?"

"That Your Grace should extend a hand of protection to the righteous, for the advocate Boblig is capable of anything: even of accusing the clergy!"

"For whom do you ask this?"

"I ask for Thomas König, priest at Gross Ullersdorf, for Johann Pabst, priest at Römerstadt, and also for myself."

The bishop was on tenterhooks. These were the very priests whom the inquisitor had wanted arrested. Boblig had accused them of being in league with the Devil, and now the dean was accusing the inquisitor of the same crime.

"Why should these priests require protection?"

The dean said nothing for a moment. He could prove nothing and only suspected what Boblig was building up to.

"The advocate Boblig knows that we are following what he is doing," he said at last, "and is finding it very unpleasant."

This did not satisfy the bishop. He knitted his brow and stared out the window for a moment, pondering the facts. Whereas he did not know Boblig at all, he had known the Dean of Schönberg for a long time. Recently, however, he had heard many unpleasant things about him and the other two priests, König and Pabst. But the dean did not behave at all like a guilty man. He spoke with assurance and no trace of fear. But then again, the Devil did grant certain powers to his disciples. So how was he to decide? He chose the easy way out.

"These matters are extremely serious," he said. "They have to be meticulously investigated, and there must be no rash action on our part. Be assured that we shall be pleased to clasp our faithful and zealous priests to our heart, if they are found to be without guilt!"

Liechtenstein spoke with a sincere voice, and Dean Lautner felt considerable relief as he heard what he wanted to hear. He smiled, but this very smile aroused the bishop's alarm.

"When you came into this office," he cried suddenly, "you spoke about indignation. But I, too, have heard indignant stories, about the people whom you represent!"

This time the dean was startled. The bishop continued.

"Although all three of you are well aware that we do not suffer any priest in our diocese to take himself a young housekeeper, this rule has been contravened by the priest at Gross Ullersdorf and the priest at Römerstadt. And even you have a young woman as a cook. *Mulier in ecclesia tacet.* Let your women keep silence in the churches. But how may they keep silence, if they share their beds with the clergy!"

Dean Lautner blushed crimson. This was what Dean Winkler had alluded to! This attack had surely been prepared long before, by Schmidt, the priest at Zöptau. The dean had been hit in his most sensitive spot, and it was only with great difficulty that he remained in control of himself.

"Was I, Your Grace, to throw out on the street the little girl who was taken in at the deanery by my own mother after the terrible fire? That little girl, grown into a maiden over the years, took my mother's place when she died. Would it be in accordance with Christian love to drive her out and put her at the mercy of poverty and of worldly temptations?"

The bishop frowned.

"You know what Saint John says! *Quoniam omne, quod est in mundo, concupiscentia carnis est, et concupiscentia oculorum et superbia vitae!*"

The bishop stressed the word *carnis*—of the flesh.

Lautner translated the full passage in his mind: All that is in the world, the lust of the flesh and the lust of the eyes and the pride of life, is not of the Father, but is of the world.

He replied, remembering in his anger that he was talking to Bishop Liechtenstein, a man whom it was not advisable to oppose:

"Your Grace will perhaps allow me to quote Saint Bernard, who says: Ideas, however impure, do not tarnish the mind, if the heart and the will do not allow them to!"

The bishop straightened up and stared sternly into the eyes of this proud man accused of witchcraft. Not even after being charged with contravening the rules of the diocese had he cowed. Was this his own strength, or did it come from the Devil? Everything had to be taken into account. He rose and announced solemnly:

"Everything, my son, will be given due consideration. Now you may go in grace."

The dean rose and bowed deeply again to kiss the bishop's ring. Then he strode out, strong and firm, almost like a victor.

Liechtenstein watched him go. Then he turned to the picture on the easel. Only now did he become aware that the old father who was welcoming his prodigal son was wearing a coat of purple, the color of bishops. And again he saw the old man's hands, touching with love the shoulder of his son.

"And what of my own?" he asked himself.

He had let the old graying priest kiss his ring, but had not offered him his hand, and he had not even said one kindly word. He had behaved like a judge to a guilty man. But what if this priest was entirely without blame, and Boblig's charge came of an impure cause? Had it truly come of hatred or greed? Why would such a man as the Dean of Schönberg make a pact with the Devil?

"*Quamdiu vivimus, peregrinamur,*" whispered the bishop. "As long as we live, we are pilgrims. But perhaps what Saint Paul really wanted to say was: As long as we live, we are wanderers!"

For one moment more the Bishop of Olomouc gazed into space. Then, abruptly, he rang the bell for his secretary.

19 ✦ *Confidential Information*

Dean Lautner sat in his heated room, Mendetz's *Travels across Europe, Asia and Africa* laid out before him. Today, however, reading was beyond his powers of concentration. Since his audience with the Bishop of Olomouc, he had been feeling out of sorts, and the reason was Susanne. Never before had he thought their living under the same roof could arouse indignation; after all, he had never heard anyone make any pointed remarks. But now it was preying on his mind. The bishop had made himself quite clear. And there was no doubt that at the present time he had to have the bishop on his side. So how was he to go about it? How was he to get Susanne out of the house and not cause her pain? There was one obvious possibility, and the dean constantly returned to it: to marry her off. But he had not yet dared to broach the subject with her.

Just then, Susanne came in to rake the coals in the hearth and to lay fresh logs on the fire. She entered on tiptoe in order not to disturb him; but the dean was aware of her every movement. Even now he found it hard to open a conversation. But he had to, and now was as good a time as any.

Just as she was finished with her work and was preparing to leave, the dean got up and said in a kindly voice: "Sit down, Susanne, I'd like to have a word with you."

Susanne raised her eyes, looked at the dean, and guessed that this was not going to be pleasant. She remained standing, wondering what she was about to hear.

"Just sit down. There's time yet, before they come for the christening."

Susanne obeyed but sat on the very edge of the chair, ready to spring up at any moment. She gazed innocently at the old dean, and it did not escape her attention that he wore an embarrassed frown. What had happened? She was not aware she had done anything wrong.

"I've been meaning to ask you, my dear: do you have a young man?"

This was the last thing Susanne had expected to hear.

"No, I haven't!"

"You don't have to deny anything! I don't want to chide you, I'm only asking."

"Well, I haven't," Susanne repeated softly.

Lautner looked away. This was a sour apple that, once bitten, had to be eaten.

"Have you thought, Susanne," he continued, pulling himself together, "that one day you'll have to get married? I'm an old man, and soon I'll be joining my Father and mother. Then what will become of you?"

It occurred to her that the dean was not saying what he really had on his mind. As if he were concealing something. Perhaps he was going to suggest a husband for her.

"Who," she said, with a hint of bitterness, "would marry a priest's cook?"

Susanne had not wanted to hurt the dean, but the words gushed out.

For the dean this was an even harder blow than his audience with the bishop. He hung his head in silence. Surely he should have known what kind of reputation a priest's housekeeper could expect, especially someone as young and pretty as Susanne! Now he knew what suffering she must have gone through. But she had never said a word.

"Has anyone hurt you?" he asked.

"Not yet."

The dean was not sure how to proceed. Only after a long pause he asked: "And don't you want to get married?"

"Want?" she scowled. "For somebody like me there can't be any wanting. I'm a priest's cook and always will be!"

"I said I might soon die. Then what will become of you?"

Lautner had never heard Susanne speak so bitterly. "Or?"

Susanne had already lost control. Her eyes filled with tears.
"I should never have come to the deanery! It was my bad luck!"
She ran out of the room, almost certainly to old Florian.

The dean was dumbfounded. After a while he rose, crossed to
the window and looked out. Outside, the wind was chasing flakes
of snow, the first of the winter.

"*Vae misero mihi,*" he whispered, "woe is me!"

He stood at the window for some time. Then he sat down and
began searching his conscience. Yes, he had always thought more
of himself than of her, but only now was he aware of it. She ought
to be married. But where could he find her a husband? He could
at least find her a position as a maid somewhere. But where, and
with whom? And who would take her place?

He would have to take advice from a levelheaded man of the
world such as Hutter, or Sattler, or Peschek. But what would the
Gross Ullersdorf parish priest, König, do with his cook, Elisabeth,
and her sister? And what about the Römerstadt priest, Pabst?

A glance at the clock reminded him it was time to go to the
church. He put on his greatcoat and fur cap and went out.

The path to the church led through the cemetery. As usual, the
dean paused at a grave by the low boundary wall that was part of
the town's ramparts. It was the last resting place of his parents,
Zacharias and Dorothea, and it was carefully tended. This also
was due to Susanne. A bird-cherry bush that she had planted was
growing by the wall; at blossomtime it spread a bittersweet fragrance over the grave.

Lautner stood bareheaded at the graveside, lost in his thoughts,
unable to tear himself away, unable even to say a prayer. The two
baptisms that awaited him in church were for the moment quite
forgotten.

Sebastian Flade, clerk to the district court, was to be godfather
to the infant son of Master Kranichl, the baker. Seeing the dean at
the graveside, he waited politely for him to remember his duty;
then he went out to meet him. He bowed from a distance.

"I have something to tell you, Father," he blurted as if his
tongue were burning with the news.

"Well, Godfather," said the dean dubiously, "go on."

"A letter has arrived at the magistrate's office, from the prince . . ."

"And not for the first time, I'll warrant!"

"Only it's not an ordinary letter, Your Reverence. His Eminence Prince Liechtenstein directs that Schönberg is to have its own inquisitorial tribunal, to be set up immediately . . ."

"What?" cried the dean.

Had he heard right? Was this a joke? Lautner had never been too fond of this sanctimonious little clerk. No, Flade was not joking. The dean felt a tightening in his chest and a pressure on his heart.

"Do you know," he asked, "who has been named director of the tribunal?"

"The advocate from Olomouc, Master Boblig of Edelstadt!"

The dean had already guessed. Yet his head still swam when he heard Flade pronounce Boblig's name. The slight figure of the clerk was blinking ridiculously in excitement. It seemed to the openmouthed Lautner that this crafty little man was actually pleased.

"And do you know who have been nominated as members of the tribunal?"

"The district judge, Master Gaup; then the Lord Mayor, Master Beck; and last of all my own self. They wouldn't be able to manage without a clerk," Flade added as if apologizing.

"So Gaup is the first associate inquisitorial judge," repeated the dean, more to himself than to the clerk.

"And there's something else I can tell you, Reverend Father, but—I beg you—in all confidence," Flade's voice softened. "I understand Master Boblig and Master Gaup have been preparing this for some time."

"But what in heaven do they want? Why an inquisitorial tribunal in Schönberg?"

The clerk shrugged his shoulders.

✦ ✦ ✦

Lautner hurried to the church, his legs trembling, his heart racing. This was the worst thing that could have happened. His audience with the bishop had been in vain. Equally, there would be no point now in visiting Prince Liechtenstein, Lord Protector of Schönberg, or his wife, Elisabeth Sidonia, by birth a Salm-Reifferscheid. Advocate Boblig was already firmly in the saddle, and Gaup was to be his henchman. A great misfortune was approaching Schönberg, perhaps even greater than the fire of '69. Then the damage had been merely material—but what now?

Lautner staggered into the sacristy and donned his surplice without even taking off his coat. Then he accompanied the sexton into the church for the baptism. Everyone there noticed the dean's absentmindedness; he very nearly mixed up the names at the christening.

After the ceremony he flatly refused the invitations to attend a little celebration, though at other times he would have gladly gone, at least for a while.

"Perhaps the dean's sickening," remarked one of the godfathers.

But it was worse than a sickness.

Dean Lautner hurried from the church to see his old friend Kaspar Hutter and give him the dreadful news. So dreadful that he quite forgot about Susanne.

20 ✦ *Half past Midnight*

As long as the old town hall had stood on the square at Schönberg, it had never taken more than a few hours for the citizens to
learn what was being discussed inside, even though the councillors were pledged to the strictest secrecy. When the old town
hall had been destroyed by the fire, a new one was built in its
place; but otherwise nothing changed. Whatever went on inside
was always the talk of the town before the day was out.

Prince Liechtenstein's order for the setting up of a special
inquisitorial tribunal in Schönberg caused considerable public un-
rest. The people of the town were well aware of a connection with
the interrogations taking place at Ullersdorf Castle. But who
among their own neighbors could possibly be accused of such
dreadful crimes? Just as much indignation was aroused by the
composition of the inquisitorial tribunal. It was generally conceded that the Lord Mayor had to be on it, and even Flade, the
court clerk; and the people could also understand the nomination
of Master Gaup, the new district judge, even though they disliked
him for his haughtiness and careerism. But why had Boblig, an
advocate from Olomouc, a stranger whom everyone found repulsive, been appointed director? Was it not enough for him that he
was directing the interrogations at Ullersdorf?

Discontent grew further when it became known what he was
to receive for his services: a comfortable apartment, three double-
thalers, and several gallons of beer per week, twelve cords of
firewood per year, and generous daily expenses besides. This advocate was certainly not cheap! Although the Lord Protector of
Schönberg was promising to cover the costs of the inquisition
from his own treasury, Prince Liechtenstein was renowned for his
miserliness—and the town would end up paying for everything!

Master Boblig would be paid three double-thalers a week, Master Gaup one thaler, and the Lord Mayor and the clerk forty-five kreuzers a day each! So much money for nothing! And that wasn't all! Guards would have to be hired, an executioner and assistant would have to be paid for, and traveling and other expenses would have to be covered. Whoever thought of this deserved a ball and chain!

Advent approached, and with it the hustle and bustle that always preceded Christmas; and because nothing in particular seemed to be happening, the discontent gradually subsided. Then, one early afternoon, a coach bearing the Zerotin crest arrived on the square and halted in front of Gaup's new house. A liveried coachman sat in front, while an enormous musketeer sat at the back. Master Boblig shot out, followed by his hunchbacked assistant Ignatius clutching a small valise—the advocate's entire fortune.

Master Simon, the cheeky shoemaker from the Schönberg suburb of Hermesdorf, pointed to the bag as he shouted from the crowd: "They won't be traveling so light when they leave, I'll be bound!"

✦ ✦ ✦

Several days passed, and nothing of consequence appeared to be happening. The advocate and his assistant remained at Gaup's house and did not set foot outside. But there was a light in their apartment until well into the night, and the cellarman from Nollbeck's had to go there every hour with a large pitcher of beer. Only once did the advocate receive anyone other than Master Gaup—and that was the Lord Mayor and the clerk Flade.

Immediately after this visit, Master Ruth, the mason, was commissioned to carry out some building work at the town hall. Two large rooms on the first floor were cleared and whitewashed. One of them was furnished with a large oak table, chairs, two strong-boxes and a reading desk, while the second was left empty. The town-hall jail—one cell for the poor, and one larger one for the wealthy burghers—was also to be rebuilt. Ruth was ordered to build new walls inside to make four cells.

People in the street scowled as they passed the town hall, which stood like a kind of fortress in the middle of the square. They even avoided the little shops of the bakers, shoemakers, potters, and grocers that huddled around it, so that the shopkeepers' earnings did not even cover the rent they had to pay for the unsightly wooden shanties they occupied. It was as if a dreadful storm were approaching, as if at any moment the town crier would roar the alarm that lightning had struck again.

The winter of this sorrowful year came a little earlier than usual. A chill wind blew insistently from the snowcapped mountains. Then light snow came also to the broad valley of the River Tess. The paths froze, and all the ponds were covered by a finger-thick crust of ice.

In any other year this mild wintry spell would have been greeted with joy. Citizens young and old would have flocked outside the town walls to savor the view of their beloved Schönberg, perched upon a small ridge and enclosed by ramparts of brick. High above was the lofty tower of the town hall, with its two onion domes and a wooden gallery for the town crier, while below it was the modest tower of the deanery church of Saint John the Baptist. Before the fire, it had boasted thirteen spires and looked from a distance like an immense Gothic monstrance. Now it was topped by a simple, makeshift flat roof, with a huge cross in the middle. But the grandest sight of all was the barrier of high mountains to the north, standing like an impenetrable wall, protecting the land of Moravia from its foes.

This year the people of Schönberg felt only a grim foreboding and preferred to stay at home or to visit friends. Many of them stopped going to their favorite taverns and tap-rooms, for rumor had it that the inquisitor was sending out spies, and many idlers, ruffians, and drunkards were said to have been given drinking money by the inquisitor's assistant.

On the last Sunday in November, a group of friends gathered at the house of Kaspar Sattler, the master dyer. The men— Peschek the clothmaker, Hutter the former district judge, and Dean Lautner—sat with him in the parlor discussing the latest events, while the womenfolk talked in the kitchen.

The dean was unusually quiet. He was of two minds whether to disclose what he had been told by the parish priest at Gross Ullersdorf. König had heard from Master Göttlicher, who in turn had heard from Zeidler the forest warden, that Boblig had been given the names of some of the ladies of Schönberg who were supposed to have been at the witch-swarms. And some of them, it was said, had been accompanied by their husbands.

Lautner was well aware that this was the reason for the new tribunal. Master Boblig was about to reveal his hand, and the trials that he would conduct in Schönberg would eclipse anything he had done at Ullersdorf. But was he to tell this to his friends? If he knew the names, he would be able to warn the right people and advise them to flee. But he did not know whom the inquisitor had in his sights and did not want to cause unnecessary panic, perhaps in the wrong place.

"We'll soon know who's to be the first victim in Schönberg," Sattler was saying. "No doubt the inquisitor has already made his choice!"

"Just look at what he's getting," said Hutter. "Three double-thalers a week in Schönberg, and at least that at Ullersdorf, too—that's six double-thalers for a start!"

"But surely," said Peschek, "Boblig is only an instrument in someone else's hands."

"If Boblig is an instrument, then it is of human folly!" said Hutter. "He's profiting from something that's been known for a very long time: Fear can lead people to commit the gravest of all crimes—the betrayal of oneself and of one's friends. All he has to do is brand two or three women as witches. Half of the people believe him straightaway, and the other half, purely out of fear that the inquisitor might turn his attention to them, testify to all kinds of nonsense. Everyone ends up trembling in fear. That's just what the inquisitor needs. All he has to do then is point his finger at someone he doesn't like. It's not so long ago that inquisitors in the German lands could destroy the population of entire villages!

"Of course," he continued, "the authorities are just as much to blame. Princes, counts, and barons—they're only concerned with hunting, sport, banquets, and making merry; it never occurs to any of them to see where the inquisitors have their fingers. The Countess of Galle at Ullersdorf is a pious old lady all right, but has she ever refused to accommodate Boblig in any way? When she couldn't bear it any longer, she left for Wiesenberg! She never had the courage to go and see for herself how the prisoners were being treated, how the interrogations were being conducted, and even how old Mistress David of Wermsdorf met her death!"

"Boblig is the judge," remarked Peschek, "but don't his verdicts have to be confirmed by the Court of Appeals in Prague?"

"That's true," smiled Hutter, who had a wealth of experience, "but you mustn't think the appeal judges behave any differently from the Countess of Galle! They're not interested in what's the truth and what's a lie. They only pay regard to the formal aspects of the case. One of them, though, did once say this publicly: I know very well that there are many innocents among the convicted, but that's not my affair. My task is to establish legal rectitude. I pay heed only to whether the verdict is in accordance with the law!"

"But that's dreadful!" Peschek gasped.

"It is indeed," affirmed the former judge. "And what makes it worse is that the people who are appointed inquisitors are usually themselves of bad character, covetous and cynical. Just look at Master Boblig of Edelstadt!"

"And what of Master Gaup?" remarked the dean.

"Much has been written of inquisitorial judges," continued Hutter as if he had not heard Lautner's remark. "The learned Adam Tanner wrote that the Faculty of Law in Ingolstadt was once called to investigate two of them, and it found that both had conducted trials that were illegal, and had sent innocent people to the stake only in order to enrich themselves. They were then put before a court themselves, condemned, and eventually put to death."

"The Jesuit Langenfeld wrote of a prince who had several inquisitors put to death for the same reason," said the dean. "Langenfeld was for a number of years a confessor to condemned witches. He declared publicly, without violating confessional secrecy, that when he weighed all the arguments for and against, he came to the inescapable conclusion that the great majority of those who had been executed were absolutely innocent."

"How is it possible?" cried Sattler.

"For several reasons, dear Kaspar," Hutter replied. "The judges' covetousness; the authorities' negligence; the appeal courts' lack of interest; the law's imperfections; and most of all, human cowardice!"

"But how can such verdicts be pronounced in God's name?" cried Peschek.

Everyone looked to the dean, who shrugged his shoulders.

"God allows even other things," he said.

"That means," said Peschek, "that whoever falls into the hands of such an inquisitor has no hope at all of saving his skin!"

"The law of the land goes hand in glove with the Inquisition," Hutter smiled bitterly. "Witchcraft is a crime paramount to heresy. And heresy is a crime against both the church and the state. In the matter of heresy, even popes favor the death sentence. And according to the law, the very fact that a person is accused of heresy is a presumption of his guilt!"

Only now did Peschek realize exactly what the inquisitorial court in Schönberg would mean. A practical man through and through, he immediately thought of defensive measures:

"We must send a deputation immediately to the prince! Or to Count Kolowrat-Libstejnsky, the provincial governor!"

"Or better still," suggested Sattler, "the High Chancery in Vienna—Count Nostitz!"

But Hutter shook his head.

"Friends," he said, "you are forgetting that Boblig is here at the orders of Prince Liechtenstein. Do you want to enter a dispute with His Eminence? And do you think that Count Kolowrat-Libstejnsky or Count Nostitz would set himself against him on our side? And finally, it would take at least three years for them to arrive at a decision. Three years! Just think what could happen in that time? Let's leave it, friends, and play some tarok instead!"

There was nothing like a game of cards to forget one's

troubles, if only for a while. And even the dean was delighted to accept the suggestion.

Kaspar Sattler took out the deck of tarot cards. Old Esther Rohmer, the maid, came in to replace the candles, and as the men launched into their game, she hurried out with a pitcher to fetch beer.

Back in the kitchen it was storytelling time. The womenfolk settled around Marie Sattler, who began to recount the old tale of the golddigger of Blumenbach, near Altstadt.

Once upon a time the miner set off to work on a night that was so beautiful he was loath to go underground. But go he did, and he dug and dug, until all of a sudden he came upon a huge nugget. It was very hard for him to remain calm enough to continue working until the morning, but remain he did, and as soon as the shift was over, he took the nugget and ran home with it. But on the way, he met a little manikin, who was none other than the *kobold*, the spirit of the mine. He asked the golddigger what he was carrying. Oh, nothing, he replied, lest he lose his treasure. If it be nothing, let it be nothing, said the *kobold* and disappeared, along with the gold.

"And the moral of the story is: Never tell lies," said the dye master's wife, concluding her tale.

Then it was the turn of Marie Peschek. Her tale was the one about how gold mining came to an end at Altstadt.

In the old days, the people had to toil very hard in the mines to eke out the barest of livelihoods. Then the *kobold* took pity on them and opened up the earth to reveal great reserves of the yellow metal. So the people easily came upon plenty of gold. They soon became rich and quite carried away with their wealth, and life became one long round of merrymaking, dancing, feasting, and drinking. One day, a little gray man appeared among the drunken miners carousing at the inn. He saw how they were throwing money about and even treading on it, and he asked them why. Why not, they replied, for it's as common as dirt! And the little man—for he was the *kobold*—said: If it be dirt, let it be dirt! And from that day, not a single vein of gold was ever found again in the district of Altstadt.

Liesel Sattler and Susanne Voglick had heard the tale before, but still they listened with rapt attention. For who did not love to hear the old stories of the *kobold*?

Esther Rohmer returned from the tavern with more than a full pitcher of beer. She also brought some news from her son Tobias, the town bailiff. Moments earlier, he said, the executioner Jakob Hay had arrived from Ullersdorf with his assistant; and they had opened the empty whitewashed room at the town hall and were working at something inside. And no one was allowed in.

The men heard Esther's loud voice from the next room, stopped their game of cards, and stared at one another in horror. One thing was clear: Master Jokl had not undertaken the night-time journey to Schönberg for nothing.

Neither Marie Sattler nor Marie Peschek was in the mood for any more stories now.

As if at a single command, Heinrich Peschek, Dean Lautner, and Kaspar Hutter stood up. Kaspar Sattler did not ask them to stay.

Moments later, Dean Lautner was on his way home, leaning on Susanne, who carried a lantern, along the arcade that lined the upper side of the town square. From this side the town hall loomed dark, like an abandoned castle. All was still, and the whole town was sleeping the sleep of the just. At the corner of the street on which his church stood, the dean paused and looked straight up the road, across the ramparts, into the distance. The night was black and starless, and a warmer breeze was blowing from the west.

"There's going to be a thaw!" Susanne announced.

"If only that were so," said the dean.

But he was not thinking of the weather; only of Master Boblig and the executioner of Ullersdorf.

✦ ✦ ✦

Several minutes after midnight, a tearful Liesel Sattler ran across the square and without a light made her way up Church Street, then along by the cemetery wall to the deanery, where she rang the bell sharply several times.

The whole house immediately woke up, but Florian was the first to the door. Someone is dying, he thought to himself, and the relatives are sending for a priest.

"All right, all right," he muttered. "As if it couldn't have waited until morning!"

The dean and Susanne, watching from an open upstairs window, recognized their visitor.

"What's the matter?" Susanne shouted.

"It's Mother. Master Gaup came with the constables and took her away!"

"Why?"

"They say she's a witch!"

Susanne hurried down and together with Florian led the exhausted Liesel upstairs.

The dean, quite devastated, remained standing at the window, whispering words from the Scripture: "O Lord, I await thy redemption . . ."

And he was thinking not only of Marie Sattler, the woman he had known since his childhood, but of all the others who were bound to tread the same road as she. And he had no doubt there would be many.

How long ago was it that Kaspar Sattler had asked who would be the first? Now he knew!

21 ✦ A Kindly Face

The lock scraped shut, the footfalls of Jakob Hay's son faded away, and a sudden stillness remained. Marie Sattler stood without moving for some time, sensing the oppression of the silent dark and the chill of the shackles on her wrists. At last she mustered the courage to take a few steps. Dry straw rustled underfoot, startling her with the sound of hissing snakes. Only then did she remember that this was what prisoners slept on. No, this was no bad dream. Marie Sattler, the wife of the master dyer, councillor, and former Lord Mayor, was in jail! She sank to touch the straw with her chained hands, and feeling a coarse blanket on the floor, pulled it over herself and closed her eyes. Thoughts chased through her gray head like white butterflies over a cabbage patch. No, not butterflies. More like biting gnats, blowflies, or hornets.

So she was being accused of witchcraft! If it had been said by someone who did not know her, it would not have been quite so bad; but Master Gaup himself had come for her. He had to know, like everyone else in Schönberg, that she had never dealt in black magic; she had never even read any book on witchcraft, save the one about Doctor Faust. Who could have been so wicked as to accuse her of such a dreadful crime? And who could have been so gullible as to believe the charge? It was nonsense!

It finally dawned on her that it had to be some kind of misunderstanding, a mistake. Her name had been confused with someone else's. A tiny spark of hope shone in the darkness. Tomorrow, when the new day came, all would be explained, and the truth would surface like oil on troubled water. Kaspar and the dean would see she was released. And Master Hutter would help them: he knew everything there was to know about the courts!

But still the dye master's wife did not fall asleep by the morning. She tried to calm herself by praying and recited the I Believe and the Lord's Prayer over and again, but it did not help. She often stopped in mid-sentence, remembering her fate and thinking of her husband and of Liesel and of old Rohmer, the maid. What good fortune is was that both her sons, Hanus and Peter, were abroad and were not to know of their mother's disgrace!

Time dragged on, and Marie's old body shivered with the cold.

At last a dim light seeped into the cell through the tiny, densely barred window. Morning was breaking.

Soon the door opened and young Hay appeared again, this time with a pitcher of water and a crust of bread.

"Don't you eat it all at once!" he said. "This has to last you all day!"

Marie was startled. Not by the prison fare, for she was not even thinking of eating; what struck her was the familiar way this little brat was addressing her. But she overcame her anger and asked whether her daughter or husband would be able to visit her.

He stared at her as if she were demented.

"What do you think this is? A public house?"

"Can't they send me something from home?"

"And what would you want?"

"Something warmer to put on. And I'd like to have my rosary. I have some beads at home that were blessed in Rome."

"Can you beat that! A witch, and she wants a rosary!"

The door slammed and Marie was alone again. A witch, the executioner's boy had said! O God, perhaps it was even worse than she had thought! She sank to her knees and began to pray.

As she prayed, the cell brightened to reveal nothing but bare walls, a straw-strewn floor, an earthenware pitcher of water by the door, and on it a hunk of bread. Next to the pitcher, its eyes observing her like two gleaming pearls, sat a mouse.

She gave a shrill scream and hammered on the door. The mouse scurried away, but no one came. It occurred to her that this was like being entombed alive. Again she shrieked, but even now no one heard. Her strength gone, she fell on the straw and burst into silent tears.

The hours passed as ever before, but Marie Sattler knew nothing of the passage of time, for she had nothing to guide her. The town hall clock did strike the quarters and the half-hours, but its chimes did not reach her cell. She had no idea whether it was noon or already the evening, but she lay and waited. Surely someone would come and release her from this cold tomb. Her husband could not leave her there! And neither could the dean!

If only she had known what excitement had seized the town that morning, when the people learned of her arrest as a witch! Everyone knew the master dyer's wife. The Spanner family had been one of the town's most noted families, and when Spanner's daughter married the rich Kaspar Sattler, there was shooting from mortars and celebrations fit for a countess's wedding. The burghers held her in esteem, while the poor weavers from the surrounding villages turned to her whenever they were in trouble. She often made good from her own purse what her husband, who watched every kreuzer, docked from their pay. Could anyone really believe that she had signed herself body and soul to the Devil?

Outside, the work of the day dragged slowly, and not only because it was Saint Monday. Knots of people stood in the street, and neighbors visited Kaspar Sattler at his home to shake his hand. The grim-faced dye master raged against the vile traitor Gaup, who for a few thalers from the villainous Boblig had stolen his wife, a respectable woman, from her bed at dead of night, as if she were some kind of common wench or murderess. But there was still justice in the world! If the prince was not able to help, he would have to go elsewhere, even to His Imperial Highness, Emperor Leopold!

People also went to the deanery and asked the dean: Could the dye master's wife indeed be in league with the Devil?

Pale through lack of sleep and desperately anxious himself, Lautner struggled to calm his parishioners, assuring them that everything would soon be explained. It was evidently some kind of mistake, the kind anyone could make. But they had to wait and trust in the Lord.

He knew his words were lighter than gossamer. But what else was he to say? Was he to tell them that Boblig would hardly be satisfied with Marie Sattler, that he would soon find others, that no one among his flock could be safe from his clutches? What about when the inquisitor really got down to work? Just as foul waters surged from the rivers at the time of floods, so now would the town be overflown with malice, hatred, and all the other human vilenesses. One man would suspect the next, neighbor would turn against neighbor, brother against brother. Calumny would flourish. Was he to tell them what dreadful things were coming? If only he knew how to prevent them or where to turn for help! Even Kaspar Hutter, a man of such experience and courage, was incapable of speech, let alone wise counsel. How firmly must Master Boblig sit in the saddle, if he dared lay a finger on the wife of Kaspar Sattler, one of the most influential men of Schönberg!

Everyone wanted to catch sight of Judge Gaup or the fat-bellied inquisitor Boblig. But neither set foot in the street, either this day or the next.

Only on Wednesday afternoon, when the wave of anger had somewhat subsided, did a few passersby chance to see the inquisitor as he strode across the square, accompanied by his hunchback assistant and Barta, the huge musketeer. Boblig looked neither to the left nor the right, but straight ahead to the town hall.

At first, the curious onlookers stopped, then daringly followed him to the town hall. But their way farther was barred by guards.

Not long afterward, the lock of Marie Sattler's cell scraped yet again. She raised her head and gave a startled shriek as, in the glare of a lantern, she saw the odious face of the inquisitor.

But when Boblig spoke, his words were warm.

"Don't be afraid, madam. I'm here to help you, to curtail your suffering."

Marie stood up and looked wide-eyed at this strange man. Was this truly Master Boblig of Edelstadt? From what she had heard of him at home, she had imagined him to be a bloodthirsty beast of prey—but opposite her stood an elderly gentleman with a face that was almost kindly.

Boblig nodded to the young Hay, who quickly removed her shackles and led her into the courtroom. The room was full of light, warmth, and cleanliness. On the wall hung a large crucifix, and underneath it a wick burned in a little oil lamp. Marie saw it and piously crossed herself.

The inquisitor threw a glance at the executioner's boy, who immediately left the room.

"Sit down, madam," said Master Boblig, taking a seat himself.

For a moment he gazed at her, as if he were making up his mind how to begin, but it was only an old trick to unnerve his victim or at least to fill her with apprehension. Thanks to Gaup, he knew everything about her. Three days in jail had already crushed her spirit. But there was no need to hurry. Haste would be a needless waste of income. Boblig's mind was estimating how long this old woman could be expected to hold out in jail. At least two years. She appeared to be quite sturdy and well preserved for her age.

"You must be very cross with me for having you dragged off to jail," he said finally with a friendly smile.

"It's a mistake, I'm sure," she said and also smiled. "Everyone can make a mistake."

"That's quite possible," affirmed the inquisitor. "All I want is for you to answer a few questions. You're a native of Schönberg?"

"Yes, I was born here," she said gladly.

"So you know everyone in town?"

"Not all of them, but I do know a lot of them!"

"That's excellent! At least you can tell me what I need to know about everyone."

"But why me, sir?"

As if not hearing her, Boblig posed her a strange question:

"I'd like to know: what kind of a man is your husband, Kaspar Sattler?"

Marie had thought he was going to ask about strangers, but he was asking about her own husband! What could he want? She fell into a long silence.

"I hear your husband is a hard-working man," said Boblig, still maintaining his friendly tone, "and that he's earned himself quite a little fortune. I hear you recently married off your daughter. Is that so?"

"Yes," she replied willingly, her eyes gleaming with pride as she remembered the celebrations.

"I hear you had a grand banquet . . ."

"There were plenty of guests!"

"Who was there?"

"Our friends."

"What if you told me some of their names?"

Marie thought it strange that Boblig should ask her these things, but for the time being she felt nothing amiss and answered willingly:

"There was Dean Lautner, Councillor Peschek, Prerovsky the soapboiler, Judge Hutter . . ."

"Are you good friends with the dean?" interrupted Boblig.

"And how shouldn't I be friends with him! He often visits us!"

"I hear that in your youth there was something more than friendship between you."

She blushed. What did this man not know? And why was he saying these things?

"We were still almost children. Christoph of the Lautners went to the Latin school in Olomouc and I attended lessons with Master Treutner, the teacher."

"And then?"

"Christoph fled from the Swedes and studied abroad. I got married to Kaspar."

Boblig smiled.

"Young blood, then. Perhaps you don't remember it anymore?"

"I'm an old woman. I have three grown-up children, and soon I'll have a grandchild."

"I hear your younger daughter Elisabeth is friendly with Susanne Voglick, the dean's cook. Is that so?"

Marie looked untrustingly at the judge. She had the unpleasant feeling that of all things he was most interested in the dean, and she didn't like it.

"Yes."

"And what can you say about Susanne?"

"She's a good girl," she replied with increasing distaste. "I'm only sorry for her, because it's difficult for her to find herself a young man."

"Why is that so, do you think? Won't the dean let her?"

"He treats her as if she were his daughter."

"As a daughter? Some people say other things! Were they together at your eldest daughter's wedding?"

Marie was finding these impertinent questions more and more repulsive.

"Yes. He takes her everywhere," she replied begrudgingly.

"Did you get very merry at the wedding?"

"It's usually merry at weddings."

"And the dean?"

"He's always in a good mood!"

The judge nodded his head, gazed into a corner, and fell silent for a moment. Marie was on tenterhooks. She was becoming increasingly dissatisfied with herself. Perhaps she had said things she should not have said.

Suddenly Boblig gave her a stern look.

"Do you know the old bathkeeper from Gross Ullersdorf, Dorothea Biedermann?" he asked.

"How could I not know her! I take baths there."

"And do you also know Mistress Göttlicher, the papermaker's wife from Gross Ullersdorf?"

Marie suddenly sensed danger. The bathkeeper and the papermaker's wife had been imprisoned as witches. Why was the judge asking her about them? But she told the truth.

"Yes, I know her."

"Do you know what they have been accused of?"

"I have heard, sir, but I don't believe they could have committed such a sin."

Boblig gave a crooked smile from the corner of his mouth.

"So you don't believe in witches?"

He fixed his gray-green eyes on her. She shivered and averted her eyes in silence.

"Do you, or don't you?"

"There are evil beings in the world, but I don't think there can be many of them," she said. "And I don't think they can do much, because the Lord God surely doesn't allow them to."

Boblig smiled to himself at the Solomonic wisdom of her reply. But he was tiring of this game; it no longer amused him.

"You know, of course," he said ominously, "why you have been imprisoned?"

She did know, but witchcraft was an unutterable word; it was better to be silent. Boblig did not press her for a reply but gazed again into a corner.

Suddenly he inhaled deeply and spoke again. But this time his voice was like the hiss of a viper:

"Dorothea Biedermann and the papermaker's wife Göttlicher admitted that they met you at the witch-swarms on the Peters-stein. That, madam, is why you are here!"

Everything went dim before Marie's eyes.

"Good God! That isn't true!"

"Both women volunteered the information." Boblig smiled. "And they confirmed it under torture."

"It's a lie!"

"Both are willing to tell it to your face, at any time!"

Marie covered her face with her hands and wept. Her whole body trembled.

Boblig was patient. He drummed his fingers wordlessly on the table. Then he stood up and touched her shoulder.

"Come with me!"

He opened the door to the neighboring room and pushed her inside. There at a small table sat Master Jokl in a red tunic and the hunchback Ignatius. The dye master's wife saw them and gasped.

"That, Marie Sattler, is the executioner from Ullersdorf," said Boblig. "I'm sure you know him."

She looked in horror first at the executioner, then at the hunchback. Her heart missed a beat.

"Master Jokl," said Boblig, opening a little snuffbox, "show the councillor's wife what instruments you have."

The executioner took a thumbscrew from a shelf, thrust it in front of her eyes, and showed her where the thumb was put in, how the screws were tightened, and where the blood ran out. Then he took out the Spanish boots, and again indicated how they were clapped onto the feet and legs of people who did not wish voluntarily to admit to their crimes. Ignatius rattled a chain.

Marie Sattler was at the point of swooning.

Boblig winked at the executioner, who placed the instrument of torture back in its place, and led the prisoner back to the courtroom.

Now the judge no longer looked like a kind, elderly gentleman, but just as Marie Sattler had imagined him—a bloodthirsty beast of prey. His voice also was no longer friendly at all. Thus, perhaps, was how the Devil spoke!

"You have seen everything, madam. Because I mean well with you, I'm going to give you time to make up your mind. When you want to tell me the truth, as during holy confession, just let your jailer know. I'll come and see you straightaway."

"But I've told you the truth!"

"You told the truth! But what else didn't you tell me? Your silence on many things means you actually lied. You didn't say a word about Dean Lautner's hocus-pocus with the sacred host in your home. You said nothing of what acts he performed with your daughter Elisabeth, with his cook Susanne, and also with you, his former lover! Just you remember . . . And when you've remembered everything, call me. I'm in no hurry. I have plenty of time. But here's another piece of advice before I go: Sincere sorrow does ease the conscience and it can even bring the Lord God's forgiveness. And do you know how to show your sorrow best of all? By remembering every detail and by giving the names of all the friends who joined with you in serving the Devil!"

Boblig clapped his hands. When the young Hay came in, he ordered him to take Marie Sattler back to her cell.

22 ✦ *A Heavenly Portent*

Alarming stories had long been circulating of a relentless advance of the Black Death in southern Europe, especially in the Turkish lands. The more remote communities of the Altvatergebirge heard these tidings from traveling people, the wanderers, jugglers, old soldiers, and poor wretches just released from Turkish captivity. But these were all mendicants, desperate for sympathy, and so were not to be trusted. Later, however, the same disturbing news was brought by the merchants and teamsters heading north to Silesia. They reported that the Plague was now raging in the Hungarian lands and that many cases had already occurred even in Vienna but had been kept secret for the sake of the Emperor. Victims of the Plague, they said, were first seized by a fever, then ugly tumors or lumps sprang up in their armpits, behind their knees, or on their loins. Finally, their bodies began to blacken, and in a few days, sometimes even a few hours, they died, and their corpses gave off an unbearable stench. These merchants and teamsters were mostly prudent folk, and they had to be believed.

The valley of the little river Tess was a healthy place. No one had ever fallen from the Black Death there. The people hoped that the Plague would continue to avoid their poor region, and they were anxious when they heard the news of its advance. Didn't they have enough troubles of their own?

Later came even more startling news: The imperial court was abandoning Vienna and moving to Prague. Eyewitnesses appeared who had seen for themselves the huge convoy of three thousand fully laden vehicles on its way from Vienna in the direction of Znaim. Emperor Leopold, the Empress, the entire royal family, all the ministers, officials, cooks, musicians, and even the servants were fleeing the Plague. This was the most telling evidence that the disease already had the Austrian capital in its grip. And how far was it from Vienna to Moravia?

Soon afterward, the soapboiler Prerovsky received a letter and a package from his brother, the parish priest at Bisenz. The letter said that the Plague had already claimed several lives in South Moravia, and inside the package was a special aromatic mixture with which he was to fumigate his abode twice each day. The mixture contained some chippings of sweet wood, juniper berries, grains of incense, and also some pieces of red resin, evidently from a black-cherry tree.

Before long, an imperial decree arrived from Sigismund, Count Sack, regional governor at Olomouc, with instructions on how to prevent the spread of the disease. At the same time, the Bishop of Olomouc gave orders for a special edict to be printed at the press of Mikulas Hradecky and distributed throughout the diocese. In this edict he exhorted the priests to appeal in their sermons for repentance, for morality, and greater austerity. At the same time he ordered that if God were to permit such a misfortune, the clergy were not to abandon their posts but were selflessly to tend to the sick and to afford them consolation. There was to be no repeat of the sad events elsewhere, where the priests had been among the first to take flight.

✦ ✦ ✦

Eusebius Leander Schmidt, parish priest at Zöptau, did not doubt for a moment, when he read the bishop's edict, that the Plague was coming as a punishment for the unrighteousness of man. Above all, of his own parishioners, whom he had never held in any high regard. The fruits of his extraordinary fervor were meager indeed. The people did go to church, attend confession, or receive the sacrament. But they lived like savages: sinned at every turn and still believed the old superstitions more than they did their own priest. It was just as Saint Cassian had written: their bodies took pleasure in lewdness and carnal lust. Now divine retribution was on its way, and Father Schmidt knew his duty.

When he ascended the pulpit the following wintry Sunday, his cheekbones seemed even more protrusive and his hair even more bristly than before. The Lord God, he said, had long endured unrighteousness, for in His goodness He gave the wicked a term of grace in which to change for the better. But if they exceeded this term, He would wreak a terrible vengeance. They would be punished, and one such punishment was the Plague.

The congregation listened with bated breath. They all knew what a scourge the Plague was, but only the older ones had experienced it for themselves. They knew that the Plague was far worse than fire or flood, hail or famine. The Plague was death's own harvest. It did not discriminate. It took the righteous as well as the wicked. It took both rich and poor, young and old. These older folk remembered that often the greatest scoundrels had been spared, while the most righteous and most honest had succumbed to the disease after only a few hours. This did not tally with what the priest was saying at all.

In Schönberg, the ominous Plague Decrees were nailed up outside the town hall, the gatehouses, and the churches, calling for sobriety and austerity; a place was set aside for a hospice; a quarantine station for travelers was set up; and Dean Lautner appealed in his sermons for repentance. Momentous things were happening and an air of fear prevailed. Commercial activity slowed, for the merchants and teamsters hardly ever came anymore.

Yet the taverns were thronging again, as if the people were eager to live life to the full before Death the Reaper came to gather his harvest. The preaching of Father Schmidt of Zöptau was the most frequent topic of conversation in the taprooms. Yes, calamity was looming, and the witches were to blame. And the dye master's wife was one of them. Most likely it was thanks to her that the taverns now closed two hours early and the stink of juniper smoke was everywhere! And what if there were more witches yet to come? Would they close the taverns completely? Where was an honest fellow to take a little comfort before the tumors and the sores were upon him?

Such were the thoughts of Hanus Vejhanka, weaver of Hermesdorf, as, smothered with pitch against the Plague, he sat in the Paradies inn.

"That's the way it is," he shouted in a whimpering voice. "The gentry want to get rid of the poor. There's a lot of us, and that bothers them. So they hire these witches to bring the Black Death on us. One of them's been caught already—the wife of that bloodsucker Sattler, who robs us poor weavers. But there's more of them yet! At least a score of them in Schönberg! Just take a look at what's in the treasure chests of the gentry—they're packed with gold and silver. And how did they come by it? From working for it? No, all you get from work is bloody calluses and poverty!"

In the corner of the taproom sat old Florian, the coachman from the deanery. Hearing Vejhanka, he took a furious pull from his wooden mug, rolled his eyes, and clenched his fists in fury. The tavern was full of gentry, the burghers of Schönberg. Their duty was to shut Vejhanka's drunken mouth, but none of them had the guts to do it. Groeger, the furrier, was even grinning, as if he were glad the weaver had slandered Mistress Sattler. Florian decided to step in himself.

"Hold your tongue, you sot!"

"Why should I hold my tongue? Am I to say good-bye to the world for the sake of a Devil's baggage?"

This was too much. Florian stood up and raised his fists to give this loudmouth something to remember, but then he felt a powerful grip on his arm. It was Riegel, the hulk of a town jailer.

"Leave him be. Vejhanka's right, you know. And wasn't your master always at the Sattlers' place?"

Florian's hands dropped. Not because he was afraid of this bully, but because Riegel's words utterly stunned him. He looked around at the other patrons of the inn, hoping that someone would stand up to defend the dean or silence Vejhanka, but no one moved.

He spat, quickly finished his drink, and stumbled outside.

Arriving back at the deanery, he crept into his room, but not for long, for his anger was almost beyond endurance. Instead, he went to the stable to be with his horses, to stroke them, pat them, treat them to some bread. They were dearer to him than all of the gentlemen at the Paradies inn.

At any other time, Florian would have confided everything to the dean, but on this occasion he was ashamed and kept quiet. Even so, Lautner knew that there had been a change among his parishioners. The neighbors no longer greeted him with the same respect, they no longer smiled when they saw him, and even the church was less well attended, and only women went to the special afternoon devotions.

Only when Christmas came did the church fill again. Since the fire, there had been neither the time nor the money to restore the church of Schönberg to its former glory, but on Christmas Eve, in the glare of the lighted wax candles, even the mock gold and silver appeared to be real. Their worries forgotten, the congregation waited solemnly for the ringing of the bell in the sacristy, for the emergence of the dean in his gold vestments, for the blare of the organ and the sweet voices of the choir.

Suddenly there was a strange stirring in the church. Winter, the gingerbread man, clearly excited, was exclaiming something to his closest neighbor. Straightaway, other members of the congregation got up and went outside, and more followed.

Florian raced breathlessly into the sacristy, where the dean was already dressing to go to the altar.

"Father, a star has appeared in the heavens!"

"What star?"

"A tailed star, a comet!"

The dean could not resist going outside. The churchyard was full of people observing the strange star that had appeared on this day of Christ's birth. It was reddish in color, with a sparkling tassel of a tail.

There could be no doubt that this was the comet they called the blood-drinker. Whenever God wanted to announce a grave misfortune, a war, famine, fire, or pestilence, this was his heavenly portent.

Like the others in the churchyard, the dean felt fear. Like

them, he believed that this comet was God's warning to the people. But of what? Was it heralding a new war against the Turks? A fire? The death of the sovereign? Or the Plague?

A cloud obscured the comet, the people made their way back to the church, and the dean began to celebrate the Midnight Mass. When the congregation prayed, it was with an unprecedented fervor; and even the dean conducted the service more piously than he had for a long time. When he sang the Gloria, his strong voice filled the whole church and moved every heart.

"Gloria in excelsis Deo et in terra pax hominibus bonae voluntatis! Glory to God in the highest, and on earth peace to men of good will!"

Pax hominibus! Peace to all men!

Hardly had the dean finished singing, when he remembered Marie Sattler. Even to her, O Lord, grant thy peace!

The organ played, and the congregation rose to sing an ancient carol of Christmas. Of all the voices, the sweetest and purest was that of Susanne Voglick.

"Lord, even to her grant the peace and happiness she deserves," whispered the dean, though it was not part of the prescribed prayers.

23 ✦ The Last Resort

Ignatius Karl Matthias, Count of Sternberg and Counselor of Appeals, scarcely showed his face at chambers after the arrival of Emperor Leopold and his court in Prague. The gloomy rooms beneath the Vladislav Hall at Prague Castle, and the even gloomier ones with the torture chambers in the basement, had never held too many attractions for him; but to find him there nowadays was yet rarer than to meet a black man on Charles Bridge.

Today, however, the noble counselor did appear and so astonished his secretary that the young jurist quite neglected to accord him the respect that was his due. So grandly attired was the count that a cock pheasant, compared to him, was as plain as a hen partridge. A shirt of rare Venetian silk; breeches of costly white cotton, beribboned in vivid red; a neckerchief of Brussels lace; a short waistcoat, the color of black cherries, crossed with a broad sash, green as a parakeet and richly embroidered with silver and gold; the red silk stockings that were prescribed by court etiquette; high-heeled shoes; a French *allonge* periwig; and a broad hat, bedecked with two huge ostrich feathers.

The count smiled, for he took pleasure in his pallid secretary's astonishment. It was a sign that he would also create the best impression at his audience with the Emperor.

"It's some time since you have been in chambers, Your Excellency," the secretary declared, bowing to his superior.

"I trust there's nothing here that cannot be held over," replied the count, a little offended that this young man should concern himself with boring official matters instead of admiring his clothes. They had cost a small fortune.

"There are a number of very complicated cases to be considered, Your Excellency."

"How long have they been here?"

"Some of them more than half a year."

"Half a year!" the count scorned. "Do you think that's a long time? You are aware, are you not, that the Court of Appeals is the last resort. Just imagine where our authority would be if we were to settle cases quickly, within a week, or a month! The longer the parties have to wait for a decision, the more clearly do they perceive that we have given long and very careful consideration to every point for and against. We gain in esteem without even lifting a finger! Your complicated cases can wait for at least half a year again!"

The secretary bowed. He had already been reaching for the files, but now he pushed them away again.

"There is, however, a little matter *ad ratificandum*. A mere formal confirmation of sentence, Your Excellency."

"What does it concern?" asked the Counselor of Appeals with evident distaste.

"An inquisitorial court at Gross Ullersdorf, Moravia, on the Zerotin estates, passed sentence of death by burning on three women for consorting with the Devil."

"Didn't they have anything better to do?"

"I have read all the papers with great attention, Your Excellency. My understanding is that the testimonies of the three women and their ultimate confessions were exacted only by severe torture. In fact the whole procedure appears to have been highly suspect . . ."

The count furrowed his brow.

"What do you find suspect? The charge? Or the use of torture to obtain a confession? That has always been the practice of inquisitorial courts. Where did this take place, did you say?"

"On the Zerotin estates, at Gross Ullersdorf."

"Zerotin? Premek of the Zerotins died some time ago and left two young sons at Ullersdorf. It occurs to me that the estates are looked after on their behalf by an aunt . . . We're relations, in a way."

"Yes, the manor is administered by the Countess of Galle."

"We cannot abandon orphans. It's our duty to protect them!"

"Your Excellency, the case has no bearing at all on the young owners of the estates. What I find suspect is the inquisitorial judge, a certain Boblig of Edelstadt. He uses the methods that were employed by the inquisitors in the German lands at the beginning of the century. But we've moved a long way since then . . ."

The furrows on the count's brow deepened and his voice reflected his annoyance: "Tell me: did these women confess, or didn't they?"

"They did confess, but only after severe torture, Your Excellency."

"So what are you worried about, young man? From a legal point of view, the thing is as plain as a pikestaff! If they confessed, then they're beyond our help!"

The secretary hung his head, not daring to oppose his superior. But it was clear that he did not agree.

"You, my friend," said the count sharply, "are unnecessarily making work for yourself and burdening your conscience. Why concern yourself with these village women? They confessed, and that's the end of the matter. It's not for us to consider whether they did or did not sign a pact with the Devil. For us the only important question is whether the trial was properly conducted! But there is one other serious consideration. You have heard, perhaps, that a disturbing discontent has recently boiled up among the laboring classes of the countryside. Peasant farmers have been writing petitions, and deputations have been taking them directly to the sovereign. Add to this the Turks, Thököly, the Plague, the King of France, the empire's poor finances! If the farmers were to revolt, that would be too much for our gracious sovereign. Our duty, therefore, is to ensure order is maintained."

"But the trial at Ullersdorf has nothing at all to do with what you have said, Your Excellency."

"What do you mean?" exploded the count. "Did the women serve the Devil? They did. They admitted it. You said so yourself. If they served the Devil, they couldn't serve the earthly authority, which comes of God. And whoever doesn't serve authority, whether or not he has a pitchfork or cudgel in his hand, is a rebel.

And rebellions have to be averted. We have to stand by those two poor orphans. Peace must prevail on their estates! And further, we must see that nothing disturbs our gracious sovereign! Do you understand what an honor it is for us that he has moved his entire court here to Prague Castle?"

The secretary hung his head still lower.

"See to the matter as soon as you can. The sentence will of course be confirmed!"

"It will be done, Your Excellency!"

"Do you have anything else?"

"May I make an observation, Your Excellency?"

"Yes, but briefly. Time is flying."

"My understanding is that the Court of Appeals must see that justice prevails. No one should be allowed to be wronged."

"Quite so," the count nodded, the ostrich feathers quivering in his hat.

"And I am almost certain that the case at Gross Ullersdorf involves three innocent women. Superstitious or aberrant, perhaps— but quite innocent, because they could not have committed the crimes of which they were accused. Common sense tells us . . ."

The young man was getting on the counselor's nerves.

"But you yourself declared that they confessed!"

"Yes. But they were compelled to."

The count shook his head.

"I don't understand you, young man. Are you a jurist, or some kind of preacher? Don't the rules of interrogation admit torture as a means to discover the truth?"

"They do. But there is something else at stake. Our conscience!"

The count sighed. This was a waste of time. He made to leave but stopped by the door.

"Conscience, you say! What's that to do with it? As a jurist you have to be guided by valid laws. To proceed otherwise would be to violate those laws. Save your conscience for the girls you go with!"

The secretary was silenced. The counselor suddenly felt sorry for him. Good-naturedly, he added: "You haven't even said how my clothes suit me!"

"Oh, they're very grand, Your Excellency!"

"Do you think the others will be jealous of me at court?"

"Most certainly, Your Excellency."

Count Sternberg left the chambers. The young jurist gazed after him for some time. Then he went to the desk and began to write the confirmation of sentence in the case of Maryna Schuch, Dorothea Groer, both of Wermsdorf, and Marie Züllich of Weikersdorf.

"Laws! Their laws conceal every conceivable villainy," he muttered as he laid down his pen.

24 ✦ A Heap of Ashes

The drums rolled darkly on the manors of Ullersdorf and Wiesenberg. Officials from the castle were riding out to all the villages, proclaiming an ordinance signed by Sheriff Vinarsky of Kreuz. Tomorrow all the serfs, led by their magistrates, were to proceed in the early hours of the morning to Ullersdorf Castle. There had not been such a drumming and a gathering of the people since the unhappy year of '62. Then, following the defeat of the peasants' revolt, the people had all had to go to the castle to renew their oath of allegiance to the authorities in the person of the regional governors, Karel Jindrich of Zerotin and Johann Kaspar, freeman of Montana. What new misfortune was to be heaped on the poor serfs of Zerotin?

The day before, a dusty coach had arrived at the castle, carrying a square-shouldered young gentleman with protruding teeth and a hooked nose. It was Master Johann Jakob Weingarten, Secretary to the Court of Appeals. Sheriff Vinarsky greeted him with great ceremony, and even Master Boblig of Edelstadt bowed his respects. The guest from Prague was tight-lipped and disposed to furtive glances as if there was something on his conscience; but some substantial refreshments were soon to change that.

The inquisitorial tribunal was convened that very evening in the courtroom. There the gentlemen of the tribunal heard the Secretary read out the solemn pronouncement of the Court of Appeals concerning Maryna Schuch, Dorothea Groer, and Marie Züllich. The verdict of the inquisitorial tribunal had been upheld *in extenso;* and since nothing had been found that could be regarded as an extenuating circumstance, there was to be no mitigation of punishment—to wit, decapitation before the ignominious burning.

The law prescribed that the sentence be announced to the condemned before the execution. The executioner was therefore ordered to bring the women before the grand inquisitorial tribunal at the hour of ten.

It was quite out of the question for the delinquents to appear before the Secretary to the Court of Appeals in their present state. Their clothes were in tattered shreds and their bodies were covered in dirt, festering sores, and human filth. So the first thing Master Jokl did was to have a bathtub and water brought into the jail. The women were ordered to wash, then each was given a long gown of coarse gray cloth to wear. Finally, Master Umlauf, the jailer, brought them beef soup from the kitchen.

Thus prepared and fortified, they were led into the courtroom, where the gentlemen of the tribunal were seated at the long table, fortifying their own good selves with wine. The executioner stood Dorothea Groer, the strongest of the women, in the middle, while the diminutive figures of Maryna Schuch and Marie Züllich were lined up to her left and right.

The condemned women stood still, and their feeble eyes, unused to daylight, looked fearfully at the gentlemen seated at the table, engaged in collegial conversation. Some of them they knew, but others not at all.

Before they had time to notice anything else, one of the unknown gentlemen got up. Puffed as a pigeon, he had a hawk's beak of a nose, and bared his huge teeth like a bulldog. Dorothea and Maryna wondered who this could be; but the miller's wife closed her eyes. She was so weak that even looking was an effort.

This gentleman did not seem to be paying them any attention. All he was doing was reading from some sort of document, full of foreign and strange words that none of the women properly understood.

To the miller's wife the Latin words sounded just like a funeral service. She, and then the beggarwoman, burst into tears. Only the sturdy Dorothea Groer remained erect, her eyes fixed on this foreign gentleman. What could he be saying? Soon she guessed he was delivering a verdict. Perhaps, it occurred to her in a flash, it promised freedom . . . But this was only a momentary thought, and her careworn mind knew immediately that it could not be. Why would Master Jokl have sent them a bathtub and water? Why would he have dressed them in these dreadful shrouds? Why would he have given them such good soup?

This was the end!

The gentleman with the huge teeth finished and sat down without even looking at them. The inquisitor, Boblig, rose to take his place. All three women knew him, but not like this. Now he was grandly dressed, and his bald head was covered with a wig. They could expect no grace from him. Dorothea lowered her eyes and sighed deeply, while Maryna moved her lips as if at silent prayer.

"Did you hear the sentence?" said the inquisitor in a loud voice.

Sentence! Now all three women knew what the gentleman with the teeth had read. Sentence! It could mean nothing other than death.

They had often spoken, during the timeless days and nights shared in the cold prison cell, of what awaited them. They had not expected mercy, and more than once they had even begged their jailers to end their suffering, for death seemed to them to be more merciful than imprisonment. But now that they were washed and clean, and strengthened by good food, that terrible word came as a blow. They stared wide-eyed at the inquisitor. Did it mean death?

The ceremony could not take long. The women were too feeble. Besides, a delicious smell of roast meats was wafting from the neighboring room.

Boblig pointed his finger at the beggarwoman of Wermsdorf.

"Maryna Schuch! Did you hear your sentence? I ask you: Do you accept it?"

The old woman trembled. She knew from the interrogations that this man was not to be opposed; otherwise the executioner would take her into the torture chamber. Rather death than that!

"Yes. Thank you kindly," she said in the voice she used to use when she went with her begging bag around the villages and was given a crust of bread.

The inquisitor looked at Secretary Weingarten and smiled faintly. Boblig was satisfied with the old hag and even more content with himself. When he saw that his guest from Prague was also smiling, he turned to the miller's wife.

"You, Marie Züllich! Did you hear the sentence? Do you accept it?"

For some time, Marie could not bring herself to open her mouth. Master Jokl, standing behind her, gave her a gentle prod of warning.

"I most humbly thank your Gracious Lordships," she whispered.

Boblig slipped a confident glance at the Secretary, but Weingarten was at that moment sipping from his glass and not listening at all.

Finally the inquisitor turned with the same questions to Dorothea Groer.

She drew herself up. Her face twitched and a flash of rage appeared in her eyes.

"What choice do I have?"

This time the inquisitor did not look for praise from his guest but ordered Jokl and his assistants to lead the women away.

The executioner took them through the torture chamber to the dark cell beyond, where the two Capuchin monks were waiting. Their task now was to try and save at least the sinners' souls, their bodies now beyond any human redemption.

Only when she saw their brown cowls did Dorothea, the boldest of the three, become clearly aware of what the sentence meant. She shrieked, but one of the monks put his hand on her mouth.

"Be not afraid," he soothed. "Open your heart to me and confess as if you were confessing to Jesus Christ Himself. Thus you may save your soul, and that is the main thing. Come!"

He took her by the hand. She fell silent and went with him like a child.

✦ ✦ ✦

It was a dull and murky morning, and a sharp, cold wind was blowing from the mountains. Processions of people were making their way along the road from the north and south, led by their village magistrates. At the crossroads, officials were giving them directions to the village of Gross Ullersdorf and to a stretch of hillside below the forest.

The farmers and cottagers already knew why the lords were herding them to Gross Ullersdorf. It was for the burning of the witches who, it was said, had caused misfortunes to be brought on the people and who would have brought the Plague also, if their intrigues with the Devil had not been revealed in time. That was what the scribes said, and it was also written in the ordinance signed by Sheriff Vinarsky. But the people, especially from Wermsdorf, Weikersdorf, and Petersdorf, had their doubts. They knew all three women very well. When had any of them done anyone any harm?

Twelve coaches were prepared in the castle courtyard, and eighty men at arms, musketeers, bailiffs, and gamekeepers were lined up, with ten mounted cavalrymen at the rear. Tucked to the side below the watchtower was a covered wagon, harnessed to which were two thin, old nags.

When the tower clock struck ten, their lordships began to troop out of the castle, dressed as if for a festival. The Secretary to the Court of Appeals, Master Weingarten, took his place in the grandest coach, accompanied on his left by Master Boblig of Edelstadt. The regional governor, Count Sack, got into the next coach with the Sheriff Vinarsky. Then the other coaches were filled, four gentlemen in each. The burgrave gave an order, the musketeers marched ahead, and the coaches moved off behind them. The gamekeepers brought up the rear.

As this was happening, the covered wagon moved to the jail, where Master Jokl, in the company of the two Capuchins, led out the condemned women. Getting them into the wagon was a task of some difficulty, for they were too feeble and overwrought to climb up themselves. The two monks clambered in with them, as well as the executioner and his two boys. Jokl was dressed in a red tunic, breeches—one leg of which was black, the other yellow—and well-greased boots.

The driver cracked his whip and the wagon moved off toward

the gate. Once on the road, it was surrounded for greater security by the cavalrymen.

The wagon jolted and clattered, and the cavalry horses pranced.

Maryna Schuch was moving her gums habitually, as if at prayer; Marie Züllich was drawing quick, deep breaths, her eyes closed; Dorothea Groer was sitting erect, staring at nothing in particular. Suddenly she gripped Father Crescentian's hand.

"Reverend Father!"

"Be afraid of nothing," the monk consoled her. "God is merciful!"

"But I lied when I confessed to you, Reverend Father. I never did any witchcraft, ever!"

The Capuchin frowned.

"To lie during holy confession is a sin!" But after a while he added in a more moderate tone: "God always finds the honest and rewards them as they deserve!"

"O God, God!" she wept.

As the procession neared the village, a death knell sounded from the bell tower of the Gross Ullersdorf parish church.

A large crowd of onlookers, mostly women and children, had gathered on a little flat area of hillside below the pine forest. The day before, young Hay and two assistants had driven three stout stakes into the ground there, and two weaver-women had piled a circle of dry pine logs around them. Beneath the logs was a quantity of oil-soaked woodchips and shavings, and also dry oat straw.

Now guards were on duty, maintaining order and determining where the people of each village were to take their places.

Someone claimed that at least three thousand people had gathered, though this was more than lived in the whole of the two manors of the Zerotin estates.

The gentry alighted from their coaches at the end of the village, from where they went on foot to the place of execution. The assembled crowds now had something to feast their eyes on, as their lordships, mostly plump and finely preened, puffed and panted their way up the steep hill, glancing loftily at the serfs as they went, as if they were so many bothersome insects. Father Schmidt, the scrawny and sunken-eyed parish priest of Zöptau, also eyed the crowds, but not harshly, or even contemptuously. His glance was rather one of reproof, as if to say to each one of them: If not for me, you would not be having this rare theater! Only Zeidler, the forest warden, looked rather to the ground than at the people and pulled on his long, squirrel-red beard.

The gentry had not yet taken their places according to their rank when the covered wagon arrived.

A hush fell upon the people. All stood on tiptoe, craning their necks in order not to miss a thing.

The first to jump down from the wagon was Jokl, as red as a bullfinch.

A whisper passed through the crowd: The executioner!

Then with the help of Jokl's boys and the Capuchins, the condemned women got down from the wagon.

The people could hardly believe what they saw. Instead of a band of dangerous witches they saw only three wretched old women, dressed in dreadful shrouds. Even those who had known them well could no longer recognize their shriveled faces, emaciated bodies, and disheveled gray hair.

The beggarwoman of Wermsdorf was the first to see the three pyres and the protruding stakes. She gripped the hand of the miller's wife and stood still. Then Dorothea Groer saw them also and froze. One of the executioner's assistants had to push them on.

The members of the inquisitorial tribunal separated from the rest of the gentry as they came to the place of concremation and stood with their backs to the stakes. The condemned women, supported by the monks and the executioner's boys, were lined up to face them.

Sheriff Vinarsky shouted an order, and the Gross Ullersdorf magistrate stepped forth to read the sentence to the crowds. But his trembling voice was weak, and the wind carried away his words; few people understood what he was saying.

After the magistrate, it was the inquisitor's turn. Everyone knew Master Boblig, for his name instilled fear far and wide. He was dressed in a new blue coat and a lace necktie, and wore a wig. He pulled in his stomach and for a moment gazed sternly at the gathered crowds. Soon, however, his face brightened. His moment had come. It was enough merely to glance at any one of the gathered thousands, and that person would tremble and would feel as small and insignificant as a pebble in the roadway, as weak as a new-hatched chick. Who could be mightier than Master Heinrich Franz Boblig of Edelstadt? The Countess of Galle, who had refused to take part in the concremation? Sheriff Vinarsky? Secretary Weingarten? Laughable!

When finally the inquisitor had finished amusing himself by observing the crowds, he turned to his victims and shouted for everyone to hear:

"Maryna Schuch, Dorothea Groer, and Marie Züllich! I ask you for the last time before the sentence is carried out, whether you stand by your testimonies to the court!"

"Yes, everything is true," replied the beggarwoman for all three, but her voice was so quiet that the Capuchins and executioner's boys could hardly hear her.

The members of the inquisitorial tribunal did not appear to be greatly interested.

Again the inquisitor's voice resounded:

"Maryna Schuch, Dorothea Groer, and Marie Züllich! I ask you: Is everything you said against your accomplices true, and do you hope to die on it?"

"Yes, it is, and we do," replied the beggarwoman again, for all three. Her voice was feeble.

Boblig smiled faintly. Everything was going like clockwork.

"Say now, in truth, and for all to hear it," the inquisitor raised his voice, "whether anyone, at any time during the investigation, subjected you to any duress!"

"No," Maryna Schuch whispered.

Marie Züllich merely shook her head. Dorothea Groer did not speak, neither did she make a move.

"Are you quite certain," continued the inquisitor, "that you brought no misfortune upon any innocent person?"

Dorothea emitted an unintelligible shriek, which the inquisitor took to indicate her agreement.

"Maryna Schuch, Dorothea Groer, and Marie Züllich!" he went on. "Do you admit that you sinned against authority? Do you acknowledge that the punishment which has been accorded to you is just?"

The women looked at one another anxiously as if not knowing which question they were supposed to answer.

The Capuchins nodded.

Having satisfied the requirements of the law and having no further questions to ask, Boblig turned to the executioner.

"Master Jokl, do your duty!"

The executioner's boys seized the condemned women and led them the few cruel steps to eternity.

Once again, Dorothea's place was in the middle. Maryna was led to her right, and Marie to her left.

Maryna Schuch, beggarwoman of Wermsdorf, halted midway, remembering Saint Laurence and the picture that hung in the church at Zöptau. O, my little saint, how sorry I was for you! Such a nice little man, and they roasted you like a goose on a gridiron! Now they're going to burn me, too! She suddenly cried out, but the executioner's boy clapped a hand over her mouth.

Jokl's helpers were experts. Dragging the women forward, they quickly chained their gaunt bodies firmly to the stakes and jumped to the ground. Then Master Jokl took up a torch and touched off the kindling at one pyre after another.

The straw and oil-soaked woodshavings immediately burst into flames with a great billowing of smoke and fire.

Shouts rang out from the crowd, but there was also the sound of women weeping.

The Capuchins loudly recited the Our Father; and several voices joined with them as the Gross Ullersdorf church bell again sounded the death knell.

The beggarwoman of Wermsdorf remained untouched by the flames for some time, for the wind was blowing them away from her. She stared wild-eyed at the crowds and caught sight of Johann Axmann, the village magistrate at Zöptau, and Bittner, the sacristan, and even the altar boy who had been the cause of her misfortune. Or perhaps she did not see them at all, but only thought she recognized them among so many people. Then she felt the searing pain. If it had not been for that boy! Or for Father Schmidt! She screamed but was swallowed by the merciful smoke. The tongues of flame licked her cheeks as the fire devoured her shroud. Then her face quite disappeared.

The wood was dry, the flames crackled merrily, and the wind bore the smoke high into the sky. The witches burned like torches.

All around, the people stared aghast and strained their ears to catch their last words, but no one heard anything but the crackling of the flames, the prayers of the Capuchin fathers, and the sound of the death knell.

Father König himself tolled the bell, for both his sexton and bellringer had gone to watch the execution.

✦ ✦ ✦

The gentry did not stay until the end but walked back to their coaches and set off at a gallop to the castle, where a grand banquet had been prepared in their honor by the countess, represented by Sheriff Vinarsky.

Some fifty guests now gathered in the banqueting hall near the courtroom to celebrate the culmination of their pious work. And with every course of food and drink their spirits rose.

The tables were piled with fish from the village ponds, trout from the mountain streams, crayfish, seven different kinds of roast meat, sweet pastries, and fruit. There was beer to drink, and wine, and brandy.

Johannes Jakob Weingarten, the distinguished Secretary to the Court of Appeals, had eyes for nothing but the feast. He perspired profusely and his ears wagged curiously as he ate and drank more voraciously than anyone else.

Everyone drank heavily, however, including the inquisitor.

Master Heinrich Franz Boblig of Edelstadt was exultant. He had attained yet another famous victory. While others of his age were content to warm themselves at the fireside, their tired limbs racked with gout, he was embarked on an enviable work. He looked around at the guests as if to say: Gentlemen, this is only the beginning!

When at last the guests were full of stomach and flushed of face and unable to accept any more choice morsels, they began exchanging stories. But none could outdo Master Boblig of Edelstadt.

"Those women whom we consigned to the fires of hell," he said, "were only small fry. Witches are usually far more dangerous. I remember one from Waldshut. There was once a wedding feast in that little town, and just about everyone was invited. The only person to be forgotten was the wife of a wheelwright from the suburbs. And she, as it happened, had signed a pact with the Devil. She was furious she hadn't been invited, so straightaway she called on the Devil to cause a hailstorm over the town. The Evil One listened and complied. Before the eyes of several shepherds, he raised her up to a great height and transported her to a little hill near the town, where she had to make a little hollow in the ground, pour water into it, and stir it with her finger. Then the demon took a handful of this broth, flew off with it over the town and cast it into the air. At that, there was a hailstorm, and the greatest damage was done in the very place where the wedding party was gathered. The wheelwright's wife later admitted everything, and having confessed, she died."

"Yes, a wondrous power is granted to such women," added Secretary Weingarten, selecting a plump joint of veal, for he was not yet replete.

"A wondrous power indeed," Boblig rejoined, "and sometimes even verging on the incredible. Perhaps, gentlemen, it's appropriate to recall an episode that was recorded by those two venerable Dominican monks, Institoris and Jakob Sprenger. Witches can do men harm by various means, but our two Dominicans tell of one who had a remarkable power. Whenever she joined carnally with a man, she deprived him of his manhood. Numerous eyewitnesses at the inquisitorial court testified that they had seen her nest, full of some twenty penises taken from the men who had known her.

They moved about as if they were alive and pecked like birds, and the witch fed them with corn and other foodstuff. The Dominicans conceded that the witnesses could have been misled, charmed by the Devil, but this is refuted by other facts. One of the unfortunate men whom the witch had afflicted turned to another witch for help. She advised him to climb a certain tree, where he would find the nest and be able to retrieve what he was missing. This he did, and he chose the biggest, but the witch admonished him for it. The largest one in the nest, apparently, belonged not to him but to a certain clergyman. Both witches were subsequently caught, voluntarily confessed to the tribunal, and rightly died at the stake."

This doubtful tale set the scene for a whole number of the most unsavory stories. Soon the hall was ringing with roars of laughter and the banging of glasses on the table.

Finally even the guest of honor from Prague was full. He washed down the last morsel with a full glass of Hungarian wine, dashed the goblet to the floor, and launched into the old *Lanzknecht** song:

> *Cannon roar, afar, afar,*
> *And the bells are tolling.*
> *Man of war, to arms, to arms,*
> *Hear the drums a-rolling.*
> *But raise a glass before you go.*
> *What brings the morrow—who's to know!*

Other drunken voices joined in, and the hall filled with shouting, as if a whole detachment of *Lanzknechts* were feasting there.

Master Boblig was exhilarated and sublimely happy. He also broke into rasping song, and his choice was the favorite drinking song of the students of Jena:

Lanzknechts, or *Landsknechts*, were mercenary footsoldiers in the German lands from the fifteenth to seventeenth centuries.—Trans.

> *O, it's no sin*
> *To fill your skin.*
> *Drink until you hit the floor.*
> *And if you spew, here's what to do:*
> *Drink again, boys, drink some more* . . .

At this, some of the gentlemen fell off their chairs, to be carried off to their rooms by footmen. The last to leave were Secretary Weingarten and the inquisitor Boblig, accompanied to the end by his hunchbacked assistant, Ignatius.

As all this was happening, the executioner's boys were retrieving the chains from the yet warm ashes of the pyres of Ullersdorf. The young Hay scattered the heap with a shovel, and the wind blew particles of ash far and wide. Some of the remains of Maryna Schuch, Dorothea Groer, and Marie Züllich were surely blown as far away as Wermsdorf and Weikersdorf, and perhaps even to the priest's house at Zöptau.

25 ✦ *The Serpent*

Kaspar Sattler and Judge Hutter did not cease urging the dean to try and influence the inquisitor to bring about Marie Sattler's release. Lautner, for his part, would have interceded on her behalf at any time, even in the middle of the night—were it not for two things. One was Master Boblig of Edelstadt, the mere memory of whose face overwhelmed him with revulsion. And the other was the unmistakable signs that the wind was turning against him at the Consistory.

Poor Marie! Lautner thought of her now almost as often as during his schooldays at the Olomouc Latin school, when he had still been in love with her.

Eventually the old memories proved to be stronger than the counsel of his wiser friends. The dean decided that he would, after all, overcome his revulsion, visit the inquisitor and exert all his eloquence and authority to help the master dyer's wife.

It was not an easy thing for him to do. Indeed, he would rather have stood before Bishop Liechtenstein, or even the Emperor himself, than look into the bloated face of this drunkard and braggart. Boblig claimed to fight the Devil, but in reality he served the forces of Satan with all manner of wickedness: violence, fraud, lies, deceit, hypocrisy. To deal with Boblig meant playing the hypocrite oneself. It meant self-humiliation: begging, pleading, whimpering. Perhaps it also meant having to endure insults and impertinences: to look, yet not to see, and to listen, yet not to hear. On top of everything, Lautner had a feeling of utter helplessness when confronted by this demon in human form. The Lord alone knew who stood by him, preparing his way, making his paths straight. It was not impossible that he was supported by the bishop, or at least by his secretary, Father Schmidt.

But further delay was out of the question. And so it was that one frosty afternoon, without telling Susanne where he was going, the dean left the house on his mission to the inquisitor. The town square at the end of Church Street was covered by a layer of frozen snow. He glanced about the square, then strode directly ahead, toward Gaup's house. Perhaps he wanted Boblig to see him from the window; or perhaps he was afraid to walk around the square under the arcades, lest he meet someone he knew and have to tell them where he was going. Lautner did not know himself why he elected to go straight across. He walked uncertainly, leaning on his stick, his eyes fixed to the ground.

Ignatius was sitting at the window of Boblig's apartment, observing the goings-on in the square and whiling away the time eating dried pears. As soon as he saw the dean, he ran smiling to his master, who was engaged in writing a long letter.

"Dean Lautner's on his way here!"

"How do you know?" the advocate muttered, not lifting his eyes from the page.

"I saw him from the window. He's heading across the square, straight for us!"

"Not very compelling evidence, Iggy," Boblig smiled. "But if he does come, do give the black magician of Schönberg a proper clergyman's welcome!"

Ignatius retired to the hallway, curious to know whether he had guessed correctly. Boblig, meanwhile, for safety's sake, stuffed the half-written letter into a drawer.

Soon there was a knock at the front door. It creaked open and Boblig heard Ignatius's welcoming voice in the hall. The inquisitor rose, opened his own door, and beamed at his visitor. The dean read a great satisfaction in his face. So, little man, you've come at last, his eyes seemed to be saying.

"What an honor! To what do I owe such a distinguished visit?" Boblig cried, scratching his chest under his friarlike robes.

"I am led to you, sir, by my duties as a spiritual pastor."

"I'm very curious. Please, come in."

Boblig admitted his guest into his spacious and richly appointed room. A large tiled stove gave out plenty of heat, but the air in the room was heavy, stale, and suffused with tobacco fumes. The inquisitor bade his guest sit down in the armchair, and for himself drew a simple rush-woven chair from under the table.

The dean was suddenly conscious that the speech he had prepared at home was now good for nothing. Boblig's eyes were razor-sharp and pierced to the quick. There was no point in playing clever. He would have to be blunt, unrestrained by social courtesies.

"I've come to ask you what interest you have in the imprisonment of Mistress Sattler," he said in a firm voice, not averting his gaze from the inquisitor's own.

Boblig clutched his chin with his fat fingers and curled his lower lip. For some time he remained silent, directing a faintly mocking gaze at this old man, who was now sweating in a fur coat that he had not even bothered to remove.

"Would you allow me, Your Reverence," he said at last, "to answer with a question? Why should you, of all people, deign to take an interest in the fate of Marie Sattler?"

Lautner was conscious his inquiry was being turned against him and that he was to be cross-examined. He ran his palm across his damp forehead.

"Marie Sattler," he said, struggling to adopt a natural tone of voice, "has always been a good Catholic and has led an exemplary life. No one in Schönberg knows what she is accused of."

Boblig smiled good-humoredly.

"You are making a grave mistake, Your Reverence. On the contrary, the whole town knows very well what she is accused of. And I am sure that you know also!"

The inquisitor's fierce gaze forced Lautner to drop his eyes. At this moment the dean felt a hatred in his heart toward this cunning and slimy man. It was impossible to look him in the face. He was a serpent, he thought to himself. A poisonous snake!

"Whatever is being said in the town is simply nonsense," he replied with considerable self-control. "I have known this woman for a great many years."

"I know." Boblig smiled indulgently. "I understand that in your youth you enjoyed some quite intimate relations with her. And that to this day you often visit her home."

"And what of it?" exploded the dean, his discretion now gone. "Is that supposed to be an aggravating circumstance for her? Or for me, even?"

"Compose yourself, Your Reverence, and look at this calmly. Is it your opinion that Marie Sattler is being held in the town jail without good reason?"

"Yes, that is my opinion!"

Boblig pulled a wry face, reached into his pocket, took out a silver snuffbox, and opened it to his guest. When Lautner declined, he took an epicurean pinch himself. Then he sighed and began to speak. It seemed that he also was straining to curb his temper.

"There are many things in this world, dean, that can remain concealed, even from one's closest kith and kin, for a very long time, but which one day have to emerge. Allow me, *carissime,* to tell you a story that actually happened some time ago in the diocese of Strasbourg. A laborer was cutting logs outside the town, when all of a sudden he began to be pestered by a large black cat. No sooner had he beaten it off than two other black cats appeared, and all three furiously attacked him. Only with great effort did he manage to drive them away with a stick. Not an hour later he was seized by two constables and hauled before a judge, who accused him of severely wounding three respected local ladies. The woodcutter said in his defense that he had never lifted his hand to any woman. 'But it happened not one hour ago!' the judge cried. Only then did the woodcutter remember the cats. Only thus *probatum fuit,* was it proved, that those three ladies were in reality witches, who for long years had contrived to conceal their allegiance to the Devil—and not only from the whole town, but even from their husbands and children. What do you say to that, Your Reverence?"

He gave a triumphant smile, but the dean cut him dead.

"Why are you telling me this, sir? I know the story. It was

recorded by the Dominican Jakob Sprenger in his dubious work *Malleus maleficarum!*"

"It appears, Your Reverence," said Boblig spitefully, "that you harbor considerable reservations about its authenticity!"

Again the dean had the feeling that he was being cross-examined.

"It's too ancient a tale!"

Boblig nodded his head a while.

"I don't think you believe in witches at all," he went on in a friendly voice. "We've already discussed this before . . ."

Lautner knew that according to Sprenger's book, this was the line of questioning an inquisitor was to follow during his first interrogation of a person charged with witchcraft. According to *The Witch Hammer*, it was not important how the suspect replied; he remained a suspect whether he said he believed in witches or not. The dean flushed hot with rage, but he suppressed his fury and replied with apparent calm.

"I believe in the Devil's influence in this world, for such is the teaching of the Holy Church, firmly grounded in the Scripture. But where witch trials are concerned, sir, as you surely know better than I, there is much that is unclear, or contrary to common sense. But I didn't come to you to dispute such questions. I wanted to find out when you are going to release Marie Sattler. She is utterly blameless, and I personally can vouch for her good character."

"You, Your Reverence?" asked Boblig, and the dean felt a diabolical laughter behind those words.

"Yes, I, her spiritual pastor!"

The inquisitor fell silent for some time.

"And what if I were to tell you, *carissime*," he said eventually, "that Marie Sattler has already confessed? She has been in league with the Devil for decades!"

The dean stared in amazement. Only a man such as Boblig could have concocted a lie like this. He sprang from his chair.

"That's utterly absurd!"

The inquisitor also rose, slowly, fixing his serpentine eyes on his guest as he spoke.

"Do you think the execution of the witches at Gross Ullersdorf was also absurd?"

Lautner did not reply. This was another question worthy of Jakob Sprenger, or his partner, Institoris.

"Is it your opinion," continued Boblig in the same tone, "that the inquisitorial court consigned those three women to the flames without clearly proving their guilt?"

"And how did it prove it?" cried Lautner angrily.

Boblig's face twisted.

"By their own confessions and also by a number of testimonies!"

"Probably from people who were also accused of the same crime! And after severe torture!"

Deep lines were now appearing on the inquisitor's brow. It was clear that he intended to deal his opponent a telling blow. But when he spoke, it was with an oily, fulsome voice.

"Your Reverence, Let me tell you something about the woman on whose behalf you are here, whose spiritual pastor you are, and whom you say you can vouch for. Marie Sattler sold herself, body and soul, to the Devil. But she was not alone. She has many helpers and friends here. For many years, Schönberg has been a den of loathsome iniquities, and I personally find it very difficult to understand why you, as a spiritual pastor"—and on these words Boblig placed especial stress—"had no idea they were going on. I am afraid you are going to face some unpleasantnesses when the Consistory finds out about this. You ought to prepare yourself for them."

But for his heaving breast, Christoph Lautner stood as motionless as a rock. Boblig's words had been no friendly warning but a clear threat. A threat such as he had made before, at the priest's house at Gross Ullersdorf.

Boblig was wicked. Not out of anger or vengefulness, but simply because his wickedness gave him pleasure or profit. For him a lie was a weapon that was the equal of truth, and deception and trickery were perfectly honorable and useful means to an end. It amused him to be able to destroy innocent people, to rob them of their serenity, their property, or their lives. His web was spun as gently and as purposefully as a spider's. And once he had selected his victim, he would never let him go. Now, it seemed, he was out to catch the Dean of Schönberg.

"I don't know much about the trial at Gross Ullersdorf," Lautner said at last.

"I'll be pleased to tell you, if you wish. Otherwise you might hear all sorts of things. But there is something you have to bear in mind. So far, this has been merely the overture. The major work is yet to come. There are at least twenty persons awaiting sentence at Ullersdorf alone."

"Twenty?" the dean gasped.

"And in Schönberg, it appears, the harvest will be even more bountiful!"

"O God!" The very ground seemed to quake beneath the dean's feet.

Boblig's face suddenly brightened.

"I see, dean, that you are horrified at the prospect. But as a spiritual pastor you ought to be pleased. Aren't we ridding your sheepfold of the wolves? Aren't we carrying out the most pious task the Holy Church could ever wish for? Aren't we doing battle with the Devil, the archenemy of mankind—and far more effectively than you do, for example, in your sermons?"

"You, you . . ." cried Lautner in indignation. But Boblig did not allow him to finish.

"I know, Your Reverence. You want to express your gratitude. But it really isn't necessary. We inquisitorial judges are modest and quiet workers. Our work is insignificant, and we lay no claim to any special credit. Perhaps when we are gone, our small contribution will be recognized. However, I do hope that in you I will find support and assistance. There is clearly much work awaiting us in Schönberg. And you, Your Reverence, are an unavoidable part of it . . ."

The dean sensed the mockery. He swallowed hard and clenched his fists. But Boblig smiled.

"Hey, Ignatius," he cried suddenly, "bring in wine! We must show some respect for the Dean of Schönberg!"

"No, no!" cried Lautner, reaching for his stick.

The inquisitor stared, a look of astonishment on his face as he urged his guest to stay.

"I do hope you're not denying us your assistance, *carissime*."

"Forgive me, I cannot. I have other duties to perform!"

"Such a pity! We could have spoken about so many things. I wanted to ask you especially about some of your friends in Schönberg, at Gross Ullersdorf, and at Römerstadt . . ."

But the dean was already fleeing from this house of Satan. It was beyond his powers of forbearance to take any more.

His head was bowed now as he made his way back across the square, his eyes fixed to the ground again. Suddenly he was struck by the words of the prophet Job: The things that my soul refused to touch are as my sorrowful meat . . .

Lautner strode directly to Church Street with not one backward glance. So he did not see the inquisitor Boblig standing at an upstairs window of Gaup's house, with a full glass of wine in his hand and a contented smile on his face.

26 ✦ Young and Beautiful

The dean resolved to tell no one in town of Boblig's threats, not even his closest friends, for he did not know whom the inquisitor had in mind. But the reference to Lautner's friends at Gross Ullersdorf and Römerstadt was undoubtedly an accusation of his brother priests, König and Pabst. They had to be warned without delay.

Directly after lunch the next day, the dean ordered Florian to harness the horses. Then he warned Susanne not to go anywhere until his return and to open the door to no one, and climbed into the fur wraps aboard the sled, bound for Gross Ullersdorf.

Florian, perched proudly on the driver's seat, was as pleased as the horses to be on the road again. They tossed their heads and snorted merrily, and the only modest aspect the sled presented was the round figure of the graying priest curled up in a corner. When they crossed the square, the dean could not resist a glance at Gaup's house. Standing at one of the windows was the crooked figure of the inquisitor's goblin, Ignatius. He was bound to go running to his master with the news that the dean was leaving. Lautner spat and turned his head the other way.

The day was sunny. Melted snow dripped from the roofs that were exposed to the sun, and water trickled along the streets. But outside the town gate there was no sign of a thaw, and the countryside remained covered in snow. The distant mountains were a clear gray-blue, the air was fresh, and all around was silence, save for the occasional cawing of the crows.

"Hey, Florian, why the haste?" the dean called out. "There's plenty of time."

"It's not me, Father, it's the horses! They're just glad to be beyond the gates of Gomorrah!"

"So give them their head, Florian!"

The dean had not been mistaken in supposing that Ignatius would rush to announce his departure.

"The dean's going somewhere by sled," he called from his place at the window.

"So let him! He won't get away!" muttered the inquisitor, who continued peering into his papers.

But Ignatius, his simian face broadened and his eyes lighted, had had an idea. He crept to his master's table on tiptoe and stood two paces from it, scratching behind one ear.

"I see you have something on your mind," said Boblig, looking up.

"I think I've just been touched by the Holy Spirit!"

"Do you really think the Holy Spirit finds you so attractive, Iggy?"

"Just imagine, master! Isn't this a glorious opportunity to pick up that pretty cook, the one who's so fond of lying with devils? The dean's away, and so's that brute Florian. Nothing could be there to stop us, and we could get her under lock and key, nice and quietly!"

The inquisitor drew himself up, eyed the hunchback for a while, and chuckled.

"You, Iggy, are a rogue. But I have to admit, it's not a bad idea!"

Boblig pondered. He had his hands full with the witches of Gross Ullersdorf; he was waiting for confirmation from Prague of the verdicts on Susanne Stubenvoll, Marie Petrova, Agneta Kopp, Anna Föbel, and Barbora Kühnel. He was also elaborating a verdict in the cases against Dorothea Biedermann, bathkeeper of Gross Ullersdorf, Barbora Göttlicher, Katerina Rabovska, and Barbora Kranichl—who still stubbornly denied her crime as soon as she was taken out of the torture chamber and thus was giving the judges much work. There was still plenty of time to deal with the witches of Schönberg; and even the most zealous of inquisitors could not work from dawn to dusk like a bondsman. But then it occurred to Boblig that many weeks had passed since Marie Sattler's arrest. The people had already half-forgotten her and had become inured to the inquisitorial tribunal. And that was undesirable. The burghers on the street had almost stopped greeting the feared inquisitor and were not even anxious to avoid him. The noble task of the Inquisition could prosper only when the people held it in dread. Throwing the cook into jail would certainly cause a stir, and it would also be a vigorous response to the dean's plea for the release of Marie Sattler. Not only would the dye master's wife not be released, but the dean's own young mistress would be locked up to join her! Boblig's eyes gleamed.

"Iggy, do you know what woman is?" he asked.

"*Opus diabolicum,* the work of the Devil," the hunchback replied with a sentence he had often heard his master use.

"If that be so, then we must act, Iggy! Besides, as I remember, that little girl from the deanery is indeed a pretty thing. And a pretty girl is always an ally of the Devil. This will be an especially tasty morsel for you, Iggy, if I know you. You're quite right! Bring my fur coat, we'll go right now to see Master Gaup. Perhaps we'll manage to catch him without his wig!"

✦ ✦ ✦

If only Susanne Voglick had suspected something! For some days she had observed that something was troubling the dean. He was off his food; his sheets were rumpled with his tossing and turning at night; he no longer joked and was forever shutting himself in his room. But he had disclosed nothing, and she was not in the practice of asking him what was on his mind.

After the dean's departure, Susanne busied herself with ironing a whole basketful of church linen. The Schönberg church was only sparsely furnished, for the burghers had paid more heed to the town hall and brewery, and had neglected the house of God, but there was still enough linen for quite a pile to have amassed since Christmas. Susanne began with a will, but she was hardly finished with the first item when the bell rang at the front door. She looked out and to her great joy saw that it was Liesel Sattler. This was good. At least Liesel would be able to sprinkle the linen for her!

The February afternoon was short, and Susanne had to catch up on quite a lot of missed work. Once her smoothing iron was hot again, both she and Liesel set to work, and soon the pile of linen, both with lace and without, was quickly disappearing. At last, only a few small items remained in the basket.

Suddenly there was another jangling of the doorbell.

"Who the devil can that be?" cried Liesel.

"Why don't you look out of the window?"

A few moments later she returned as white as a sheet.

"Master Gaup is standing outside," she whispered.

Liesel's good mood was now utterly gone. She was remembering the dreadful night when Gaup had come to take her mother away. Susanne, however, did not make the connection.

"Gaup? What does he want here?"

Not noticing her frightened friend, she ran to the window herself. There outside stood the district judge, looking up at her, dressed in a fur-lined coat of blue woolen cloth. She opened the window and shouted down.

"The dean's not at home! He'll be back at suppertime!"

"I've not come to see the dean. It's you I want to speak to!"

Susanne closed the window and ran downstairs. Only when she was standing at the door did she remember what the dean had ordered: not to open it to anyone. But surely he had strangers in mind, and not Master Gaup!

She slid the heavy key into the lock, turned it, and opened one leaf of the double oak doors. But it was a mistake, as she immediately saw. Master Gaup was accompanied by two constables. Susanne was not fainthearted, and perhaps she would not have been so startled were it not for the sight of a familiar, hideous hunchback hiding behind a tree. She wanted to slam the door, but one of the constables was quicker and jammed his foot inside. She turned and fled up the wooden stairs, pursued by heavy footfalls. Her only thought was to reach the kitchen, but it was impossible. Liesel appeared in the doorway to see what was going on and blocked her way. Susanne suddenly felt a heavy hand grip her shoulder.

"That's a fine way to greet us, sweetheart!" smiled the unshaven constable, showing his protruding teeth.

Seeing there was no escape, Susanne stared contemptuously at the intruder before looking down the stairs at Master Gaup, who was panting his way to the top. Only he would be able to give her an explanation. Surely it was not done for the district judge to storm the dean's home in such a manner!

Gaup, followed by the other armed man, was already on the last step. He smiled faintly.

"Are you Susanne Voglick?"

"But you know me, Master Gaup," she replied, her lips pursed.

"You're coming with us!"

"Me? Why? And where?"

"No questions, and put on your coat!"

"I'm not going anywhere. I have to wait for the dean with his supper!" said Susanne loudly, but there were tears in her voice.

"Something far more important is waiting for you. If you don't go voluntarily, you'll be taken away by the guards!"

The housekeeper noticed that someone else also was standing on the stairs: the hunchback.

"Don't be afraid!" Ignatius said in a squeaking voice. "No one will bite you, even if you do look nice enough to eat."

Her heart missed a beat.

"But I didn't do anything!"

"No one says you did," said Gaup in a rather more kindly tone. "All we want is for you to make a deposition."

Susanne felt some relief at this, but still she did not trust him.

"What deposition?"

"Mistress Sattler wants you to give evidence!"

Her best friend's mother! How long had that good lady been in jail! Susanne realized that her testimony could help both Mistress Sattler and Liesel. She no longer resisted, pulled her coat from its hook, and put on her woolen head scarf.

"Lock everything up here and give the key to Liesel," said Gaup. "She'll hand it over to the dean when he arrives."

This was suspicious. Was her testimony to last so long? The dean would have to have his supper!

"I have to be home before the dean gets back!" she said, looking into the judge's eyes.

His face twisted into a wry smile.

"You can be sure we won't let the dean go without his supper."

Susanne realized he was lying and felt a terror that turned her legs to wood. Her sole salvation lay with Liesel. She looked to her and saw that her friend was pale and trembling, her eyes full of tears. Liesel was reliving the time that Master Gaup broke into the Sattlers' home and dragged away her mother.

The judge was in a hurry. He issued an order to the unshaven constable, and before Susanne knew what was happening, he seized her roughly and painfully by one arm, while the second constable grasped her by the other.

And then it all went quickly at once. The constables carried rather than led her down the creaking wooden stairs, while the apelike Ignatius scampered ahead and the district judge strode behind. But he ran a finger behind his collar as he walked, as if it were suddenly too tight for him.

At the front door he turned around. Liesel also was coming down the stairs. She had stuffed one corner of her apron into her mouth to stop herself crying out.

"Lock up and run home!" he ordered her sternly.

The procession made its way quickly along the wall of the graveyard and into Church Street. There was not a living soul to be seen, and not until the corner of the square did they come across old Mistress Rollepatz, leaning on her stick.

She realized immediately what was happening and began screaming.

"The dean's cook! They've arrested the dean's cook!"

"Quiet, you hag!" one of the constables shouted. But Mistress Rollepatz ran off along Church Street and carried on shrieking until people started coming out of their houses.

"Quickly, quickly!" urged Gaup. Nothing frightened him more than a mob.

It was not far to the town hall, and before the people had discovered what was going on, the procession had already disappeared inside.

A moment later, Susanne Voglick found herself in the court-room, confronted by the dreaded inquisitor. The very sight of him was as if someone had suddenly touched her with a hot iron. He was even more loathsome in the gloom, even though he tried to assume the friendliest of faces. He walked across to her and chucked her under the chin.

"We already know each other, my dear. Don't you remember my visit?"

Susanne gritted her teeth and made no reply. How could she fail to remember this man!

Boblig glanced at Master Gaup.

"Leave us alone, please. I won't be needing you now."

"Not even my men?"

"I doubt it. The dear girl is as gentle as a lamb. And, of course, we're not going to hurt her! We're just going to ask a few ques-tions and then send her home again. It must be much more pleas-ant at the deanery than here, am I not right, Susanne Voglick? This cold chills me to the marrow."

Again, Susanne made no reply. Master Gaup ushered his con-stables outside and turned at the door.

"Just in case, though, we'll stay in the corridor."

Only now did Susanne notice that Ignatius had remained in the room. His simian features, illuminated by an oil lamp that swung back and forth beneath a huge crucifix, appeared even more ghastly than in the light of day. Susanne realized she was utterly in the power of these two wicked people, about whom she had heard such terrible things. But she would not let them get away with it so easily. She would tell everything to the dean, and he would know immediately how they were to be punished.

So far Ignatius did not dare approach her and remained in a corner, feasting his greedy eyes on her beautiful, perfectly formed body. If Susanne had taken more notice of the hunchback, she would certainly have been more frightened of him than of Boblig. But now she was looking at the inquisitor.

"Sit down, my dear. I see you're trembling," he said.

Susanne sat down on the very edge of the rough chair and placed her hands on her shaking knees.

Finally the interrogation began.

"Do you know at all why I sent for you?"

"Master Gaup said it was because of Mistress Sattler . . ."

"We'll leave that for later," the judge smiled. "First I'd like to ask how you are doing at the deanery. Is the dean good to you?"

Though she had no experience of such investigations, Susanne realized this question was designed only to win her trust and confidence. Only later would Boblig proceed to the heart of the matter.

"The dean is a nice man," she replied.

"So he's fond of you?"

Susanne frowned, sensing the double entendre in Boblig's otherwise friendly voice. She fell silent, and Boblig did not press her for an answer. He tugged his lower lip, took a pinch of snuff, and continued gazing at his victim. He was in a good mood. It was a long time since he had last investigated such a comely young thing.

"When I look at you," he said, "I quite understand why the dean is fond of you. I hear that wherever he goes, he makes quite a show of his pride in you! And so would I!"

"That's not true! He doesn't make a show of pride in me!"

"Come, come, now!" The inquisitor smiled. "Doesn't he take you everywhere with him? Visits, weddings, baptisms, feast days . . ."

"I carry the lantern and he leans on my arm. He doesn't see very well in the dark!"

Boblig burst into laughter.

"Your master does have things arranged nicely! If only I had a guardian angel like you, instead of Ignatius. Look what a handsome fellow he is!"

Susanne did not even turn her eyes. She was increasingly confused and had no idea where this talk was leading.

The inquisitor suddenly became serious.

"Do you know Mistress Sattler, the wife of the master dyer?"

Susanne nodded. This is it, she thought.

"I hear you and the dean used to be frequent guests at the Sattlers'. Is that so?"

Susanne nodded again.

"And things used to get quite merry there, I hear."

"Sometimes."

"And what did you do, when you were merry?"

"We sang, sometimes the dean told us stories from the days when he studied at Landshut or Graz. And we used to play cards . . ."

"And didn't you do something else?"

Susanne, uncomprehending, shook her head.

The inquisitor lifted her head.

"And now," he said sternly, "tell me, as if you were at holy confession: Did the dean often have his way with you?"

Susanne leaped up as if she had been bitten by a snake. Her cheeks were crimson and her brow was deeply furrowed.

"What do you mean?"

No sooner had she said it than a chortling rang out from the corner. None but the hunchback could laugh like that. Susanne felt as if she had fallen into a lion's den. The ground on which she stood burned into her feet.

"Tell me, then, at least, Susanne Voglick," resounded the croaking voice of the inquisitor, "whether the dean often had his way with Mistress Sattler?"

"How can you think such things, sir!" she sobbed.

"But at least you're going to tell me why the two of you used to go to the cellar so often?"

"The only person who went there was old Miss Rohmer!"

"All right," said the judge, shrugging his shoulders. "If you don't want to talk about these things, I'll ask you about something else!"

For a while he paced up and down the darkened room as Susanne followed him with her fearful eyes. For the first time she realized with a pounding heart that it was perhaps the dean whom Boblig was interested in, more than herself or Mistress Sattler.

Boblig suddenly halted and gave her a piercing stare.

"It is true that you are still able to blush, my dear, but you have long not been so innocent as you would have us believe. We know that on more than one occasion you attended a gathering of witches on the Petersstein and that your gallant was Lautner, Dean of Schönberg. And we also know that you defiled the sacrament by taking the sacred host there in your shoe!"

Stunned to hear such a dreadful charge, Susanne sank desperately to her knees and raised her right hand.

"I swear before Almighty God that everything you said, sir, is an untruth. I was never ever with the dean on the Petersstein and I never defiled the sacrament!"

"We shall see!" smiled the inquisitor.

Now it seemed to the hunchback that his moment had come. He emerged impatiently from the corner.

"You know, my dear," he said, going straight to her, "every witch has on her body a witchmark, the sign of the Devil, so that others of her kind may know her . . ."

Seeing agreement in his master's eyes, Ignatius stretched out a hand to Susanne. His fingers were like claws.

She guessed what this creature was itching to do. He wanted to paw her body with those filthy fingers, looking for signs in the shape of freckles, moles, warts, or pockmarks.

"I don't have any marks!"

"That's something we must see for ourselves, my dear," said the inquisitor slowly. He was looking forward to seeing Ignatius tear the clothes from this beautiful girl, to seeing her young naked form gleam in the dim light.

But Susanne was determined to fight. She backed nimbly to the wall and waited.

The hunchback bore down on her, his mouth agape, his tongue half protruding. Suddenly he pounced.

He expected no resistance at all. But Susanne was a head taller and far stronger than he. She tore herself away and punched him hard, full in his twisted face.

"Bitch!"

He took a pace back, but then rushed headlong at her again.

Master Boblig of Edelstadt prepared to help his assistant, reaching out his long arms and seizing the dean's housekeeper firmly by the shoulder, while Ignatius grabbed her by the waist.

Susanne was strong, but not strong enough for two. She saw the disfigured face of the hunchback and smelt the tobacco-laden breath of the inquisitor. No longer did she think of her honor; now she was in fear of her life. She began to scream.

Out in the corridor, Judge Gaup gave a start. He burst into the courtroom with both constables.

Quite breathless, the inquisitor fretted and fumed, shouting at Gaup as if he were a small boy.

"Take this viper to the cells straightaway. Give her the black hole, and no food. And on no account let her have any contact with the Sattler woman!"

The constables hurled themselves on her. But she put up no resistance, for she no longer had any strength. They led her away like a lamb.

Meanwhile Master Boblig of Edelstadt pulled himself together, explaining to Gaup that cases like this, when a young and beautiful girl was possessed by the Devil, were the toughest of all.

The hunchback, clutching his bruised face, fervently agreed.

The district judge looked from one to the other. He had his own ideas, but he kept them to himself.

✦ ✦ ✦

Dean Lautner stopped by at the Sattlers on his way home, to find Kaspar sitting in the living room with his back to the tiled stove, his head in his hands. He did not even look up when his guest walked in.

Liesel stood crying by the window. When she caught sight of the dean, she went to him and handed him the keys of the deanery.

Lautner did not understand.

"What in the Lord's name has happened?"

Only now did the master dyer lift his head.

"Gaup and two constables took Susanne away."

"My God! Susanne!"

The dean clutched at his heart. At the last moment Liesel pushed a chair beneath him to break his fall.

27 ✦ *Next in Line*

Lautner had not left his bed for two days. The town surgeon, Doctor Mauer, had hurried to the deanery, lanced a vein in the dean's left shoulder, and let a full pint of blood to alleviate his heart. Since then he had lain almost motionless, his eyes closed. Dorothea, Kaspar Hutter's wife, had kept house for him. She was a good woman and not too talkative, and she let no one near him.

Only at the end of the second day did the dean open his eyes, gazing about the room as if not recognizing it. Dorothea immediately went to his bedside, placed her hand on his forehead, and gave him a kind smile.

"Are you feeling better?"

But the dean had no thoughts for his own health. Now, just as throughout the two preceding days, he was remembering Susanne. His reply was quite different from what Dorothea expected.

"What do you think, Dorothea? Is it at all possible that Susanne was in league with the Devil?"

Dorothea laughed.

"That could only be said by a dimwit, a dunderhead who doesn't know his left from his right. Don't even think about such things, Father. It's madness!"

"Madness," repeated Lautner. "It certainly *is* madness, but how, Dorothea, do you explain that so many people, many of them with doctors' titles even, believe in this madness? I'm not thinking of Master Boblig of Edelstadt—he's made a lucrative living out of superstition—but of those who make the decisions at the Prague Court of Appeals, at the imperial court in Vienna, at the Consistory, at the provincial tribunal, at the universities, Catholic or Lutheran . . ."

"Kaspar says the Devil's just an invention of the gentry to help them keep the common folk under control."

Lautner shook his head feebly.

"If it were only so simple, dear Dorothea! It is true that many recent rulers have used the struggle against necromancy above all to control their subjects—but belief in witches is far, far more ancient. The Greek philosopher Plato spoke of witches, and others before him. Demons are mentioned in many places in the Bible. A woman was executed as a witch in Europe at the beginning of the twelfth century . . ."

"That's because people have always been foolish. That's what Kaspar says. But don't you pay it a thought, Father. Rather you tell me what you'd like me to cook for you."

But the dean had no thoughts of food.

"Perhaps it's because people would rather serve evil than good. And the Devil is only the embodiment of evil!"

"And you should rather be silent than talk in this way, Father. The surgeon ordered strict rest!"

Lautner fell silent for a while, then sighed loudly.

"Poor Susanne! How could they say she was a servant of Satan?"

The dean's head sank into the pillow, and his sinewy hand thrust away the heavy eiderdown to reveal his heaving breast.

Dorothea sat next to the bed and grasped his hand.

"Please, Father, try not to think of her . . ."

"Why didn't Boblig rather arrest an old man like me? Why did he take her, young and fresh, her whole life still ahead of her?"

"Perhaps he wanted to kill two birds with one stone. Susanne, and you, too. Don't let him get what he wanted, Father! Anyway, Susanne isn't lost yet. Kaspar will see to that!"

"Kaspar," the dean smiled faintly. "I know he's not short of courage. But what can he do against the baseness of humanity? Lest he too fall into the spider's web!"

"Don't you worry about Kaspar, the main thing is for you to get better!"

Neither Dorothea Hutter nor Mauer the surgeon told the dean of the commotion caused by his housekeeper's arrest. He had no inkling, therefore, of the tumult, which was perhaps even greater than that caused by Gaup's earlier arrest of Marie Sattler. But this time it was different.

If Susanne had been only an ordinary priest's cook, no one would have paid much heed. Priests' cooks generally stood only a smidgen higher than common servant girls on the social ladder and never enjoyed a high reputation. But Susanne was one of the most beautiful girls of Schönberg, and the very reverend dean had always accorded her respect, treating her as his own daughter or granddaughter. Her arrest had to cast a dark shadow on him also, for he was surely involved in everything she did. If Susanne Voglick were guilty, he had to be guilty, too, for instead of thwarting her schemes, he must have turned a blind eye to them. Did this not prove that one must never trust the wiles of a woman? And were we not all mere flesh and blood?

Gossip spreads fast, like a lighted splint cast into a heap of pea straw, besmirching even the most innocent. Poor Susanne was unable to defend herself; and the dean, confined to his bed, was unaware of the slanderous rumors. Only the courageous Kaspar Hutter, who had known Susanne since her childhood, had the awareness and the resolve to stand up for her—and before the whole of Schönberg, if need be.

First of all, however, he had to find out why the inquisitorial tribunal had thrown her into jail. The most straightforward approach would have been to ask Master Boblig of Edelstadt, except that this would have been like asking a wolf why he had savaged a sheep. So Hutter set out to see another member of the tribunal— Sebastian Flade, clerk to the district court.

Flade was one of those people who have no enemies. Not because he was an especially pious and honest man, but because he never publicly opposed anyone. On the contrary, he sought to be on good terms with everyone, whoever they were, according them far more respect than he ever took away. So long as Kaspar Hutter was in the service of Prince Liechtenstein, Flade bowed deeply before him, and in all of Schönberg there was no more respectful man; when Hutter was removed from office, the clerk's respect did not disappear but merely cooled by a few degrees. Who was to know, after all, whether Master Hutter would not soon occupy another influential position?

When the former district judge appeared before him, Sebastian Flade knew just what to say.

"So the dean is still gravely ill," he said, a martyrlike expression on his face. "We missed him again at church this morning. It's such a pity he couldn't celebrate Holy Mass for us. We had to make do with silent prayer. Of course we all prayed for his health."

Hutter saw through to the very bowels of this sanctimonious little man. But he maintained a solemn tone.

"You surely know, Master Flade, what led to his condition? The arrest of his housekeeper at the orders of the inquisitorial tribunal. You are a member of the tribunal, and the reason for my visit is to ask you why she was imprisoned. If you will be so kind and tell me, I am sure the dean will soon regain his health and will be able to celebrate Mass again."

The clerk's expression now was as if someone had squeezed a lemon in front of his face.

"I, too, have heard about the arrest of the cook from the deanery, and I must say it caused me some surprise. I always regarded her as a decent and respectable girl."

"Master Flade, you are not replying to my question. I am asking you why she was imprisoned. Weren't you, and aren't you still, a member of the inquisitorial tribunal?"

Flade had to show his true colors, and that was always a difficult thing for him to do. He forced a reply.

"I'm a sort of superfluous member. Do you know how I found out about Susanne Voglick's arrest? From my own wife! My dear friend, the inquisitorial tribunal hasn't actually met yet, because so far it has had no case to judge. Master Boblig of Edelstadt has made certain arrests, and Master Gaup has been assisting him. There is nothing more I can tell you."

This was exactly what Hutter had expected, for he knew something of the work of inquisitorial judges. But he sensed a note of dissatisfaction in Flade's tone.

"I would refer you to Master Boblig of Edelstadt or to Master Gaup," the clerk continued in a kindly voice.

"Thank you for your excellent advice." Hutter smiled and left. But he did not go to see Boblig, of course, or even Gaup. Instead he went to visit Heinrich Peschek. The clothmaker would surely help. He was a man of experience, judicious, yet fearless.

Besides, he was also a councillor, though he only intervened in community affairs when it was really necessary, for there was nothing he despised so much as idle prattle about stupidities and trivialities. His main concern was to devote himself to his trade. His merchandise, be it linen or tripp, enjoyed a fine reputation, and merchants came from far and wide to do business with him.

Peschek was not at home. His wife, Marie Sattler's sister, was very upset by Susanne's arrest and would have welcomed the chance to talk about it, but the former district judge had no time to waste. He hurried to Nollbeck's, where, Mistress Peschek had told him, he would find Heinrich with the Viennese cloth merchant, Jakob Langweil.

The inn was a hive of activity. Although it was a weekday, the workshops were empty and the drinking places were full to overflowing. And in every tavern, including Nollbeck's, there was only one topic of conversation—the young cook from the deanery and the dean himself.

Heinrich Peschek was sitting with his business partner from Vienna. Kaspar joined them at their table and soon found the remarkably young Langweil to be an agreeable character. He was a witty man, and despite his youth he appeared to have considerable experience and worldly wisdom.

At the neighboring table was a company of carousers headed by the furrier, Thomas Gröger. He was already the worse for wear and appeared to be staring at them, looking for an excuse to start an argument.

Gröger was a fool and was fond of showing it. He was also a

confirmed enemy of the former district judge, ever since his acquittal of the superstitious countrywomen on charges of witchcraft. It was Gröger who had incited half the town against Hutter and had most contributed to his removal from office.

Langweil could not help overhearing the talk of the cook from the deanery and asked what it was all about. When Peschek briefly told him, he shook his head.

"Anyone would think this place has been asleep for a whole century! If this were the year 1600 I wouldn't be surprised—but nowadays?"

Hutter leaned over to him.

"Just look at that pockmarked ignoramus at the next table. The one that looks like a bull with its horns drawn. If he were given the chance, he'd have all the fools of the town stone that poor girl to death!"

"There are fools everywhere, sometimes even in the highest positions. It's up to you as cleverer folk to get the better of them!"

"But how?"

"By ridiculing them, showing them as the fools they are!"

Gröger rose unsteadily to his feet, staggered over to their table, bent down so that his face almost touched Hutter's, and in a slurred voice began making a speech.

"So what do you say about that cook from the deanery, Kaspar? You're a bit quiet! If you had your way, you'd set her free, wouldn't you, and maybe even kiss her little hand. What I say is, it's a good thing it's Master Boblig of Edelstadt who's judging her. Boblig! You know who he is? He's a smart fellow, not a godless character like you, who doesn't believe in the Devil. But there is a Devil, and that Devil, my boy, is a beast. As an old judge and a friend of the dean's you surely know that Lucifer and his angel friends weren't satisfied with what the good Lord had given them. They wanted more and more, higher and higher, like Master Gaup. They wanted to be even higher than the stars in heaven. They wanted a place next to the Lord Himself and to be His equal in all things. That's why the Lord cast the Devil out. And that's why the beast now takes his revenge wherever he can and seeks out disciples all over the world. You, Kaspar, you're godless, you don't believe any of it, but let me tell you, if you were touched by the Holy Spirit, you'd see, even with your eyes closed, that there's thousands and thousands of them. And mostly women. Perhaps your eyes are going to be opened now by that little cook from the deanery. From the deanery! Even into that holy place, where the light of the Lord is supposed to shine, did the Devil find his way! You often visit the deanery. Did you ever see anybody there with horns on his head? Didn't you ever play cards with him? I hear the dean's taken sick from it. But what else could he expect, warming such a viper on his own breast . . ."

Kaspar Hutter fought to overcome his fury, to stop himself from making a rash move that he would later regret. Heinrich Peschek had also heard enough.

"Go and sit down at your own table, Thomas, and don't pester us any more," he said gently. "You don't know what you're saying. The best thing you can do is go home!"

But Gröger appeared to take no notice. He stared vacantly for a while, then dumped himself like a sack of corn on the empty chair next to Jakob Langweil. And only now did he get a good look at Peschek's visitor.

"And who are you? I don't know you."

The curly-haired merchant with the long black beard raised his eyebrows, turned up his nose, and bared his teeth.

"Don't you know me?" he said in a deep bass voice. "I am Satanas Urias, flown from the furnace of hell, blown from a fiery volcano, and come straight to Schönberg, to this inn, to see what you are about. I have listened to your blathering, and I have heard enough. Abracadabraca. Are you Thomas Gröger, ignoramus?"

The furrier was dumbstruck. And even his drink-sodden companions fell silent, for all had heard the stranger's words.

"It appears you do not believe me, Thomas Gröger," continued Langweil. "So look under the table, and see my hooves. Or touch my head, and feel the horns under my hair. Or better still, touch my behind, and you'll find the coil of my tail. Why are you sitting there like a bag of bran? You look as if you've swallowed a tomcat, fur and all!"

The merchant spoke very loudly. All the people in the inn were now listening to this stranger and were already sensing some kind of fun. Gröger, meanwhile, swallowed hard, afraid to make a move.

"You still don't believe me? Don't you smell the stink of brimstone? Smell my hands!"

"No!" the furrier gasped at last.

"But I must say there is a strong smell here!" came the voice of Simon the shoemaker from the window seat. "Isn't something sticking Thomas to his seat?"

Only now did Thomas Gröger begin to emerge from his drunken stupor, to see it was all only a joke. The whole inn was shaking with laughter at his expense. He rushed out without even paying his bill.

After a while, Jakob Langweil decided to go to his room at the inn.

"That's the way to treat such fools," he remarked as he said good-bye.

Outside on the street, Heinrich Peschek and Kaspar Hutter could now talk.

Kaspar wanted Heinrich, as a councillor, to support his idea that a deputation of eminent citizens be dispatched to Prince Liechtenstein's castle at Eisgrub in South Moravia, and perhaps also to the emperor. But the prudent clothmaker did not agree.

"My dear Kaspar," he said, "the prince and Master Boblig are both whistling the same tune. If it were a case involving someone who mattered to the prince, your idea might be a good one, but Susanne is a common priest's cook as far as he is concerned. She's far too small a fry for such a great man. The prince's court would see this only as an excuse to grind us down even more. Remember, they instituted this tribunal as a means to tap the wealth of Schönberg. We'll have to wait."

"You're forgetting Marie Sattler. How long has she been in jail?"

Peschek frowned.

"That's a sad business, but what do we know of her so far? All we know is that Boblig has had her locked up and that he's investigating her. The good news is that so far she hasn't been tortured. That's not enough to warrant our sending a deputation."

Hutter was angered by this display of passivity.

"So are we to wait until Boblig arrests you? Or Kaspar Sattler? Or me?"

"There's nothing else we can do for the time being."

The friends parted coldly.

Kaspar Hutter hurried to the deanery to pick up his wife and pay his respects to his friend Christoph.

Heinrich Peschek made his own way home, all thoughts of Hutter, Susanne, and even Marie Sattler now put firmly behind him. Now his head was full of the good business he had done with the Viennese merchant, Jakob Langweil.

✦ ✦ ✦

It was gone midnight, and the whole town was asleep. The constables left the town hall and went straight to the Sattlers' house to arrest the master dyer and his younger daughter, Liesel.

This time they searched every corner of the house, opening every door and drawer. Many valuable things disappeared during their search, and all that they found was a small wooden box, full of a foul-smelling black ointment.

The talk of the town later was that this was magic ointment, containing quicksilver, old boar's fat, dry-rotted wood, pulverized dried frog, and the sacred host from the church altar. The dye master's wife, and even the dye master himself, had anointed themselves with it to render themselves invisible when they flew to the witch-swarms.

28 ✦ *A Fateful Word*

The countryside was resonant with the twittering of starlings and the warbling of blackbird, thrush, and lark, and the chatter of woodpeckers from the forest. But the joyful chorus was soon disturbed by the bellowing of bailiffs and magistrates, routing out the weary peasants and cottagers to work. The long winter had weakened their limbs, and their bellies were sunken; luckily the sun shone for them as they bent their backs in hated feudal labor on the lords' lands. But they were still hungry, for the gentry gave them nothing to eat for their toil, even though their larders at home were scavenged bare.

Kaspar Hutter, the former district judge, was also downcast as he walked the streets of Schönberg. All in vain had he attempted to persuade several of his bolder neighbors to join a deputation to Prince Liechtenstein or at least to the members of the provincial council in Olomouc, who had always helped the people of Schönberg when they were in trouble. Following Kaspar Sattler's arrest, no one dared draw the unwelcome attention of Master Boblig of Edelstadt. On the contrary, they now vied with one another in their shows of respect for the inquisitor, hailing their greetings and bowing deeply to him, and only the most courageous gave him a wide berth. There were even those who insinuated themselves into his favor, and yet others who at least tried to get on the good side of his assistant and were pleased when they could pay for his drinks.

The cautious clothmaker, Heinrich Peschek, now relinquished his proverbial equanimity. Originally he had wanted to wait until Boblig dared lay his hands on some eminent member of the citizenry, but now that his brother-in-law was in jail he was at his wit's end, unsure whether to undertake something with Kaspar

Hutter or do something on his own. Only the rebellious shoe-maker Simon was bold enough to drop the occasional poisonous comment at the expense of the inquisitorial tribunal or the town councillors; but on hearing such remarks, even his friends distanced themselves from him as fast as they could, keeping a watchful eye on all sides as they did. Sometimes fear is a greater contagion than the Plague.

Kaspar Hutter was not the kind of character who would simply fold his hands in his lap. Without discussing his plans with anyone, he set off alone to Olomouc to see the renowned advocate Maixner.

The advocate heard him out most attentively, agreed with everything Hutter told him, but in the end, like Peschek, recommended that nothing should be done that might be construed as opposition to Prince Liechtenstein. Maixner knew very well that it was the prince's will that had placed Boblig so firmly in the saddle. And he knew also that the inquisitor had many friends close to the Bishop of Olomouc. He hesitated, therefore, to undertake any action at all. Instead, he turned the conversation to other pressing matters—news of which had so far not reached the remote community of Schönberg. Thököly was leading a new rebellion against the Austrian crown in the northern Hungarian territories, and shipments of military materiel were being rushed to Austrian strongholds there. Meanwhile, the perfidious Turks were said to be massing enormous new concentrations of troops on the northern frontiers of their empire. A new and ferocious war was looming. Why else would even the bishop be concerned about strengthening the castle defenses at Mürau?

Hutter, more contrite than ever before, told Dean Lautner on his return how he had fared. The dean gave a bitter smile and replied with a quotation:

"*Anima esuriens etiam amarum pro dulci sumet.* Even the bitter comes as sweetness to the hungry soul!"

How Christoph Lautner had changed! It was as if he were waiting for a miracle, though he knew that the days of miracles were long gone.

✦ ✦ ✦

The fifth day of April brought another witch-burning at Gross Ullersdorf. The executions followed the same course as those of August the year before. Five stakes were driven into the centers of five pyres of dry wood, but only four condemned witches were tied to them—Marie Petrova, the jolly wife of the estates manager at Johrnsdorf; old Agneta Kopp of Gross Ullersdorf; Anna Föbel, the sister of Dorothea David of Wermsdorf, who had died after torture, her back allegedly broken by the Devil himself to prevent her testifying; and finally Barbora Kühnel, the former priest's cook at Gross Ullersdorf. The condemned Susanne Stubenvoll, wife of the castle cellarman at Gross Ullersdorf, was granted special mercy; before her body was consigned to the flames, Master Jokl cut off her head with one blow.

This time the Court of Appeals in Prague was not represented by Secretary Weingarten, but by Dr. David Wenzel Mirabel of Freiberg, Counselor of Appeals, who was even fatter and more gluttonous than his predecessor. The overrighteous Schmidt, parish priest at Zöptau, also attended, and at the last moment Canon Peter Rehramont, Master of Ceremonies of the Bishop of Olomouc, announced his arrival. Father König, parish priest at Gross Ullersdorf, was not invited, and neither was the Dean of Schönberg. The old Countess of Galle again apologized for her nonattendance through illness, but at the same time she did not allow her two nephews to take part in the dreadful theater. As before, she was represented by the castle sheriff, Master Vinarsky of Kreuz.

After the execution, the gentry repaired to the castle, where a lavish banquet was ready for them. But the mood was not as exuberant as the last time. Especially Master Boblig of Edelstadt was not at all satisfied. The only guests of honor to show up had been Canon Rehramont and the Prague Counselor of Appeals; all the others, and a score of invitations had been sent out, had sent apologies. But that was not all. Neither Dr. Mirabel nor Canon Rehramont had deemed it appropriate to stand up at the beginning of the banquet and pay tribute to the great works of the inquisitor.

Boblig ate little but drank a lot. And at the end of the evening, when the heedful Ignatius stowed him in his carriage for the long journey back to Schönberg, he took a whole flask of fiery Hungarian wine with him.

It was almost midnight when they reached the town. To the hunchback's greatest surprise the inquisitor did not have himself driven to their apartment but to the town hall. Pursued by his assistant, he staggered inside and ordered the startled guards to bring Marie Sattler into the courtroom without delay.

Before they brought her in, Boblig sprawled onto a chair and waited while Ignatius foraged for a glass. His eyes were bleary and he reeked like a wine barrel.

When the dye master's wife appeared, all reduced to skin and bone, he eyed her mockingly.

"You Devil's baggage! I've come to ask you whether you'd like to see your hardheaded husband?"

A spark appeared in her terror-stricken eyes.

"See, woman, I'm not so bad, am I?"

"Sir!"

"There's just one thing, however, I'd ask of you. You must tell your husband to his face what you said to the court!"

Marie Sattler had long lost all her self-will, and fear of torture had made her a submissive instrument in Boblig's hands. Now at last she had the chance to meet her husband.

"I'll tell everything . . ."

Boblig ordered the master dyer to be brought in.

After a while, the jailer pushed him into the room. He was stooped, thin, and morose. When the jailer had awakened him, he knew that an interrogation awaited him, and perhaps even torture. So far he had confessed to nothing, but imprisonment, hunger, cross-examinations, and fear of torture had considerably weakened his resistance. Now he was standing, staring, just three paces away from the terrible inquisitor. He did not even notice his own wife.

"Master Sattler, I am giving you your last chance," the inquisitor began. "We have counted your fortune. Mark my words, you will lose it to the last penny, and your head besides, if you do not confess. I want you to understand: we don't really need your confession at all. Just two concurrent sworn testimonies are all we need, and we already have at least a dozen, among them one from your own wife. No; what is at stake now is the redemption of your soul. Besides, we would not like from *confessionem delicti* to proceed *ad gradus torturae*, when you are, after all, a former Lord Mayor of Schönberg. You still have a chance to save not only your soul but also your personal fortune, or at least a substantial part of it for your children. And all you have to do is confirm what the others have said against Dean Lautner."

Kaspar Sattler's strength was ebbing away. He had expected no mercy, yet now he was being offered an opportunity to save at least his property for his sons. But could the villain Boblig be believed?

The inquisitor seemed to be in no hurry for an answer. He motioned Marie to step forward. Now Kaspar saw her and was not sure if it was his wife. Until he heard her voice.

"My Kaspar!"

Yes, it was her, but God, what had they done to her! His heart gave a leap, and tears welled in his eyes. He raised his hands to embrace her, but the jangling shackles restrained him, and the jailer quickly pushed him back.

It was a moving scene even for the drunken Boblig. He needed to bolster his courage with brutality.

"Come on, you old bawd, tell him the truth to his face!"

The master dyer was staggered to hear such vulgarity, but his wife had already become accustomed to worse names. She stood eye to eye with Kaspar and began to recite what they had taught her. She spoke as if from delirium, her eyes flaming like two burning coals, confessing to things that Kaspar knew with utter certainty she could never have done. She spoke of nighttime flights to the Petersstein, and of dancing and frolicking there; she admitted to fornication with other men and said that their house had often been a place of witch revels, where Lucifer himself was represented by Dean Lautner. And shamelessly she told how she herself had let Lautner have his way with her and how she had taken even Liesel to him, and how even her husband Kaspar had fornicated with Susanne the cook, and even with his own daughter, Liesel.

It occurred to Sattler that his wife must have lost her mind in jail. Or had he himself gone mad?

"What are you saying, Marie?" he said in a trembling voice.

But his wife seemed not to have heard.

"The greatest villain is the dean," she went on. "He dresses in priestly robes, but he only does it to avoid suspicion. Kaspar, tell the judge the truth that he wants to hear. You have to, otherwise you'll lose your life, and so will our Liesel. And they'll take all your money . . ."

She could not be in her right mind, the master dyer thought to himself. He spoke to her as if she were a child.

"Marie, you know you're not speaking the truth!"

She gave a start, stared vacantly, and then burst into uncontrolled weeping. Boblig decided to intervene. He rose and staggered toward Sattler.

"I repeat, Sattler, this is your last chance. I want to hear nothing from you but one word. Either yes, or no. Is Dean Lautner a disciple of the Devil?"

Sattler gritted his teeth and said nothing.

"Yes, or no?"

Still he did not reply.

Marie cried out in desperation.

"Speak, Kaspar, for God's sake, speak! Save Liesel! And save something for our sons!"

The master dyer stared from the judge to his wife, realizing in horror that one way or the other he had already lost his life. No one could save him now, not when even his own wife had turned against him. But if he were to give false testimony, he might avoid further torment. And perhaps also some of his property would remain for his children. If only he could believe this demon!"

"Kaspar!" his wife implored him.

At last the fateful word escaped his lips.

"Yes."

Boblig looked to Ignatius with a smile.

"Take this down!"

The hunchback rose to the writing desk and took up a sharpened quill.

29 ✦ *Signum Diabolicum*

There were times when the inquisitor could not endure solitude, and others when he found even his best friends repugnant. Then he closeted himself with Ignatius and drank; and when his belly refused more wine, he became maudlin, his eyes glistened, he began to remember and yearned for the old days.

Now was just such a time.

That evening, Boblig unceremoniously ejected Judge Gaup, made sure the musketeer Barta was at his post outside the door, turned the key twice in the lock, and ordered:

"Wine, Ignatius, a sea of wine!"

Outside, the evening was warm, as before a storm, and the sky was like the vault of a crypt; but inside the inquisitor's apartment the air was stale, for all the windows were shuttered. A heavy candelabrum, evidently meant for a church, stood on the table, and in it, burning with a smoky flame, was a thick church candle.

Boblig drank in silence for some time. Eventually he turned to his assistant.

"Iggy, do you know what I'm thinking?"

The hunchback did not.

"I'll tell you. It's a long time ago now, maybe thirty years. A Gypsy woman read my palm. She said I'd have a long life but unhappiness in love. Fiddle faddle, who'd believe a Gypsy woman anyway? But she told me something else as well. Whenever I was in dire straits, I was to turn my face to the north. Then I'd see who my friends were. They'd be standing to my right, while my enemies would be on the left. It's nonsense, I know, and I forgot it long ago. But last night I had a strange dream that reminded me of that Gypsy woman. I dreamed I really was standing with my face to the north, and on my left stretched a long line of people,

264

all colored a grim brown. And on my right also stood a great crowd, mostly women, all cast in a clear emerald green light . . ."

"And were they beautiful, these women?"

"Some were, and some were plain. I recognized some of them as women I'd condemned to the stake."

"Nice friends," chuckled Ignatius. "The Gypsy lied!"

"Don't laugh, Iggy. My flesh still creeps when I remember that dream."

"Perhaps it's time we went back to Olomouc and you became an honest advocate again. It looks as if your conscience is beginning to speak out."

Boblig glared at the hunchback, quaffed a full glass of wine, then pounded his fist on the table.

"Oh no! There's work to be finished here! Think of all our reports to Prince Liechtenstein and to the Bishop of Olomouc and the Prague Court of Appeals, and still we don't have our hands on the sorcerer priest. Maybe he's up to something and we don't know it. Or maybe the authorities are just slow. I'd love to know, Iggy!"

"Perhaps," suggested his assistant, "they don't believe our witnesses."

"That's not possible! Are you saying they wouldn't believe Sattler?"

"Do you know whose testimony would get the bishop moving?

"Whose?" Boblig snorted.

"The cook's!"

"Susanne Voglick? But all she says is: I don't know, and that's not true!"

"Because we're too gentle with her."

"Gentle. You're right, Iggy. But I still can't bring myself to have her put to torture. When I see her I always remember the wife of a certain member of Saint Luke's Guild of Artists, who used her as a model for his Madonnas. I've told you about her . . ."

"And yet we'll have to squeeze her eventually!"

"I know, Iggy. If only she were an ugly hag, I wouldn't hesitate for a minute. I don't give a fig for old crones. But beauty unnerves me. When I behold beauty, I'm as soft as clay. Top up my glass, Iggy. I know it has to be, but *ultra posse nemo tenetur*, no one is obliged to do more than he is able . . . Do you understand, Iggy?"

"But Susanne isn't an artist's wife, she's a priest's cook!"

"So be it, then! Pour me another, Iggy!"

But this was one glass Master Boblig of Edelstadt did not finish. Dribbling the wine as he did, he laid his head on the table and fell asleep.

✦ ✦ ✦

The inquisitorial tribunal was convened in Schönberg the very next day. The members took their places at the table in the court-room: Beck, the Lord Mayor; Gaup, the district judge, proud as a pigeon; Sebastian Flade, the clerk, a pained look on his face as if he were suffering from toothache; and Master Boblig of Edelstadt, ashen faced, bleary-eyed, and with a voice like a cracked pot.

The inquisitor ordered wine to be brought in. The others raised their glasses with him out of courtesy; but this was early morning and they had no taste for wine.

Boblig first advised his associate judges of their responsibilities, stressing especially that everything they were about to hear and see was to remain a strict secret. Then he announced that Susanne Voglick, the cook from the deanery, was to be interrogated, and added straightaway that her case was especially grave.

"You all know her. She is young and very comely, and it could be assumed that she would regret her actions and facilitate the work of the investigator by confessing. But even though we interrogated her several times, she has remained obdurate and continues to give negative replies. Quite evidently, she is under the influence of the Devil, who holds her in his power. Such obduracy is known as *malitia taciturnitatis*. It rarely happens to young and beautiful women before inquisitorial courts, though many years ago there was a similar case in the town of Wasungen. That was a young and beautiful witch who refused to confess, even when she was put on the rack. Between tortures, she was warned she would be stretched a second time on the rack if she didn't volunteer a confession. She didn't even reply. So the executioner went ahead. As he did, she finally opened her mouth and mumbled something quite unintelligible. So, thinking she wanted to speak at last, the judge had her taken down, but she lost consciousness as soon as they untied her. The executioner began to wash her down with wine, but he found she'd expired. The Devil had silenced her by breaking her back."

The other judges stared in horror; no one among them wanted to witness the Devil breaking the back of Susanne Voglick. As soon as the Devil was mentioned, Sebastian Flade made a large sign of the cross.

"Do you think, Master Boblig," asked Judge Gaup, "it will be necessary to put our own prisoner on the rack?"

Boblig shrugged his shoulders.

"That depends on her. And yet more so on the Evil Spirit who has her in his power!"

In the absence of any more questions, Boblig directed that Susanne Voglick be brought before the court.

Jokl led her in, and the judges held their breath. Even the inquisitor, his eyes glistening, licked his lips. Tall and slender, with her long hair tied in a bun, she had become even more beautiful in jail; her skin was now finer and her eyes had acquired a peculiar gleam. Barefoot under her coarse black shift, she walked with silent strides as if gliding above the ground. Now she stood before the tribunal and stared at her judges, all of whom she knew well. Longest of all she stared at Master Gaup, until he could endure it no longer and lowered his eyes.

Boblig turned to Ignatius to see whether he was ready to write everything down. Then, in the name of God the Father, the Son, and the Holy Spirit, he began his examination. First of all he asked Susanne her name, age, status, and whether she attended confession and holy communion.

She replied as briefly as possible, in a deep, mellow, and somewhat stifled voice.

Then the inquisitor posed the usual question. Did she, or did she not, believe in witches?

The answer rang clear.

"No!"

"But the testimony of many people proves that you often took part yourself in the gathering of witches on the Petersstein. Do you admit that, Susanne Voglick?"

"That's not true!"

"But it has been proved quite clearly by many witnesses, among them Kaspar Sattler and his wife Marie, that you used to go there with Dean Lautner!"

"Not true!"

"Also it is proved that you carried the sacred host there in your shoe!"

"No!"

Boblig glanced at the judges' table, shrugged his shoulders, and said: "*Malitia taciturnitatis.* The Devil is preventing her from speaking!"

Sebestian Flade felt sorry for her. He rose and spoke with a trembling voice.

"Susanne, I've known you since you were a little girl, and I've always been fond of you. Tell the truth. If you admit your sins and express sorrow, the Lord God will forgive you. And even the court can be merciful!"

Even Judge Gaup had his say:

"Tell the truth and ease your burden!"

Susanne had not deigned to look at the clerk, but now she fixed a silent and contemptuous stare at this shameful traitor. This was Master Gaup who had had the dean be godfather to his firstborn son; this was the man who had tricked his way into the deanery; this was the man who now wanted, by hook or by crook, to convict even the dean of witchcraft.

The inquisitor glared at his victim. It seemed to him at this moment that Susanne was even more beautiful than artist's wife whom he had remembered the day before. Beauty and the Devil! Were they not two words for the same thing? What was the use— the duty of an inquisitor was to battle with the Devil. And so the courtroom resounded with Boblig's harsh voice:

"Susanne Voglick! So far we have taken your tender age into account and we have shown patience. We hoped you would at least save your own soul by confessing. But your persistent refusal to do that has only added weight to your terrible guilt, and this compels the court to proceed to the use of torture. You have yet one more opportunity to think again, but in a moment our patience will be at an end!"

None of those present had ever heard Boblig speak so softly as this. All eyes now turned to the wretched Susanne. The gaze of the Lord Mayor seemed to speak for all the members of the tribunal: Submit and spare yourself, and us, this terrible spectacle!

"So go on, speak!" cried Flade.

Susanne finally forced herself to speak.

"I can say nothing other than what is true."

Boblig turned to the judges.

"Did you hear? She didn't say that! It was the Devil speaking with her tongue!"

But the other judges did not look as if they were in agreement. Susanne did not appear to them to be possessed by the Devil. Indeed, she reminded the pious Flade of the Bavarian martyr, Saint Afra, whose picture had hung behind the pulpit of the Dominican church before the fire. The picture had shown Saint Afra tied to a burning stake. Her face was just like Susanne Voglick's now.

The silence was broken by the inquisitor:

"Master Jokl, fetch the thumbscrew!"

The executioner brought a shapeless iron instrument from the next room, bowed deeply to the court, and finally looked at the prisoner.

"Master Jokl, do your duty!" said Boblig.

The executioner motioned to the nearest jailer, who lifted up

Susanne's hands. She, meanwhile, looked at the opposite wall, over the heads of the judges, where a black crucifix hung.

"Help me, Jesus," she whispered.

The executioner pushed her thumbs into the holes at each end of the instrument.

"I ask you for the last time, Susanne Voglick, whether you wish voluntarily to confess to your union with the Devil?"

Susanne was unable in her fear to utter a word, but only shook her head. She did not know where she found so much strength.

"Master Jokl, begin!"

Without even looking at his victim, the executioner began gradually to tighten the screw. Susanne felt a pressure on her thumbs. Once, a long time ago, she had caught her finger in the door, and it had hurt more than this. She did not look at the thumbscrew but continued to face the figure on the cross. Her heart rejoiced, for it occurred to her that He had spared her the pain.

But how she was mistaken! The executioner tightened the screw further, and both the pressure and pain increased. Now it was a hundred times worse than when she had caught her finger in the door. Her face contorted with the agony and she foamed at the mouth.

The inquisitor ordered the executioner to pause.

"Do you wish to confess, Susanne?"

She looked at Boblig, and as she did, she glimpsed the gaping face of Master Gaup and was seized with rage against her torturers.

"No!"

"Master Jokl, another turn of the screw, if you please!"

The executioner was willing, but his instrument was not made for such tiny fingers. Blood dripped steadily from Susanne's crushed thumbs, but the screw could not tighten the irons enough to smash them to a pulp.

Even so, the pain was dreadful. Susanne gritted her teeth and howled. She no longer looked at the figure on the cross. Even He would not help her. Her eyes were closed.

"Do you wish to make a confession, Susanne Voglick?" she heard. Boblig's voice seemed to be a long way off.

"No!"

The inquisitor ordered Jokl to stop.

"She's innocent! She withstood the torture!" This time it was the relieved voice of Beck, the Lord Mayor.

"She passed the test," agreed Flade, the clerk.

Boblig gave them both a look of disdain.

"Not at all. Her gallant is standing beside her, willing her body to feel no pain."

"And who is her gallant?" asked Gaup.

"Have patience, and she'll tell us herself," said the inquisitor, smiling. And turning to the executioner, he ordered him to bring in the Spanish boots.

Susanne watched the blood dripping from her thumbs. She had felt a surge of relief as the thumbscrew was removed; perhaps she did not hear what new torture the inquisitor had ordered.

Jokl carried in another, bulkier instrument of torture, while his assistant brought in a sturdy chair on which Susanne was forced to sit. The assistant pulled up her shift to reveal her slender legs. Then, while his assistant and one of the jailers held her down, the executioner clapped her feet into the iron form and drew it shut.

An immediate and dreadful shriek burst from Susanne's breast. Sharp iron protuberances inside the form were piercing her calves and shins, and a terrible pain was permeating her whole body. She screamed like a wounded animal, and her body coursed with sweat, but the executioner did not stop. On the contrary, he went on tightening the form.

This was the moment the inquisitor had been waiting for. "Do you wish the executioner to stop the torture?" he whispered gently.

Without thought, she nodded. Anything to escape the pain!

The executioner loosened the screw, and the pain eased.

"Will you make a confession?"

"Yes."

She no longer had the strength to resist. Christ on the cross had not helped. No one would help her.

Master Jokl quickly opened the iron form.

"Be it known to you, Susanne Voglick, that there is yet a third degree of torture, the most severe. If you do not confess now, you will be put on the rack. So speak! Were you in league with the Devil?"

Her crushed thumbs hurt with a gnawing pain, and her injured shinbones and torn calves burned as if someone were touching them with a hot iron. And Susanne had heard that the rack was yet worse! O God! If only at least she could have something to slake her thirst!

Ignatius, his mouth open, his tongue resting on his lip, was not writing but staring intently, watching her every move. He knew what she needed and offered her his glass of wine. She seized it ravenously, drank it in one draft and then drank another. She felt a droning in her ears, her head spun, but at least the pain eased, and that was the main thing. Only indistinctly did she hear the inquisitor's next question.

"Susanne Voglick, who was your gallant? Lautner, Dean of Schönberg?"

"Yes."

Even if she had been asked whether she had killed her own mother, she would have made the same reply.

"Did you enjoin him in sinful and carnal union?"

"Yes."

Susanne's strength was absolutely exhausted. The wine had sapped her senses and her will. Nothing mattered any more . . .

For a whole hour, Boblig plied her with questions, and she replied to all of them.

The gentlemen at the table listened in astonishment to Susanne's testimony. Though everything defied belief, they believed it all the same, for they were hearing it with their own ears: yes, yes, yes . . .

Once the interrogation was over, there was nothing to prevent Boblig from sending Susanne back to her cell, but at the last moment it struck him that here was yet another chance to astound the tribunal, besides satisfying his own curiosity. The day before, his head had been full of memories of the artist's wife. Now he could see for himself which of them was more beautiful. He turned to his associates.

"The confession of the accused is surely sufficient. But we would be incautious if we were not to consider one other piece of evidence—something that inquisitorial courts generally consider first of all: whether the accused has on her body the *signum diabolicum.*"

Master Jokl knew, as he lifted Susanne from her chair, what he was to do. No sooner was she on her feet than his practiced hand tore off her black gown. Suddenly the gloom was pierced by the dazzling sight of a naked and extraordinarily beautiful body. The members of the tribunal caught their breath, and even Flade, the pious clerk, suddenly saw not Afra the martyr but Eve amid the Garden of Eden.

Ignatius sprang up from his papers; searching for the Devil's mark was his specialty.

Dulled by the pain and the wine, Susanne stood rooted to the spot like a Greek statue of marble or alabaster. She trembled but did not cry out and did not even defend herself but gazed with glistening eyes at her still bleeding crushed thumbs and legs.

The hunchback was already touching her body. This time it did not enrage her, and Ignatius was not afraid she would hit him.

"Seek, Ignatius, seek!" cried Master Boblig of Edelstadt, standing on tiptoe. "You know where young witches most often bear the Devil's mark!"

And the hunchback sought. He traced his trembling fingers across Susanne's body, his head bent ever closer, until he was almost touching her skin with the tip of his nose. Now the gentlemen at the judges' table were excited, and they, too, were rising to their feet in order not to miss anything.

"Ah, here it is!" the hunchback cried at last. "The *signum diabolicum!* On the inside of her left thigh!"

Master Boblig motioned the judges to go and see for themselves. They gladly obeyed; even the pious clerk, who was in such a rush that he almost knocked over Susanne's chair.

"Do you see it?" Ignatius asked. "It's a wart, the size of a pea."

Yes, they all saw it, though they were looking elsewhere.

Susanne's eyes were closed. Still she made no effort to cover herself or cry out.

"If this truly is the *signum diabolicum*," Boblig explained, "then no blood will flow from it, even if we prick it!"

The executioner pulled a long needle from his pocket, took the wart skillfully between the fingers of his left hand, and with his right hand he pricked the needle into the Devil's mark. And— wonder of wonders!—not one drop of blood spurted from it!

"A proof more convincing than any confession!" stated the inquisitor dryly.

The members of the tribunal could do nothing but agree; they did not know that the upper part of the needle was hollow and that the blunt point retracted into it on contact with the wart. They returned to their table in high excitement.

Susanne suddenly emerged from her unconscious state and, aware what they had done to her, began to scream:

"It's a lie! A lie! It's all a lie!"

Humiliated by her own nakedness, she loosened the knot of her luxuriant hair, shook her head, and at least partly covered her breasts with her long black tresses.

"Take her away, Jokl, and give her something to eat!" Boblig ordered.

The executioner threw her the shreds of her clothes, and he and the jailer carried her, rather than led her, outside. Now, for the first time, Susanne Voglick, a proven witch, was weeping.

Inside the courtroom, all was quiet for some time. Eventually, Master Boblig of Edelstadt helped himself to a hefty pinch of snuff and broke the silence.

"*Amice,* in all of my life I saw the Devil but twice. Once when I had to judge a certain artist's wife, and the second time was today . . ."

30 ✦ *Decision*

Karl, Count of Liechtenstein-Castelkorn and Bishop of Olomouc, was sitting by himself in the spacious study of his new residence. His face was gaunt, his dry skin an unhealthy gray, and two deep furrows ran from the root of his nose to his sagging jowls. It was a warm day outside, but his knees were covered with a fur rug. His wrinkled hands, the hands of an old man, rested on a bundle of papers that lay on the intricately carved table.

The bishop was neither reading nor writing at this moment, nor was he studying his walls full of pictures of the saints by renowned artists, or even treating himself to a look at his delightful French tapestry depicting the siege of Troy. Instead, his clouded eyes were staring into the distance. Through the window, white clouds were scudding against the azure sky. A moment before, one of them was shaped like an enormous bat with outspread wings; then a fantastic seagoing vessel had glided in from the west with a full spread of sail. And now something yet more wondrous had appeared in the heavens: a skeleton wielding a scythe. Death the Reaper.

Death!

For an instant the bishop caught his breath. Death was something he thought of very often these days. Not that he wished cravenly to surrender to it or even yearned for it come. No, he loved life. But recently he had sensed a waning of his strength. More than once he had noticed how even inspecting his pictures tired him and how sometimes he found it difficult to grasp what people were saying.

Death. The bishop knew that however people tried to hide from it or plead with it, death was inescapable, inexorable. It was senseless even to fight it. Sometimes righteous, sometimes unjust, death was uncompromising. With some it was the crowning point of a lifetime of work, others it struck down in their prime. But to him, the bishop, it had been merciful. He had been granted a long life and he had been allowed to complete the work he had resolved to do. He was grateful for that. And yet there was still so much that could be done! If only death could wait for him, at least five more years!

Bishop Liechtenstein often probed his conscience nowadays, preparing himself for the questions he would have to face when he met his Maker. Until recently he had not been afraid, but now he was not so sure.

His gaze shifted to the table and the pile of documents on it, brought in by his secretary, Elias Isidor Schmidt. Instinctively, he pushed the papers aside but immediately drew them back.

"You did not fight a good fight, Bishop of Olomouc!" he whispered to himself. "How will you reply to these charges?"

The very utterance of these words seemed to imbue his feeble body with some of its old energy. The trembling fingers took up the papers again, and the bishop applied himself once more to careful study of the long passages of underlined text. And the further he read, the more worried was his brow and the deeper were the furrows of his jowls.

The papers had been submitted by Boblig of Edelstadt, inquisitor, in the matter of the witch trials at Gross Ullersdorf, with special regard to three clergymen, above all the Dean of Schönberg, Christoph Alois Lautner, who appeared constantly in the testimonies of the accused. But they also included several pages of a denunciatory character from Brother Schmidt, parish priest at Zöptau, and an urgent request from the Prague Court of Appeals, signed by Count Nostitz, Count Lazansky, and the Lord of the Manor of Walldorf, calling for the said dean to be turned over to the inquisitorial court. The bishop read the dreadful indictment many times, but it was the last page that he found most profoundly striking. This was Boblig's detailed transcript of the testimony of Susanne Voglick, cook and housekeeper to the Dean of Schönberg.

"O God!"

How certain he had been that heresy had been eradicated from his diocese and that his merits would be acknowledged and rewarded. And now this!

The bishop's hand clenched involuntarily into a fist. Half-closing his eyes, he imagined the Dean of Schönberg, as he remembered him from his last audience. In no way did he look like an arch-heretic. He had conducted himself with assurance, without the slightest shadow of the sycophancy that usually marked those with something to hide. Lautner had appeared to be speaking the truth. He had not even denied he had a young cook, and the kindly way he had described her had carried no hint of lechery. He had not even attacked Master Boblig of Edelstadt but merely begged protection for himself and for his fellow priests, König and Pabst. True enough, some scoundrels did have honest faces, and tricksters often wore masks of the highest respectability, but Lautner had not appeared to be acting. That was why he had rather inclined to his side and encouraged him that he would always be pleased to clasp his faithful and zealous priests to his heart. In fact, he had almost embraced him there and then!

What a disappointment the dean had turned out to be! According to the most respected citizen of Schönberg and his wife, and now, even according to the testimony of the dean's cook herself, he was an apostate, a disciple of the Devil, a heretic of the most despicable sort, a liar, a hypocrite, a trickster, a far more villainous scoundrel than any who were crucified at the Savior's side. And the Bishop of Olomouc had almost clasped him to his heart!

Soon, however, the dean's honest face appeared once more before the bishop's half-closed eyes, and he began to consider matters more calmly. Perhaps, he thought, the dean could not be held entirely to blame. Perhaps it was the cook who was the originator of all the evil that had befallen him.

Could the Dean of Schönberg have resisted at all? After all, Master Boblig had written that Susanne Voglick was a young woman of exceeding beauty. Had the bishop himself, when his limbs were not yet stiffened with age, always been able to resist temptation? There had been times, he remembered, when the young priest Liechtenstein had had to fight temptation through hours of prayer, until his knees, like Saint James's, were as calloused as the skin of a camel. Would it not be Christian to send to Schönberg for Lautner, have him confess his sins, and then grant him absolution? To forgive him like the father of the Prodigal Son, who eventually returned home?

The bishop glanced at the picture that had captivated him for so long.

But was he allowed to do such a thing? Could a bishop grant forgiveness to a heretic? Was it allowed to absolve someone who was in league with the Devil? Thou shalt not suffer a witch to live, said Moses. And had not he, the Bishop of Olomouc, always fought bitterly against heresy? Was he to change his ways now? How could he explain that to his Maker?

A heretic was the worst criminal ever born to woman. No death was ignominious enough for a heretic, as the Holy Fathers had so often said. Heretics and witches were worse than the Devil himself; for the Devil, when he was once cast out of heaven, had no original innocence, whereas witches and heretics, by virtue of their holy baptism and Christ's redemption, had once been without sin. The witch, therefore, was guilty of sinning not only against the Creator but also the Redeemer! And above all that, the Dean of Schönberg had also desecrated his holy orders!

Could such a loathsome sinner be worthy of mercy? It was clear: There could be no valid mitigating circumstance. *Habeat sibi!* May he not be spared!

The bishop gave a shrill ring on his silver bell.

Secretary Schmidt came in humbly; his cunning head was bowed, and he raised it only when he stood before his superior. Not a muscle of his face moved, and yet he knew what decision had been reached.

"We have scrutinized these papers," began the bishop with some solemnity, "and long deliberated . . ."

The secretary ventured to interrupt:

"Might I point out to Your Grace that Master Boblig of Edelstadt is sitting in my room? He is prepared to inform Your Grace of yet further details."

The bishop frowned. An odd thought had struck him: Had all this been arranged by the secretary and this advocate Boblig themselves for some unknown reason? Surely not.

"No," he said curtly. "That is not necessary. I do not wish to see him."

Secretary Schmidt was furious with himself for being such a fool. How could he have forgotten? The bishop could not forgive Boblig for being even more zealous than himself in the pursuit of heretics in his diocese!

"We have decided," continued the bishop, "that there can be no further delay in sanctions against the treacherous priest, the Dean of Schönberg. May he be taken into custody. Furthermore, may there be established forthwith an inquisitorial commission for the most vigorous investigation of his case!"

The secretary was unable entirely to suppress a satisfied smile.

"Does Your Grace have in mind the persons who will comprise the inquisitorial collegium?" he inquired.

"Yes, I nominate Canon Rehramont, Secretary Schmidt . . ."

Schmidt bowed deeply.

" . . . and then this Doctor Boblig of yours, who appears to be an experienced man," added Liechtenstein with some distaste.

The secretary repeated all the names.

But the bishop was not listening. He was looking at a picture that hung on the wall: *The Return of the Prodigal Son*. He stared at the old man's hands and suddenly winced. Something inside him moved, and he felt, quite against his will, a softening of his heart. He turned to his secretary.

"We shall complete the collegium with one more member: our dear Brother Winkler, Dean of Müglitz!"

Schmidt looked at the bishop in surprise.

"Winkler is an old friend of the Dean of Schönberg," explained Liechtenstein as if by way of an apology. "Let the heretic also have his advocate in the commission, lest he complain we are not fair to him!"

"Your Grace's heart is too kind!" the secretary said in a sanctimonious voice.

The bishop ignored the remark.

"But everything," he continued, "must be done with no fuss. Upon my faith, we have nothing to be proud of in this case!"

Schmidt stood motionless, for he had not yet been dismissed.

"Do you know, my son, what thought occurs to me? The words of our Savior as presented by Saint Matthew in his Gospel: Whosoever is angry with his brother shall be in danger of the judgment! We shall have to judge without anger. Now go!"

The secretary left, nodding his head. This was not the bishop he knew. He had never seen such clemency from him before. And yet this case involved no mere misdemeanor but the gravest of all crimes, a proven alliance with the Devil!

31 ✦ A Brotherly Kiss

Someone was hammering on Kaspar Hutter's door. It was night, but even in the dark, the former judge recognized Tobias Rohmer. The young town constable declined an invitation to come in. He was on duty, he said, and had left his post only for a moment. Hutter guessed he was bringing bad news.

"So what can I do for you?"

"I just wanted to tell you what I heard the jailers saying. Susanne Voglick has confessed to witchcraft and named the dean as her gallant . . ."

"And did you speak to her?"

"I'm no longer allowed near the prisoners."

The young man disappeared into the darkness, leaving Hutter in the doorway, rooted to the spot.

He said nothing of what he had heard to Dorothea but spent a sleepless night racking his brains whether to tell his friend the dean.

Better not. Christoph was ill, and his weak heart might not withstand another heavy blow.

Late next morning, however, Hutter did visit the deanery, to find his friend brooding in silence over an open, but perhaps unread, book. Lautner refused his offer of a game of chess and showed no interest either in news of the town.

Kaspar feigned anger.

"You can't go on like this! As soon as you are able, you must request an audience with the bishop. You said yourself last time that he was as kind as he was stern. Anyway, he has no other priest like you in all of the diocese!"

Before the dean could reply, Florian brought in a new visitor. It was Georg Kress, the church schoolmaster and preceptor from

Müglitz. He bowed most respectfully, boomed the most cordial greetings from the very reverend Dean Winkler, and held out a sealed letter.

Lautner took it, crooked his head, and glanced inquisitively at his friend Kaspar.

"From Vojtech?"

It was difficult to believe that the Dean of Müglitz could suddenly be so well disposed to his brother priest in Schönberg, especially now that Susanne was in the clutches of the inquisitor. Since Lautner's last trip to Müglitz, there had been no contact between the old friends.

He anxiously unsealed the letter and read the few lines:

> Carissime frater! *Our feast day is approaching, and you are very much in my thoughts. Please be assured that you are most welcome to visit us in Müglitz. I trust you will accept this invitation* per amicitiam nostram *and so see for yourself that nothing of our feelings has changed. Please be so kind as to come. Let me know via our preceptor whether to expect you.* Ad amicitiam nostram contestandum.* *J. V. Winkler.*

Lautner could not believe his eyes. He read the note once again, shook his head, and turned to the preceptor.

"Is there something the matter with my brother dean? Is he ill, perhaps?"

"Ill? Why, no! Now he's as fit as a fiddle!"

Lautner stared into the preceptor's broad, honest face and saw no sign of insincerity. Surely even he knew what troubles he had had, yet he was behaving with utmost respect. Vojtech Winkler also knew of his plight, yet he had sent him the kindest of invitations as if nothing had happened.

The dean's heart was suddenly seized with a warm glow. How wrong he had been to doubt his old friend! While others had begun to avoid him, Winkler was now publicly saying that he was

---

*In affirmation of our friendship.

on his side! His good heart had spoken, and not the illness that had evidently affected him at their last meeting.

Lautner handed the note to his friend.

"Read this, Kaspar! Vojtech invites me to Müglitz for their feast day!"

Hutter read it and was also taken by surprise. He was well aware of Winkler's cowardice and knew that he would go to any lengths to curry favor with the bishop. Could it really be that he was siding with a friend who was under grave suspicion?

"Are you going?" he asked dryly.

"How could I refuse?" said Lautner, wondering at such a question.

Hutter shrugged his shoulders.

"If I were in your place, I would rather stay at home."

The dean frowned.

"I know, Kaspar, you would prefer me to go to see His Grace the Bishop, but there's time for that. Someone from the bishop's palace will be going to Müglitz anyway. Canon Rehramont might be there, or Schröffel, the bishop's notary. If so, I probably won't have to go to the bishop at all!"

Kress interrupted:

"Both the canon and the notary have promised to come."

"You see?"

Lautner turned to the preceptor, thanked him for delivering the letter, then set about preparing refreshments for his honored visitor.

Hutter took advantage of the opportunity to take his leave.

"As long as you manage," he said as he went out.

The former judge had grave misgivings, and they would not go away. How could Winkler, of all people, so ostentatiously reaffirm his friendship with Christoph, whom the inquisitor wanted to convict of witchcraft through testimony exacted by torture?

Two days later, the Dean of Schönberg set off for Müglitz.

Florian had not been overjoyed when he was told where they were going. He had had his own experiences of feast days in Müglitz and knew that coachmen and servants such as he would hardly get to lick a bone. His mood, therefore, was one of sullen silence. But not for long. He had some news to tell, and once they had passed through the town gates, he turned to speak to the dean.

"That Boblig has had the Sattlers' house sealed, Father!"

But the dean was thinking of more pleasurable things, and not even the fate of his unfortunate friend seemed to move him.

"Oh, they'll unseal it again!"

"Lots of things have gone missing there . . ."

"Master Sattler will get everything back one day, and with interest!"

Florian stared. This was not like the dean at all.

It was a warm, golden day, and every sound in the thin autumn air was like music. Somewhere, a peal of bells resounded like a harp playing in the distance. The clear green color of the woods had already given way to ocher and crimson, and here and there appeared the deep black of freshly plowed fallow land. Spotted cows roamed the pastures, adding further life to the vivid landscape.

After a while, it was the dean's turn to address his driver.

"Don't you think, Florian, that the Lord is exceedingly good? Just look at this beauty all around! Soon it will be covered with snow, of course. But then we'll have the spring; every seed and every shoot will sprout new life. And not a man exists who could stop it!"

Florian did not reply immediately but stared at the rise and fall of the horses' hindquarters. Then he turned his head.

"And what good is all that beauty to us? The Turks are threatening the Emperor again. They say there are already skirmishes on the border!"

The dean was disagreeably disturbed from his reverie.

"There are no Turks on our borders with the Hungarian lands, Florian. The only fighting is with Count Thököly and his rebels."

"Demon, Devil, what's the difference!"

"At least you have nothing to be afraid of. You won't have to go and fight anyone, Turk or rebel."

"Who knows? Since the time they took our Susanne away, there's nothing that ties me to Schönberg any more."

Florian's words fell upon the dean like salt in an open wound. Susanne! He would have to put in a word for her with Canon Rehramont. But he could not get this business with the Turks out of his head.

"And where would you go if you left Schönberg, Florian?" he said after a while. "Who would look after the horses?"

"Do you think I'm too old to go, Father? I am quite old, but I'm still worth two of the kind of youngsters they put into the army these days. I'd miss your horses, true enough, but the Emperor would give me another."

The journey went quickly, and soon the silver ribbon of the River March appeared and then the red tower of the Müglitz deanery church. Florian gave a crack of the whip.

Dean Winkler, dressed in a new cassock, was standing in front of the deanery, waiting for Lautner with open arms. As soon as Lautner alighted, he was greeted with a warm hug and a brotherly kiss on both cheeks. He thought of Hutter's warning, and how ridiculous it had been! No, this was good old Vojtech. The last time they had met, the harsh words had come not from him but his illness!

The religious ceremonies had finished before Lautner's arrival, and the guests were already assembling in the large hall of the deanery. This had been turned into a banqueting room, decorated with pinewood branches and scented with juniper smoke. All the guests hailed the honored guest from Schönberg. Apart from parish priests from the deanery district of Müglitz, there was Jiri Cicatka, priest at Geppersdorf, Brother Pudlo, priest at Postrelmov, and Brother Sustek; there was Master Nekvapil, Lord Mayor of Müglitz, and a number of councillors, and there were several officials of the diocese, especially Master Kotulinsky of Kotulin, Sheriff of Mürau, and Master Kress, the preceptor. But Lautner looked in vain for Canon Rehramont and the bishop's notary.

Winkler asked everyone to take their places at the table and invited his special friend, the Dean of Schönberg, to sit on his left.

The banquet proved to be excellent. Merry chatter and laughter was soon resounding on all quarters, and one toast followed another. Dean Winkler, usually so morose, fairly beamed, constantly urging his guests to eat, offering them some capital snuff and raising his glass more often than was appropriate for a man of his age and infirmity.

Even the Dean of Schönberg forgot his troubles and grew merry in such good company. He ate and drank with gusto, and his good friend Vojtech never ceased plying him with the choicest of morsels, until he finally had to resist:

"At my age, Brother, I have to be guided by the words of our Savior: Neither too much, nor too little. The middle of the road is the best place to be. Remember, where did the infant Jesus lay in the stable at Bethlehem? In the middle, between the ox and the ass! And where did they find Our Lord as a boy, in the temple at Jerusalem? In the midst of the teachers! And when he died, was it not on the cross in the middle, between two thieves? So even I, when offered this beautiful little goose, shall take the middle portion, the part that bears such a beautiful name—the Pope's nose!"

The guests laughed. Only Winkler frowned faintly, not because of the ox or ass in the stable at Bethlehem or the two robbers, but it seemed to him quite disrespectful to speak of a goose's rear end as a Pope's nose.

Throughout the banquet, no one mentioned the witch trials at Gross Ullersdorf, the inquisition in Schönberg, or Master Boblig of Edelstadt. Lautner regarded this as a great considerateness toward his person. He was grateful and all the merrier for it.

Conversation passed to the Turks, to Thököly, and also to the latest prohibition on imports of French goods. The French influence had been encroaching everywhere: the French mode of dress was replacing the old Spanish fashions; new French dances, such as *retirades, reverences, caprioles,* and *menuets d'amour,* were being introduced, and the nobility were taking lessons in elegant deportment, in how to offer ladies their arm, how to take snuff, and even how to handle their spectacles to be à la mode. But what other than Sodom could one expect from France?

Twilight fell, the first candles were already burned to the stumps, and some of the guests from more distant places readied themselves to go. It was time for the parting cup.

Dean Winkler brought out a great flagon of aromatic, honey-colored spirit and began pouring it out to the guests gathered about him.

"I trust I'll come in for some praise for this," Winkler smiled blissfully. "A fine brandy-wine, distilled from calamus root."

No one had drunk such a drink before, and even the name was new.

"Calamus is the sweet sedge, a spice plant from Turkey," explained Winkler. "Its beneficial effects were known to the ancient Greeks and Romans. They say it's a wonderful aid to the digestion!"

"That's just what we're going to need," said Dean Lautner, sniffing the fragrant spirit before taking a sip and rolling it on his tongue.

"Excellent but dangerous," he remarked. *"Vivat decanus Georgius Adalbertus Winklerus!"*

His brother dean refilled his glass. As Lautner raised it to his lips again, he noticed a gamekeeper enter the room with a letter on a plate, which he set down at the place where he had been sitting.

Another surprise! He went to the table and took the large envelope into his hands. Yes, his name was on it. He turned it over. On the other side was the red seal of the bishop. This did not appear to be a joke. He looked up, uneasily. The others were watching him tensely, not a smile on any face he saw. What could this mean? Could it be something unpleasant?

"A letter from His Grace!" he exclaimed.

"Break the seal and read it!" suggested the Dean of Müglitz.

Lautner unsealed the letter with trembling hands, opened it, and began to read. After the first few words, his eyes gaped. Black

magic . . . Crimes against Almighty God . . . Renunciation of the
Holy Church . . . the Petersstein . . . This was impossible! Lautner examined the seal again, and then the letter. The seal was indeed the bishop's and so was the signature: *D.G. Episcopus Carolus Secundus comes de comitibus de Liechtenstein-Castelcorn.*

For one instant, his heart stopped. Then he began to shake as if
struck by the ague. His legs could no longer bear him, and he had
to lean on the table to prevent himself from falling. He looked
desperately from one to another, but everyone's eyes were
lowered.

"What is all this supposed to mean?"

A voice rang out. It was the burly Sheriff Kotulinsky from
Mürau.

"It means, Your Reverence, that on the orders of His Grace
you are under arrest. I have been charged to take you without
delay to Mürau!"

Only now did Lautner fully comprehend what had happened.
They had laid a trap for him. That was the only reason why
Winkler had lured him to Müglitz. His Grace had been afraid to
have him arrested in Schönberg. Everyone at the table had known,
and yet throughout the banquet they had behaved as if they were
his best friends! They were traitors all, and the greatest traitor
among them was Vojtech. What baseness! Among so many
brethren there had been not one who, by the slightest word or
gesture, had even attempted to warn him. Who could have con-
ceived of such baseness? None but the Devil himself, or Boblig!
And Winkler was merely doing just what he was told.

Lautner pulled himself together, went up to Winkler, and
looked him in the eye.

"You lured an old friend to your house for the sole purpose of
delivering him into the hands of the bishop's men. You have done
a mean and evil deed. You have betrayed a friend and sullied the
honor of the entire priesthood!"

Winkler, speechless, merely swallowed. Lautner turned to the
others.

"And what about you, my dumbstruck friends? Instead of

defending a man who has been wronged, you look the other way. The Sheriff of Mürau intends to dishonor this house, and you make no move to prevent him!"

No one said a word. Lautner turned to Winkler again.

"If this is all your doing, then you are worse than Judas! You kissed me on both cheeks and sat me down at the table in the place of honor. You even called me brother!"

Winkler, quite red in the face, was finally able to speak.

"Yes, you were my brother once, but not any longer."

"Why?" Lautner interrupted him. "Because I've been wrongfully charged? No one has proved me guilty yet! So much for brotherly love!"

"If your innocence is proved, I shall be the first to beg your forgiveness. I shall go down on my knees before you. But now I am merely carrying out the orders of His Grace the bishop."

"You cannot justify a betrayal!"

Four gamekeepers, armed with loaded muskets, entered the room and surrounded the Dean of Schönberg. At the order of the sheriff they seized him and marched him outside. Lautner no longer protested or even defended himself.

A covered wagon had been prepared in front of the deanery. The gamekeepers bundled him inside and then climbed in themselves. The driver cracked his whip, and they set off. The town gate was open, and beyond it eight armed horsemen stood waiting. They immediately surrounded the wagon, and for a short while they all waited until Sheriff Kotulinsky rode out to join them on a beautiful black horse. Then the whole convoy moved off in the moonlight along the valley road to Mürau, the fortress stronghold of the Bishop of Olomouc.

✦ ✦ ✦

Old Florian was astonished to find that this time even the coachmen and servants were given plenty of food and drink. Even more astonishing, however, was the presence of so many gamekeepers from Mürau. When Master Kotulinsky, Sheriff of Mürau, went into the servants' quarters during the evening and called on the gamekeepers to be prepared, Florian became uneasy. He went outside and was surprised to see a covered wagon standing by the wall of the graveyard. None of the guests, certainly, had arrived in such an ordinary vehicle. Why was it there?

The dean's coachman did not go back inside but waited in the shadows in front of the deanery to see what would happen next.

He did not have long to wait. Soon, four gamekeepers emerged, escorting the dean himself!

Before Florian knew what was happening, his master was bundled into the wagon and the driver was whipping the horses.

Everything was over in a matter of minutes.

Florian stood petrified for a moment, but then, like the old soldier he was, he began to think quickly. He hurried into the stable and harnessed his own horses to the dean's carriage. Then, without a word to anyone, he set off for Schönberg.

The dawn was already breaking when he stood before Kaspar Hutter.

When he heard what had happened, the former district judge of Schönberg gritted his teeth. Everything was far worse than he had expected. He thought for a moment, then ordered:

"There's something you ought to do, Florian. Go to Father König, to Gross Ullersdorf. Perhaps it's not too late!"

"And then?"

"Then you'll see!"

Florian did not move.

"And what am I going to do without His Reverence?"

"You'll know what to do!"

The old soldier muttered under his breath, returned to the carriage, climbed onto the box seat, whipped the horses, which he had never done before, and drove them to Gross Ullersdorf.

32 ✦ *A Dangerous Business*

No one knew quite where the report of the dean's arrest had come from, and neither did anyone know the exact details; but all of Schönberg was shocked and perturbed. Craftsmen left their workplaces, shopkeepers their counters, housewives their housework, to share the astonishing news, but only half of them believed it. They were fond of the dean in their hearts, they had a great respect for him and had been sorry to see how ill he had become in recent times. Surely the Inquisition could not have charged him with witchcraft. Didn't a priest have power over the Devil? Why would he have put himself in the Devil's service?

Bittner the weaver and Welzel the clothier decided to go to the deanery themselves to see if there was any truth behind the reports. On the way they were joined by Fritz Winter the gingerbread man, the shoemaker Simon, and several others, so that by the time they reached Church Street, the crowd already numbered several dozen people.

The door to the deanery was locked. Fritz Winter rang the bell fit to break it, but no one appeared at the window. Simon the shoemaker managed to get into the stables. The horses were gone, the carriage also, and there was no trace of old Florian. That proved the dean had not yet returned from Müglitz.

Then the sacristan appeared. The dean should have been at home long ago, he said, because he had promised before his departure that today he would celebrate morning Mass at the usual time. Something had to be wrong when he did not come. Either he was detained or had fallen ill, or something had happened to him on the way.

Someone else announced that the wife of one of the town gatekeepers had twice let Florian through during the night, once into the town and once out again. Where had he gone? Had he been carrying someone or something? If Florian had been in Schönberg without the dean and had departed again without leaving any message, it was very suspicious. No one could come up with a satisfactory explanation. Mystery surrounded the dean's disappearance.

The crowd returned to the square. Outside the town hall, Fritz Winter proposed that they visit Flade, the court clerk. He might know something. So, accompanied by several other citizens, the gingerbread man entered the town hall and demanded to know where the dean was.

"I know nothing, neighbors," the hangdog clerk told them. "All I heard was he went to Müglitz for the feast."

"What we've heard, all over town, is that once he got to Müglitz, they locked him up!"

"So my wife tells me," Flade admitted.

"Why would they have locked him up? Does the inquisitor have anything to do with this?"

Flade tried to keep calm, but the high-backed chair on which he sat was suddenly like the chair in the torture chamber, run through with dozens of nails. His pores welled with sweat, for he knew well that the dean's arrest, if indeed he had been arrested, could only be the inquisitor's work. As a member of the inquisitorial commission, he had heard Boblig address questions about the dean to Kaspar Sattler, Marie Sattler, and even Susanne Voglick and young Liesel. He looked out of the window. There were already around a hundred angry people outside. It would take only one of them to hurl a few inflammatory words, and the men could take the town hall by storm and free the prisoners. Flade knew the constables' courage. Not one of them would resist. The mob had to be got as far as possible from the town hall. But how?

"Perhaps the district judge will know more. You should ask him," he suggested unhappily.

"So we'll go and see Master Gaup."

The deputation thundered out of the office. Flade mopped

his brow; he had gained time, and perhaps he had saved the town hall.

There was a roar outside, and he heard the mob chanting Gaup's name. But one voice rose above all the others. It was Simon, the shoemaker.

"Why go to Gaup, when we can ask the inquisitor himself?"

The mob agreed and surged toward Gaup's new house, where Boblig had his apartment.

Barta the musketeer was not standing guard in the arcade outside, and the house itself was locked. The inquisitor and his assistant, their consciences evidently unclear, had decided to stay away. So what now?

"Gaup!"

Someone shouted out the judge's name as the crowd turned to face a lone figure approaching the house. It was indeed Ferdinand Gaup, dressed in a white wig, a blue woolen coat, and shiny shoes. He was trying to look as dignified as he could, but the color of his face betrayed his fear.

"What's going on here?"

Suddenly there was no one in all the crowd who would dare interrogate the district judge. Gaup realized the power of his authority, and the color returned to his cheeks.

"Clear the way, neighbors! Back to work, now, every one of you!"

But then a woman's voice rang out from the back of the crowd.

"We want our dean back! If he was arrested in Müglitz, you have them set him free right now!"

"What makes you think he was arrested?" thundered Gaup, his face now crimson. "That's just old wives' gossip. You know what they say: Geese cackle, women prattle! Get yourselves home, the dean will come back!"

But now Fritz Winter plucked up courage:

"How do we know that? They say the inquisitor wanted to have our dean arrested. We lived in holy peace and harmony until he and his hunchback came to town. Now nobody can believe anything or anybody any more . . ."

Simon the shoemaker joined in:

"And certainly not the inquisitor or his men! They're only in it for what they can get!"

"While we're left with nothing!" added Winter as other voices chimed in:

"They grab every kreuzer that's going!"

"Kreuzers? More like whole thalers!"

Judge Gaup nervously stood his ground. Such seditious talk on the town square, and in his presence! Perspiration trickled from beneath his heavy wig.

More citizens were arriving. The mob was growing, and the bigger it became, the more threatening it was.

"All sorts of things have been stolen from the Sattlers' house!" piped another voice from the crowd.

It was old Esther Rohmer, who had served the Sattlers for so many years. She had to know! On more than one occasion, Gaup had accompanied Boblig in breaking into the dye master's home regardless of the seal. He recognized the Sattlers' maid and also the message of her words. It was a direct attack against him personally. Come what may, he had to frighten her into silence.

"Show yourself, woman, and tell me exactly what you mean!"

But the mob was seething. Fists were being raised. Suddenly Gaup's courage was gone. He looked around, intent on escape.

Then, unexpectedly, help came. A man was running across the square. It was Thomas Gröger, the furrier, and he was shouting:

"The dean's coming!"

The color returned to Gaup's face yet again. He wiped his cheeks with a large handkerchief.

"So there you see, fools!"

But no one was listening to him. They were all running to the other end of the square to greet the dean.

A carriage drawn by two horses was jolting up the hill at walking speed. But it was not Lautner's, as the people were to see. The Dean of Schönberg had never kept such underfed nags as these.

It was Father Schmidt, the priest from the parish of Zöptau, accompanied by Chaplain Mosig. Schmidt drew himself erect as the carriage entered the square, full of so many people apparently gathered to greet him. His long neck stretched, and his lizardlike eyes shone brightly from his thin, sallow face. But he soon noticed that no one was shouting *Vivat!*—and no one even doffed his cap.

Gaup had recognized the carriage from the outset and had wasted no time. He was already racing down the street alongside the ramparts directly to the deanery, and by the time the carriage arrived there, he was waiting outside the door.

"Allow me, Your Reverence, to greet you in place of the dean, who has not yet returned from Müglitz," Gaup said as if he knew nothing of Lautner's fate.

Schmidt's reply was curt:

"Don't expect him!"

"I see Your Reverence would like to visit the deanery. But the door is locked."

"I have the key!"

A look of feigned amazement appeared on Gaup's face.

"How?"

Schmidt raised his eyebrows loftily. Evidently this was meant to signify a smile.

"I have been charged by His Grace the Bishop to administer the deanery at Schönberg in the absence of Christoph Lautner."

"Does this mean the dean will not be returning so soon?"

"I trust that is the case!"

Mosig managed to open the door, and both priests entered the deanery.

✦ ✦ ✦

Father Schmidt's move to the deanery was a clear sign that the reports of the dean's arrest had not been unfounded. It was a crushing blow to the people of Schönberg and also to their mood of belligerence, of which not a trace remained. Life suddenly returned almost to normal, except that everyone was even more downcast and unhappy than before. Even Fritz Winter lost heart, retiring in silence to his pastry kitchen and his gingerbread hearts and gingerbread men.

At first sight it might have appeared that nothing extraordinary had happened. But when the sun sank to the horizon and the parish church bell clanged the evening hour, the drinking places filled, as the people drowned their sorrows and their rage, and gathered to hear the latest news, though there was little hope the tidings would bring any comfort or joy.

Kaspar Hutter, who could satisfy the citizens' curiosity, was engaged in the most confidential conversation with councillor Heinrich Peschek. Not in a tavern, but in the little back room of the linenmaker's apartment. Not even Peschek's wife Marie was permitted to hear what Kaspar had to say, which was everything he knew about the dean's arrest.

"And has Florian returned?" asked the linenmaker when Hutter had finished speaking. He would have wanted to hear about the events in Müglitz from the coachman himself.

"I hardly think he will come back again!"

Peschek tended to have a ready solution for everything, but this time he fell silent. He was pondering what could possibly be done. Could they send a deputation to Prince Liechtenstein? Or to the Emperor? And whom could they send? Who would be bold enough to go?

Hutter broke the silence.

"We have to bear in mind that everyone who used to keep company with the dean is under threat. Boblig will need more witnesses."

"So we shall bear witness ourselves!" Peschek almost snapped. "It's our duty to tell everyone to their face that there's not a jot of truth in the charges against the dean!"

Hutter smiled bitterly.

"You're forgetting that we're dealing with an inquisitorial court and that Boblig is its director. He won't accept your testimony unless you confess to serving the Devil yourself!"

The linenmaker understood. He pursed his lips and scratched his head.

"Do you think he could force even me to testify to something that wasn't true?"

"I don't know, Heinrich. Until someone's actually faced torture, they can't tell how strong they are. But that's not the point. The important thing is, Boblig does need more witnesses, and he'll hardly want to content himself with the kind of people he already has!"

Peschek looked sharply at Hutter.

"Are you trying to warn me, Kaspar, as you did the dean? Did you come to tell me I'm under some sort of threat?"

Kaspar merely shrugged his shoulders and lowered his eyes.

"I think you should bear that possibility in mind. If I were in your place, I'd lose no time. First thing, tomorrow, if I could, I'd set out on a long business trip. And I'd make sure to deposit most of my money with trustworthy friends, as far from Schönberg as possible."

Peschek rose and for a moment paced the little room, frowning and deep in thought. Finally he halted.

"Tell me, why don't you run away yourself? You were the dean's closest friend."

"I can rely on just one thing," Hutter smiled. "I have no property that Boblig thinks is worth having!"

Peschek walked the room again for a very long time. Then he looked Hutter in the eye.

"Thank you for your advice, but I'm not going to run away! It's all nonsense! Who can prove I was in league with some evil power? Really, I'd like to see anyone try!"

"I advised Christoph," Hutter sighed. "He didn't listen . . ."

Peschek seemed not to be listening. He spoke, but it was rather to himself than his guest.

"Am I a small boy that I should run away from such a scoundrel? What would I become in my own eyes if I did? No, no, dear Kaspar, Heinrich Peschek will not run away from Boblig of Edelstadt. If need be, I shall stand up to him. Someone has to make a stand!"

"This is a very dangerous business, Heinrich!"

"Do you know what this reminds me of?" the linenmaker smiled. "Long ago, Lautner preached of the commotion Saint

Paul caused when he went to the Temple of Diana at Ephesus. The traders were selling all kinds of miraculous pictures and talismans, and they accused him of discrediting their wares by destroying the people's faith in their miraculous powers. Isn't it time something like that happened here, Kaspar? Isn't it time someone stood up to discredit this loathsome advocate, Boblig, as the cheat and impostor that he is?"

The former judge stared in admiration. Until now, his level-headed friend Heinrich had devoted himself solely to his business, and only quite exceptionally had he taken an active part in public affairs. Now he had shown himself to be a man of even greater resolve than Dean Lautner. Still, Hutter felt he had to repeat the warning:

"This could be your devastation, Heinrich!"

"Perhaps it could. But it could also be my victory. And then again, it could be nothing at all!"

"I doubt that very much."

"All the more reason why there should be someone in Schönberg who will not flinch from his responsibilities!"

"I understand."

Kaspar Hutter grasped Heinrich Peschek's right hand and pressed it firmly, deeply moved.

33 ✦ *So Many Lies!*

The days sped by, and each was the same as the next, like grains of wheat in the palm of one's hand. The Dean of Schönberg spent all of them behind the thick walls of Mürau Castle, locked in a wretched cell that was furnished with only a simple bed and a small table and chair. During this time he overcame the fury of disgrace he had felt at the Müglitz deanery and was now able to contemplate his fate with a degree of calmness. He drew strength from the Bible, which was part of the inventory of his cell, and also from his conviction that he would not be abandoned by his friends.

He was paid two visits by the director of the episcopal inquisitorial commission. On the first occasion, Master Boblig of Edelstadt was fulsomely persuasive. The court would certainly look kindly on a penitent confession, he cajoled, and it could even spare his life. But Lautner did not consider such talk worthy of a reply. The second time, Boblig resorted to threats. But they, too, achieved nothing.

Lautner obtained paper, pens, and ink from Sheriff Kotulinsky and spent days composing a compendious apologia for the bishop. How he regretted he did not have his library to hand!

Then Boblig came to see him a third time, to show him copies of depositions from witnesses, proving him guilty of practicing black magic. But even this did not break Lautner's faith in his eventual acquittal. He knew he could not expect justice from Boblig, but he was convinced the bishop would ultimately see through the inquisitor's deceit. And then there was Kaspar Hutter; he would most certainly stand by him.

Christmas was approaching. One bitterly cold day, the dean was taken out of the castle, bundled into a cart, and driven to

Gross Ullersdorf. Four of the prisoners there had testified to his guilt, and he was to be confronted with their testimony.

Boblig's most pliant witness for the prosecution was Stubenvoll, the former castle cellarman. His testimony, addressed directly to the dean before the full commission, was so absurdly untrue that no child could have given it credit. But Canon Rehramont, Dean Winkler, and Secretary Schmidt listened quite gravely. When Lautner pointed out that he was taking part in a repulsive comedy, the canon adjourned the proceedings and had the prisoner taken away.

Several more weeks followed. Then the gamekeepers came for the prisoner again. This time, at dead of night, he was taken to Schönberg.

The first witness to appear at this further confrontation was a wizened and bent old man. Shackled hand and foot, it was all he could do to stagger into the courtroom, where he stood staring stubbornly at the floor.

"Kaspar Sattler," the inquisitor warned him, "if you wish to achieve eternal salvation, you must give the truth, the whole truth, and nothing but the truth!"

Lautner stared in astonishment. The master dyer that he knew had always stood erect, his back ramrod-straight; his face had always worn a sly grin. Could this decrepit old man really be Kaspar Sattler? And what would he say?

"I've already told the whole truth!"

It was Kaspar's voice, sure enough, but as if from beyond the grave. Lautner trembled. All the prosecution witnesses at Ullersdorf had been strangers. Would his friend Kaspar Sattler testify as they had done? Would he, the dean, have strength enough to endure such a confrontation?

"Kaspar Sattler, do you recognize Dean Christoph Lautner? Lift your head and look him in the eye!"

The master dyer obeyed. His gaze met the dean's, but it was the glassy-eyed stare of a corpse. There was no trace of movement in his face.

"I recognize him. It is Dean Lautner of Schönberg."

"Tell us, truthfully, what you know about him!"

Sattler hesitated for a moment, then he unleashed a flow of words like a schoolboy reciting a task learned by heart.

"It is the truth! The dean was in league with the Evil One. He went to the witch-swarms on the Petersstein, but even more often he attended gatherings of witches at my house . . ."

Lautner was aghast.

"Kaspar, what are you saying?"

"Yes, it is true. You often used to be at the gathering of witches at my house. You used to join carnally with Marie, my wife, or Liesel, my daughter, or Susanne, your cook. Sometimes, *in nomine Atris,* you would crown my wife Queen of the Witches, sometimes you would crown Liesel . . ."

"Kaspar, pull yourself together! What have I done to you that you so falsely testify against me?"

But Sattler's ears seemed to be stopped with wax. He merely hung his head lower and continued his recital:

"You, Dean Lautner, carried the sacred host in your pocket, and your cook carried it in her shoe. You boasted that you baptized children in your church in the name of the Evil One, *in nomine Atris* . . ."

"You're lying, Kaspar!"

Lautner was overwhelmed. It was impossible, he told himself, that Kaspar was in his right mind. Boblig had surely given him some potion to cloud his senses and deprive him of his will; otherwise he could not be saying these things.

Sattler fell silent. The inquisitor looked at the other judges and observed the devastating effect with satisfaction. This had not been the testimony of the Ullersdorf cellarman or of some muddled countrywoman but of Lautner's best friend!

"Tell us, Kaspar Sattler," he said, turning to the witness again: "is your testimony not tainted by some hostility toward the dean?"

"No. We were good friends for many years. I harbor no hostility toward him, neither for the sake of my wife, nor for the sake of my daughter. We both served the Evil One and we both have to suffer for it!"

Lautner attempted yet one more time to bring Sattler to his senses.

"Kaspar, for the Lord's sake, pull yourself together. You sound as if you've drunk henbane or some such potion. I've always regarded you as a brother. We've been friends since boyhood . . ."

Sattler turned to face Lautner and raised his head. His eyes were dulled, and bulging veins throbbed on his temples. His brow was drenched with sweat. Boblig spurred him on.

"Just look him in the eye, Sattler!"

He opened his mouth but only with great effort.

"I am telling the truth, dean. Why do you go on denying it? You'll regret it one day. For a long time I denied the charges, too, because I thought I could get away with it. Until the inquisitor and Master Jokl used their powers of persuasion. At least now I live in hope that my soul will be saved."

Kaspar had said it clearly: the inquisitor and Master Jokl had used their powers of persuasion . . . Did Canon Rehramont understand? The dean looked at him. The canon was sniffing a small vial of scent and was looking neither at Kaspar nor at Lautner. *Vanitas vanitatum et omnia vanitas.* Vanity of vanities, and all is vanity.

Lautner could restrain himself no longer and howled in a voice steeped in tears:

"Kaspar, I'm not angry with you and I gladly forgive you everything, for I know, and the good Lord knows, how you were forced to testify the way you did. I wouldn't like to be in the judges' shoes when the Lord calls them to account for their sins. But we two have no reason to fear. Perhaps this is the last time we'll see each other in this worldly life. Brother, forgive me if in any way I have ever hurt you, just as I forgive you."

The wretched Sattler forgot his shackles and the two jailers behind him. He stretched out his hands to approach his friend, but the jailers roughly held him back. Tears streamed from his eyes. He opened his mouth and would certainly have said something other than the words he had been taught. But the inquisitor stopped him in time.

"Take him away!"

The bishop's secretary, Schmidt, could not resist thundering at Lautner:

"Enough of this comedy, Christoph Lautner! Your crimes are an insult to the divine majesty of the Lord."

Dean Winkler leaned over to him and excitedly whispered something in his ear. Evidently only he had understood why the inquisitor had sent Sattler away so quickly.

Marie Sattler was supposed to be brought in as the second witness. But she proved to be in such a bad physical and mental state that she was not fit to be examined. Instead, the jailers brought in her daughter Liesel.

What had become of the chirpy, delicate girl that Lautner had known? She was but a shadow of her former self. Her dark eyes flamed feverishly from an almost translucent face; her mouth was twisted, her beautiful hair disheveled, and her shoulders twitched in terror as she faced the inquisitor. Then she gave her testimony, confirming everything her father had said, adding only that in the name of the Evil One, the dean had wanted to betroth her to the soapboiler Prerovsky, and he, too, was a disciple of the Devil.

"Look the dean in the eye!"

She turned to Lautner and repeated everything to his face.

The dean replied, addressing her kindly as if she were a small child:

"But Liesel, you know very well it was I who persuaded your father not to marry you off to Master Prerovsky!"

Liesel stared at the dean as if she did not know him. Then she suddenly burst into heartrending tears. Her whole body shook convulsively, and she was unable to say another word.

Even Canon Rehramont was moved and called on the inquisitor to spare Liesel further questioning.

Susanne Voglick was the last witness to be brought in.

Even after her incarceration in a foul prison and despite her gauntness, her pallor, and her tattered clothes and shoes, Lautner's housekeeper was still strikingly beautiful. Nor was her spirit completely broken; when she saw the dean she attempted a smile.

"Susanne!"

"Father!"

The inquisitor could not allow this.

"Susanne Voglick," he rasped, "you were brought here to give evidence against Dean Lautner. Do you wish to tell him, to his face and before the full episcopal commission, what on many occasions you have already told me?"

So even Susanne had been forced to testify as the inquisitor had wanted! What must she have suffered! Lautner looked at her and waited with apprehension for her to speak.

But she said nothing. Instead, she gazed from one judge to another as if she wanted to discover whether she could expect justice from any one of them.

Boblig grew impatient:

"Tell what you know of the banquet that took place at the Sattlers' house!"

She did not reply. The inquisitor raised his voice.

"Speak! You know we have means to loosen your tongue!"

A frown fleeted across the beautiful vault of her forehead, but still she was silent.

Lautner could hardly breathe; so great was the tension. She surely knew Boblig's tortures, yet still she hesitated! How courageous she was! Far more courageous than Sattler!

Susanne suddenly raised her hands and turned them so that the dean could see her crushed thumbs. If she could, she would have lifted the hem of her dress and also shown him her mutilated legs and their still open wounds. Then she spoke:

"My misfortune was that I came to be at the deanery in Schönberg in the first place, after the fire. If only I'd perished behind a fence somewhere, like a dog . . ."

"Susanne!" sighed the dean, deeply touched by the bitterness of her words.

"The Sattlers' banquet!" Boblig warned her sternly.

"Banquet? Yes, I was at the banquet when Marie was married. I came to the deanery, and there they made a witch of me . . . And that's why I have to burn in the flames . . ."

Boblig was visibly growing nervous, for Susanne was replying quite differently from the way she should have done. He went up to her and gripped her arm.

"Calm down," he said, and his voice was remarkably kind. "All you have to do is repeat what you've already told me. Except that today you have to say it to the dean's face!"

Her testimony was vital. Boblig depended on it, for it was to be decisive for the bishop.

Susanne slowly turned to face the dean. Only now did she seem to realize what had happened to him. She opened her mouth, but instead of words, it emitted a dreadful shriek. She screamed and shook, and beat her own head with her shackled hands.

The distinguished members of the inquisitorial commission sprang from their chairs in agitation at such a display of insanity. Boblig attempted to seize her, but her eyes widened at his touch—and she burst into demented laughter, far more dreadful than any of her weeping or screaming.

Even now Boblig remained calm.

"Nothing unusual, gentlemen," he observed. "Simply the Devil preventing his diabolical follower from speaking!"

"Perhaps," suggested the canon, "she's gone mad!"

"No, the Devil has her in his power. *Malitia taciturnitatis* . . ."

Secretary Schmidt blanched white as chalk on hearing of the Devil's presence and began to make the sign of the cross in the air:

"*Apage satanas. In nomine Patris et Filii et Spiritus sancti . . .*"

But Susanne did not cease her demoniacal laughter. Except that it was no longer laughter—only wild, inhuman screaming.

Suddenly, in the midst of the chaos, the dean's firm voice rang out.

"This is your doing, gentlemen judges! You have killed her! Killed her!"

Canon Rehramont was the first to pull himself together.

"Take her away!"

Susanne suddenly fell quiet. Tears streamed from her eyes and she left quietly, without another look at the judges or at her former master.

It took quite a while for calm to return to the courtroom. Then Boblig turned furiously on the dean.

"Christoph Lautner, do you still refuse to admit your guilt?"

The Dean of Schönberg fixed his eyes on this beast in human form. Was he to be less courageous than Susanne?

"Yes! There is no truth in the testimony of Master Sattler, nor that of his daughter, nor even of the poor girl whom we have just seen and whom you stripped of her senses."

"Silence!" shouted the bishop's secretary.

Boblig, red in the face, blubbered:

"You've had a comfortable imprisonment so far. We've been far too gentle with you!"

But the dean was unfazed.

"The episcopal commission is mighty, but might and right are two quite different things."

Without even asking the canon's consent, Boblig nodded to the jailers, who led Lautner away.

A heavy silence remained. Canon Rehramont frowned vacantly, then turned hesitantly to the inquisitor.

"I once read that the Devil can assume the form of any person he wishes, creating a doppelganger, or duplicate. Can't this Lautner be some kind of duplicate?"

"Not at all," the inquisitor snapped. "We're not dealing with a duplicate but a genuine original!"

34 ✦ *Bitter Experience*

The Countess of Galle fell ill. She felt no particular pains; simply her strength seemed slowly to be ebbing away. Her complexion became ashen gray, her eyes sank, and her movements became torpid. Perhaps Mistress Biedermann could have cured her in the healing springs, but the bathkeeper of Gross Ullersdorf was long dead. The countess's personal physician from Olomouc administered various potions and assured her she would recover as soon as the spring sun appeared. But bold enough, at her age, to contemplate the worst, she only partially believed him.

When had she actually become aware that all was not well with her? Yes, it had been the day she received the last letter from Father König. The poor priest had died just a few days after hearing from Florian what had happened to the dean. Sudden pains in his right side were accompanied by vomiting and a high fever. The pains grew worse. One old granny advised cold compresses, another hot poultices. By the time the countess could send for her own physician, the priest was no more.

But before he fell ill, he had written her a letter. It was a letter of farewell, saying that he had to go away quickly, to escape the same fate as Dean Lautner. But the letter did not stop there; it went on to issue the countess a grave warning. She was to beware of people who were so zealous in hunting and burning those whom they deemed to be witches. She was to take great heed especially of Master Boblig of Edelstadt; to question what he was doing, the methods he employed in his interrogations, the way the confessions were arrived at, and the increasing number of people involved in his trials. The letter urged her to investigate carefully whether the people who were being burned were not in fact innocent or had done nothing of any harm. One day, she was reminded, God would call all men and women to account for their sins. As the secular authority, the countess was responsible before God for the well-being of her subjects. And she should remember that there could be no condonation of injustice, even that which was committed in the belief that some good could become of it.

Until now the Countess of Galle had had a clear conscience. A pious woman, she had observed all the laws of the Church and had given a decent upbringing to the two young Zerotins. The only thing was she had not spared too many thoughts for her feudal subjects—but wasn't that what her officials were for?

Now, suddenly, she was dismayed. Had she neglected her responsibilities? Hadn't it been her duty to see for herself what was going on in the courtroom, the torture chamber, and the prison cells of Ullersdorf Castle? Shouldn't she have been suspicious when the inquisitor arrested Stubenvoll the cellarman, Mistress Drechsler the castle housekeeper, Mistress Göttlicher the papermaker, or Mistress Biedermann the bathkeeper? She had known them for many years; they had served her faithfully and she had been utterly satisfied by them. Every one of them had attended church and received the holy sacrament. Yet Boblig made witches of them all. And though it caused the countess concern, she kept silent, and this in itself was an expression of assent. The fact was she had transferred her authority to Sheriff Vinarsky, for she flinched from dealing personally with an inquisitor whom she found repulsive. Perhaps her very distaste for him had cost nine people their lives!

How she now missed little Father König! Who was to put her mind at ease now, who was to advise her? Whom could she turn to? Whom could she confide in? Jiri Cicatka, the new parish priest at Gross Ullersdorf, was nothing like his predecessor, and she had no confidence in the Capuchins. Even Sheriff Vinarsky was not the man he used to be. He had become a stranger, paying greater heed to the wishes of Master Boblig than to hers. But who was to bear responsibility before God? It had to be her, the Countess of Galle, as Father König had written. And, given that the blame was hers, how was she to make atonement?

She summoned the sheriff. But Master Vinarsky of Kreuz seemed unwilling and evasive. When questioned about Boblig, he neither spoke well of him nor ill, but merely complained that yet more cells had to be built, for the number of prisoners was rising. And he told her who the inquisitor's latest prisoners were: Johann Axmann, the old Zöptau magistrate, and his wife.

Now the countess was even more dismayed. The sheriff had not told her all he knew and was concealing many things. But why?

She summoned her treasurer. Little Frantisek Vaclav Vrany bowed low, but he also was consistent in his evasion of any direct questions about the inquisitor. Instead, he seemed preoccupied with economic affairs, which his doleful face indicated were less than encouraging. This came to the countess as something of a jolt. Was she not supposed to be administering the manor of Zerotin for the benefit of its young heirs? What if her custodianship were to leave the estates indebted or reduced in any way?

The treasurer spoke expansively about the previous year's poor harvest; the low income from the iron-forges; the feudal subjects who neglected their work; the taxes that were already too high but would be yet higher, for a new war against the Turks was threatening; and he complained that serfs were fleeing the estates and crossing the border. Finally, he mentioned the extraordinary items of expenditure that were constantly increasing.

The countess wanted to know what those special items were. Like it or not, the treasurer had to tell her.

"They are the expenses connected with the unfortunate witch trials . . ."

"You will have to explain!"

The treasurer began enumerating the costs: the inquisitor's pay, his frequent journeys, his servants, food, drink . . .

"Mainly the drink," the countess observed with some malice.

Master Vrany continued:

" . . . the building of the new jail, wages for eight jailers, the cost of keeping the prisoners, even though it's only one kreuzer a day per person . . ."

"How much a day does it cost to keep a draft horse?"

"More, Your Ladyship, much more. Then we have to add the fees for the executioner and his assistants, wood for the con-cremation, payments for numerous messengers, arrangements for the guests who attend the executions, the frequent banquets . . ."

"Yes, the unfortunate banquets!"

"Many eminent people come here, some even from Prague, Your Ladyship. Guests have to be honored. And everything is far more expensive nowadays, with a war on the way. The treasury is diminishing, Your Ladyship."

The treasurer lowered his head as if expecting a blow. The countess stared at the peeling blue wallpaper and pursed her lips.

"There'll be more executions soon, I understand."

"Yes, Your Ladyship. They're just waiting for confirmation of sentence from the Court of Appeals. A further five persons are to be concremated . . ."

"But this time there'll be no banquet!"

The treasurer looked up, startled by this outburst.

"I trust Your Ladyship will forgive me for pointing out that a great number of eminent guests are coming. The reputation of the house of Zerotin is at stake, a name which is beyond compare in all of Moravia."

The countess realized she had overshot the mark.

"All right, so there will be a banquet, but you will have to cut some corners!"

Vrany did not show any enthusiasm.

"You can put it down to the Turks!"

"It will be done, Your Ladyship!"

✦ ✦ ✦

Spring arrived not long afterward and confirmed that for once the physician from Olomouc had not been mistaken. The Countess of Galle did indeed revive, and her strength seemed to return. Sud-denly the castle was full of her presence and nothing happened that did not escape her sharp eyes.

The confirmation of sentence on four condemned persons ar-rived from Prague, and preparations were immediately begun at the castle, including the arrangements for the banquet. The inquisitor became very glum when he heard about the austerity measures and requested an audience with the countess.

She could not refuse to see him but was determined to put up a fight.

When Master Boblig arrived in her room, she graciously allowed him to kiss her hand but then waved him loftily to a chair on the far side of the room.

"What is your wish, sir?"

The inquisitor knitted his brow and gave her a mocking gaze.

"I understand Your Ladyship saw fit to issue some kind of new directives regarding banquets."

He was not beating about the bush, and this pleased the countess.

"I consider it improper to celebrate the death of those unfortunates with a lavish banquet. A Requiem Mass and prayers would surely be more appropriate."

Boblig gave one of his wry smiles.

"We are not in the habit of celebrating the death of the—as you put it—unfortunates, but a triumph over the Devil. Did our Savior Himself not command us to do battle with the Devil? And when we do and defeat him, should we not be jubilant?"

The countess was confused. Fortunately, she remembered the letter from Father König.

"Are you quite sure, sir, that all the persons whom you have condemned to death are truly guilty of the dreadful crime of witchcraft?"

Boblig sat up, suddenly worrying about where this conversation was leading.

"You need have no fear, milady. All were properly convicted. Besides, they all volunteered full confessions, either in the course of straightforward examinations or under torture. The inquisitorial tribunal always abides by the law, proceeding on the sole basis of what is admitted voluntarily by the accused, or is proved by the testimony of witnesses. Besides, the entire process must be carefully scrutinized by the Court of Appeals."

"And yet, what if they are still innocent?"

Boblig laughed.

"Could Almighty God allow innocent people to go to such a terrible death?"

This was an argument to which the countess had no answer.

"My God, when will there be an end to these trials?"

"I am afraid, milady, that this is only the beginning!"

The countess could not help gasping:

"But it's costing so much money!"

"Money?" the inquisitor said contemptuously. "What is a few paltry groschen compared with eternal bliss? When your Day of Judgment comes, milady, every one of those witches will be a great weight in your favor on the scales of divine justice."

The Countess of Galle could hardly contain her rage.

"You may go, sir," she said.

35 ✦ *Divine Ordinance*

It was with a heavy heart that Count Liechtenstein-Castelkorn, Bishop of Olomouc, followed the events that were unfolding in the Hungarian lands. Count Thököly, who had repudiated obedience to the Emperor, was pressing ever westward, while the Turks, the age-old enemy of the Hapsburg Empire, were massing their forces and were bound to launch an attack soon. Would they be held back by the imperial army? Would the monarch be supported by the royal houses of Christendom? As always, the French were more on the side of the Turks than the Emperor; and the other kings and princes, because they did not consider themselves to be in immediate danger, were showing their usual culpable lack of action. The only exception was the Polish king, Jan Sobieski, who had had his own experiences with the savage Turks. But would his help be enough? All too often, it seemed, God allowed victory to the heathen, and it was difficult to see the sense of it. If the hordes of Hungarian rebels and Turkish invaders were to spill across the frontiers of Moravia, if Kromeriz were to fall, and if the enemy were to reach as far as Olomouc, half of the territory of Moravia would be left a wasteland for years. Liechtenstein's heart was gripped with anxiety. All too clearly was he conscious that if this were to happen, everything he had built up so laboriously over so many years would fall to wrack and ruin. Even he, the bishop, was in grave danger. Unless, of course, he took refuge at Mürau. By some divine inspiration he had had the castle fortified in good time, well armed, and provisioned for a siege.

The thought of the castle at Mürau immediately reminded the bishop of Lautner, Dean of Schönberg, for it was there he was imprisoned. And he was an even more loathsome matter than the war with the Turks.

Long into the previous night, the bishop had gone through the numerous letters, reports, and protocols that the inquisitor Boblig had sent him. They had not made pleasant reading. The documents made it as clear as day that the former Dean of Schönberg had devoted himself to the occult for years, apparently ever since he was visited by the legendary arch-heretic, Doctor Borri of Milan. Of course, it was easy to point a finger at anyone, and a simple accusation would have meant little—except that Boblig had given the names of a full thirty-six witnesses and had sent copies of their depositions, proofs of Lautner's guilt. So far, however, the most substantial proof was missing: the confession of the accused himself. The inquisitor conceded that all examinations and confrontations so far had had a negative result. That was why he was requesting permission to use torture.

Besides the papers from Boblig, the bishop also had an apologia written by Lautner himself from his cell at Mürau, and several reports from Sheriff Kotulinsky. These reports were favorable: throughout the dean's period of imprisonment, the sheriff had found nothing untoward in his cell, and the prisoner's conduct had always been exemplary. Lautner's own defense document, meanwhile, utterly denied his guilt, claiming that all the charges against him were mere concoctions of the inquisitor, stemming from his thirst for glory and, perhaps even more so, from his material greed. Further, the dean declared that confessions exacted by torture were worthless, and so were any charges that were grounded in such forced confessions. Anyone, wrote Lautner, could be accused by an inquisitorial court, but no one could be purged of false charges made by that court. There would be greater justice in freeing, say, thirty guilty people and one innocent among them, than for all of them, regardless of blame, to face cruel punishment. The dean besought His Grace, therefore, to review the entire case, to be guided above all by the soundness of reason and by the warmth of his heart, and not to be influenced by arguments that had long been repudiated by innumerable learned authorities in both theological and legal matters.

The Bishop half closed his eyes and vividly imagined the two men, the accuser and the accused. Boblig's letters were as repulsive in tone as he was in his appearance; there was something about them that was impure or contrived. On the other hand, the dean's apologia, written from prison, seemed to be just as sincere as the Christoph Lautner the bishop had once known. The dean was a little country fellow, clumsy and impertinent perhaps, but clever and courageous, and never inclining to falseness, hypocrisy, or sycophancy. But the question remained: was it not all a kind of mask? According to Boblig, the dean had been practicing black magic for at least ten years. If that were so, and he had managed to deceive everyone for such a long time, then he was an extraordinarily great sinner.

Although the inquisitor's evidence was quite devastating, the bishop was still not entirely sure.

Secretary Schmidt entered, his face careworn. He bowed deeply.

"Your Grace deigned to invite Canon Rehramont and Dean Winkler of Müglitz. They have been waiting for some time."

The bishop sighed.

"Send them straight in."

The bishop's secretary led the two clergymen into the study, where the bishop directed them to armchairs at the round table; and even Schmidt was told to take a seat. Apart from Master Boblig of Edelstadt, whom the bishop had deliberately not invited, these three men comprised the episcopal commission—the inquisitorial tribunal that was to judge Christoph Lautner, Dean of Schönberg.

A brief silence reigned as Count Liechtenstein rested his thin and veiny hands on the table, the sapphire of his bishop's ring casting a dull reflection from its finely polished surface. He stared out the window into the distance before turning his gaze to Rehramont:

"Brother Canon, I would be pleased if in all conscience you answered me this question: Is Christoph Lautner guilty of the crime of which he is charged before the commission?"

The canon was surprised by the clarity and directness of the question. This was not to his liking. A frown flew across his high forehead.

"There can be no disputing the fact that Master Boblig of Edelstadt has amassed some damning material," he stalled.

"I am aware of that," said the bishop with impatience, "but I would like to hear your own personal opinion!"

Now Canon Rehramont had things under control. If His Grace was asking for his opinion, then it could only be because he was not sufficiently convinced himself.

"I must say, however," he continued cautiously, "that even despite this damning material, I am not unconditionally convinced of Lautner's guilt. Above all, I think we lack proof of a motive. Why would Lautner commit such deeds?"

The bishop did not show whether he was satisfied or not with the canon's reply, but turned without comment to Secretary Schmidt.

"And what is your opinion, Brother?"

The secretary did not hesitate for a moment. His mouselike eyes lighted up and he spoke quickly as if he had learned his speech in advance:

"I am of quite the opposite opinion, Your Grace. I am utterly convinced that Christoph Lautner is guilty. Thirty-six witnesses clearly confirmed that they met with him on the Petersstein or at the home of the Sattlers. Some of the witnesses reaffirmed their accounts at their hour of death, and others did so to his face during confrontation. The accused was not able to disprove their testimonies. So far, the accused has not confessed. If he refuses to do so voluntarily, the law directs but one course of action against him—the use of torture!"

"But he is still a priest," remarked the canon.

Schmidt had a ready answer.

"It's not unknown for priests to be arrested and subjected to torture by the secular authorities. It's happened on more than one occasion without their bishop's consent. So why should it not happen with episcopal approval?"

The bishop said not a word, one way or the other, but stared penetratingly at the Dean of Müglitz.

"And what is your opinion, Brother?"

Winkler was in a nervous quandary, not knowing until the last moment what he was going to say. Above all else, he wanted to remain in His Grace's favor, but without knowing what the bishop himself thought, it was very difficult to say anything. The fact was, during the confrontation in Schönberg, Winkler had been racked with doubt about Lautner's guilt. It seemed to him that it was all a premeditated farce; that it was despicable for Boblig to use force against a member of the priesthood, and even more so if it was done in the bishop's name. But could he dare say such a thing to His Grace?

"To err is human," he said at last.

The bishop knew well that Lautner and Winkler were former friends. That, after all, was why he had nominated the Dean of Müglitz as a member of this inquisitorial commission.

"I wouldn't say that was a particularly good speech for the defense!" he said with a smile.

Winkler was alarmed. He dearly wanted to say the right thing, yet even now he could not detect from Liechtenstein's voice exactly what the bishop wanted.

"I wouldn't think of playing the role of advocate, Your Grace," he squirmed. "I would only wish to recall the words of our Savior: All manner of sin and blasphemy shall be forgiven unto men: but the blasphemy against the Holy Ghost—against reason, that is—shall not be forgiven unto man!"

Bishop Liechtenstein gazed with interest at this old priest. He knew him well and was therefore aware what courage his comment had required.

If the Dean of Schönberg were to confess, the whole case would soon be concluded. But the investigations so far made it clear there would be no confession without torture. Deep in his heart, the bishop could not condone the use of such obsolete and brutal means, but was he allowed to avoid it? The easiest course was to leave others to make the decision.

"Are you of the opinion, friends, that torture is to be used against our priest, Christoph Lautner?" he said in a quiet voice that betrayed nothing of his thoughts.

Protocol demanded that the canon, as the most senior member, should reply first. But the bishop's secretary beat him to it: "I'm all for it, Your Grace!"

Only then did Canon Rehramont reluctantly concur: "If the law admits it and if there is no other more appropriate means . . ."

Dean Winkler wavered for some time before his reply. Again he reminded himself of the scene in the Schönberg courtroom when Lautner had been confronted by Susanne Voglick. It seemed to him now that the moment had come for him to say something that had long been troubling his mind. Perhaps it was the very thing His Grace wanted to hear.

"It is almost certain, Your Grace, that Dean Lautner will indeed confess if all three degrees of torture are used against him. However, may I put it to Your Grace: Is torture truly the most reliable means of finding the truth? Some eminent jurists, Baldus, Marsitius, and Cataldus among them, acknowledge the usual torture and even recommend more kinds of coercion. Their argument is that people rather admit the truth than endure agonizing pain. On the other hand, other authorities teach that for the same reason—fear of pain—people would equally admit untruths also. Eventually, with repeated torture, Christoph Lautner will indeed confess, and the inevitable verdict will be that he is a witch or sorcerer. But will he have confessed according to the first example, or the second? There is no certainty at all. And if he does not confess, let us say, during the first and second degrees of torture—will he be regarded as innocent and therefore released?"

At last, Dean Winkler, who had studied law in his youth, had said what he thought was required. He looked at the others and was dismayed to see that he had evidently said quite the wrong thing. Not only was Secretary Schmidt clearly indignant, so was His Grace the bishop. Count Liechtenstein was showing his displeasure by drumming his fingers on the table. Winkler would rather have been a hundred miles away.

"It has been proven by the highest authorities," said the secretary sternly, "that silence can be maintained under torture only with the help of the Devil!"

The bishop knew about *malitia taciturnitatis*. But he was reluctant to admit that Satan possessed such power. God had to be far more powerful. On the other hand, he did believe firmly that nothing ever happened except with God's indulgence. The point, therefore, was not whether the Dean of Schönberg confessed or whether his replies continued to be negative; the main thing was that whatever happened, it was God's will. Then again, every bishop was duty-bound to carry out his pastoral office, and that also included the struggle against heresy and all manner of other disorders in the Church. It had to be left to God. He would show whether Christoph Lautner was a disciple of the Devil.

Count Liechtenstein gazed into the distance through the window. Then he said, rather more solemnly than usual:

"Christoph Lautner is a priest. For this very reason it greatly behooves us to find the truth. It is claimed that his guilt is proved by the testimony of thirty-six witnesses, but he denies the charges. What he does under torture remains to be seen. However he behaves, it will be in accordance with God's will. If he confesses, we shall have no alternative but to be guided by the words of Saint Matthew: Whosoever does not obey the Church is but a heathen and a publican. It is not for us to decide but for the Lord Himself. We can, of course, admit the possibility that he is not guilty. If that be so, we need have no fear that the torture will do him harm. None of us knows the dispensations of the Lord, and it may be that God will reward him all the more generously in the hereafter. Whatever the case, as the learned Delrio says clearly: By divine ordinance is innocence always divulged. We have nothing to add. So we shall give our gracious consent that our priest, Christoph Alois Lautner, be subject to torture of the usual kind."

"Amen," cried Canon Rehramont, eager as always to win the bishop's favor.

Secretary Schmidt also gave voice to his satisfaction. Only the Dean of Müglitz was close to tears. Not because of what awaited his former boyhood friend, but because he had probably ruined his reputation with His Grace the bishop.

36 ✦ The Hailstorm

The heat wave that came at the end of the summer was like nothing in living memory. The wells dried, the water quite vanished from the streams, and all that was left of the River Tess was a succession of foul-smelling, stagnant puddles full of dead fish. Even the brewery stopped making beer for lack of water. The parched earth cracked, and its dry surface crumbled to a swirl of smothering dust. There was a great threat of fire, and the citizens of Schönberg kept vigil both day and night, though if God had indeed permitted fire to break out, no one could have extinguished the flames without water.

It was on one such scorching day that the inquisitor and his assistant returned from Ullersdorf to their apartment in Schönberg. Although the journey did not last long, Boblig and Ignatius arrived covered with dust, tired, and very thirsty. As soon as they were at home, they flung open the windows and threw off their coats. The hunchback took some pears from a bag: round bergamots with a fine, spicy flavor. The inquisitor grabbed one, lay down on his bed, and bit into the fruit; but it was still too hard for the ruins of his teeth, so he threw it aside and ordered Ignatius to fetch wine from the cellar. One full glass of wine later he was streaming with perspiration and was obliged to ask Ignatius to bring him a towel. Further speech then apparently beyond his powers of exertion, the old inquisitor slumped languidly back on his bed, his shirt opened wide to reveal a broad, heaving chest, thickly matted with hair. Only his eyes, half closed, continued to observe his miserable assistant.

Someone hammered on the door.

"Go and see who the devil it is!" Boblig said.

Ignatius ushered in Franz Ferdinand Gaup.

The sweltering heat had also rid the district judge of all sense of decorum regarding his attire. He had no wig and was clad only in an open blouse, light breeches, and old slippers.

"Such an oppressive heat, Master Boblig! Please forgive my appearance, sir," he said, mopping his fat neck with a handkerchief, "but I've brought you the mail that came when you were away."

Gaup handed over three sealed letters. The inquisitor tossed them carelessly to Ignatius.

"Who's written to us, Iggy?"

The hunchback examined the seals.

"There's a letter from His Eminence Prince Liechtenstein, from Eisgrub."

Gaup was already well aware that one of the letters had come from the prince's court; even so, he straightened his back and adopted a respectful expression on hearing such an exalted name. What surprised him very much was that Master Boblig appeared to show no curiosity at all.

"Who else?"

"An episcopal red seal, master," said Ignatius. "This one's from His Grace the Bishop of Olomouc."

Gaup leaned over, clearly envious of Master Boblig's highly impressive correspondence.

"And the other one?"

"A black seal, master, no crest. Another vulgar scribbler, perhaps, wanting to bother you."

"Vulgar, you say? They're the kind of letters I like. Open it up, Ignatius. And you can read it in front of Master Gaup. It won't hurt him to learn something new!"

The hunchback broke the seal, opened the letter and scanned it in silence.

"Out loud!"

"It's nothing of importance, master. Just the husband of one of the Gross Ullersdorf witches, asking for clemency through the office of his magistrate. They want her beheaded mercifully before concremation."

"Tiresome fools! What would I give for their problems!"

Gaup had still not been offered a seat or even a little wine. He guessed he had probably come at an inopportune time and said good-bye. No one asked him to remain.

But no sooner had the door closed behind him than the inquisitor clamored impatiently for Ignatius to unseal the letter from Prince Liechtenstein.

"Perhaps the prince had a little shock when we submitted our accounts," said Boblig. "It's easier to squeeze oil from a stone than to get a few groschen out of that cavalier!"

Boblig was not mistaken. The prince's letter, written in his own hand, expressed grave concern over the high expenses incurred by the inquisitorial proceedings in Schönberg. The investigations had been under way for an inordinately long time, he wrote, and still without result. He went on to inquire whether the accused would be able to pay the court costs themselves from their own resources. He would be pleased to receive a report about this very soon. True, he wrote, he had committed himself to cover the court costs from his own treasury, if such expenses could not be met by the hereditaments of the condemned, but the proceedings had proven to be unexpectedly protracted, and the costs were rising at an alarming rate. The prince concluded by offering some wise advice: that before instituting proceedings against anyone, the master inquisitor should first thoroughly investigate that person's pecuniary circumstances, namely whether the likely hereditaments would suffice to cover all the court costs.

Boblig chuckled as he heard the prince's submission. How thoughtful of His Eminence! This was his advice to an inquisitor of forty years' standing! It was like teaching a horse to tell the difference between oats and bran!

Soon, however, Master Boblig stopped laughing and furrowed his brow. He recalled the famous inquisitorial judges who had used the witch trials in German Silesia to amass great fortunes, to acquire houses and estates and all manner of lucrative positions. He, Boblig, the keenest judge of all, could also have become rich long ago, if he had not spent so much. But now it was too late. He would have to be satisfied with just the bones instead of the meat. *Tempora mutantur*.

"Tell me, Ignatius," he said after a while, "whom do we serve? God or Mammon?"

The hunchback shifted from one foot to the other.

"My opinion, master," he said after a while, "is that we are serving God through Mammon."

"You're an artful one! You'd make a good presiding judge at the Court of Appeals!"

The pot-bellied Boblig roared with laughter until once more he was streaming with perspiration and had to mop himself with a towel.

"What does the bishop say?"

Ignatius carefully peeled off the episcopal red seal and glanced at the brief letter.

"Eureka! At last, master!"

"What at last?"

"His Grace Count Liechtenstein, Bishop of Olomouc, graciously informs us that he is placing Christoph Alois Lautner, Dean of Schönberg, at the disposition of the secular authorities and *ipso facto* accords his consent to the use of torture as a means to investigate the said person's involvement in crimes of black magic and vile sacrilege."

Boblig sprang up with remarkable agility, snatched the document from the hunchback's hand, and studied it carefully. But not for long, for suddenly the room darkened and he could hardly see to read.

"Bring a candle!"

Not stopping even to wonder why it was so dark, he took the letter to the window, but there, too, he had but little light.

The hunchback came in with a burning candle and a terrified look on his face.

"A storm's brewing, master."

"So what!" Boblig waved a dismissive hand. "We have a candle, don't we?"

And he began to read the letter carefully. It bore all the hallmarks of being drafted by the bishop's secretary, Schmidt. The more Boblig read, the more satisfied he was. But it had certainly taken some time for Olomouc to come to a decision! All the same, the impenitent Lautner was now at last utterly in his power, and the final triumph was at hand. *Qui vivra verra!* The inquisitor remained staring at the letter, rejoicing at the thought of the bishop's face on reading a copy of the dean's eventual confession.

Ignatius was becoming impatient.

"What reply do we give to the tiresome fool?" he asked after a while.

"Which one?" The inquisitor had quite forgotten.

"The one who wants mercy for his wife."

"Six ducats on the nail, and we'll do just what he wants. Before Jokl ties her to the stake, he'll lop off her head. That's three ducats for me, two for you, and one for the executioner!"

"There were times we'd charge nine ducats for that kind of mercy!" Ignatius laughed, though his smile vanished as a bolt of lightning struck close by, suddenly filling the room with a blinding flash of light.

But his master noticed nothing. He was reading Prince Liechtenstein's letter again.

"His Eminence complains about our slowness, Ignatius," he said. "So we'll have to show him we're not idling our time away. Bring the list of Schönberg witches, and we'll pick ten of them to keep him happy. Anyway, it's time we took someone else in!"

Ignatius brought the list.

"Read!"

"First of all, there's the soapboiler, Prerovsky. Wealthy. Very wealthy. Denounced by Marie Sattler, Kaspar Sattler, and their daughter Liesel."

"Good. That's one."

"Then there's his old mother . . ."

"That's two!"

"Further, Dorothea Peschek, wife of Councillor Peschek, the linenmaker, and sister of Kaspar Sattler. Very well-off . . ."

"That's three. But she should have been at the top of the list, Ignatius!"

"Then there's Manda Bock, widow. Poor."

"Leave her be. His Eminence can't waste money on her."

"Old Mistress Bernhardt, wife of the locksmith from the Old Gate. Propertied."

"That makes four then."

"What about Dorothea Partsch, the cooper's wife?"

"The young one, good looking? Most certainly!"

At this there was another flash of lightning and an immediate crash of rolling thunder as if the town hall tower were falling about their ears. Even Master Boblig of Edelstadt caught his breath. But surely no thunderbolt would strike the house of the district judge! Nevertheless, the inquisitor crossed himself and stepped back from the window.

"Am I to read on?" asked Ignatius, his teeth chattering.

"Try praying!"

No sooner had the inquisitor spoken than a new flash of lightning illuminated the room with a dazzling glare, followed immediately by a terrifying clap of thunder. The wind howled fit to tear the window from its hinges. And then the hailstorm began. Lumps of ice as big as hen's eggs began to shower the town, drumming into the roofs and beating into the pavements. This was surely a calamity: the dispensation of God; the crack of doom.

The inquisitor sank onto the couch and buried his head in the pillows, while the hunchback, still clutching the candlestick, knelt down and with a quaking voice recited all the prayers he knew.

The storm quickly passed, and when it did, Ignatius opened the window to let the freshness into the room. As he did so, he was stunned to see a gang of people shouting their way from Monastery Street.

"What's going on?" Boblig asked gruffly.

"I'll go and see," the hunchback replied and ran out onto the square.

He soon returned with the news:

"It's old Mistress Rohmer, who used to be the Sattlers' maid. Master Gröger, the furrier, caught her weaving spells. They say it was she who conjured up the hailstorm. Master Gaup's taking her to the lockup!"

"Idiot!" The inquisitor exploded. "Does he think that's the way to win praise from the prince?"

37 ✦ The Seven-Headed Beast

In some places the hailstorm utterly destroyed the crops, while elsewhere the devastation was only partial; substantial damage was also caused to the town. This was not the first such calamity to visit the district of Schönberg, but it was quite different from anything that had happened before. This was no act of retribution from the Lord but a work of the Devil, wrought by a witch. Master Gröger, the furrier, had seen her with his own eyes. Old Esther Rohmer, once a maid at the Sattlers', had invoked the storm with the help of the Evil One.

The next day, when the people were still counting the costs of the damage, ten persons were arrested on the orders of the inquisitorial tribunal. So Mistress Rohmer had not been acting alone! Even the wife of the rich councillor Peschek was involved; even the soapboiler, Prerovsky, and his mother; even the beautiful cooper's wife, Mistress Partsch! No one thought too deeply why even their houses, their gardens, and their fields had also suffered in the storm.

Popular belief in the supernatural power of witches was vigorous and had never smoldered far below the surface; now it blazed into the open. This belief was forcefully heightened by Administrator Schmidt in his Sunday sermon, which was followed by a wave of hatred directed especially against Esther Rohmer. The town-hall guard had to be strengthened, for there was a danger that the mob would drag her out. But the hatred was also directed at the other prisoners who had been jailed at the same time, even though none of them could be shown to have had any part in the calamity.

When it was widely reported that Esther Rohmer had admitted everything in her prison cell, the whole town was gripped with an intense and unprecedented fervor. Gangs gathered in the streets and indulged in wild talk. No one dared defend those who had been placed under arrest, no one dared argue reason to the tumultuous mob. Even formerly mild-mannered and peaceable citizens were joining in the cries. Burn them! Stone them! And the more eminent the accused were, the more hateful was the talk. Look how the soapboiler Prerovsky had shown his true colors! No wonder the good Lord had marked him with such an ugly bald head! God alone knew where that interloper had come from! How could he have come by such property in so short a time? And why had he never married? Though why should he, when he could have his way with all the witches he wanted! And his mother? What a hag she was! She spoke to no one unless she had to, and when she did, it was such a jabber that no one understood her. That was the tongue she must have used with her gallant! Or Katharina Klug. Supposedly a respectable widow, she had survived two husbands—plainly dispatched from this world by her spells so she might go roving with her vile gallants! And who but they would go with her! Or Mistress Bernhardt, the locksmith's wife. Now it was clear why she had lost three children in a year. They had simply got in her way, and she had disposed of them! And Dorothea Partsch, the cooper's wife? Just think of the way she deported herself, how provocatively she dressed and walked, how she tossed her trim little rump to lure the menfolk into her clutches. Two devils stared out from each of her sparkling eyes. Her gallant was a powerful demon to be sure!

The greatest calumnies were poured on Marie Peschek, wife of the linenmaker. She had always appeared to be so saintly, making sure to go to church every day, sprinkling herself with holy water, distributing alms, and helping the needy, but all that had been a kind of mask, to allay suspicion! Not for nothing was she the sister of the Kaspar Sattler who had confessed that he was leader of the witches on the Petersstein! Now it was plain to see why the Sattlers and the Pescheks were so prosperous! Whatever those two families turned their hands to, it always brought them profit—and how could it be otherwise when they were helped by the Devil himself!

The town was awash with a stinking mire of lies, slander, concocted stories and pure rage. No one was spared, for the filth of rumor spattered everyone, and especially those whom the inquisitor had had arrested at the same time as Esther Rohmer. What an opportunity the hailstorm had been!

It was as if Schönberg had seen a fulfillment of the Revelation of Saint John, that a beast with seven heads and ten horns had indeed arisen on the land, and the world was worshipping the beast.

It so happened that this was the very day the out-of-town weavers were due to hand in their cloth in return for a few groschen and to take new yarn home. Many of them had worked for Kaspar Sattler, and his arrest had threatened their livelihood; but as soon as the official red seals appeared on the master-dyer's house, Heinrich Peschek had taken them onto his own books.

Though devastated by the arrest of his wife, the linenmaker accepted the cloth and paid them in full, without even his customary examination of their work. But he gave them no new yarn. Thoroughly preoccupied with his wife's arrest, it did not occur to him that the weavers would not be able to support their children without more work. He was so upset that it did not occur to him he was depriving the poorest of the poor of their daily bread— and that at the very time the hailstorm had ruined their meager harvest.

The weavers left to roam the town in desperate search of work elsewhere. Some went to the taverns to drown their sorrows with a glass of brandy or a pot of beer.

Hanus Vejhanka, weaver of Hermesdorf, had already been drinking before handing in his cloth, for he was again in one of his moods. He also received no new yarn and resolved to wash down his rage with more drink at Nollbeck's. Outside the taproom on the square he met several acquaintances and began to broadcast his ideas loudly. The weavers, he told them, were not to take such injustice lying down. Were they like calves to allow their throats to be slit without a murmur? They were to join together against the gentry, for they were even worse than witches!

"Out in the open they all make a show of how godly they are, but at home they're servants of Satan! Who other than disciples of the Devil would deprive the poor weavers of their last crust of bread?"

This also happened to be market day. The square was full, so there was no dearth of an audience. People gathered round as the drunken weaver became even more talkative.

"Not long ago, I heard a sermon from a reverend gentleman who compared the poor to dry wood, and the rich to green wood. The word of the Lord, he said, was fire. Dry wood, he said, is quick to catch fire, while the green merely smolders and resists the flames. So do the rich resist the word of the Lord, while every day they feast on fine food and gather gold into their treasury. They resist the word of the Lord and they make deals with the Devil. True, some of them have been thrown into prison, but how many of them are still free? Brethren, the time has come."

The district judge, accompanied by three constables, emerged from the town hall and approached the inn, intent on restoring order.

The warier ones among the crowd immediately dispersed, but the weaver had no thoughts of escape. Especially when he saw another figure approaching. It was the man who, more than anyone else, had caused his gorge to rise: Heinrich Peschek.

Now he shouted even louder:

"Master magistrate, do you see that man? That thieving robber, cheat, swindler, Mammon worshipper, Devil's baggage? His wife's imprisoned as a witch, but what of him? Brethren, let us demand the return of the money he extorted from us. Our own money, stained with our own blood!"

Peschek continued striding toward the town hall, quite lost in thought. He noticed the crowd of people in front of the inn and also heard the weaver's provocative voice, but he had no idea what he was saying or that it had anything to do with him until a clenched fist was brandished in front of his face. He stopped short in alarm.

"Thief, scourge of the poor weavers! You joined with the Devil against us!"

Now he heard it clearly and also recognized the speaker.

He gritted his teeth. He was unused to giving way to anyone, least of all now. No one was going to obstruct his way to the town hall.

Fortunately, three guards arrived on the scene, muskets at the ready, to drive back the clamoring crowd. Peschek strode on resolutely, ignoring the shouting. Only when he reached the town hall did he turn around, to see the musketeers dispersing the crowd with liberal blows. He sighed. What things were happening in the quiet town of Schönberg! The people seemed to have taken leave of their senses.

Peschek detained himself no further but entered the town hall to lodge his protest with Master Dominik Beck, the Lord Mayor, against his wife's imprisonment.

Just a few days before, the Lord Mayor would have beamed with pleasure at the sight of his fellow councillor. This time, however, his facial expression was more that of a man on whose neck a boil had just burst.

"Dominik, I wish to protest against the arrest of my wife. Our town must not put up with such violence, not even from an inquisitorial tribunal."

"And what do you want to do?"

"At the very least, to complain to the prince. And to resort, if need be, to the monarch himself. Are we village serfs, or what?"

Beck tugged at his beard and stared into a corner for a while. Then he spoke.

"Heinrich, let me give you a piece of advice. Hold your tongue!"

"Hold my tongue? When I am so sorely wronged? What would I be worth then?"

"Just hold your tongue, Heinrich. Don't make it worse!"

"You mean for myself?"

The Lord Mayor knitted his brow. Perhaps he had given away more than he had to.

Realizing that further talk was a waste of words, Peschek turned without proffering his hand and went out.

Before he left the building, however, he went to see Sebastian

Flade, who had always shown himself to be respectful and willing. He found the court clerk to be even more jittery than the Lord Mayor. As soon as the linenmaker walked in, he turned his eyes heavenward.

"What a misfortune the Almighty has sent upon us!"

Peschek glowered.

"Don't you bring the Almighty into this, Sebastian. You know just as well as I that this suffering has been brought upon us by the inquisitor Boblig. And you others are helping him!"

Flade pretended not to have heard.

"Poor Marie! How I'd love to do something for her! But believe me, there's nothing I can do. Except pray for her. The only man who could do anything is Master Boblig of Edelstadt."

"Thank you for your advice," he snarled and left.

Peschek had the feeling he had touched something slimy; his head fumed, his blood seethed. Are we but sheep to the slaughter, merely waiting for the butcher to cut our throats?

A number of people were milling around the door outside, townspeople and countryfolk. Peschek knew most of them well, but they turned their faces away from him as he emerged. Only here and there did someone nod his head in acknowledgment before plunging into conversation with his neighbors. At that moment the linenmaker despised them all.

Was he such a lousy cur, he thought, that they should shun him so? But then he raised his head aloft and thrust out his chest. No one, he determined, was going to see how he felt.

Suddenly he spotted Master Heinel. The Schönberg jailer was winking surreptitiously. At the same time Peschek felt Heinel pushing some kind of soft object into his hand. His fingers closed around it, and he thanked the jailer with his eyes. Then, his fist clasped tight, he hurried home.

When he arrived home, he opened his hand to see what Heinel had given him: a ball of crumpled paper. He unwrapped it with trembling hands. One side of the paper was blank, but on the other side were a few hurriedly penciled words. There could be no doubt that this was a note from Marie.

"Dear Heinrich," his wife had written, "things are bad. They want to make a witch of me. Please see Kaspar Hutter or Master Maixner and ask them what we are to do."

Heinrich Peschek was a hard and resolute man, but now he found himself shaking. Sinking onto a chair, he closed his hand around the smuggled scrap of crumpled paper as if it were a sacred relic. He also closed his eyes, but it was not in time to stem the flood of tears. O God! How was he to help her?

It seemed he was in a quicksand. The ground beneath him had opened up and he was sinking deeper and deeper, with no one anywhere to offer him a helping hand. At one fell swoop, all the friends he had known at the town hall had become people without hearts, utterly indifferent to his misfortune. The weavers to whom he gave work had branded him a thief and extortioner. If it had not been for the musketeers, perhaps they would have trampled him to death. Perhaps his house would have been ransacked or razed by fire. And why?

A few days before, he would have been able to face up to anyone. His word had been like gold, valued and respected; now he was sitting at home, abandoned by everyone, not knowing which way to turn. They had accused his wife Marie of witchcraft; and they would torture her to force a confession. True, she was strong and would surely not succumb as easily as her brother Kaspar, but would she ultimately endure? Wouldn't she confess, like the others? Shame on those who wrought such violence! Shame on those who did not oppose the real villains. Beck the Lord Mayor and Flade the clerk were mere reeds in the wind, servants of Boblig! So what was to be done? How was poor Marie to be saved? Could Kaspar Hutter really help? Or Master Maixner, the advocate in Olomouc?

Peschek was still sitting motionless when nightfall came.

Someone hammered at the door. He rose to open it, but it was not on the latch. Kaspar Hutter stepped inside, to be greeted with a bitter smile.

"At least someone doesn't shrink from me!"

"But even I had to wait until dark, Heinrich. And I had to

sneak here like a thief. No one trusts anyone. Everyone's under
suspicion—rich or poor, healthy or sick, young or old, crippled or
cross-eyed."

"Look," said Peschek, handing his friend the smuggled message. "Heinel gave it to me."

Kaspar Hutter read it.

"Poor woman!" he whispered.

"Marie's thinking of you. She hopes you'll be able to help her;
you or Maixner."

Hutter shook his head.

"Maixner won't be able to help, not now!"

"And you?"

The former judge stared out the window. Outside was impenetrable darkness. After a while he sighed.

"But what can I do?"

"You used to be such a fighter!"

"I want to fight now, but we've lost so much time. It's all far
more difficult than before. In all of Schönberg you'd find no one
who'd put his signature to a complaint and you'd certainly find
no one who'd take part in a deputation to the Lord Mayor of
Olomouc or to Prince Liechtenstein. No man is safe, and all are
afraid. Today you may be master in your own house, but tomorrow you could be languishing in jail. Yes, even you, Heinrich, or I
or my wife!"

"But that's the very reason we have to act quickly! Go and see
the prince, Kaspar! I'll stay here, whatever happens. Someone has
to be in contact with the prisoners."

"I'll go, of course I'll go, but . . ."

"You need money, perhaps? How much? I'll give you all you
need. This isn't just about Marie. It's about me, you, everyone and
everything!"

"I'll go, Heinrich. But it will take a long time, too long. I'll
have to go higher than the prince to get anything done. And it's
hard enough simply getting to the people at the top. Making them
listen is even more difficult. They have hearts of iron!"

His hopes raised, however, Heinrich Peschek was not going to
give in.

"Any day now, I'm expecting Master Langweil to arrive. Perhaps you remember him, the merchant from Vienna. You could leave town in his wagon, no one would see a thing. I'll entrust all my money to him and give him goods on credit, as much as he can take. You'll have the right to use the money as you see fit. First you'll go to Olomouc, then to the prince at Eisgrub; and if you don't arrange anything there, you'll go to the provincial governor in Brünn or to the Emperor in Vienna. Go, Kaspar! Spare neither yourself nor the money, spare nothing."

Kaspar Hutter hardly recognized his old friend. Before his family became directly involved, Heinrich had always stalled for time. But now he was full of energy.

"That's a good idea of yours, to travel with the merchant," Hutter said. "But my advice, in any case, is to give him all the money you have. You're not to leave any at home. Boblig knows about it, that's for sure, and he'll come looking for it. He's like a terrier; he never lets his quarry go but chases him through bramble and thorn until he drops from exhaustion. But there's one thing you've forgotten, Heinrich. I have a wife. And if I were to disappear, Boblig would take revenge on Dorothea."

Peschek lowered his head as if he had been dealt a blow. "I'll look after her, don't you worry," he said, though he felt only too keenly what little comfort this was.

"Some responsibilities weigh very light, Heinrich. Others weigh heavy. This is heaviest of all!"

"I know. But someone has to do it!"

"All right, Heinrich. I'll go!"

The two men shook hands.

Langweil arrived from Vienna the very next day. And just one day after that, laden with tripp and ordinary linen cloth, his wagon was already leaving town again. It did not occur to anyone, as it clattered through the Old Gate, to check whether woven goods were indeed all it was carrying.

Someone else disappeared that day: Tobias, the son of old Mistress Rohmer, the constable who had helped the poor prisoners in jail in whatever way he could. He was hurrying to Brünn, to see Master Prerovsky's brother.

38 ✦ *The Leopard and The Kid*

One dank day, Sheriff Kotulinsky appeared in Lautner's cell to announce the arrival of new orders from His Grace. The dean was no longer to be regarded as a prisoner of the bishop but was to be held in custody as a common criminal.

Lautner knew this was a turn for the worse; the prospects of a happy conclusion to his trial were now even further removed than before.

"And you, master sheriff," he asked sadly, "do you still regard me as the kind of person they say I am?"

Kotulinsky hung his head and did not reply.

"Don't you have at least some doubts? Has it not occurred to you that if I were truly a sorcerer, the Devil would surely have helped me escape from your prison?"

This time Kotulinsky did reply, though it was not an answer to the dean's question:

"I really should not be saying this, but there is one thing I'd like to tell you. Be ready, for yet worse things are to come."

Lautner caught his breath.

"What are you preparing me for?"

"Please don't ask me. I can tell you nothing."

The sheriff went out, and once more the prisoner was alone. When he completed his apologia, Lautner had felt himself imbued with an inner calm, but now this was scattered to the winds. Just what was Kotulinsky preparing him for? Had Boblig already elaborated a verdict? If he had, then all was lost! After a while, however, Lautner's dread gave way to doubt. Boblig, after all, was not just any sort of inquisitor; plainly, he wished to assure himself of a complete and utter confession. And because he would not get one voluntarily, he would have to proceed to torture, for such was the practice of the Inquisition. But torture could not be carried out by a secular court on a prisoner of the bishop unless the bishop renounced his protection—which he had done. This was Boblig's opportunity! This, surely, was what the sheriff had wanted to warn him of! They were going to torture him. They were going to torture him just as they had tortured Kaspar, Marie and Liesel Sattler and poor Susanne Voglick and Johann Stubenvoll, the Ullersdorf cellarman. Would he endure, or would he fall?

Outside, the wind moaned, and somewhere in the village a dog howled. Night had fallen, and from time to time, the half-moon was obscured by fleeting clouds. Christoph Lautner stood watching by the window of his cell. There was the moon, shining and glistening like molten gold, yet a moment later, along sped a cloud and the brightness was gone. Was the cloud therefore mightier than the moon? No, for it was bound to dissolve or fly away, but the moon would remain. Light was more powerful than darkness. But now, unfortunately, darkness prevailed, for a heavy cloud covered the crescent of the moon, and the wind was moaning and rustling through the trees, their bare branches rattling like dead men's bones. Perhaps it was no dog howling in the village but wolves coming down from the mountains.

The whole region had now lain for long weeks in a profound darkness. Thick clouds covered both the moon and the sun, for what was the Inquisition but a cloud? It could not be for eternity; one day the sun would emerge again and cast its golden beams over the land. But why the dreadful darkness now? What was the meaning of it?

Lautner recalled something he had read long before about King Solomon, the wisest man of all. Solomon, it was written, could not understand four things: how a bird could fly in the air, how a serpent could creep across a rock, how a boat could sail in the middle of the sea, and how it was that not even such a wise king as Solomon could understand these three things! How little did Solomon wish to know! If only he had rather used his wisdom to tell future generations why the world was visited by such darkness, why people took leave of their senses and killed one another, why there were times when even wise men could not see the difference between fairness and injustice, and why even honest folk could worship murderers and thieves, regarding them as benefactors.

The night passed without sleep for the former Dean of Schönberg. When morning came, he felt weaker and unhappier than before. He ate nothing, not even a crumb of bread, but only drank cold water. Then he opened the well-thumbed Bible, and his eyes chanced to fall on a verse from the prophet Isaiah:

"The wolf also shall dwell with the lamb, and the leopard shall lie down with the kid; and the calf and the young lion and the fatling together; and a little child shall lead them . . ."

A magical vision of peace, serenity, love, and mutual respect arose in his mind. "And they shall beat their swords into plowshares," he read on, "and their spears into pruning hooks: nation shall not lift up sword against nation, neither shall they learn war anymore . . ." Yes, one day such a time would surely come to pass. And there would be neither prisons nor the suffering within them, and there would be neither judges nor accused. All people would be brothers and sisters . . .

Then came the sound of footsteps at the door, followed by the grating of a key in the lock. The door flew open, to reveal a jailer and two armed gamekeepers.

"You're coming with us," said the jailer.

The dean shivered and looked around for his fur coat.

"You won't need your coat, you won't be going far!"

The gamekeepers led him out of the cell and marched him down a long passage, the sound of their footsteps crashing against the stone walls. At the end of the passage they went down some steps, then along another passage and down yet another flight of stone steps. Lautner was quite certain what awaited him in the basement. The only thing that surprised him was that even a bishop's castle had a torture chamber.

The procession stopped at a heavy ironclad door. The passage wall, built of unrendered stone, was a good yard thick. There was a mustiness in the air and a bone-chilling coldness.

The jailer opened the door. Beyond it was a narrow chamber with a cross-vaulted ceiling and blackened walls, illuminated by several candles on a bare table. The air was heavy and acrid with smoke. Some people in fur coats sat at the table, and opposite them a cruel rack and pulley reared out of the gloom.

No longer could there be the slightest doubt about the prisoner's fate. He looked to the people at the table and recognized the entire inquisitorial commission; also, nearest the door, sat Sheriff Kotulinsky. In the yellowish glare of the wax lights, the judges' faces reminded Lautner of a picture that hung in the Dominican monastery in Schönberg; it showed the soldiers at the foot of the cross, casting lots for the coat of Christ. But the vision lasted only an instant, for Lautner found himself focusing his gaze on the inquisitor's face. Suddenly it was the face of a leopard. Not the one the prophet Isaiah had spoken about, lying down peacefully with the kid, but a real leopard. A dangerous beast of prey, a savage brute, thirsting for blood and utterly without mercy.

It was cold in the basement. Kotulinsky had omitted to tell the servants to bring cinnamon-spiced mulled wine, so Boblig opened the interrogation without delay:

"Christoph Lautner, you are hereby granted your last chance voluntarily to make a confession. Do you wish so to do?"

Steam billowed from the inquisitor's mouth, and the candle flames flickered.

The prisoner was no longer staring into Boblig's leopard face but at the sheet of blank paper spread out in front of the hunchbacked clerk, whom he now noticed for the first time. What did this godforsaken monster intend to write?

"Answer!"

"I have told you many times," Lautner said at last in a choking voice, "that I cannot confess to things I did not commit . . ."

Lautner noticed, as he spoke, how Boblig's face twisted, how the bishop's secretary frowned, and how Sheriff Kotulinsky scratched nervously at his beard.

The inquisitor rasped: "Master Jokl!"

Jakob Hay, the Ullersdorf executioner, emerged from the shadows, accompanied by his son.

"The thumbscrew!"

Expectation had become certainty. The Dean of Schönberg was about to embark on the same road as Kaspar and Marie Sattler and their daughter Liesel—yes, and even dear Susanne Voglick. He had been so careful to look after her, to see that she should never know poverty, and yet she had so bitterly regretted ever crossing the threshold of his deanery. It couldn't be helped now. Once more, a dark cloud covered the clear round of the moon. The leopard was not lying peacefully with the kid; it was preparing to drink its blood.

Lautner half raised his hands to the executioner. And as he did so, he heard the shrill voice of the bishop's secretary, Schmidt: "Confess, Christoph Lautner! Spare us, and yourself . . ."

The prisoner gave a wry smile. Secretary Schmidt was afraid of the blood that would spurt from his crushed thumbs. But he was not afraid to take the life of an innocent man!

"Rather should I be saying unto you, Brother: Spare the innocent!"

Boblig ignored this exchange and gave an order to the executioner.

Now the cold metal was clamped onto the prisoner's hands. Perhaps this, he thought, was the very instrument used on little Susanne.

Then came a painful pressure on his thumbs. He gritted his teeth, half closing his eyes. He had to be brave. The beasts were thirsting for his blood and his suffering, and he was determined to give them no pleasure.

"Master Jokl, begin!"

The leopard bared its fangs, or rather the hollow stumps of its teeth. Steam billowed from its mouth. Surely it stank of blood.

The pressure on his thumbs increased, and an excruciating pain spread from his hands to all of his body.

"O God!"

Boblig gave a sign to the executioner, and Master Jokl stopped turning the screw.

"Christoph Lautner, I ask you again: do you wish voluntarily to confess to your sorcery?"

"No!"

"Master Jokl, continue!"

The pain doubled, then trebled. Lautner longed to lift this piece of iron with his tortured hands and smash it against Boblig's head. But the inquisitor had been careful to take account of such a natural reaction; the young Hay was ready to restrain the prisoner if he made any move against his tormentor.

"Yet more, Jokl, if you can!"

An inhuman shriek burst from the dean's lips as the agony of the torture began to overwhelm the power of his will.

Again he heard the shrill voice of Secretary Schmidt, whose own spirit could no longer endure even the sight of such horror:

"Confess your guilt, Lautner! End your suffering!" A small voice inside his head seemed to be echoing Schmidt's words. End your suffering! Just one word is enough, Christoph Lautner! Just one little word! But the dean ignored the whisperings in his mind, for he knew still that he had to resist. He was defending his life and all it stood for. He was defending the truth against lies!

"I can't!"

Lautner's voice was steeped in tears. The experienced Boblig knew his prisoner was near breaking point, and the crisis was coming. He looked to the executioner. He was giving yet one more turn of the screw. Lautner's blood was now spilling onto the stone floor, his body convulsing, an inhuman roar gushing from his lips. But he was resisting, with all the reserves of strength that he possessed.

A smile appeared on Boblig's face. This was the kind of song he liked to hear. Another minute, two maybe, and the hardheaded dean would cave in, like Kaspar Sattler before him.

The inquisitor did not want to shout in order to make himself heard, so he went quite close to the prisoner:

"Do you finally wish to make a confession, Christoph? If you

don't do so now, then after a while, we'll resume the torture.
After the thumbscrew come the Spanish boots, and after them the
rack . . ."

This was the first time the inquisitor had addressed the dean
by his Christian name alone. He was now quite certain of
victory.

Impossible as it seemed, Jokl now tightened the screw yet
further.

Boblig pressed his face into that of his prisoner.

"Tell me, Christoph," he said, "did you engage in black magic
and make pacts with the Devil?"

This was Lautner's moral breaking point, the culmination of
his crisis. Everything else was of no consequence now; all that
mattered was to stop the pain.

He nodded his head twice.

"Master Jokl," Boblig cried gleefully, "enough!"

Then he turned to the judges:

"You all saw that! The accused nodded twice at my clear
question. A nod of the head is quite the equal of any verbal
confession. And that's how it will go down in the court record.
We may therefore state that the former Dean of Schönberg,
Christoph Alois Lautner, this day finally made a confession."

Lautner heard all this as if from afar; even so, he well understood. He stared at this beast in human form, forgot the pain in
his thumbs, and saw only the jaws of the leopard, thirsting for
blood. Thrusting himself away from young Hay's grasp, he sprang
to the table.

"That's a lie! It's not true I confessed! I am not guilty of the
crimes that you ascribe to me!"

"It's too late!" frowned Boblig. "Everyone saw it!"

"It's a lie! A lie!"

The inquisitor pursed his lips and turned to Master Jokl.

"Put him on the rack!"

But Canon Rehramont was already on his feet.

"That's enough for today, Master Boblig!"

Sheriff Kotulinsky seized the opportunity and went outside to summon the gamekeepers.

They came in, positioned themselves on either side of the prisoner and escorted him out of the chamber.

Again the cold passages, the stone steps, the crashing of footsteps from the stone walls. Finally the little room with the barred window, through which the sun was already peering.

Once inside, the first thing Lautner did was plunge his smashed thumbs into the pitcher of cold water, to ease the pain and stanch the bleeding.

Then he threw himself on the bed, and for a while lay quietly; but soon he raised himself and began loudly to accuse the four unhearing walls of his cell.

"*Vae misero mihi!* Woe is poor me! What a disgrace! What ignominy. I did not endure even as much as Susanne! My thumbs are perhaps too soft, unaccustomed to pain. I have lived in great comfort. I'm a coward. I've pronounced sentence on my own treacherous self!"

Then he calmed down and buried his face in the pillow. A saying of Horace's emerged from his memory: *Est modus in rebus, sunt certi denique fines,* there is a measure in things, there are definite bounds.

He thought of his mother. How little had he remembered her in prison, until now. If she were here, she would kiss his pain better, just as she used to when he was a little boy.

"O Mother!"

Tears streamed from his eyes.

Eventually, the door opened softly. It was the jailer, bringing in a large glass of mulled wine.

"The sheriff sends you this."

"The sheriff?"

"Yes. Drink it down at once. It will send you to sleep!"

"Please give him my thanks."

The jailer loitered in the doorway. Suddenly he reached into his pocket and took out a little wooden box.

"I've brought you some ointment. Put some of this on your thumbs. It'll stop them hurting and help them heal."

Then he left. He had never been a man of many words.

Lautner felt he was in a trance. The sheriff was sending him wine, and even the jailer, out of the goodness of his own heart, was bringing ointment . . .

He looked out the window. Outside, the sun was shining. Once more, the tears flowed. He stood holding his hands in front of him and looked into the brightness of the sun.

"And yet one day," he whispered, "even the leopard and the kid shall lie down in peace . . ."

39 ✦ *Forgiveness*

Beyond the window, spring was already ablaze in all its colors, but inside Lautner's cell at Mürau Castle, the days were becoming ever gloomier. His long term of imprisonment had gradually deadened his hopes. The solitary confinement had had its effect, and the lack of any kind of news had instilled within him a resignation to his fate. Even so, his spirits had enjoyed something of a revival in recent times, for he was sure a reply from the bishop was forthcoming. Whenever the sheriff entered his cell, Lautner's first question was always whether a letter had arrived from His Grace. The sheriff did not want to dash the prisoner's hopes. He himself had supposed there would be a long wait for the bishop's answer to Lautner's apologia; but that term had long expired, and still there was no trace of a reply. The explanation, he suggested to Lautner, could be the new and terrible Turkish onslaught upon Christendom.

This was a fresh blow for the dean. For who, in these troubled times, could still be interested in the fate of an unfortunate old man imprisoned at Mürau?

Before long, the otherwise laconic jailer let slip the news that they had burned two witches in Schönberg just before Christmas. One was old, the other young. He even remembered their names: the older one was a Mistress Sattler, the younger one was a Miss Voglick.

The revelation cast Lautner's entire world into new turmoil. His own fate now appeared so clear that all further hope was in vain. What sense would it have? Was not death itself a release?

Not long afterward, the inquisitor Boblig returned with the entire commission, and the prisoner was led to the torture chamber a second time.

Once again the thumbscrew was fitted, and the scarcely healed thumbs were again crushed into a pulp. Yet Lautner still refused to confess. Perhaps Hay the younger, this time stepping in for his father, had a greater compassion for the former dean and did not turn the screw as tightly as he might. More likely, Lautner had discovered new reserves of morale to deny victory to the inquisitor. Certainly, the news of the death of Marie Sattler and Susanne Voglick had heightened his resistance. Rather than elect, by dint of a confession, the same death as dear Marie and Susanne, he was determined to die under torture.

Boblig was enraged. Seeing that the thumbscrew was to no avail, he ordered the executioner to put the prisoner on the rack.

Against all expectations, one member of the commission stood up to protest: Winkler, Dean of Müglitz. The rules of the Inquisition, he declared, and also the Papal Bull of Paul III, decreed that periods of torture were to be brief. Also, it was forbidden to use torture several times in the course of one day, or even one hour, or to use torture for several days in succession.

Boblig bit into his fleshy upper lip. He knew that Winkler was correct, and he saw also that the other clergymen agreed with their brother from Müglitz.

"Anyway," said the bishop's secretary, who could hardly stand the sight of blood, "the testimony of thirty-six persons is quite sufficient proof for a conviction, and it is therefore unnecessary to exact a confession!"

Boblig frowned.

"Some theologians," the Dean of Müglitz was continuing, "claim that if there are two opinions which are contradictory but equally credible, it is quite possible, in all good conscience, to incline to one or the other!"

"And what, Dean," challenged the inquisitor, "am I to understand by that? Are you trying to say the claims of this sorcerer are just as credible as the depositions of three dozen witnesses? That would be making a mockery of the entire inquisitorial process!"

Winkler was quite distraught. He had certainly not intended to say anything like that. He turned for help to Canon Rehramont, but he merely shrugged his shoulders.

Despite his suffering, Lautner well understood Winkler's words and was filled with joy at Boblig's defeat and Winkler's unexpectedly courageous part in it. He gazed thankfully at his former friend. So even he was doubting his guilt! Or perhaps a fresh wind was blowing from sources close to the bishop!

After the second torture, the Dean of Schönberg was taken with a fever and fell into a delirium that lasted all day and all night. He cried out for his mother and spoke to Marie Sattler, Liesel, and Susanne; he wandered about the town of Landshut; he found himself in Vienna, repulsing the Turkish assault on the ramparts. He shouted, he laughed, he wept.

But in the morning the fever subsided, and soon everything seemed to return to the old routine. One day followed another like the seconds and the hours on a timepiece. No one brought any news, the jailer spoke not one word more than he had to, and Sheriff Kotulinsky avoided seeing the prisoner at all. There was no reply from the bishop; and probably never would be. As Secretary Schmidt had said, thirty-six witnesses were quite enough for the pronouncement of a verdict. It seemed the former Dean of Schönberg would soon be joining his departed friends. Some days later, Sheriff Kotulinsky finally came to Lautner's cell.

"The Turks have taken Raab," he said. "His Grace is making his way here to Mürau for greater security."

A gleam appeared in the prisoner's eyes. If Bishop Liechtenstein was on his way to Mürau, the two were bound to meet!

Seeing what was on his mind, the sheriff hastened to add the bitter truth to the sweetness of Lautner's thoughts.

"I have to tell you that His Grace does not want to be under the same roof as a prisoner accused of witchcraft. He directs you to be transferred elsewhere."

"Where?"

"To Müglitz. The bishop has had a new prison made ready for you."

Müglitz! The very name aroused all the shameful memories of Lautner's deepest dishonor.

"This is the end of me!" he said.

The following day, Christoph Lautner was taken to the new

prison, built by the burghers of Müglitz from a semicircular bastion that jutted out from the town ramparts. Inside was a cramped chamber with a low ceiling and stone walls that exuded cold. There was a bed, a table, and a chair. And what was once a slit embrasure in the rounded wall was now a narrow window, fitted with stout iron bars.

The dean went straight to it and looked out. There, somewhere to the north, below the distant mountains, lay his native Schönberg. The countryside stretched out before him: meadows, fields, scattered villages with familiar names, the white high road. This was a precious landscape, full of memories of his youth, and the very opportunity to see it again was cause for joy. At Mürau he had seen only tall trees below the castle walls and black squirrels. He would not miss them.

In front of the cell was a narrow passage patrolled by the guards. At Mürau he had known only silence. Here in Müglitz, the echo of footsteps on the brick floor would be a constant reminder that he was a prisoner, the sound of every footfall taking him one moment of time nearer to his death. But what kind of death? By burning at the stake like Susanne Voglick and Marie Sattler? Lautner sighed deeply, lay down on the hard bed, and closed his eyes.

Now he thought of Vojtech Winkler, his boyhood friend, and he felt him to be very near, as if once again they were sitting on the same bench at school in Olomouc. Except that their friendship had ended forever. Vojtech had turned into a Judas, and then even one of his judges. What had this judge done for his old friend? Had he defended him against the inveterate Secretary Schmidt or the complacent Canon Rehramont? True, he had never heaped fuel on the inquisitorial fires, but then again he had never shown concern for his friend's fate, not until the last round of torture. Then he had even dared to oppose Boblig. So what was happening? Had Vojtech changed?

Suddenly the footsteps in the passage stopped, and an uneasy silence followed. Lautner rose, returned to the window, and again looked out at the landscape. Dusk was falling. For some time his gaze was held by a coach moving along the white high road. The last time he had traveled that road, it had been as the Dean of Schönberg, with old Florian. What had become of his faithful servant? Florian had never enjoyed going to Müglitz on account of Winkler's miserliness. If only that had been his only imperfection!

✦ ✦ ✦

A few paces away from the bastion-turned-prison were the sprawling premises of the Müglitz deanery. In one of the large rooms inside, on a bed by the window, Winkler lay moaning. His old illness, gout, had made a return, this time with extreme ferocity, and it felt to him as if someone were driving red-hot nails into his legs. The medicinal powders that had helped him before were now without effect. Kathy, his housekeeper, wrapped his legs in warm poultices, but even this did not dull the pain.

No sooner had she left the room than Stephan raced in.

"They've brought the Dean of Schönberg, Father!"

Winkler groaned. He remembered the torture chamber at Mürau; how the blood had spilled from the prisoner's smashed thumbs; and how Christoph, his teeth gritted, had borne the pain. He heard his inhuman shrieks. He wanted to spring up, but the pain in his own limbs forced him back onto the bed.

"Tell Kathy to come in!"

When she appeared, he said: "Did you know Dean Lautner is in the new prison?"

"The sorcerer?"

"Do not pass judgment lest you be judged yourself! His trial isn't over yet. Now he's our neighbor. You ought to send Stephan over to him with something to eat."

The housekeeper tossed her head, and even Stephan stared in amazement. What had become of the dean that he should ask for such a thing?

But Kathy did not dare disobey; a short while later, Stephan left for the bastion, carrying a large platter of good food.

✦ ✦ ✦

Florian had never been fond of Dean Winkler's coachman, but Lautner was quite overwhelmed with joy when Stephan arrived in his cell.

"Stephan! How are you? Do you know anything about Florian?"

The coachman gave him a bewildered smile. This wild man, long unshaven and unshorn, bore little resemblance to the Dean of Schönberg who had always given him such generous tips.

"I'm just the same as ever, Father. As for Florian, they say he ran off and took the horses with him," he said, forcing himself to add: "I've brought you something from the dean."

Lautner stared hungrily at the enticing food.

"Are you sure it's from the dean, Stephan? Not from Kathy?"

"It's from the dean all right, Father!"

No, brother, thought Lautner to himself, you will not buy my indulgence as cheaply as this!

"Stephan, please tell your master that I, a scoundrel in his eyes, can accept nothing from him," he said. "Tell him I thank him. But I will have to be content with bread and water."

"But the Reverend Father himself . . ."

"No, Stephan, I can accept nothing from Dean Winkler. The comedy he played with me during your feast day was quite enough for me. You remember, don't you! I would take the food if it came from you, but not from him. Off you go, and take it back with you!"

Night came, full of the moon's silver brightness. Inside the new prison, Lautner did not sleep, for he could not rid his mind of thoughts of his old friend. Had Vojtech changed? Or had there perhaps been a change of mind in Olomouc? A faint hope stirred in the prisoner's heart like a tiny plant sprouting roots into the rock.

Neither could Dean Winkler sleep that night. Not only was he still racked with pain, but his thoughts, too, were constantly returning to his former boyhood friend. Christoph had rejected his charity, renounced him as a friend, and—epicurean that he was—he had even rejected his offer of food. Christoph could not forgive him for luring him to Müglitz and handing him over to the bishop's men; he could not forgive him for his disgraceful pretense, throughout the feast, that he was his best friend, though he knew what was being prepared. Yes, I was wrong, Winkler admitted to himself. *Mea culpa, mea maxima culpa,* I behaved despicably. Like Judas.

"But for God's sake, what was I supposed to do?" he cried, as if Christoph Lautner were standing at his bedside. "Was I to go against the orders of His Grace the bishop, and even bring suspicion on myself?"

The sick old man tossed and turned on his bed. It was true that he had behaved disgracefully, but could he alone have taken Christoph's side? After all, he knew and trusted the testimonies of the witches of Ullersdorf. And those testimonies, clear and detailed, were believed also by Canon Rehramont and certainly by the bishop. And yet something else weighted the scales against his former friend: ever since boyhood, Christoph had been captivated by the strangest things; at one time alchemy, at another astrology, then the science of healing with herbs, curative waters, roots, all manner of potions and purgations. And he often studied books, many of which were on the Index.

Only later, when Christoph stood accused by Kaspar and Liesel Sattler and by Susanne, had a note of doubt stolen into Winkler's mind. He had known Lautner for many years; he knew him to be forthright and truthful and never inclined to tell lies, except in jest. The confrontations with his accusers saw him behave with distinction. He could hardly be lying. Even graver doubts had set in during Christoph's second period of torture at Mürau. If he were entirely guilty of all charges, he would surely have succumbed to the agony of the torture and confessed like the witches before him. Surely, such power of will could be possessed only by someone who was defending the truth! Or—and now Winkler seemed to hear again the voice of the inquisitor—someone to whom the Devil had given superhuman strength!

"God, O God, what is the truth?"

The Dean of Müglitz was stretched on the rack of his own

conscience. If Christoph were innocent, then he, Vojtech Winkler, man, priest, and judge, was guilty of a foul crime against his old friend.

Throughout the next day and night, tormented by the pain of his condition and the pangs of his conscience, he sought a solution. Then suddenly he found one. Come what may, he had to renounce his membership on the inquisitorial commission; his illness would be sufficient reason.

The following day, Winkler sat down at his desk and with a firm hand and the choicest Latin wrote a letter of resignation to His Grace the bishop.

Then, overcoming his pain, he left the deanery and, letter in hand, went straight to the prison, where the guards took him inside.

Lautner was standing at the window, staring toward the distant mountains. He turned as the door scraped, and was stunned. There, bent over a stick, sallow-faced, wretched, and humble, stood Vojtech.

It was some time before Winkler was capable of speech. Then at last he spoke with a trembling voice:

"Christoph!"

"What do you want, Dean?"

"God is punishing me with my illness . . ."

"See, Dean, how God is punishing me!" said Lautner, lifting up his crippled thumbs.

"I've come to beg your forgiveness, Christoph."

"My forgiveness?"

"Once, Christoph, you said something that I took care never to forget. Love is like the salt that gives savor to what we eat; it's like the light that gives form to what we see . . ."

Lautner interrupted:

"You remembered the wise words, Dean, but you have not abided by them, neither as a friend, nor as a priest. You have not behaved like a jurist who treats an accused man as innocent until and unless he is proven guilty. You may object, if you please, that this principle is not valid at an inquisitorial court. But did Boblig prove my guilt? It is true that he submitted to you the testimony of thirty-six persons who bore witness against me. But perhaps it escaped your notice that all those witnesses accused of witchcraft gave their testimony only after several tortures. Were you present when they gave those testimonies? You assisted when they crushed my thumbs. Did your conscience not cry out? Did your old sense of friendship not stir within you? What else do you want from me, Dean?"

"I will no longer stand by and watch you be tortured. I don't want to be your judge anymore!"

Lautner frowned:

"What are you trying to say?"

Winkler withdrew from his sleeve the sheet of paper addressed to the Bishop of Olomouc.

"Read it yourself, Christoph!"

Lautner took the letter begrudgingly and stared at it in surprise. He handed it back with some scorn.

"One can never be too cautious. Even illness is sometimes a boon!"

"You must understand, Christoph, that I cannot say everything I would like . . ."

Lautner laughed bitterly.

"I know, you wouldn't like to lose the bishop's favor. And neither would you wish to incur the wrath of Master Boblig. I do appreciate how difficult it is for you. You would like to cry out, for all to hear: Christoph Lautner is innocent! But you can't, because you, and the Very Reverend Canon Rehramont, are assisting the inquisitor in his foul comedy. And if you cried out: Put an end to the rampages of the Silesian criminal and murderer of innocents, the inquisitor Boblig! Give the people their freedom!— That would be even more dangerous, wouldn't it?"

Dean Winkler was horrified. What if someone were listening at the door!

"Christoph," he sobbed, "I know I've done you a great wrong . . . But *per amicitiam nostram,* Christoph . . . For the sake of our old friendship . . ."

Lautner saw the tears in the eyes of his former friend and knew that Vojtech was neither lying nor pretending. This poor old unhappy man was actually in an even more wretched state than he, the bishop's prisoner, who was accused of witchcraft. Winkler alone, though a free man, bore a burden of genuine guilt.

Lautner stretched out his hands.

"Did we not always teach that we were to forgive even our enemies, Vojtech?"

And Dean Winkler sank into his arms.

40 ✦ *Gallows Hill*

There was yet plenty of time before the execution, but little knots of people were already grouping on the square; the men tight-lipped, the women muffle-voiced, sharing the latest gossip.

When the inquisitor appeared, accompanied by his hunchback assistant, the women fell silent and everyone watched tensely his movements. He was on his way to pay a surprise visit to the district judge at his grand new house in New Gate Street.

As soon as he arrived, Franz Ferdinand Gaup sent for some good Hungarian wine from the cellar, then began giving Boblig all the latest news from the town. But the inquisitor expressed no great interest. He frowned and gazed at his host with a faintly mocking smile.

Gaup called his wife and asked her to show Master Boblig their latest infant, his godson.

The inquisitor could not resist an acerbic comment:

"Wouldn't you like to tell me, Master Gaup, whom you have in mind as godfather to your next son, when he is born? The first one's was Dean Lautner, wasn't it? Then it was my turn . . ."

Gaup bit his lip. Over the past two years, the ruthless judge had changed considerably. His belly had become bloated, his chest arched, and his face now rarely assumed the lickspittle grin that had once marked his dealings with Master Boblig. He had seen too closely the practices of the old inquisitor and was not amused when he occasionally became the butt of Boblig's jokes.

The inquisitor usually sent for him when he needed something. Today he had come himself. Why? And why the ugly mood?

The inquisitor did not keep him guessing.

"The prince wrote," he said, tipping a brim-filled glass of wine down his throat.

Gaup pricked up his ears.

"It will be of interest to you, judge, that the heirs to the master dyer Sattler have lodged a complaint against us."

"But Sattler's not dead yet!"

"The two hours of life he has left are neither here nor there. The heirs are complaining to the prince that we removed the seals from his house, had a locksmith open the door, forced open the strongboxes, and removed cash and valuables."

The judge broke out in a sweat of nervous indignation.

"Who is it that dares to complain?"

"It's not too important, but I'll satisfy your curiosity, if you wish: it's a certain Johannes Georg Weber, Salzschreiber* of the district of Glatz in Silesia."

"That's his eldest daughter's husband. Used to be a silversmith."

"A legitimate heir. This Weber urgently requests also that he be given a precise list of all the things we confiscated from Sattler's house."

"The impertinence!"

"If you like, impertinence. Fine," said Boblig with a smile. "But the prince directs that we do draw up such an inventory forthwith, that the original be sent to his office, and a copy of it to Weber as the representative of all of Sattler's heirs!"

Gaup mopped his fat neck with a handkerchief.

"That," he sighed, "is going to be very difficult."

Boblig said nothing for a while. Then his face dissolved into an increasingly enigmatic smile.

"If I am not mistaken," he said, "you have had your eyes on quite a large part of the Sattler estates: the Klug farmhouse and land. How much did you want to give for it?"

"Five hundred gulden."

"Sattler gave fourteen hundred gulden for it some years ago. What's more, he carried out improvements to the house and also bought more land to go with it."

---

*Literally: salt-clerk, a senior official at a salt mine.

"But I'm buying it under special circumstances!"

"That's true, but now we have the letter from His Eminence!"

This was a pretty mess. Gaup gazed anxiously at his visitor. "What if the prince wants to know what price I'm paying?"

"Never you mind!" said Boblig. "The prince has worries enough as it is, with the war on. Let's not give him any more cause for concern!"

Then he turned to Ignatius.

"First thing tomorrow, Iggy, you will reply to His Eminence. As regards the seals, write him that we were entitled to remove them, because we sealed the house in the first place."

"Yes," said Gaup gleefully, "that's quite right."

"As regards the cash and valuables, we were entitled to take them into safekeeping to prevent their theft from the premises. We used them to cover expenses connected with the inquisitorial process against Kaspar Sattler, his wife, and daughter. In cash we found only thirteen hundred gulden, which sum does not cover even one half of the costs of the court proceedings."

A great weight seemed to fall from Gaup's chest.

"Yesterday," he told the inquisitor, "Sattler invited Master Flade and another councillor to help write his will."

"All in vain," remarked Boblig dryly. "The inquisitorial court, or rather the prince, has prior claim to his property, to cover the costs of the case. Our Salzschreiber Weber will hardly inherit as much as it cost him to write the complaint. And Sattler's sons? They'll be too late in the field to get anything!"

"But what of the Klug farmhouse?"

"Never you mind about that either, *amice*. It will have to be sold to cover the court costs. And so far as I know, there is no other interested purchaser in the district than Judge Franz Ferdinand Gaup."

Gaup understood and was happy. He raised his glass. "There are always lessons to be learned from a wise man!"

"Unfortunately," sighed Boblig, "people often forget the value of wise counsel."

Gaup wanted to run for money straightaway, but the inquisitor restrained him with a smile.

"There's no hurry, *amice*. We have yet another unpleasant matter to discuss. It concerns the soapboiler, Master Prerovsky. A brother of his, the prior of the Carthusian monastery at Königsfeld, has lodged a complaint about us with the Emperor himself. His majesty has passed that complaint to Prince Liechtenstein, and now the prince wants an explanation."

Gaup flew into a rage:

"It's all young Rohmer's fault! Prerovsky gave him a letter, and he ran away to Brünn with it. Otherwise everything would have been taken care of by now. Have you seen Prerovsky's new house below the New Gate? It's a proper palace!"

"Don't have any thoughts about that house yet, Master Gaup. Prerovsky is a tough and stubborn fellow. He's already withstood two tortures."

"If only he didn't have those brothers in the priesthood . . ."

"But he'll still confess eventually. It'll just take more effort, that's all. As they say, for every finger a ring may be found. But we have to hurry, we have to act while the authorities in Vienna still have other things to worry about!"

Suddenly the conversation was interrupted by the tolling of a bell.

Boblig finished his drink. Then he, his assistant, and Judge Gaup rose and left the house. Outside, a coach was already waiting. They got in and set off for the *Galgenhügel*—Gallows Hill.

Marie Peschek, Liesel Sattler, and the master dyer Kaspar Sattler, all of them duly convicted of being in league with the Devil, were to be consigned to the flames. And once again, the whole town was going to the execution. Except Heinrich Peschek.

The rich linenmaker had already had to move out of his house; the inquisitorial tribunal had ordered it to be sealed, as if someone inside had died of the Plague. But he had not sought refuge with any of his fellow councillors or relatives. He knew how they would have behaved toward him. Instead, he took shelter with the poor shoemaker Simon, a man who was both bold and cheerful, and who had not lost his profound sense of reason, even in these terrible times.

Simon lived alone in a humble wooden dwelling by the brook on the northern outskirts of town, with only the songbirds—siskins, goldfinches, and hedge warblers—to keep him company. He willingly granted refuge to the rich linenmaker and shared with him as a brother the little food that he had. But not only that: he was also an inspiration for his guest, a source of trust that one day change would come; for it was not possible that truth should not ultimately triumph over the most shameful of lies.

But Peschek proved hard to placate. Knowing Kaspar Hutter's tenacity, experience, and reliability, he had placed all his faith in the former judge's mission to the south. But the days had passed and no news had come, good or bad. Kaspar had not returned to Schönberg, and neither had Langweil, the merchant. It was as if they had vanished from the face of the earth.

Turkish troops were marching on Vienna, which was now reported to be under siege, encircled by a ring of iron. All sorts of things could have happened to the rich merchant. Robbers could have ambushed him, killed him, and stolen what he was carrying; even soldiers were capable of such deeds. It was also possible that Langweil and Kaspar were stranded in the beleaguered capital. So many things could have happened to them in these turbulent times.

The death knell sounding from the deanery church was a sign that the long procession was leaving the town square for Gallows Hill. The shoemaker quickly slammed the window of his parlor, quite frightening the songbirds. But Peschek opened it again.

"We mustn't be afraid of the ringing of a bell, Master Simon," he said.

Then he sat on a low stool and put his head into his hands, following the procession in his thoughts. Now it had to be approaching the New Gate. From there it was going down, below the town walls. In a while it would be winding north along the bank of the brook, quite near Simon's house. So near that he might even go into the little garden and hide in the spindle-tree bush to catch a last glimpse of his dear, brave wife. How he would love to stroke her graying hair as he used to when it was the color of old rye straw and soft and smooth to the touch; how he would love to press her hand good-bye. But all he could do was watch. Still he did not go. He knew that if he did, he would be unable to restrain himself and would try to drag her from her captors.

✦ ✦ ✦

Now they could both hear the singing and the tumult of a great crowd.

Simon sprang up from the table and again slammed the window.

This time the linenmaker did not open it again but huddled on his stool and turned to face the corner. He was weeping and did not want Simon to see.

The procession stopped and silence fell. Marie, Liesel, and Kaspar Sattler were already ascending the hill, with all Schönberg behind them. Simon and Peschek said not a word; even the birds were quiet, as if someone had startled them.

The two men continued to follow the procession in their minds. Surely it was at the top of the hill by now. Perhaps Boblig or Gaup was already reading the sentence. Now the inquisitor was putting his final questions to the condemned prisoners. The order was given. One mighty swing of the sword—and Kaspar's head fell from his shoulders. Now the executioner's boys were lifting Kaspar's torso and Marie and Liesel, both alive, onto the pyres. One of the boys was lighting the straw with a torch. A plume of black smoke curled from the dry wood . . .

The shoemaker slowly opened the window.

"Now you can say good-bye to your good wife's soul, Heinrich," he said, uttering the Christian name of the rich linenmaker and town councillor for the very first time.

At that instant, a goldfinch burst into song.

41 ✦ *Truth on the Rack*

Suddenly, in the middle of September, all the bells of Müglitz began to ring. Christoph Lautner gazed out over the landscape and listened to their solemn peals with a heavy heart. But not until the evening did he hear what they meant. Mates Kekule, the old guard who occasionally kept the night watch on the bishop's prisoner, told him His Grace had ordered all the bells of the diocese to be rung to celebrate the great victory over the Turks. On the twelfth day of September, 1683, the allied armies of imperial Austria and Poland, under the leadership of Charles of Lorraine and the Polish King Jan Sobieski, had put the enemy to rout below Vienna, saved Europe from the horrors of war, seized rich spoils, and were now driving the heathen hordes back into the Hungarian lands, toward Neuhäusel and Pest.

That night, the tolling of the bells continued to ring in Lautner's ears, filling him with a strange foreboding. He knew it was only due to the war against the Turks that he had been forgotten in Olomouc and elsewhere; perhaps now his case would be brought forward in rapid order.

Many months had passed since Dean Winkler's visit. Vojtech was surely regretting it now. What dread he must have suffered lest anyone discover how he had bared his soul to the heretic, how he had begged forgiveness! How unhappy he would be that he sent his letter of resignation—if he had indeed sent it at all! Since their last meeting, Vojtech had not sent him so much as a book to read, nor even a little snuff; only Stephan still paid his regular calls with food. How much more, then, did Lautner appreciate the friendship of the old guard, Mates Kekule!

Not long before, Mates had also brought news of a new execution at Schönberg. They had burned Master Sattler, the rich master dyer, he told the prisoner. And they had burned his daughter, too, and Mistress Peschek, the wife of the linenmaker. Lautner felt his heart in his throat.

Mates saw straightaway that he had made a mistake and tried to cheer up the prisoner by telling him how the people of Müglitz had expected Bishop Liechtenstein to stop by on his way back from Mürau to Olomouc. The musicians were ready with their long trumpets, flutes, and drums, the Guild banners were flying. Master Nekvapil, the Lord Mayor, was dressed in his finery. But nothing came of the town's day of glory, because when the bishop came, he entered through one gate and immediately left through the other, without even stopping.

But Lautner was not listening to this small talk. He was thinking of Kaspar Sattler, thanks to whom he had become Dean of Schönberg in the first place. He was thinking also of Kaspar's daughter Liesel, who had always reminded him of a little bird. And he was thinking of Marie Peschek.

These three friends had gone, and he would have to follow. O God! What were our sins that you so persecute us? Can this truly be your will?

That was the last night Christoph Lautner had the pleasure of Mates's company, for his place was taken by another guard. Was this also an ill omen?

Time passed, fast for some and slowly for others. Autumn gave way to winter, and with it the snow. The whole countryside was thickly covered, and when the sun shone on it, Lautner's eyes ached from his constant gazing into the distance. Inside the prison it was cold, bone-chillingly cold. How grateful, therefore, was the prisoner that he still had his old sheepskin coat—retrieved not by the Dean of Müglitz, nor by Master Nekvapil, but by old Mates in the fall, before he was relieved of his post. The coat was warm, but even warmer was Lautner's memory of the kindhearted soul who had been his guard.

One day Lautner happened to hear an unusual noise in the passageway and was more than a little alarmed. His ailing heart thumped and his legs so trembled that he was obliged to steady himself against the wall.

The key grated in the lock, and the door opened.

Standing outside was Father Schröffel of Schröffenheim, the bishop's notary. A large and bespectacled nose between a pair of pale and bewildered eyes. Behind him stood Master Nekvapil, the Lord Mayor, and Hildenbrandt, the town magistrate, and Wild-holz, the municipal court clerk.

It was hard to tell from the notary's cold eyes what he was bringing. Lautner waited.

Father Schröffel took some time to get used to the gloom of the little cell with its low, vaulted ceiling. He merely stared at the prisoner inside as if not quite able to believe his eyes. It was a strange look, and it made Lautner ill at ease. The notary's face would have worn quite a different expression if he had been bringing good tidings.

At last, now accustomed to the dim light, he spoke. His voice was deep and seemed quite out of place with his slight figure.

"Christoph Lautner, did you request His Grace's permission to turn to the Holy Father in Rome?"

"Yes," the prisoner said, his voice barely audible.

Before the notary opened his mouth again, Lautner knew what he was about to say.

"Christoph Lautner, we did not presume to disturb the Holy Father with your case; we ourselves investigated it fully in all its points. We perceived you would persist in your obduracy. For your own sake it would be better for you to make a humble confession."

Lautner stared into the watery eyes behind the eyeglasses. His heart pounded and his hands shook.

"All I want," he said, his voice choking, "is right and justice."

"Better to repent. Remember the words of Saint Matthew: The enemy that sowed the tares is the Devil!"

These words brought Lautner to his senses. His weakness passed, and it was with a loud and indignant voice that he cried out to all his visitors: "But in the same Gospel it is also written: I will have mercy, and not sacrifice!"

The episcopal notary blinked, groping for suitable words of reply, but before he found them, Lautner spoke out again:

"And there is yet another verse from the Gospel of Saint Matthew that I would like to remind you of: Blessed are they which do hunger and thirst after righteousness!"

"From your mouth," shouted the notary, "that is blasphemy!"

And having said that, which was indeed all he could find to say, he turned his back on the prisoner and left, followed by his entourage.

Father Schröffel left behind a thick sheet of paper, bearing the seal of the Bishop of Olomouc. Lautner, still remarkably calm, seized it and began to read. Latin was an everyday tongue for the former dean, yet he found the content and form of the long and convoluted paragraphs scarcely comprehensible. Finally his gaze rested on a few lines written in another hand, evidently that of the Vicar-General, Count Bräuner, the suffragan bishop. These words were quite understandable:

"Even if I myself were weighed down by such burdens of guilt, sacred justice would require that I be publicly burned as an example to the whole world!"

Lautner dropped the paper and went to the window to take a breath of fresh air, involuntarily grinding the document with his heel as he did so.

The last glimmer of hope was extinguished. The sentence, albeit indirectly, had been pronounced. And there could be no appeal.

Death! Perhaps they were already looking at their victim through the crevices in the door. Kaspar, Susanne, Marie Sattler, Marie Peschek, Liesel. They had all gone. And Christoph Lautner was about to follow.

He gazed again at the landscape and whispered the words of Saint Paul:

"*Infelix ego homo!* Unhappy man am I!"

Then he remembered his mother.

"O Mother! Why did you suffer the pain of my birth? Why was I born? Why did you rear me?"

His heart was gripped with sorrow far greater than he had ever known before. He looked out at the countryside but saw nothing.

"*Quos amo, arguo, castigo,*" he whispered, remembering the Scriptures. "Whomsoever I love, I reproach and admonish!"

And then he remembered also a verse from the Revelation of Saint John the Divine: He that is unjust, let him be unjust still: and he that is filthy, let him be filthy still: and he that is righteous, let him be righteous still: and he that is holy, let him be holy still!

He burst into sobbing peals of embittered laughter. How long had he believed in those words! Now he felt them to be but barren sounds.

Lautner lay down on the bed and closed his eyes. His head was empty of everything but a rushing noise as when a river gushes through the rocks. Once, when he was a student at Graz, the River Mur had burst its banks in high flood. The rushing noise was just the same.

So he did not even notice when, after a while, the door of his cell opened. Only the presence of strangers already in his room awoke him from his torpor. He raised himself up, to see two constables accompanied by a man with a beard and a leather apron, and a young apprentice.

He understood straightaway why the man in the leather apron had come.

"I have orders," said the locksmith as if apologizing.

The prisoner said not a word but held out his arms. Once the manacles had been put on his wrists, he sat down so the locksmith could attach the fetters to his ankles.

The men left. Lautner rose and walked around his cell. The chains on his hands and feet jangled.

"Now I'm no longer alone," he told himself. "I suppose I have these two noisy friends with me for the rest of my days!"

✦ ✦ ✦

The weather changed, and so did the countryside seen through the narrow window of Lautner's prison. But one thing remained: the prisoner's desire for freedom and his yearning to see his native town once more. It was to Schönberg now that the dean's thoughts were most frequently directed. If he only knew what was happening there!

The bells had of course rung also in Schönberg when the victory over the Turks was celebrated. All the citizens gathered in the deanery church, and not only did they give thanks to God for the victory; even more fervently than that, they prayed that peace should come at last to their own town also.

But how mistaken their hopes were! The very next day, the constables arrested the papermaker's widow, Mistress Weillemann; and Dorothea Hutter, the wife of the former judge who had disappeared to an unknown place; and Christiane Reinhold. Then it was the turn of the ever-cheerful Fritz Winter, without whom no banquet was complete; then old Mistress Rollepatz; Master Bittner, the maker of gold lace; and ultimately even the hapless linenmaker, Heinrich Peschek, who had long awaited his arrest with certainty but—though he had plenty of opportunities—had never run away.

Once again, the town was to know sorrow, suffering, and fear.

Many people fled from the manor of Zerotin to the nearby region of Glatz, to Silesia, or to the Dietrichstein manor of Janowitz. Worst affected by the flight were the poor weavers from the mountains, who worked at home for the linenmakers, traders, and rich merchants of Schönberg. All of a sudden no one had any work for them. Kaspar Sattler was dead; Heinrich Peschek was in prison and his house was sealed, and the smaller merchants had no one to sell to. The weavers begged in vain for yarn and all in vain reduced their already paltry rates of pay. Dire poverty was knocking at the cottage doors.

Even the unruly Hanus Vejhanka of Hermesdorf was at the end of his tether and began to recall the years spent working for Heinrich Peschek as an age of plenty. True, the linenmaker had nitpicked, checking for the tiniest of faults in the work, but he always paid up, and when he sometimes docked a copper heller or two, his wife always made up for it in some other way.

Hunger stalked the wooden cottages of the weavers, and there was nothing they could do to turn it away. The magistrates from the villages sent earnest entreaties to the authorities, begging for help on their behalf, but it was not the custom of the officials of the manor to reply to such supplications from the peasantry.

Throughout the region, the people were finally beginning to realize who was the real cause of their misfortune. But who would have enough courage to undertake anything against the almighty Boblig? After all, he had the support of Prince Liechtenstein and of the Bishop of Olomouc, the Law Lords of the Prague Court of Appeals, the provincial officials, and even the old Countess of Galle, whose illness was again worsening daily. Never before had the master inquisitor enjoyed such power and glory.

He had the air of a king. He could do anything. Everyone with whom he dealt prostrated themselves before him, agreeing in advance with everything he said, however nonsensical it might be.

"Did you ever believe, Iggy," he would ask his faithful assistant, "that such a bright star as this would ever rise for us again?"

"I always believed it, master," the hunchback replied. "But this isn't a star, it's a comet!"

Christoph Lautner, prisoner of Müglitz, had no news of Boblig. Nor did he know what the inquisitorial commission, which was conducting his trial, was working on. What did it intend to do with him? Did it want to torment him with uncertainty? To leave him locked up for the rest of his days? Or had the gentlemen of the commission forgotten about him on account of more urgent matters?

That was not the case. On the contrary, Bishop Liechtenstein himself had ordered that the trial of the former Dean of Schönberg be concluded as soon as possible. He stressed this point especially to Doctor Mayer, the new member of the commission, whom he had nominated to replace Dean Winkler of Müglitz. Doctor Mayer threw himself into the work with great energy.

Now Christoph Lautner could have no cause to believe he had been forgotten.

One day the constables arrived to escort him to the torture chamber at the town hall. Come what may, it was the commission's resolve that a confession be exacted. And as the thumbscrew had not been enough, the court would proceed straight to the third degree of torture—the rack.

As the executioner tied his wrists to the ladder of the rack and his ankles to the pulley-rope, Master Boblig repeated the question he had asked so many times before:

"Do you wish to make a confession?"

"I am innocent," Lautner replied, his voice firm. "I cannot lose my soul through a lie!"

Boblig gave a signal.

The executioner's boy grasped the rope. Lautner moaned as his body tightened.

"My God!"

"Will you confess?" This time it was Doctor Mayer who was asking.

"I can't!"

"Be reasonable," Mayer went on, now standing at Lautner's side. "The Inquisition can never turn back. The torture will be repeated for as long as . . ."

"I can't lie in the face of death!"

Doctor Mayer shrugged his shoulders and looked to the executioner, who again pulled the rope taut. Then he hauled.

An inhuman scream filled the chamber. Lautner's arms had been torn from their joints.

"Will you confess?" Again it was the voice of the leering inquisitor.

"No!"

Nevertheless, the court directed after a brief consultation that the prisoner be taken down from the rack. The executioner pushed Lautner's arms back into joint, and his boys doused him with water. Then they offered him a glass of wine.

The judges were still conferring.

"I say no innocent man could stand such pain," Boblig of Edelstadt declared. "Lautner can endure it only with the help of the Devil. I speak from many years of experience."

Secretary Schmidt agreed.

"Truly, it could not be otherwise."

But they did not proceed to further torture that day. Instead, the prisoner was taken back to the bastion jail in a basket-carriage and laid on his bed, utterly exhausted.

Lautner was long afraid to move at all lest the excruciating pain begin again. His mind was working feverishly, constantly returning to the words of Doctor Mayer: The Inquisition can never turn back. So they would torture him again and again. The judges were not concerned with the truth, only a confession. So let them torture him! To death, if need be!

But even as Lautner thought, someone seemed to be whispering into his ear: And what will you achieve by that? Resistance is folly! Even if they did torture you to death, no one would ever be the wiser; no one would ever hear that you didn't confess. Only that the Devil didn't permit you to speak! God has abandoned you! Even he wants you to confess to something you never did! So why endure such suffering? How many times will they yet stretch you on the rack before you yield up the ghost? You can't escape death, so why endure the torment? Confess! Kaspar Sattler did, and so did Marie and Susanne!

But then Lautner was seized with fresh hope. Perhaps Doctor Mayer's words were just an empty phrase. Surely, when Bishop Liechtenstein heard that Lautner had not even confessed on the rack, he would understand. He would know that only a man who was innocent could resist such tortures. Therefore, Christoph, you must endure! You must hold on until the end! There is no other way!

The next day, Lautner was taken for more torture. This time the executioner barely pulled the rope tight, and the pains were even worse than before. He implored them to take him down.

Master Boblig went up to the rack and stood by his head.

"Do you confirm that the testimonies of thirty-six witnesses, of whom five have already died by burning, are truthful?"

"I confirm that they did so testify, but I cannot confirm what they testified about me."

"He thinks we're fools! Executioner!"

This time the master executioner spared no effort. The chamber filled with an inhuman roar.

"Will you confess?" It was Doctor Mayer again.

"Yes . . ."

The pitiful prisoner was taken down.

"Yes, I am guilty," he said with a feeble voice. "Susanne Voglick introduced me to the Evil One . . . He had a woman's body and his name was also Susanne . . . I signed a pact with this demon . . . Yes, I renounced the Lord God, the Virgin Mary, all the saints and our Holy Church . . ."

That day Christoph Lautner accepted no food; only water, to quench his raging thirst. Fever tormented him. At times he wept. He knew he had lost his life, and he had also lost his honor. He had sustained the vile and despicable superstition against which he had fought. He had relied on God, but God had set himself on the side of his enemies.

The next day, Lautner was taken back to the court for further interrogation and was graciously allowed to sit down. But one look at Master Boblig renewed his determination. Before the first question was put to him, he said:

"I declare that nothing of what I testified yesterday is true. Only the pain of torture forced me to testify as I did."

"Executioner!" shouted the inquisitor.

Lautner began to tremble.

"Tell me," asked Doctor Mayer in a voice that would cut butter, "is yesterday's testimony true, or is it not?"

"It is . . ."

Lautner was no longer able to put up any resistance. To all the nonsenses that Boblig had put into the mouths of his witnesses, Lautner confessed, for he was no longer responsible for his actions. He confessed to everything and anything.

At the end of the day, in a shaking scrawl, he affixed his own note to the record of the court:

"Everything is true. In witness thereof I hereunto set my hand. Christoph Alois Lautner."

42 ✦ *Found by Law*

Several more weeks were to pass before the collegium, headed by Doctor Mayer, elaborated its verdict and Count Liechtenstein, Bishop of Olomouc, affixed to it his signature and seal.

So it was not until the middle of September that the prisoner of Müglitz heard the inquisitor's croaking voice pronounce the final judgment. Boblig read out the sentence in the jail with all the members of the judicial collegium crammed into Lautner's cell behind him.

"Almost five long years have passed since Christoph Alois Lautner, erstwhile Dean of the town of Schönberg, first stood accused by divers persons, both male and female, on the manor of Gross Ullersdorf and also in the aforesaid town of Schönberg, six and thirty persons in total, as with one voice—*uno quasi ore*—of engaging in sorcery, of committing for long years the most enormous and unforgivable crimes—*enorma et nefanda scelera*—and of taking part many times in great gatherings of witches in the company of the said six and thirty. These persons, among whom were the culprit's closest friends, steadfastly insisted on their confessions, and even after pronouncement of sentence did stand by them until their death . . ."

The inquisitor paused for a while, but the wild eyes that stared from the unkempt bearded face of the condemned man compelled him to continue:

"Even the former Dean of Schönberg did himself voluntarily confess after torture, and by his testimonies and by depositions made in his own hand did confirm, that he was guilty of the most dreadful and loathsome crimes against the Divine Majesty; that he took part many times in congregations of witches on the Petersstein; that he devoted himself to the Evil Spirit; that he

renounced the Lord God and his beloved saints; that he dishon-
ored the sacred hosts when he carried them in his shoe and
danced on them with his female companions and partners in sin,
and that with the aforesaid sacred hosts he committed lewdnesses
so wanton that they do not bear recounting. Further, he confessed
that he celebrated Holy Masses to the Devil; that he sacrilegiously
confessed; that to dishonor the suffering of Our Lord he smote
with a rod the lamp hung below the Crucifixion; that he sacrificed
young children to the Devil and invalidly baptized; that he did not
absolve the penitents who made confessions to him and that he
joined carnally with many mothers and their daughters. Moreover, he often willfully revoked his testimonies and admissions
and appeared more and more obdurate and impenitent . . ."

A somewhat bitter smile appeared on the prisoner's face, but
otherwise Lautner stood without movement.

"On considering these crimes and depravities, the episcopal
commission, formerly the inquisitorial and now judicial collegium, set up to pronounce judgment and to execute sentence—
collegium pro ferenda sententia eiusdem executione—has found by
law that the said Christoph Alois Lautner is to be stripped of all
clerical rank and office, and that in accordance with canon law he
is to be unfrocked and handed over to the executioner, and that
his body, in a public place and while still alive, is to be burned to
ashes, that justice thereby be done."

The inquisitor's voice softened, and a deathly hush prevailed in
the cell.

Lautner's heart pounded beneath his ragged shirt and his
breathing quickened, but no one saw or heard, for it seemed no
one cared what was going on in his inner self.

"This verdict, arrived at without exception or dissent, and
without any pressure whatsoever, we consider to be correct," the
inquisitor was concluding. "In witness thereof we have caused our
seal to be affixed, and also set our hand. *Fiat iustitia! Carolus, Dei
et Sedis Apostolicae Gratia Episcopus Olomucensis.* Karl, by the
Grace of God and of the Apostolic See, Bishop of Olomouc."

After an almost interminable pause, Boblig spoke again: "I ask
you, Christoph Lautner: Do you accept the verdict?"

All eyes were fixed on the condemned man, but he remained silent. He knew that if he were to utter but one word, his voice would choke with tears.

The inquisitor shrugged his shoulders and would have asked another question. But before he was ready to do so, Canon Rehramont took a hesitant step forward and said in a voice full of emotion:

"Christoph Lautner, we would like to pray for you. But for this to be possible, you must express sincere sorrow for your deeds . . ."

"What deeds?" Lautner snapped.

The canon stepped back. Now Doctor Mayer spoke:

"The sentence is just. The court took account of all the testimonies . . ."

"Court?" interrupted Lautner. "What court? *Beati, qui faciunt iudicium et iustiticiam in omni tempore.* Blessed be they who utter righteous judgments at all times. But that cannot be said about your judicial collegium. What you have presented as the truth is nothing but utter concoctions and nonsense!"

Secretary Schmidt gasped:

"What an impenitent sinner!"

The canon waved his hand and the court collegium went out. Boblig, the last to leave, no longer dared ask the remaining question: whether the condemned man wished to thank His Grace the bishop for his just sentence.

But before he went out, he turned back from the door and spat venomously:

"See where your learned books got you!"

"Get out!" cried Lautner, raising his hands and rattling his chains.

Master Boblig of Edelstadt hastened after the others.

Lautner went to the window and looked out, but his dull eyes saw nothing. Only the grim future.

His fate was sealed. The Dean of Schönberg had become a sorcerer. One day, generations hence, people would examine the court records and find a signature there in his own hand, confirming all the nonsenses of which he was unjustly accused . . .

Meanwhile, he would burn like the other innocents who had fallen victim to the inquisitor, and there would be no avengers to rise from the ashes.

But future generations had to be told the truth!

The bishop's correspondence was carefully filed and stored for posterity. A letter to him was bound to be preserved.

Lautner sat down and wrote with a trembling hand:

"Your Episcopal Grace! I, a poor wretch, downtrodden by false imprisonment, stand before Your Eminence, condemned by your sentence to death at the stake for the crime of sorcery to which I perfidiously confessed, and this against my conscience and only out of fear of new torture. Face to face with death I repeat to Your Eminence: I never did commit the crimes for which I am condemned to so dreadful a death . . ."

43 ✦ *Per Aspera ad Astra*

Death was at hand. It was leaning against the door, baring its fangs. Lautner could touch it with his fingers, yet he did not see it for Boblig's monstrous face. Though he had left long ago, the inquisitor seemed to be with him still in his cell.

The prisoner shrieked:

"Liar! Ghoul!"

The sound of his own voice brought Lautner once more to his senses. He sat on the bed and felt the searing pain from the inflamed wounds caused by the iron shackles on his wrists and ankles. It was as if someone had driven a wooden wedge into the crown of his head.

"O God, why was I chosen as a victim?"

After a while, he felt a dryness in his mouth and longed to drink, but the pitcher of water was far away, and walking to it was difficult. Still, he rose to his feet but was startled by a strange noise in the passage. He guessed what was happening. They were installing yet another lock on the door and perhaps also securing it with an iron bar! They were afraid the prisoner would escape. Fools!

That day Stephan from the deanery brought him nothing to eat. Also, instead of one guard in the passage outside, there were now two men keeping watch. Their speech indicated that they were not local people and were evidently soldiers. From time to time one of them would pound on the door:

"Hey, old man, couldn't you conjure up at least a tot of brandy for us?"

"Or a pretty wench! Do you hear, old man?" the other said.

Night came. Lautner lay spread-eagled on the bed, afraid to move lest he reopen his wounds. He could not sleep.

Outside, a gale was blowing up. The prisoner overcame himself and hobbled to the window. The moon was shining, but every little while it was obscured as the clouds sped across the sky like a flight of fantastic birds. The wind howled and shrieked. Yet more evidence, perhaps, of the guilt of the former Dean of Schönberg! Boblig would certainly trumpet that the tempest had been aroused by the sorcerer's diabolical powers!

Toward morning came the great downpour. Immense quantities of water gushed from the low clouds as if the deluge were about to come. Further proof of the guilt of the *maleficant* Lautner!

Throughout the next week there was no end to the rain. From the window of the jail, Lautner could see how the roads had turned into streams and the meadows and fields into lakes. The River March, surely, had already burst its banks.

Even the prisoner was disturbed by such signs. Was the Lord God issuing a warning to the people that they might come to their senses?

In the forenoon the bishop's secretary Schmidt, Boblig's faithful ally, entered the jail. He was drenched to the skin, and his mouse-eyes peered everywhere. Everywhere, that is, except into the face of the condemned man.

Lautner stared at him with a superior, malicious sneer.

"I come on behalf of His Grace the Bishop."

It was as if someone had touched the prisoner with cold steel. He remembered the stern old man in the purple robe who had signed the sentence that was so cruel and so unjust. Bishop Liechtenstein.

"The man who, without exception, dissent, or any pressure whatsoever confirmed the sentence on me?" asked Lautner, with no trace of irony. "What could he possibly want from me?"

Pretending not to have heard, the secretary continued in his official tone:

"His Grace is gravely concerned for your soul. Should you make a penitent confession before death, he wishes to order all the clergy of the diocese of Olomouc to pray for the salvation of your soul for an entire octave. Further, he will grant you this mercy, that he will consent in advance to whomsoever you choose to be your confessor."

Lautner vividly remembered his last audience with the bishop. Once again his mind's eye saw the stern old man with his clear, penetrating gaze. He had begged the bishop in vain for his help and for his protection. Now the bishop was concerned for Lautner's soul! Was this perhaps a response to his last letter? How comfortably he had arranged things, how complacent he was!

"My dear Father Schmidt," he said firmly. "I do not need the intercession of either priest or bishop, for I hope to find better intercessors before the throne of the Almighty. He alone is the supreme arbiter!"

Secretary Schmidt was horrified, but he still managed to control himself.

"Don't you even want a confessor?"

"If I were malevolent, I would choose you or Canon Rehramont, who so eagerly assisted this entire comedy!"

The bishop's secretary lowered his eyes. Had his conscience stirred? Lautner suppressed his rage and moderated his tone.

"We are here alone, just you and I. And above us, our Father in heaven. It's not necessary to lie or to pretend. Tell me, in all conscience: Do you truly believe all the charges brought against me? I won't tell anyone what you say—I wouldn't even have time for it. But I'd like to hear it. I'm asking you more for your own sake than mine. Do you truly believe all those nonsenses?"

"Faith is one thing, evidence is another," the secretary replied evasively.

"Do you truly believe?" Lautner raised his voice.

Even now, Schmidt gave no clear reply.

"It was not I who decided but the judicial collegium and the Vicar-General!"

"But in accordance with the wishes of the inquisitor Boblig! Have you ever considered how you would testify if you were put on the rack?"

Schmidt covered his ears and quickly retreated to the door.

"You don't believe it, do you?" Lautner called after him.

But even after this episode, the prisoner was still given no peace. The next visitors were the two round-bellied, bearded Capuchins from Olomouc, Father Crescentianus and Father Carolus. Initially, it was Crescentianus, the elder and more experienced, who did the talking:

"We have come to visit you, Brother, so that we may pray together and prepare you for the journey that awaits you."

Lautner smiled a wry smile.

"Why so suddenly? You didn't even think to bring me a breviary before!"

But the monk pretended not to have heard:

"One must be prepared. You don't have much time left!"

Lautner detected the fragrance of snuff tobacco. How long had he been without so much as a pinch of snuff! He interrupted:

"Wouldn't you have a little snuff for me, Father?"

The monk's first reaction was one of astonishment at such insensibility. But because he enjoyed taking snuff himself, he knew what it was like to be without. So he reached into his pouch for his silver snuff bottle, unscrewed it, and sprinkled the little that remained into the prisoner's outstretched palm. Lautner sniffed it straight away. What a delight! It was as if his brain were cleansed through and through.

Now the second Capuchin spoke:

"You are making a grave error! You are dwelling upon earthly things, yet you should be opening your heart, pouring out your sorrows, and beseeching the Lord for his forgiveness; for only by so doing will you cause the demon to relinquish his power over you. You can yet save your soul, even if you can no longer save your body. There's not much time left!"

The prisoner looked into the monk's round, red face.

"First, you tell me, Father, whether all the persons whom you accompanied to their place of execution confessed the monstrous sins for which they were condemned. Did Mistress Sattler, the master dyer's wife, confess? Or her daughter? Or Susanne, my housekeeper? Did they confirm before their death that they really did commit the crimes for which they were about to be burned?"

"You know that a confessor priest is bound by a vow of secrecy!"

"You must not avoid the question, Father. I know you don't wish to tell me the truth, but your evasive reply is by itself enough. It tells me that all those three women recanted everything that they had testified under torture!"

Father Crescentianus frowned deeply; never before had he met such recalcitrance in a condemned man. He was sorry he had given him so much snuff.

"When do you want to confess your sins, if not now?"

"I committed other sins than those which you would wish to hear!"

"But think of the salvation of your soul!"

"You would do far better, Father, to try and confess Master Boblig of Edelstadt. His soul needs it more than mine!"

The deep bass voice of Father Carolus interrupted:

"Reprobate! You will soon stand accused before God!"

"I have had plenty of time to think about eternity," smiled Lautner. "I am not afraid of the Lord's judgment!"

"Brother Christoph," sighed Crescentianus, and now his voice was sobbing, "your impenitence will be your destruction. I am afraid for you. Surely, therefore, you will allow us to spend the last few days of your life in prayer with you."

Lautner shook his head.

"No, I'd rather sleep!"

"Aren't you afraid of God?" cried Carolus.

"You are the ones who should be afraid of him!"

The two monks left in indignation, Crescentianus more in sorrow and Carolus in fury.

Lautner stared long after them. His self-assurance was now more buoyant than before. Death no longer seemed to him such a dreadful thing as the pitiful existence of these two monks who lived either in constant pretense or in ignorance.

✦ ✦ ✦

Meanwhile, the town seethed with an extraordinary hustle and bustle. An abundance of coaches, carts, horsemen, and foot passengers jammed all the gates of the town, for word had spread far and wide that on Tuesday the eighteenth day of September would be the execution of an arch-heretic, the former Dean of Schönberg. Noblemen were arriving in splendid Viennese coaches, accompanied by their ladies and their children; there were gentlemen judges and rich burghers; countless men of the Church, both common clergymen and members of religious orders; there were innumerable officials of all kinds, and common people from town and country. Müglitz could not hope to accommodate so many people, not even when several guests were crammed into each and every room, barn, or shack in town. Many people, therefore, slept out under the ramparts, alongside a detachment of the Hannoverian regiment, which had already encamped there for several days en route from the Hungarian lands.

On Monday they were joined also by a company of troops from Olomouc, sent to secure a semblance of law and order, for the burghers themselves could no longer cope, though they were all armed with whatever they had in the way of old halberds, sabers, or muskets. The town was like an ants' nest, with people scurrying hither and thither, foraging and scavenging food and drink. Even the more cautious observers estimated the number of visitors gathered to see the execution at some twenty thousand.

Not far from the town, the executioner's boys were building a great pyre, and everyone who was able to go there, went to see them at work.

Toward evening, a coach arrived from Olomouc, carrying Lieutenant Gregor Kliper, accompanied by his wife. It was driven by an old soldier who seemed to know the town very well. When he found a long line waiting to get in at the Lower Gate, he drove instead to the Hohenstadt Gate, but even there he got no farther than Hildenbrandt's bakery. His passengers had to proceed on foot to the school where accommodation had been prepared for them. Meanwhile, the driver entrusted the coach and horses to the soldiers encamped below the ramparts, then hied into town and straight to the bastion. On the way he bumped into Katharina, the housekeeper from the deanery.

"Good Lord! Florian!"

But the soldier only stormed off, disappearing into the crowd.

Night came, dark but warm. Campfires burned all around the town, and sheep, chickens, and geese were roasted on them. Drunken cries mingled with the sounds of singing and laughter as if a great celebration were being prepared.

There was a similar clamor inside the town, though the hour had long passed when the houses and taprooms were due to close. By far the greatest noise, of course, was at the deanery, where a number of clergymen had gathered, headed by the Right Reverend Vicar-General and Suffragan Bishop, Count Bräuner. Most talk was about the condemned man who had so despicably besmirched the good name of the priesthood. But all, including the Right Reverend Vicar-General, were engrossed by the two Capuchins' account of their last visit to the loathsome heretic. Father Crescentianus recalled in graphic detail how, when he returned from the jail to his little room at the school and took the little bottle from his pouch to fill it with snuff, such a dreadful smell had suddenly sprung from it that not only he but also Father Carolus and the dean's servant and the schoolmaster and his wife—everyone had all but been cast into a swoon.

At the bottom of the pouch was something that strongly resembled demon dung.

"I regard this," he announced, "as the most convincing evidence of his guilt."

✦ ✦ ✦

Hardly had the sun of the morning peered above the horizon, when the prisoner was disturbed by another visit—one that he had least expected. It was Dean Winkler of Müglitz. Where had he found the courage? Had he come to say good-bye? He looked sickly, his fat jowls hung flabbily from his face, his eyes roamed.

"Vojtech!" cried Lautner, touched by his friend's courage.

But Winkler only shook his head sadly.

"I have been sent by the Right Reverend Count Bräuner. His Grace wishes to have all deans, parish priests, and other clergy of the diocese celebrate Holy Mass for you and to pray to Almighty God for the salvation of your soul. I am to persuade you to repudiate what you wrote in your last letter to His Grace. If you do it, the Right Reverend Vicar-General himself will visit you in prison and grant you solace. So what is your reply?"

Lautner was saddened. Vojtech had not come to say good-bye, but only to curry favor with the suffragan bishop!

"What am I to say?" he said. "That I present the Vicar-General my respects and that I thank him. If he did not know of me during my trial, then I no longer need anything from him now. Especially, I no longer need anyone to celebrate Mass or to pray on my behalf. No, that would be too easy for Count Bräuner—sending an innocent man to his death and then redeeming his guilt through prayer for the victim. Tell him I thank him, but the answer is no!"

"But Christoph, who do you think you are?" cried the Dean of Müglitz in consternation. "Even many saints had to beg on their knees for such intercession! There is no greater sacrifice than the Holy Mass!"

Lautner gave one of his faint smiles.

"My dear friend," he said, "remember the words from the Gospel of Saint Matthew: Blessed are ye, when men shall revile you, and persecute you, and shall say all manner of evil against you falsely!"

"Reprobate!" erupted the Dean of Müglitz, aggrieved that he had not managed to satisfy the wishes of the Right Reverend.

But Lautner had nothing more to say.

Winkler's eyes suddenly welled up with tears. He left the room without even offering his old friend his hand.

Lautner sighed deeply.

The Dean of Müglitz was the last visitor to make any attempt to save the prisoner's soul. After him came Master Hildenbrandt, the municipal judge, with a locksmith and two constables. The locksmith broke the prisoner's shackles. Then the judge ordered him to dress in the robe that one of the constables had brought with him. It was a long gown, like a Jewish caftan, made of a coarse serge cloth of a dirty gray color. When Lautner was dressed, the second constable placed a brimless broad hat on his head. They are making a carnival buffoon of me, he thought. But it did not matter now.

Then the guards led him out of the jail. Lautner knew where they were taking him—to be unfrocked. But he was not sure whether he would return to his cell or whether perhaps they would lead him from the church straight to the stake. He took a last glance out the window to the mountains. He wanted to say good-bye to the countryside he regarded as his own.

It was only a short way from the bastion to the graveyard, in the middle of which stood the parish church of Müglitz. Many people were gathered around it, waiting for the sorcerer to be taken out. Soldiers and municipal guards had strung chains along the route, but it made little difference; the crowd pressed so forward that the soldiers could hardly keep a path clear. But the people were strangely quiet; they were so surprised by Lautner's appearance that they could not bring themselves to shout any abuse at all.

The common people were not permitted entry to the church, which was filled only with high dignitaries and all manner of noble personages, both men and women. Some said there were even close aides of the Pope and the Emperor. The door of the church was locked and was opened only at the behest of the judge. Inside, in order that the heretic's feet should not sully the hallowed ground of the church, new planks had been laid on the square stone flags of the floor. Only on them was the heretic allowed to tread. His head was bowed when he went inside; but when he saw that hundreds of pairs of eyes were observing him as if he were some kind of wild and exotic beast, he deliberately raised it. He stared at the altar with its quantity of lighted candles. Before it was gathered a crowd of clergymen around a raised chair, where sat Count Bräuner, the Suffragan Bishop of Olomouc.

Lautner was led to the screen that separated the presbytery from the nave of the church, to a small white-clothed table bearing a chalice with a paten, chasuble, and stole. But Lautner's eyes remained fixed on the assembly of clergymen surrounding the purple-robed and mitered Vicar-General. Then he looked to the left, at the inquisitor Boblig. How he had bedecked himself for this great occasion! He looked like a parrot, with a green coat, richly embroidered with gold; a red neckerchief; red stockings, and shiny shoes. On the right stood the priest Cicatka with Dean Winkler. Vojtech was leaning against the wall, his lips moving; he was evidently praying.

The suffragan bishop gave a signal to two clerics, who immediately advanced to the prisoner and began dressing him in the priestly vestments as if he were about to celebrate Holy Mass. Once dressed, he was led before the suffragan and ordered to kneel.

The suffragan bishop rose, and with a strong voice that echoed from the vaulted ceiling opened a ceremony which had never taken place before in the parish church of Müglitz:

"In nomine Patris et Filii et Spiritus sancti . . ."

A murmur rolled around the church. The noble bewigged gentlemen with their gold-embroidered coats and silk neckerchiefs, and their ladies with their painted faces and costly dresses, all bedecked with bows and other adornments, rose and made the sign of the cross. And so did the priests at the altar, except the former Dean of Schönberg. He did not move. Not out of defiance, but because he did not know whether he had the right to make the sign of the cross anymore. He was aware that for him this was the end of the priesthood that he had been so pleased and proud to serve. Never again would he open the Mass with the words that the Vicar-General had just uttered. Never again would he bless the believers!

But the clear and resonant voice of the Right Reverend was already reciting his part:

"Whereas by way of denunciation and investigation we have apprised ourselves of the dreadful crimes of the priest Christoph

Alois Lautner, and whereas by an appropriate court it was clearly established and proven that the aforesaid priest did truly commit those crimes, which are themselves both so grave and so immense that they shake the very Majesty of the Lord and all mankind, and whereas it was perceived that the aforesaid priest was and remains unworthy of the office and dignity of the Church. Therefore by the authority of Almighty God the Father, Son, and Holy Ghost, and by our own authority also, we do deprive Christoph Alois Lautner of his priestly office and of all ecclesiastical dignities, and this for evermore. Solemnly do we divest him of them and declare him in truth, in reality and actually, according to all the traditions of canon law, to be unfrocked and degraded."

Every word of church Latin stabbed like a sharp needle into Lautner's soul. His head hung lower and lower, and only with great effort did he stem the flow of tears. Now he was worse than a miserable cur.

A humming of voices swept the church. Lautner was still kneeling on the step, resting his forehead on the cold stone screen. He was still hearing the dreadful words of the suffragan bishop. Suddenly his heart was filled with fury. He lifted his head and wanted to shout: Lies! Everything is a lie! Even the suffragan is lying, and he's unashamed to lie even before the altar!

But the clerics were already lifting him up and leading him to the little table in front of the screen. There they placed in his hands the chalice, filled with water and wine and covered by the paten with the host. Then the suffragan bishop took both objects from the hands of the unworthy priest.

"We solemnly declare that you are deprived of the power to do service to God and to offer up the missal sacrifice!"

Then, taking up a fragment of brick, he scraped with it a shaven patch on the degraded man's head and the tips of his thumbs and forefingers, declaring:

"By this scouring do we cancel the power to offer sacrifices, to transmute the bread and wine into the body of Christ, and to give blessing, with which power you were invested upon your ordination."

Then, in like fashion, he was deprived of his chasuble and stole.

When it was over, he stood before the altar in his plain gray serge robe, gazing at the ground, deeply moved. But no one could observe anything of this on his bearded face. He lifted his head only as the suffragan bishop began to perform the final act of excommunication. He grimaced in pain as he heard the words, though some regarded it as yet another sign of his impenitence.

"Seduced by the Devil, he abandoned his Christian baptismal vows," Suffragan Bräuner intoned. "He laid waste to the Church. Therefore, in accordance with the commandments of the Lord and the holy apostles, do we extirpate this rotten and incurable member from the body of the Church by the iron of excommunication that the other members be not infected by its poison."

"*Fiat!* May it come to pass!" responded the congregation of priests at the high altar.

Lautner knew them all well; he also knew their sins. Who were they to damn him? O God!

"We cast him out from the society of all Christians," the bishop was declaring, his voice growing ever mightier. "We banish him from the threshold of the Holy Mother Church in heaven and on earth, and do hereby declare him anathema, damned with the Devil and his angels, and condemned to the eternal fires of hell."

Lautner half opened his mouth. He wanted to shout out, to stop the excommunication. But then he suddenly realized that all was in vain, that this was the way everything had to be, right to the end. If there was a God, then he was watching and listening. And if there was not, what was the use? Whatever the suffragan said, it was only words, a sound, a momentary disturbance of the air.

Count Bräuner was continuing the ceremony, though now his voice was softer than before:

"Unless he release himself from the snares of Satan and unless he be reformed, and unless he apologize to the Church of the Lord, may he be borne off by demons that his soul be not saved on the Day of Judgment."

"Fiat! Fiat!" This time the voices of the priestly congregation were joined by some of the gentlemen standing in the body of the church. Even the members of the judicial collegium cried out with them, and so did the inquisitor, Heinrich Boblig of Edelstadt: *"Fiat! Fiat!"*

Christoph Lautner gritted his teeth. The Jews, instead of *"Fiat,"* had shouted at Christ: Crucify him! Stone him! Kill him! The ceremony ended. Everyone was astonished that this despicable anathema was by no means crushed by his experience. He had not even sunk to his knees. He stood erect and shed no tears.

According to the principle that the Church does not yearn for blood—*Ecclesia non sibit sanguinem*—the living body of the anathema was handed over to the secular authority, represented in church by the municipal judge of Müglitz. He gave a signal to the two guards, who immediately seized the former dean and bundled him roughly out of the church. Even now Lautner conducted himself with dignity. Everyone wanted to have a look at this loathsome heretic, this repulsive beast, this man who was worse than a pagan; yet all they saw was an old man with long graying hair and a straggly beard, marching with a firm stride and with clear eyes fixed firmly on the window behind the choir, through which rays of sunlight were beaming their way into the church. It seemed to the people that Lautner was lifting his head with deliberate pride. But it was not pride. Lautner was merely delighting in the brightness of the sun, so many times clearer and truer than the gleam of gold on the pluvials and dalmatics of the priestly robes, than the finery of the noble lords and their ladies, and the glare of the countless candles at the altar. He knew that everyone was observing his every move, but what was it to him anymore? He did not belong to them anymore, for they were not real people. If they were real, like the old women, the prim young ladies, the surly old men, and unruly youth of Schönberg, it would be different. Real people would kneel and sob and shed real tears. And he would bless them, even with these deconsecrated fingers. But these unfeeling parasites and their dainty little ladies? They were not worth as much as a glance!

In front of the church, the yard was overflowing with spectators. Everyone wanted to see the foul sorcerer, whom the Devil had granted such great power. But they saw only an old man dressed in a plain cloak and a hideous hat. There was nothing dreadful about him at all.

But his head was no longer held high. Instead, he was looking to the ground, for he was afraid of seeing someone dear to his heart. Like old Mates Kekule.

Outside the graveyard stood a cart for the condemned man and by it two of the executioner's boys. As he arrived, they hurled themselves on him and tied him with ropes. By the time they bundled him into the cart, the two Capuchins, Father Crescentianus and Father Carolus, were already sitting in it, waiting for him. Lautner saw them and sighed, but he said nothing.

Then the vehicle was surrounded by soldiers with muskets and a squadron of dragoons with sabers drawn.

Outside the town, amid the countless throng of spectators, a great pyre loomed high, with a tall stake in the middle.

Lautner half closed his eyes when he saw the stake of red pinewood. There was a rushing and a roaring in his head, and he felt a faintness in his heart.

Once again, Crescentianus began to cajole him.

"I beg you," Lautner moaned, "spare me at least now."

His lips continued to move, even as he stopped speaking. Thinking he was praying, the monk moved a crucifix to his lips, but the prisoner thrust it away:

"That's quite unnecessary!"

The vehicle halted near the pyre. In the clearing in the crowd stood Jokl, the executioner of Ullersdorf, Nekvapil, the Lord Mayor of Müglitz, and the entire judicial collegium with Master Boblig of Edelstadt to the very fore.

The boys threw the condemned man from the cart, then helped him up the few steps to the stake, to which they secured him firmly with rope. They tied him so that his face looked to the north. How grateful he was to them for that! He threw a brief glance at the sea of spectators but then moved his gaze to the distant mountains. Somewhere out there, below those peaks, was his native town of Schönberg.

For greater security, one of the executioner's boys also fastened a chain around the condemned man's body. It touched the inflamed wounds on his wrists.

"Ow!" cried Lautner. "Why pull it so tightly?"

Crescentianus also clambered up on the pyre and for the last time attempted to persuade the sinner to repent. But Lautner did not see him or even hear him. For him the world had ceased to exist. Remembering a Latin verse, he whispered the words:

"*Ad coelos propero*, I am marching to heaven . . ."

He fixed his gaze on the countryside ahead of him—the countryside that he had come to love so well from the window of his cell.

"Good-bye," he whispered.

Now, as if in a dream, it seemed to him that he heard a rumbling of discontent at the edge of the crowd. Perhaps there were people who loved him there. Perhaps, somewhere out there, was Mates Kekule, the jailer from Mürau, perhaps even Master Kotulinsky. Suddenly, from one point in the crowd, there was a piercing yell. Lautner shifted his gaze to the source of the sound. Good Lord! Florian! He was wearing a military tunic and waving his hat high above his head.

"Florian!" Lautner wanted to cry, but his voice broke and he felt a choking in his throat.

It was at this moment that one of the executioner's boys hung a bag of gunpowder from the neck of Boblig's victim. This was a special mercy that the judicial collegium had proposed. The powder would be ignited by a hot iron, it would explode, and the victim would suffocate.

Boblig signaled to the monk to get down. When he did, the executioner's boy thrust a lighted torch into the dry straw at the bottom of the pyre, then Master Jokl took a pole with a red-hot iron spike and pierced the bag hanging from Lautner's neck.

The powder exploded, and a cloud of smoke billowed out from the burning stake.

There was a great hubbub among the crowd, but only those spectators nearest the flames saw there was no longer a living man at the stake but rather something that only resembled a man. The hair and the beard of the former Dean of Schönberg were quite burned away, and his face was like the sole of an old shoe.

The lords and ladies gaped, for they had never seen such a spectacle before. But right at the back, where the simple folk stood, there was weeping. Someone cried:

"Holy martyr!"

The inquisitor Boblig scowled.

44 ✦ *The Prodigal Son*

Outside, delicate films of gossamer floated in the thin, sun-warmed air of fall. The day was mild, but inside his residence, the Bishop of Olomouc felt cold even though a pine log burned in the hearth, filling the spacious study with a penetrating, resinous scent.

Bishop Count Liechtenstein sat bent over Master Boblig's account of the execution of the unworthy priest Christoph Alois Lautner, former Dean of Schönberg. The bishop had already been fully informed by the Vicar-General and by Secretary Schmidt, but this report from the inquisitor presented many details that had escaped the others' attention. Words and sentences were deeply ingraining themselves into his memory.

Impenitent and proud sorcerer . . . suffocated after the explosion of the gunpowder . . . Some, however, opined that he lived yet half an hour after the lighting of the pyre . . . Some claim he died with God, for he cried out the holy names: Jesus, Mary . . . Some regarded him as a martyr . . .

The old man in the purple robe shivered. Perhaps it was the cold, perhaps something else. He pictured the former Dean of Schönberg next to Master Boblig of Edelstadt; an honest peasant face next to the disagreeable visage of the feared advocate, radiating cunning and sly deceit.

From the outset, it was Boblig who had led the main attack against Lautner. He constantly persuaded us of his guilt, forcing decisions on us by the power of his reports. We merely approved what he wrote and affixed our seal and signature. We did not personally examine the accused Lautner, though he did ask us for protection. We preferred to place our trust in the suspicious advocate rather than our own dean. The Devil, it is true, could manifest himself in the most varied forms and select all manner of people as his disciples. He could indeed take possession of an old and respected priest, but he could just as soon assume the form of the suspicious advocate! That would make the whole legal process the work of the Devil! The bishop recalled Lautner's last letter after the pronouncement of sentence: "I never did commit the crimes for which I am condemned to death. I confessed against my conscience only out of fear of new torture . . ."

"My God!" the bishop sighed and shuddered once again.

His sight turned to the opposite wall and a canvas depicting the biblical story of the return of the Prodigal Son. He remembered he had acquired the picture shortly before his last audience with the Dean of Schönberg.

What a resemblance! The bishop had gazed on this picture almost every day, and every time he did, he had marveled at the artistry that had expressed so graphically the idea behind the biblical story. Had he not admired the painter's art more than the idea?

Was not the Dean of Schönberg also such a Lost Son? The court had found by law that he was a maleficant, a grand sorcerer. But others knew him as a holy martyr!

The Lost Son of the Old Testament—and the Lost Son who was the Dean of Schönberg. The first returned to be clasped with love to the bosom of his father; the second was burned at the stake and would never come back.

Lost Son, Christoph Alois Lautner! Lost Son, *Carolus, Dei et Sedis Apostolicae Gratia Episcopus Olomoucensis* . . .

The bishop hung his head.

✦ *Epilogue*

Eight long, sad years passed.

Then, one clear-skied September day, an old foot traveler, bent over a stout, gnarled stick, arrived at the episcopal city of Olomouc.

He seemed to know the town well, for without asking anyone the way, he went straight to the square, where he stopped outside the large house of Master Maixner, the advocate. Without more ado, he stepped inside.

He went through the dark sitting room and pressed on up the worn wooden stairs. Once at the top, he paused to catch his breath; then with a gaunt hand he rapped on the door.

He swept off his shapeless hat and waited.

A servant woman opened the door and, seeing his ragged clothes, glared:

"No alms today, if you please!"

"I am not begging," replied the old man with a certain dignity. "I should like to speak to Doctor Maixner. Does he still live here?"

"He does, but . . ." The maid paused and looked the strange visitor up and down with yet greater distrust.

"Tell him one of his old friends wishes to speak to him!"

The maid hesitated, but at last she went to fetch her master.

After a while, the advocate appeared. He was an elderly fellow, quite obese, and wore eyeglasses. Not a kindly face at all.

"The maid says you want to speak to me. Who are you?"

There was not a sign of encouragement in his voice.

"I am Hutter, from Schönberg. Don't you recognize me?"

"That's impossible! Hutter's been dead for years!"

Surely this wretched creature could not be the former district judge! But there was something about his voice . . .

"Just look me over! It really is me. Kaspar Hutter!"

Yes, the eyes were his also. Not just the voice.

"Good Lord, what's happened to you? Everyone thought you died years ago. Come in, *amice,* and tell me about yourself!"

The wealthy advocate took his visitor by the arm, led him into his room, and sat him down into the best chair. Then he called his maid to bring refreshments.

"Can it really be you, my friend? But it's so unbelievable!"

"My outward appearance has utterly changed, I know," Hutter said smiling, "but even the inner me is also quite different. I've known terrible suffering. When I went with Langweil the merchant to Vienna to seek an audience with the Emperor, we had to cross the Hungarian lands. And there we were attacked by the Turks. They killed the merchant, took the money and the goods, and carried me off into bondage. A mule would not have endured what I have been through. But I have not come to tell you of my fortunes. I have many things I would like to ask you. Above all: May I return to Schönberg?"

"Why not? You'll be greeted like someone who's risen from the grave!"

A gleam of joy appeared in the old man's eyes.

"So the inquisitor Boblig is no longer on the rampage?"

"That villain! God knows what became of him! His fraudulent trials were halted in the end, on the orders of the Emperor."

"That good news makes up for all of my sufferings. I'll detain you no further but be on my way home. How I'm looking forward to seeing my wife and Dean Lautner! And I have to explain things to Heinrich Peschek. He entrusted us with his entire fortune!"

The guest rose as if he wanted to set off immediately, but the advocate again sat him down, this time rather more forcefully. The old man noticed the worried frown on his face.

"Don't hurry, *amice.* You have nowhere to hurry to," Maixner said, and his voice was soft and sad.

"How much I have looked forward to seeing them! There were times when I had already lost hope . . ."

"It grieves me to say it, my friend, but I must. Your wife is dead. Even the Dean of Schönberg is dead these eight years past. And Master Peschek, too, is no longer among the living."

"O God!"

The advocate nodded his head sadly.

"You would have to find out, anyway. And it's better if you hear it from me. Everyone you inquired about was burned at the stake as a witch. And forty-five other persons from Schönberg with them. And another fifty-six at Ullersdorf!"

Hutter rose. His whole body was shaking.

"You say he had Dorothea burned? And Councillor Peschek? And even Dean Lautner?"

The maid brought in beef liver pâté, wine, and some beautifully colored red apples and pears in a basket.

"Fortify yourself a little after such a long journey, and meanwhile let me tell you everything that happened in Schönberg."

"Please, go on," said the guest, taking no notice of the food.

"At the beginning, while you were still here, Boblig kept himself within certain bounds and abided by the legal regulations, at least in a rough-and-ready way. But then he became quite reckless, hurling into jail just anyone who took his fancy—though mainly, of course, people with a hint of property or wealth. Next to Master Peschek, your wife Dorothea showed the greatest courage. Not even the three kinds of torture, not even a dozen false witnesses, not even brutal treatment in jail—nothing could break her resistance. When she was under interrogation, she threw the charges straight back into the inquisitor's face. She called him such names that the clerk didn't even dare write them down in the court record. She didn't even spare the members of the inquisitorial tribunal. She told every one of them to their face, especially Gaup, just what she thought. Your wife Dorothea and Marie Peschek behaved more courageously than many men. But you are not eating or drinking, my friend!"

How could the old man think of food when he was hearing such things!

"Poor Dorothea!"

"Do you remember Fritz Winter, the gingerbread man? Boblig had him burned also."

"Even Fritz? He had no property, only a houseful of children. But you said even Christoph Lautner was burned. A priest! How was that possible?"

"Unfortunately, it happened. Boblig was mightier than the bishop. Or, rather, the bishop was unable to extricate himself from his evil influence. They burned the Dean of Schönberg in Müglitz in front of a crowd of thousands. The very memory is shameful. The dean's best friends renounced him out of fear that they themselves might fall under suspicion. Even Winkler, Dean of Müglitz, let him down, though even his days as a dean came to an end!

"Boblig's most awkward victim was the soapboiler, Prerovsky. His brother, the prior, took the case to Prince Liechtenstein, then even to the Emperor, and he kicked up a terrible fuss. We were jubilant, sure that Boblig's days were numbered, but even then that villain triumphed. He tortured Prerovsky for so long that his will was utterly broken. When he was at his weakest ebb, Boblig promised him his freedom. There was only one thing he had to do, a mere formality, just sign a declaration. That poor man signed a full confession, without even reading it. After that, neither his brother prior, nor even the Emperor, could be of any help to him at all."

"Even among the Turks there is greater justice!"

"But I have to say that of all of Boblig's victims, the toughest was Heinrich Peschek. He was a true hero. For almost eight years he refused to be broken. Though Boblig constantly confronted him with witnesses who swore his guilt, and though he was subjected to unbearable tortures, he never confessed. It was Peschek whom he described in a letter to Prince Liechtenstein as the *Magnus magus!* The great sorcerer. Peschek was one of the very last victims of the Schönberg Inquisition."

"Heinrich!" Hutter shook his head. "There was a time when for him business was everything. He certainly thought twice about standing up to Boblig. What changed him was when they imprisoned his wife, Marie. After that, he told me that even if everyone else were to hide away out of fear, he would stand and fight that monster. He lost his fortune, his wife, and then his life. I often thought of him when I was in captivity. But what became of Boblig and his assistant?"

Maixner's voice cheered up.

"The hunchback met a very sudden end. He and his master were on their way by coach from Ullersdorf to Schönberg. Both were drunk, maybe the driver, too. The horses bolted, the coach overturned, and Ignatius was crushed against a tree. He was dead before they got him to Schönberg. But nothing happened to Boblig. He remained director of the inquisitorial tribunal to the end. When the trials were halted, he stayed on for some time in Schönberg, but then he suddenly disappeared. Some people say he was carried off by Beelzebub himself."

"And no one in Schönberg settled accounts with him? Perhaps he's already directing another tribunal, somewhere else!"

"Hardly, *amice*. The wind is blowing another way now. Old Prince Liechtenstein died, and his successor is quite different. Even the Countess of Galle died. And Bishop Liechtenstein? It seems he was already full of remorse for ever allying himself with Boblig in the first place. Toward the end, everyone kept well away from the trials anyway. No one wanted to have anything to do with them. Even the Capuchins from Olomouc stopped attending the executions. Of course, that would hardly have been enough in itself to stop the trials—were it not that wiser counsel prevailed in Vienna."

Hutter moistened his lips in the wine.

"How did that happen?"

"There were several reasons, but the main one, I think, is that Boblig himself cut through the branch on which he had been sitting so firmly and so long. He was too insatiable; to him nothing was impossible any more. Especially after Dean Lautner's execution. It was as if he had mounted a wild horse and was even furiously spurring it on. His voracity no longer knew any bounds.

The manor of Ullersdorf and the town of Schönberg were no longer big enough for him, and he extorted denunciations of people from farther afield. He began to encroach on the Dietrichstein manor of Janowitz and he extended his claws to the city of Olomouc. He even had his eye on Sheriff Hassnik of Janowitz, one of Dietrichstein's most influential officials; he accused Master Sebest, councillor at Römerstadt, who had married the sheriff's daughter; and Pabst, the priest, who managed to escape in time. Boblig accused him of consorting with a demon in the form of the wife of the sheriff of Gross Ullersdorf. Vinarsky himself, it seems, escaped arrest only thanks to his sudden death."

"But Vinarsky was a member of the Ullersdorf inquisitorial tribunal."

"Certainly. In the early days he was one of Boblig's right-hand men, but he must have become wise to the inquisitor's practices, and later he refused to do his bidding. But by then, Boblig had his eyes on Olomouc. His list of intended victims included my own mother; also the city court clerk, whom he couldn't forget for his vigorous defense of Heinrich Peschek; Councillor Sommer, and at least two dozen of the most respected gentlemen of Olomouc. He simply bit off more than he could chew, and eventually it choked him. His mass accusations became so far-fetched and fantastic that no one with at least a scrap of common sense could believe him any more. Of course, we in Olomouc were not so intimidated as the burghers of Schönberg. We managed to acquire powerful intercessors: Count Lazansky and Count Sack and also Prince Dietrichstein, thanks to Sheriff Hassnik of Janowitz. The prince supported the two young Zerotins, who found the manor of Ullersdorf impoverished after the death of their aunt. Prince Dietrichstein also had powerful friends at the imperial court.

"In the end, the sorcery and black magic quite lost their significance. Money is what counts the most. No one wanted to go on putting more money into the trials. The manor of Ullersdorf was utterly in debt, and Schönberg was in an even more wretched state than after the great fire."

"Tyrants and thieves," remarked Hutter, "have always lived well among fools!"

"And among cowards, too, my friend!"

Suddenly, the visitor rose, clearly intent on leaving.

"Where are you going, *amice?*"

"Home."

"Now? But what's come over you? Rest with us, at least until tomorrow morning. You've yet to tell me about your adventures . . ."

"Please don't be angry, but I can't. Everything draws me homeward."

Maixner's pleas were in vain. Hutter took his stick, rammed his old military hat on his head, and set off on the last leg of his long pilgrimage.

The journey now was far worse than before. During his long march through foreign lands, he had been swept on by the power of hope, by the strength of his yearning to see his dear wife and friends. But now that was gone.

His bed that night was a cattle stall on a lonely farm. He did not even get as far as Neustadt.

Only toward evening on the second day did he finally see Schönberg, far away to the west. He stopped and for a long time stared at his native town on the horizon. But then, instead of going directly toward it, he veered to the north, treading the byways and field boundary paths until he came to a hill that he knew, high above the little brook that ran into the town. There, from time immemorial, had stood a gallows tree. The hill was steep and hard to climb. His feet hurt him, and he could hardly get his breath, but still he pushed on, stopping only when he was under the gallows. Then he looked around, until he saw a spot that was still only sparsely overgrown by grass. This was where the fires had burned.

He swept off his hat, sank to his knees, and bent his head to the black earth and ash. He took a pinch of it into his hand and pressed it to his crusted lips.

"O Dorothea! Dorothea!"

He remained on his knees for some time. Then he got up and turned to face the town for the first time.

It lay as he remembered it, on a slight mound, surrounded by low stone walls, with the tall tower of the town hall and the squat spire of the parish church in the middle. High above was the vast vault of the heavens. The sun had already set, but its traces remained, a pool of molten gold and a band of deep ruby red. The color of blood.

✦ ✦ ✦

The nearest entrance to the town was the New Gate. Below it, down by the brook, used to be the dye works that belonged to Kaspar Sattler, Hutter's faithful friend. And nearby used to be Prerovsky's workshop, where he boiled soap. His ashes, too, were now on the hill. Dorothea had passed through the New Gate on her last journey. So had Marie Peschek, Heinrich Peschek, Fritz Winter, Marie Sattler, little Liesel, and dear Susanne Voglick. Forty-eight of them, Master Maixner had counted. But who was to know how many more there might be? And then there was his dear, dear friend, Dean Christoph Alois Lautner, burned to death in Müglitz.

"O God."

Suddenly, through his tear-stained eyes, Hutter had a vision. He saw before him the figure of Master Boblig of Edelstadt, and the inquisitor's dark shadow fell on the town he would have murdered. He would have killed everyone in it, and half the manor of Ullersdorf, and still it would not have been enough. He had sat in judgment, and his court had been that of the executioner's sword, torture, and fire. Thus he had fought the Devil, and the Devil had surely danced with glee!

But had Boblig alone been responsible for all the evil that had been done? Had not many learned and wise men approved his crimes? Prince Liechtenstein, the judges at the Court of Appeals, the Bishop of Olomouc, Judge Gaup of Schönberg, Flade, the court clerk, and so many others. Was their guilt lesser than Boblig's? For without their assistance, Boblig's power would have come to nought.

"And what about us?" the old man found himself shouting. "Aren't we also not without blame? I, Christoph Lautner, Kaspar Sattler, Heinrich Peschek. How did we defend ourselves? Instead of rousing the world to fight, we waited for a miracle. It is our guilt, too. Our great guilt!"

For a few moments, his silent fingers crushed the ash and earth he had plucked from the place of execution. Then he cried again:

"We go on about the villain Boblig. Yes, he was an evil man, but was he not also a tool of something yet more monstrous than himself? A tool of our own superstition that catches up with us when we overindulge in comfort and indifference, and when we too willingly allow ourselves to be slaves?"

The old man leaned on his stick and made his laborious way down the hill to the muddy Hermesdorf road, before setting off along it to the town that was his home. Only now did it occur to him to wonder what had become of his house. He would probably have to go to court to get it back from Master Gaup. And what of Gaup? In all likelihood he was now the Lord Mayor.

1960–1962

✦ Glossary of Place Names

Towns, villages, and other places with German names, in alphabetical order, followed by their Czech or other names as used on modern maps. Locations mentioned in the book but not on this list may be found on modern maps under their given names.

Altvater	Praděd (mountain, the highest peak in the Altvatergebirge, or Jeseníky, range)
Altstadt	Staré Město
Bisenz	Bzenec
Blumenbach	Květná
Brünn	Brno
Eisgrub	Lednice
Freiberg	Příbor
Freiwaldau	Jeseník
Geppersdorf	Kopřivná
Glatz	Kłodzko (Polish)
Görlitz	Görlitz/Zgorzelec (German/Polish)
Gross Ullersdorf	Velké Losiny
Hermesdorf	Temenice
Hohenstadt	Zábřeh
Janowitz	Janovice
Johrnsdorf	Třemešek
Kleppel	Klepáčov
Königsfeld	Královo pole

Kreuz	Křížov
March	Morava (river)
Marschendorf	Maršíkov
Müglitz	Mohelnice
Mürau	Mírov
Neisse	Nysa (Polish)
Neuhäusel	Nové Zámky
Neustadt	Uničov
Nieder Mohrau	Dolní Moravice
Petersdorf	Petrov
Petersstein	Petrovy kameny (mountain)
Reigersdorf	Rejchartice
Reitendorf	Rapotín
Reitenhau	Rejhotice
Römerstadt	Rýmařov
Schönberg	Šumperk
Sternberg	Šternberk
Tess	Desná (river)
Weikersdorf	Vikýřovice
Wermsdorf	Vernířovice
Wiesenberg	Vízmberg
Znaim	Znojmo
Zöptau	Sobotín
Zuckmantel	Zlaté Hory